"By all that is cursed and holy!" he swore, suddenly rushing to her and falling to his knees behind her. "Ravenna, what in the Great Being's name happened?" Why did he even ask? He already knew, even before he brushed her hair away with both hands as gingerly as he could. The strands, delicate as they were, clung to the wounds, stuck to the dried blood on her back. She had been whipped. There was no mistaking such wounds. No mistaking the ragged tearing of her silken gown down its back.

"Please, don't . . . " she whispered.

Bronse could not grant her the request. In their short, vague acquaintance, he had come to know her as a proud beauty who knew her mind and how to express her convictions. She was gentle by nature in spite of that. She was not the type to give anyone cause to do such a thing, not that anyone ever deserved it. He knew it hurt her to be seen like this by him, to be shamed and weakened before him, and he felt his throat closing with fury and sympathetic pain for her because he would feel exactly the same way. He, too, would have tried to push her away, had the situation been reversed. Yet he would have secretly welcomed what he was about to do for her.

"Hush," he soothed her gently, reaching to cup her chin in his fingers, his thumb stroking her cheek from his position behind her. "There is no shame between friends, Ravenna. No shame when we are abused in ways we do not deserve."

By Jacquelyn Frank

THREE WORLDS
Seduce Me in Dreams

NIGHTWALKERS
Jacob
Gideon
Elijah
Damien
Noah

SHADOWDWELLERS
Ecstasy
Rapture
Pleasure

SEDUCE ME IN DREAMS

A THREE WORLDS NOVEL

JACQUELYN FRANK

BALLANTINE BOOKS • NEW YORK

Seduce Me in Dreams is a work of fiction. Names, characters, places, and incidents are the products of the author's imagination or are used fictitiously. Any resemblance to actual events, locales, or persons, living or dead, is entirely coincidental.

A Ballantine Books Mass Market Original

Copyright © 2011 by Jacquelyn Frank
Excerpt from *Seduce Me in Flames* copyright © 2011 by Jacquelyn Frank
Excerpt from *Supernatural* copyright © 2011 by Jacquelyn Frank

Published in the United States by Ballantine Books, an imprint of The Random House Publishing Group, a division of Random House, Inc., New York.

BALLANTINE and colophon are registered trademarks of Random House, Inc.

This book contains excerpts from the forthcoming books *Seduce Me in Flames* and *Supernatural* by Jacquelyn Frank. These excerpts has been set for this edition only and may not reflect the final content of the forthcoming editions.

ISBN 978-0-345-51767-8
eBook ISBN 978-0-345-51770-8

Printed in the United States of America

www.ballantinebooks.com

9 8 7 6 5 4 3 2 1

For Kate,
My fairy godmother

For my team at Random House/Ballantine.
You make me feel special . . .
and that's worth a thousand words.
(Well, more like a hundred thousand!)

CHAPTER
ONE

It pissed him off royally, but Commander Bronse Chapel couldn't help stumbling once again as the sand shifted from under his fast-paced footing. He corrected himself with a hard, jolting body movement in order to keep his balance, and the jerking motion elicited a soft, barely discernable groan from the burden on his back.

"How goes it, Chief?" he asked, pausing in his stride to request the answer and to allow his fellow soldier a few beats to grit out the agony that had to be washing through him by then.

"Just waiting on my encore, sir," Chief Trick Hwenk responded with the traditional gung-ho attitude of an ETF officer, his young voice sounding suddenly much younger and far weaker than it had two miles back.

Chapel hesitated and then shifted the weight of his human burden up a little higher against his spine and shoulders, wishing that the grip Trick had on him was not getting so obviously lax. Bronse could smell the injured soldier's blood just as easily as he could feel it soaking through his gear where the man was slumped over his back. The commander had a well-powered grip around the younger man's thighs and knees as the soldier rode piggyback. But if the kid couldn't hold on to his shoulders, they'd be in deep shit, and Bronse felt that fact clear to his straining bones.

"All right, Chief. Just hang by your grip for three more miles and we'll be in the nest. Of course, that means you'll have to listen to the medics bitch at you for a few days," Bronse noted, using the jovial reminder as a cover for restarting their staggering progress across the ever-shifting sand. Bronse narrowed his eyes behind his goggles, peering at the west sandline. The wind was getting antsy, but he couldn't yet see a cloud forming on the line. *That* was a blessing, at least. Provided it stayed that way. The last thing they needed to contend with was a sand hurricane.

Bronse went back to concentrating on where he was putting his feet, and how fast he could risk going without jostling his precious burden too dangerously. His every muscle burned from the exertion, but he welcomed it. He preferred being soaked in sweat, working himself to the limit of his endurance and pounding out whatever was necessary to see a certain goal achieved. He'd always felt the most in control when he had that kind of dedicated focus, and he supposed that was what had gotten him the command position on the First Active squad of the ETF in the first place.

Then again, he had wanted to be an Interplanetary Militia soldier since . . .

Well, his *matra* would swear it was since they cut the cord, and his *patra* would have proudly boasted that it was set down in his very genes, but Bronse remembered the first time he had seen a BioVid of the history of the Interplanetary Militia's ETF when he was six years old. The IM was an intra/interplanetary peacekeeping and defensive military outfit, and it had existed for well over a century. The IM had been created as a joint military effort among the three inhabited planets in the system: Tari, Ulrike, and Ebbany. It had more or less succeeded in its charter of keeping the treatises of coexistence among the three entities, as well as managing missions of peace and humanity on and among the individual planets.

The IM had several specialized branches, but nothing compared to the Special Operations sector known as the Extreme Tactics Force. To a six-year-old the ETF had sounded deadly, dangerous, and exciting as all hell. Watching the BioVid had only confirmed what Bronse had already dreamed of. Being in the ETF was a good way to get an adrenaline rush and have an opportunity to do things with nothing but your balls and your skills to get you out of hellish situations. Not to mention that it was an excellent way to get important body parts blown off.

Unfazed, Bronse had known right then that he was destined to be one of those elite soldiers, and nothing would stop him. Learning that kind of goal setting and determination at that young an age had served him well. Now, here he was, commander of the crack team of the First Active ETF soldiers. First Active meant they were the lead team and were always called first for an assignment, and it meant that his team was the best of the best. They were the ones who went to do the impossible in the worst situations, maintaining a no fear/no fail/no fatality motto that was rarely betrayed.

That motto was balanced on Bronse's back at the moment, losing blood too fast for what remained of a three-mile hike. But Bronse was doing his damndest to make them the fastest miles ever to be hiked on sand. He'd never lost a team member in the field, and he wasn't about to start with a rookie communications officer who had balls the size of jumbo adder crystals. The kid had more than proved his grit today. Trick might be their newest and youngest member, but Bronse had known the minute he'd laid eyes on him that he was the perfect fifth for his group. They'd been searching for a communications officer for a whipsnout's age, going through three washouts before Trick had sauntered onto the base, fresh out of the grueling ETF training program.

Trick had those blond boy-next-door good looks that you could see a block away, riveting blue eyes that penetrated at every glance, and the disarming manners and engaging charm to go with them. He'd been in the mess hall hardly ten minutes before he'd had a small harem of female officers and noncoms all around him. They had been laughing and flirting with him like they weren't already surrounded by a cafe overflowing with virile, accessible men. Keeping in mind that militia women were not something one toyed with lightly, or at all for that matter, Trick's magnetism was impressive.

Bronse had turned to Lasher and said that any boy who could communicate that well with IM women deserved their team position as communications officer. Lasher had agreed, looking mighty impressed himself. Another recommendation in and of itself because very little impressed Bronse's second in command. So Trick had joined Bronse, Lasher, Justice, and Ender's First Active ETF team all of two months back, and this had been their third mission out since the team had been locked in. The first two missions had been sterling. Chief Hwenk had proved himself capable of jacking into everything from TransTel satellites to the antennae of a Flibbean ground slug. The boy was a damn miracle worker.

The third mission, however, had run into a bit of a snafu.

Bronse had to stop again, this time so they both could toss back a few gulps of nutria-treated water. The sand and sun, not to mention Bronse's labors, were sucking the hydration right out of his body. The Grinpar Desert on Ebbany was merciless in that respect. Actually, it was merciless in all respects. Only the Great Being knew why anyone would want to fight over the right to live on such a forsaken piece of hell-acre. The sand hurricanes alone could rip solid stone out of the ground. A person caught aboveground was as good as dead, or at least scoured to a bloody stump.

To make matters worse, the sand was black.

That meant it soaked up the rays of the sun all day and could melt or burn the hell out of anything that touched it, stumbled in it, or outright fell down looking to bake their face. Only the special protection of the soldiers' boots and clothes kept them from this type of fate. That and Bronse's impressive sense of balance.

The faster they were out of that hostile environment, the better, Bronse thought as he began to trek off again.

For this mission, the team had split up to do reconnaissance at two separate locations. Bronse hadn't recommended or approved of that plan. However, due to the sand hurricanes and an awkwardly timed insert by their command center, they hadn't had the time to recon their target sites in succession. Their limited circumstances had meant hitting the recon objectives simultaneously, which meant either aborting to a later mission or splitting up a single team right then. Abortion meant doubling the danger of detection, doubling the risk to lives. Bronse had given in to his upper command and split his team. Justice, Lasher, and Ender had taken the north site, and Bronse and Trick had taken the northwest target. Bronse and Trick had been filling PhotoVids with recon information when they'd been made. Bronse still couldn't figure out how it had happened. They'd been silent and—wearing black—all but invisible. The Nomaad patrol had jumped them from behind, six to two, and the indigenous life-form's guards had been very skilled in hand-to-hand fighting.

Still, nothing compared to ETF training. Especially when it came to hand-to-hand fighting. Bronse and the kid had moved like lightning to eliminate their threat, working silently so as not to alert any other patrols.

Trick hadn't even cried out when he'd been pig-stuck by a wicked Nomaadic knife with a dual edge and hooks in the hilt meant to either hold the knife in, or rip flesh violently away if the wielder recalled the blade. Trick had done the smart thing, bracing a hand to hold the knife in place as he cut off the Nomaad's hand at the wrist. No small feat that, Bronse knew.

Though he rarely made a sound to reflect it, Trick still had the six-inch blade stuck deep in his gut, the hilt of which Bronse could see if he glanced past his arm on the left-hand side. Removing the blade would guarantee Trick's death. Moving Trick, every step and every slide in the sand, jiggled sharpened metal against the fragile pink tissue inside the young soldier's belly. But Bronse had no choice. The area had been too hot for a pickup with the light transport ship they'd brought for the recon. Plus, covert reconnaissance produced little advantage if you announced you'd been there with the screaming engines of a flight ship.

With luck, a sand hurricane would hit within a couple of hours and the patrol that had jumped them would be considered lost to it. There certainly wouldn't be any traces of bodies or blood. Bronse had already seen to that. In and out like ghosts—that was how ETF preferred to do their work. It was such a habit for Bronse to cover his own tracks that he could cook a four-course meal in a stranger's house and leave them none the wiser for it by the time he'd finished. His ex-wife, Liely, claimed he'd done the same thing to their marriage. She'd insisted that, for the two years they had been wed, she had hardly known he was there.

He'd never understood why she'd been so surprised by that. What had she expected it to be like? He'd been ETF born and bred—ate it, breathed it, practically made love to it—and she'd always told him that this was a major turn-on for her. *She* had sought *him* out, not the other way around. Having a relationship had been nowhere on Bronse's radar. He'd learned years ago that the Extreme Tactics Force and long-term liaisons did not mix. But Liely had come on strong, oozing attractive enticement, hero worship, and a hell-acre of wild and adventurous sex. It wasn't often that a soldier argued with that kind of easy fortune. She'd been smart, witty, and sizzling hot, seemingly with a good head on her about what it meant to hang around with a First Active soldier who shipped off in a heartbeat when called. With the volatile politics and disturbances of three planets to manage, that tended to be fairly often. Hell, she'd waved him off and hugged him hello every time without a single complaint, and after a while he believed that he'd found the rare fortune of a woman worth asking to marry. She'd said yes before he'd even finished popping the question.

And that was when everything changed. Or nothing changed, according to his discontented wife. Liely had bitched and moaned nonstop about his "inaccessibility" and how lonely she was all the time. Why wasn't he home more often? He had a family now, so why didn't he change—work a desk, get promoted so he'd make more money. Her logic was lost on him when she told him she'd expected it to be "different" once they were married. He'd been dumbfounded. He'd never once intimated that he saw himself changing for any reason. Still, Liely thought he should make concessions to coddle a whining wife—just because.

Grounds for a segregation? Yeah, inevitably it had been. Like every other fight, he'd done it quickly and quietly, putting an end to his mistake as soon as he legally could.

Bronse wasn't introspective at heart. He had a very basic makeup and that never required much self-discovery. However, he moved better when he kept his mind occupied with a lot of things at once. He kept his attention on the terrain, checked the sandline, and kept an ear out for any agony on Trick's part, but the rest of him did whatever it took to make travel through the awful conditions fly by faster.

The transport was waiting another mile and a half away now, the closest they could get and stay undercover. Justice and Lasher had wanted to trek out to meet him, but he didn't want them in the sand so close to a hurricane event. Bronse's equipment had read the storm forming an hour ago. By now it was fast approaching, and he'd soon see it on the sandline. He wouldn't risk them as well as himself and Trick. He knew that his decision had burned them, knew they were furious with him, but they'd obeyed and would continue to obey unless he said otherwise.

It rubbed them the wrong way, though—this group who lived by the motto no fear/no fail/no fatality—to be coddled by their commanding officer like a father protecting his children.

Bronse looked over to the distant sandline. The sky was becoming obscured with swirling black and violet clouds, and ground lightning was illuminating the funnels and downdrafts of the approaching hurricane.

"Hey, Boss," Trick spoke up in a rasp of repressed pain, "not that I'm complaining, but I hope I won't be washing sand out of every crack and crevice for the next few weeks."

"Can you think of a better way to encourage you to take a bath once in a while?" Bronse retorted breathlessly as he tried to pick up his pace and keep jostling to a minimum. "Gonna need a sand hurricane to scour the stink off you, boy."

"That's just—" Trick broke off his riposte to grit a low sound of agony through his throat. "Arrrhh!"

"Hang on, kid. Last leg. And I'll beat the storm with at least a minute to spare."

Trick's forehead fell limply against the back of Bronse's

neck. The pain had to be horrible, Bronse knew, even though Trick had barely made a sound.. The pain was communicated in the feel of the boy's skin—both clammy and hot—and in the slackening of Trick's strength and grip. He was losing consciousness, and Bronse wasn't sure that it wouldn't be the kinder thing, as long as the kid didn't slip off his back. Bronse leaned into his trek, keeping Trick pitched forward against his spine and balancing him even more as he went limper, finally falling unconscious.

Deadweight.

Trick was out, and Bronse could feel it in every ounce of the body on his back. He had always been fascinated by why that made a difference. It was a balance and weight distribution factor, he knew logically. The person wasn't awake to best center himself on the person who carried him. Still, it was remarkable how consciousness, or lack thereof, made such a difference in the feel of their weight.

Bronse realized he was grasping for thoughts. Practically babbling in his own mind, really. But he had to do something to make himself move faster, maintaining burden and strength, beating out the storm, and not second-guessing himself about why he wouldn't have the rest of the team come out to meet them.

"That was cutting it close!"

Justice made the declaration seconds before she yanked and banked the transport away from the approach of the storm. She pitched up toward the higher atmosphere of Ebbany, the gravity decks working hard to compensate so the team didn't end up spilled across the flooring. But it wasn't Justice that Bronse was worried about. All of his concern was aft, in medbay, with Trick and the medic. But because he needed to hear his team's report, he had to fulfill command first and let the others get back to him as to Trick's progress.

"I sure hope we don't have to find another nav/com officer," Justice quipped over her shoulder. "They come and go so fast around here; I'm getting tired of wiping the butt streaks off this chair." She nodded to the empty chair behind her and to her right.

"That isn't funny, Captain," Bronse said sternly, looking up from his VidPad, where he was recording his portion of the report before transmission.

"You're right, sir. I'm sorry, sir," she agreed quickly.

Captain Justice Mulettere was looking straight ahead, piloting them out of the atmosphere and into the starred darkness of space, but she was also glancing in her backview disc. She kept the little shiny disc clipped to her console so she could see the activity behind her. Not having to turn around to see what her crewmates were up to made for better piloting. The ship's designers could have set the pilot's chair farther back, she supposed, but she preferred models like the transport which let her feel the nose of the craft around her rather than the pilot's chair being muffled in its mid-section.

So she could clearly see Commander Chapel's reflection in her shiny disc as he sat sprawled in the command chair behind her. He hadn't even paused to breathe after dropping Trick on the medbay table and ordering her to get the transport out of there. The commander had come forward, sat down still drenched in sweat and blood and caked black sand, and gone right to his report. The trek had been brutal on him, and she could see the tremors in his overexerted muscles, even via the disc. She wasn't one to second-guess her commanding officer, but she hadn't understood why he wouldn't let them meet up with him so they could help bring Trick in. Was Bronse protecting them? They were ETF, for Great Being's sake. They were *supposed* to stick their necks out. But she'd known her superior officer for a while now, and she suspected that Bronse had been a little wrecked up about letting the new kid get tanked. The commander got very strict after one of them got hurt. His personal motto, they had learned, was no fear/no fail/no fatality, and no fuckups.

Justice sighed. The episode with Trick meant they'd be running rigorous drills and extreme training again during their next downtime. Not that she minded, because a girl had to do something to keep her figure, but she did wish that Bronse would parallel that way of thinking with other things sometimes. Like snapping a bootlace would mean a day of intensive shoe shopping. She chuckled noiselessly to herself, trying to picture the hulking men she was teamed with sitting in a shoe emporium, eating canapés and sipping Lathe wine, while salers slid the latest in fashionable shoes onto their feet, one after another. Actually, Lasher was a mighty fine fashion plate when he was out of uniform, Justice mused. He would probably get a kick out of a day of shoe shopping.

But Commander Chapel was plainly not in a mood to appreciate her humorous ideas on these matters, so she kept them to herself. Perhaps she would share them later with Lasher. And Trick would get a kick out of them for sure.

Justice frowned, hoping that Trick would be all right. She had faith in their medic; he could hold the kid over until they returned to Ulrike. The best medical care in the tri-planet system was on their base planet. Once they got the kid there, he would be good as new.

Of the three worlds, Ulrike was the most advanced and civilized in many ways besides medical care. The ETF was based there, as was IM headquarters. Although the planet was half land and half water, most of the landmass was settled and there were few uninhabited areas.

Not like Ebbany, the planet they had just left. Ebbany was mostly landmass, with little in the way of water and oceans. That made for a high percentage of deserts covering the face of the planet. However, the Ebbanites had managed to eke out an impressive civilization along the edges of the waters. Yet the bane of the peace seekers were the barbarians of the wilderness areas and the Nomaad populations wandering the desert highlands and the lowlands of belowground caverns that stretched for hundreds of miles in all directions. The endless squabbles and arming for war, especially in the Grinpar Desert, had begun to make Justice feel like she would be wearing black camouflage for the rest of her life.

If Ulrike and Ebbany were polar opposites in civilization, however, Tari had to be the middle ground. Living there was rough, whether you chose jungle or desert, city or country, or life on the many colony platforms sharing the planetary orbits and sight line between Tari and its forested moon of Adia. The platforms were situated in a line from Tari to Adia like metallic stepping-stones, each one housing tens of thousands of citizens. They had the best advantages and technologies that life had to offer, their supplies often coming straight from Ulrike, where they got first dibs on imports before they even filtered down to the planet itself.

The trouble with Tari was that each colony was a faction unto itself, and they were always squabbling over trading rights or imagined slights from another colony. Feuding was frequent, and policing the colonies was difficult because it was hard to blend in on a floating piece of metal where everyone lived in close quarters and was wary of strangers. Planetside wasn't much better. Trading rights were a bone of contention there too. Traders figured, why spend time flying all the way to the planet surface when they could simply go to the nearest platform colony. This meant that by the time goods filtered down the line to the planet, the prices were exorbitant.

Only half the planet was settled; the other half was a wild frontier that drew adventurers, troublemakers, and a serious criminal element.

Tari was one of Justice's favorite places. She had grown up on one of its platforms—a middle-class upbringing in a place that, to be frank, had been flat, cold and gray. Still it had had more than its share of dangers for a young girl. A contrast to platform life, the wilderness on Tari held a wild, colorful appeal for her. It was a matter of honesty, she thought. At least when you went to the Tari plains and rises, you knew you were headed into blatant dangers, unlike space colony life, where you thought you were safe, yet good faces held hazards in camouflage. Justice had always preferred the honesty of knowing you were in constant jeopardy.

Rather like her career choice.

She had enlisted in the IM right out of school, letting them teach and train her, letting herself be the perfect lump of clay for them to mold into the perfect soldier. Now she was one of the top five pilots in the Special Forces communities; she was one of only ten female ETF officers, and she was on Commander Bronse Chapel's First Active ETF team. Chapel was a legend in his own time, and there wasn't an ETF soldier who wouldn't give his right arm to be on his elite team. Justice had been in her exalted position for three years now, and she had thrilled in every minute of it.

"Out of atmosphere; out of orbit traffic, Commander," she reported automatically as they pulled away from Ebbany and headed fast toward Ulrike.

"ETA?"

"Thirty-two hours, sir."

"That long?" came the sharp demand.

"This is only an XJL transport, sir," she reminded him with gentle respect. "I don't have any zip. Just handling for best travel and evasion on the planetary surfaces. I can do only thirty-two hours at top mach."

Bronse's jaw clenched, and Justice could see a nerve tick angrily in his temple. The one thing none of them ever had to doubt was that their best interests and safety were at the heart of Commander Chapel's every motivation. The entire team trusted their lives to him, and with good reason. They had seen Chapel do much more miraculous things to save the lives of his crew than humping out a kid with a six-inch blade in his belly, over black sand, in hostile territory, and a sand hurricane nipping at his heels.

Justice tired of watching her commander in the disc. Now that they were in the void of space, she flipped on her autopilot and swung out of her chair as if she were dismounting a horse. She strolled back to the supplies chest secured against the rear deck plates, and unlatched it with a hiss as it released its airtight seal. She fished out a first-aid case and resealed the chest. Then she walked up to the commander, who had gone back to typing his report, the blunt tips of his fingers dashing over the electronic keyboard of the handheld VidPad. She opened the kit and, without bothering to ask for permission, she began to tend the wounds he had sustained in his fight.

He had a cut over his left eye that would need knitting, a great deal of generalized bruising that a heal patch would take care of over the next twenty-four hours, and a bitching case of sunburn that was already beginning to blister. He had apparently lost his protective headgear in the fight, which had left him exposed to the sun. Justice would bet he had a hell-acre of a sun-induced headache as well. He had the misfortune of having coal black hair, and, like the black sand, it had absorbed every ray of brutal sun that had beaten down on him. Justice selected two heal patches from the kit and slapped one on Bronse's left arm and the other under the hair on the back of his thick neck. When she pulled back, he was looking at her, a brow quirked up in curiosity. A light scar cut through the peak of his brow, accentuating the arch.

"Two?" he asked dryly.

"Yeah." She grinned, pausing briefly to nibble on the gum between her back teeth. "One for reabsorption and swelling reduction."

"And the other?"

"To cut the pain of the headache and sunburn."

She looked studiously into the first-aid case as she spoke, so she could only feel the narrowing of his eyes on her at first. Not one to give in to cowardice, not even in the face of Commander Chapel's disapproval, she smiled sweetly at him as she looked up.

"You gave me a narcotic?" he growled dangerously, reaching for the patch on the back of his neck. He looked up in surprise when she caught his huge fist in her palm, staying his actions. "Back off, Captain," he barked shortly.

"Uh . . . with all due respect . . . bite me, Commander," she retorted with lazy, unconcerned wit. "It's only a low dose, meant to counter the dip when your adrenaline plummets. Which will be any minute now. When it drops, your pain will kick in. I've been around this block enough to know. If you want to stay lucid, you have to let me cut away at your nerves a little. Otherwise, you won't be able to focus and stay alert with us."

"I don't like my reflexes being diminished or my perceptions screwed around with," he argued predictably.

"That's why it's a low dose," she reiterated. "And that's why I used a patch and not a hyperspray. If we run into trouble, you just yank it off and you'll be right in ten minutes, fifteen tops.

"I know." She held up a hand to forestall his coming argument. "A lot can happen in ten minutes. But you have to trust me. I'd rather you be half-narced without pain than blinded by the agony that we both know is coming. If I let the medic look at you, he'd lock you in medbay. At least this way I can tell him I gave you first aid and he can focus solely on Trick. Don't you think I know that's why you ran out of medbay—before the medic could get a look at you?"

"Fine. I'll leave it for now," he acquiesced as if it were a heavy travail. "But next time, ask and present arguments before just doing it, okay? I'm not ignorant. I can listen to reason."

"Yes, sir. Sorry, sir."

"Jus, I want you to stay at the stick for a while. I know you're tired and the autopilot could get us there in its sleep, but I have . . . I have a strange feeling. Let's just keep alert, okay?"

"Roger that, sir."

Justice put away the case and slung herself back into her seat, keeping her eyes on her monitors.

Despite Bronse's worries, they reached Ulrike without mishap or event. Justice swung into port on the IM space station that rotated in Ulrike's orbit with smooth grace in spite of its enormity. Thousands of troops moved in and out of the station, known as Station Zero, every day, at all hours, and the time of their approach was no different. Since IM acted in the role of law enforcement as well as militia, personnel were constantly shifting. Station Zero was a major exchange port, situated equidistant from Tari and Ebbany and practically on top of Ulrike.

Shortly after the XJL landed on the tarmac, the doors of the cargo hold lowered to reveal the entire squad standing at the ready. Trick was supported on each side by two team members, their arms linked to form a human sedan chair of sorts to support their injured comrade.

Justice and Lasher stood on the right, Bronse and Ender on the left. Bronse was, of course, in front, his thick wrist and forearm linked beneath Trick's thighs with Lasher's equally powerful grasp. At a soft sound from their commander, the team strode forward in a perfectly timed march, cushioning Trick, yet precise and proud in step so no one could mistake them for anything but the mighty warriors they were. Wounded team members of the ETF had always been brought home in such a manner, their heads held high, keeping them from being the object of pity or dismay, something every soldier dreaded in moments like this.

Silence fell over the soldiers crowded around waiting for their departing flights. A respectful silence. All braced their legs and linked their hands behind their backs in honorable attention as the ETF officers carried their injured man past them, heading for the station medical facilities.

CHAPTER
TWO

Masin "Lasher" Morse was not famous for his conversation. He was even less renowned for actually initiating one. So when Lasher asked Bronse a leading question, the commander blinked at him in surprise for a long moment. They were sharing a meal in Bronse's quarters, something they did often when they weren't in the mess with other bored officers who were on downtime, or when they weren't in the mood to search for more intimate company. Bronse's fork hung suspended between his plate and his mouth, the rich juice of the steak he was enjoying dripping with little plops onto his potatoes.

"I'm sorry," Bronse murmured after a moment, blinking and refocusing his disbelieving attention. "Could you repeat the question?"

Unperturbed, Lasher did so, grinning the entire time. He knew full well that Bronse had heard him and comprehended. "I asked you what you were thinking."

Bronse laughed suddenly, half with humor, half with that same sense of disbelief. "I am suddenly having a flashback to my marriage. Liely asked me that question a hundred times a night when I was off-mission. Do I have to worry that we've been on-mission together too long?"

Lasher responded by throwing a bread roll at Bronse's head. It hit him in the center of his forehead when he couldn't be bothered to duck, then bounced off and slid under the table. "Don't be a jackass." Lasher grinned, making his companion laugh. "I only meant to say that something is bugging you, and I know enough after all these years that it's a good idea to get a handle on your thoughts if I want to protect my own ass. Your instincts are uncanny and rarely wrong."

"We're on downtime, Morse. My instincts are going to kick back and relax until such time as we go on-mission again." Bronse set down his fork and leaned back with a deep sigh and a long, casual sprawl of well-muscled legs. There was hardly a trace left on his body of the fight he had been in, or the trek he'd been forced to make. Masin's boss was freshly shaved and showered and even wearing civilian clothes. That in and of itself was strange, come to think of it. Bronse never wore civvies on the station. He always waited until he was planetside. It was allowed in the privacy of their quarters, of course, where they were now, but once they crossed the threshold into public areas, they were expected to be in uniform unless briefly traveling for social purposes from one place to another.

"Are you going out somewhere?" Lasher asked, again surprising his commander with his attempt to generate a conversation. Or, in this case, an information-gathering session.

"Am I being interrogated?" Bronse countered.

"You are being observed as acting out of normal character by a man who has been by your side since enlistment ten years ago. And before then, if you count officers' college. If you didn't want me to know that something was going on, you wouldn't have invited me to dinner dressed in civvies, partner. Why in hell are you toying with me? Save the head games for the enemy, friend."

Bronse fixed his unusual eyes on his second in command for a long minute. Lasher met his stare dead on and with no hint of his previous humor. Neither man blinked.

The disconcerting thing about Bronse's eyes, Lasher noted wryly, was that they were an unexpected periwinkle color. A cross between light blue and light lavender. Like hazel eyes that switched between green, gold, and brown, Bronse's eyes would shift between sky blue, light violet, and the periwinkle or lavender combination of the two. They were like a woman's eyes, some would say, for their sheer prettiness.

Actually, no one would say that. They wouldn't dare.

But their lightness and the habitually perceived gentleness of color gave Bronse an unsettling edge when he fixed his eyes on strangers. They would be so busy trying to wrap their minds around the incongruity of a mountainous, deadly man with forget-me-not eyes that they would end up blabbing all kinds of information without even realizing it.

Lasher, however, was no longer unbalanced by Bronse's delicately colored eyes. That wasn't to say that a warning or smoldering threat that could be seen from time to time did not give Lasher pause. He was, after all, a very intelligent man. But at the moment there was only reluctance warring with confusion in Bronse's gaze, and Masin knew that he simply needed to exhibit patience and persistence.

"I don't think I can explain it," Bronse said at last, the words coming in an uncontrolled rush, as if he were unburdening himself of a great secret. "I'm afraid if I start to, I will sound like the Ebbany sun has fried my brain."

"Maybe it did," his second speculated with a crooked grin as he reached casually for his beer and took a swig. "I'm not used to you prevaricating, so it would make me wonder."

"I know," Bronse grumbled with dissatisfaction.

"But crazy people never think they're crazy. You're sane just by virtue of the question. So, what are you thinking? Spit it out. Let's see if I can do anything for you."

Bronse's troubled gaze flicked up to Lasher's with penetrating lavender pupils.

"One of us is going to die."

"Just what exactly does that mean?" Lasher asked, all traces of humor vanishing. "Are you talking about Trick? You heard what the doctors said—"

"No. Not Trick. Not now at least." Bronse exhaled sharply, running frustrated hands over his face and through his jet hair until the short cut spiked up even though it was slightly longer than military length at the moment. "I don't know who, or how, or anything else. I just have a sick gut feeling that we're going to lose someone on an imminent mission."

Lasher settled back in his chair again, studying his commanding officer quietly for a long minute.

"If it were anyone else, I would call Psyche Services and get you wired and decompressed," Lasher said darkly. "Going into a mission with that attitude stuck in your head is going to make it happen. You know that, right?"

"I know that," Bronse barked. "Why do you think I've been smacking the feeling down for the past two days? I thought for certain that something was going to happen on the way back to base. When it didn't, the feeling just seemed to grow in intensity." Bronse's voice lowered to a dark passion. "Part of me thinks I should be decompressing in Psyche Services, too, but another part of me is screaming out that if I leave my team I'm going to be leaving you all to get your fucking heads blown off. I don't mean that to be a disparagement against *you*, either. I've never once doubted your ability to command in the event of my absence, Masin."

Lasher took the compliment seriously, especially when Bronse forewent his militia nickname and called him by his given name, an occasion reserved for the most serious of conversations.

"I can only explain it as masculine intuition, if such a

thing exists. A soldier's intuition," he corrected himself, looking better satisfied with that. "Masin, something very unusual is about to occur, and we're going to get thrust up in the middle of it. Now, that's fine by me. That's what we do, right?" Bronse didn't wait for Lasher's nod. "But somewhere along the line, I'm sure that two things are going to happen. First, something is going to attempt to separate me from the rest of the group, and if that happens, you all are as good as dead. Second, if we manage to thwart that and make it to the end of the mission, we will lose someone no matter what. That's an idea I cannot stomach or accept. I have never lost a man in the field, and I'll be damned if I'm going to start now."

Lasher was quiet for a long time as he absorbed this proclamation. Although Bronse had a gut instinct that bordered on precognition at times, never before had he presented Masin with something as specific as this. Clearly the commander was just as disturbed by this as Lasher was. But he was disturbed to a point of determination, not panic, and that was an important distinction. It told Lasher that Bronse was still in command of his perspective and able to remain in command of his group.

"And the civvies?" Lasher pressed, getting back to that question.

"I just had to get out of uniform," Bronse said dismissively. "It helped dissuade this sense of needing to be battle ready. I need to relax and sleep if I'm going to be at the top of my game when it's needed, and I haven't been able to do that since we got off Ebbany. The civvies and your company . . . and confessing this feeling to you . . . have made me feel a little better."

"I can imagine," Lasher murmured. It bothered the lieutenant commander that this had been disturbing Bronse since Ebbany. Could the close call with Trick's life have unsettled Bronse enough to make him paranoid?

Lasher found it hard to conceive that Bronse Chapel would ever come close to the deep end, never mind jumping in. Was all of this surfacing only since Ebbany? Bronse's gut instincts had been around for quite some time though. Was that why Bronse had refused to let the team meet him in the desert, when it would have been faster and easier to rescue Trick if they had? Lasher didn't often question Bronse, never having had reason to, and it disturbed him to find himself doing so now.

"Masin, you're being transparent," Bronse said with wry observation as he slowly sipped his beer. "You think I'm a few cards short of a deck."

Lasher smiled crookedly and chuckled softly. "I'd be stupid not to consider it. But I've trusted you for every single minute of the past ten years, and I'm incapable of doing otherwise now. You've always been able to think circles around me and everyone else. Maybe your brain is evolving to a higher level, and now you can sense trouble even *before* the mission."

"Go ahead, make jokes," Bronse snorted derisively.

"Seriously," Lasher said, "I put as much stock in gut feelings, hunches, and instinct as the next soldier. It has saved my life on more than enough occasions. Your feelings just happen to be a bit more specific than the average, and, eerie as it may feel, I think I can accept that. I just need to know how much you want me to share with the crew. Frankly, I think Justice is already on edge. She spent a lot of time with you on deck and assimilated your tension and wariness. Ender was born paranoid, so he's never *not* on alert. Trick isn't going anywhere anytime soon, so I don't see any point in stressing out the kid while he heals."

"I know. I plan to keep this between you and me. Between the two of us, we can keep the others on their toes and pointed in the right direction. If I get separated from you, I know you'll know that making sure we regroup is what I want at all costs unless I clearly order otherwise. I just feel better knowing that *you* know where my mind is on this."

"I'm rock solid clear on it. Now," Lasher mused, "all we need is a mission."

Forty-eight hours later and with only three consecutive hours of deep sleep under his eyelids, Bronse was brutalizing his body in the officer's gym, trying to burn himself into some kind of exhaustive state that would allow him to fall asleep and stay that way.

It was some awful hour during the base's night cycle because the gym was abandoned, only the sickly bluish-white artificial lighting keeping him company. Even that was iffy in places, bulbs close to needing changing giving off occasional warning flickers, announcing their imminent demise. He was glad for the quiet, though, and the desolate feeling of the empty gym suited his mood.

Bronse was currently pitting himself against the gravity mats, which increased the pull of gravity in proportion to the user's strength and level of skill. Any exercise he chose would be made tougher to do as he worked against his own increasing body weight. The mats were designed to avoid causing severe injuries or stress fractures, but right up until that point they would push the limit.

Bronse had decided on some basic floor exercises. They were what had strengthened him enough to carry a 205-pound man across five miles of broiling desert, so they would damn well be enough to get him to fall asleep for at least a good eight hours. Though the crew members were trained to function at peak levels under the duress of very little sleep, when downtime came, crashing was imperative to rejuvenating and maintaining health and strength. Undergoing hard-core conditions was something best left to the battlefield and bad situations.

Reaching the limits of his stamina, Bronse finally dropped to his hands and knees in a panting sweat on the black gravity mat, his teeth gritting against the aches of his body as sinew twitched in protest and relief. It would take the mat a few more minutes to gear back its gravitational resistance after sensing that he'd stopped his workout. So Bronse rolled over onto his back and bore the strangely comforting pressure of his body being drawn toward the floor as if he were being sucked down into the mat. But then the pull of it released so suddenly that Bronse had a momentary sensation of zero-g, the illusion of near weightlessness that seemed so real that he wondered why he didn't float away. He adjusted after a moment, of course, his breathing regulating as well, but he didn't get up off the floor. He lay staring at the ceiling, somehow fascinated by the intermittent flicker of the dying bulbs in the lighting units.

"Bronse . . ."

Bronse turned his head when he heard his name being called, looking toward the entrance of the gym. He sat up abruptly when all he saw was rows of quiet exercise equipment and neatly stacked weight-sims.

"Jus?"

Not that it had to be Justice because it was a woman's voice, but he could see no cause for any other woman to seek him out at this hour. Considering the rigors of their training earlier, Justice always liked to get solid time in her rack. She wasn't the type for the restless nights that he was struggling with, so it would have surprised him to see her. But there was no sign of her or a messenger, certainly no sign of anyone on an IM base who would have dared to use his given name with such soft familiarity as he'd just heard.

More than likely he'd mistaken stray noises on Zero Station for the sound of a voice calling him. Why he'd thought it was female . . . well, he mused with a wry, self-deprecating smile, that didn't take a psychology degree to figure out, considering how long it had been since they'd had a decent planetside leave.

Keeping half an eye on the entrance to the room, he lay back on the mat again, indulging in a lackadaisical moment.

"Bronse."

Bronse froze when the very clear repeat of his name and the distinctly accented female voice flowed all around him, followed by the curious sensation of fingertips drifting down the side of his face.

"By the Being!" Bronse swore as he lurched to his feet, staggering back a step until his back hit a wall. He braced himself there for a moment, his heart pounding in shock, a half-dozen other emotions and thoughts crowding in on him.

He'd seen some pretty hair-raising stuff in his career, from cannibals to alien invaders from another galaxy, but invisible women? A ghost? Anything was possible, he supposed, and as a soldier he rapidly got past the strangeness of it and went right to the next step.

"Whoever you are, you're trespassing on a military installation. Show yourself," he demanded.

To his infinite shock, she did.

She was turning toward him as she materialized out of thin air. Details were blurred at first; only the burgundy color of the flowing fabric she wore and the darkness of her hair registered with any clarity. By the time she came fully about, however, the details were crystal clear, although she was more a holographic image than real. A very detailed ghost.

She was tall, not more than a head shorter than he was, and he was six foot four. Her features were sweeping and exotic—good bone structure and sly sensuality. Her mouth was generous, and her chin had a natural dimple. Her cheekbones were pronounced, elegant, drawing attention to the delicacy of her slim nose and the upward tilt at the corners of her eyes. All that facial exotica was foiled, however, by a simple pair of brown eyes, a cross between leather and topaz, although she got points for expressiveness because he could see wide-eyed curiosity and surprise within them. Her hair was deep, dark brown, he noted now that he could see it at its part against her scalp. It looked almost black in the cascading loops of small braids it had been styled into. Considering that the tightly trussed looping braids nearly reached the small of her back, Bronse expected that her hair was extremely long when unbound. In its current intricacy of design, however, it was utilitarian as well as pleasing to the eye.

Her figure was hidden by the free-flowing shape of the wine-colored burnoose she wore. The fabric parted in the center, giving him a glimpse of white clothing beneath. This half-hidden shift was made of a very light-weight fabric that revealed her darkly tanned skin. She wore knee-high boots and breeches beneath the ankle-length outer garment as well, and he caught flashing glimpses of Delran platinum in thin chains decorating the span between her hips and the tops of her boots. The beautiful precious metal was unmistakable, its rose-tinted glimmer blinding because of its infamous purity. On her wrists she wore a multitude of bangle bracelets made of the same metal, which was easily the most expensive natural element in the galaxy. Bronse realized that the clips binding her hair were also made of the valued metal.

Regardless of how she had appeared, Bronse was able to gather a great deal of information about her in just those few seconds. She was wealthy; only the very rich could afford Delran platinum. She was someone of import; he could sense it in her carriage and bearing. Never before in his career had he seen her type of features or her clearly cultural dress, making it possible that she was not from their system. Maybe she was from one of the wilderness areas on Ebbany or Tari, where not every culture was yet recorded.

The manner of her appearance still bothered him, though. It wasn't that he hadn't received his share of holographic messages in his time. That wasn't what was keeping him edgy and spooked. It was that there was no holographic reception pad in the middle of the floor of the officer's gym. Technologically speaking, her presence wasn't possible. One pad was needed to send and another to receive. At least, that was the *known* technology. Known technology also didn't allow for her very physical touch against his face. Bronse was damn sure he hadn't imagined that. He could still feel the path of her fingertips on his face as if his skin were hyperaware.

While he was making his observations, he could see her making her own. Her eyes moved over him with slow and blatant curiosity, shyness obviously not a factor in her makeup. She took in his hair, spiking haphazardly no doubt from being drenched in sweat, and the bluntly squared strength of his features. No one had ever called him handsome, and he didn't much care either way, but he wasn't unattractive either and he accepted that with a mental shrug.

She hesitated, as everyone did, at the lancing pastel stare of his eyes, a look of fascination spreading over her features as she leaned eagerly forward for a moment before catching herself. Bronse tried not to smile. His eyes had that effect on women, no matter who they were. She swept her gaze over the enormous breadth of his shoulders, the powerful sculpture of his chest, the smooth narrowing of his waist and hips, and the iron-hard thickness of his thighs and calves. He wore only the body-hugging black Skintex shorts that were usual for his workouts, so she was getting a highly unimpeded view of his body.

Bronse didn't mind. He was a big man, intimidating as hell, and in awesome physical shape. All of his crew maintained daunting physiques, each unique to their body structure. Bronse didn't believe in overdeveloping just for looks, however. He focused on strength, endurance, and the all-important agility needed for his job. None of his muscle got in the way of his movement, and none of it was for show. It was all about top performance under fire. He demanded the same of his entire crew.

"Who *are* you?" she asked.

Bronse was surprised by her question, his hands settling on his hips as he regarded her. He wondered how she could see him. He wasn't on a hologram pad, nor would he even know how to dial out a connection to this stranger.

"I think I asked you first," he said in his sharpest military tone.

She lifted a single brow, the delicate arch rising in an expression of amusement and surprise. It was the humor that threw him. Mainly because he was used to receiving respect and even intimidation in reaction to his military attitude. He'd perfected it during a short stint as an ETF training officer.

"My name is Ravenna. Somehow I know that your name is Bronse, though I do not know how. Now we have exchanged names, but it is unsatisfying, is it not? There is nothing to be learned from a name."

It was a good observation. He had learned more about her while she had stood silently before him. Although the unusual name could come in handy later when he got his hands on the Universal Database.

"Why did you come to me?" she asked.

Again, she had beaten him to the punch. He was bemused to the point of smiling slightly as he ran a hand through his wet hair, sending sweat bouncing off the ends.

"I didn't come to you. I think it was the other way around."

Now it was her turn to look bewildered. She recovered fast though.

"Who are you really," she demanded, narrowing her eyes. "Why do you taunt me like this?"

The question gave Bronse pause. There was the contempt of history in that strange remark. It was as if she was accusing him of . . .

Bronse straightened suddenly, flashes of memory swimming through him. "I've seen you before," he uttered in surprise.

"I cannot sleep because of you," she accused softly.

Dread chilled its way down Bronse's spine as he understood that the situation was mutual. "You," he said in quiet shock. "You're the one who keeps warning me about danger."

"No, I—" She broke off, startled out of her knee-jerk denial. "Yes," she uttered in reversal, "you are in danger. I had to tell you."

"Why? What do you know?" he demanded suddenly, stepping closer to the image of her, his fists clenching with anxiety.

To his surprise, she suddenly reached out to touch him, her left hand wrapping around the back of his neck, the other settling on his left pectoral muscle as she drew up flush to his body. It was shockingly intimate, a lover's embrace, as if she were going to pull him into a kiss. When he reacted, his hands passed right through her image. How was she able to touch him, yet he couldn't touch her in return? It was disconcerting, and he suddenly felt as though he could no longer easily defend himself.

However, she was gentle and otherwise benign as she settled against him. He could even feel her body warmth, the brush of the fabric of her clothes. Strange to feel her weight, yet it wasn't there. He had a sense of the figure hidden beneath the loose folds of the burnoose. He felt her ample breasts against his chest. A taut, flat belly touched his, and strong thighs slid long and lean over his own as they braced close to him. Bronse was astonished by the prickles of attentiveness that made themselves known up and down his body. He was already on edge, and he was aware from a militaristic perspective, but this was something far more intimate. He recognized it as a strictly male response, though he was baffled by his own uncontrolled reaction. Long stretches between planetside leaves or not, he did not usually react this casually to women. He made calculated, conscious choices in such matters. It was a lifelong habit that he had considered wise and logical for dozens of reasons.

Hell, she was hardly even a woman! Not a real one in any event. But she was still a threat, provided this wasn't a hallucination. Great Being, he hoped he wouldn't wake up in Medbay with heatstroke and a hard-on for an imaginary goddess.

The goddess, meanwhile, was looking directly into his eyes, her height placing her extremely close—just a minor head tilt away from eye level. He felt the grip of her hands tightening on his neck and chest, then her fingers turning chill as she seemed to disconnect from herself. A faraway but troubled expression passed over her.

"Do not let them leave you," she whispered, her breath warm and sweet as it flowed over his face. "They will die without you," she said urgently. Her eyes flickered behind their lids, her lashes fluttering as if she were in REM sleep and watching a dream. "And you will die without them. You must stay together."

"It's you. You're the reason I can't shake this feeling of danger." Bronse could hear the rush of his own breathing in his head, and suddenly his hands were closing around her back. He wasn't even aware that he was actually touching her now. "You keep coming to warn me."

"Yes," she said in a low voice, her tongue sliding anxiously between her lips to moisten them, the action drawing his swift attention as more powerful prickles of sexual awareness sparked through him. His body stirred against her, apparently with a mind of its own, intent on making its interests known. Yet something about all of this was terribly familiar. It was as if this impulsive arousal were a habit, a very enjoyable one.

"How do you know?" he heard himself asking her, his voice gruff, as her soft, sensual perfume—an aroma of gently exotic flowers and the undercurrent of erotic Ayalya spice—drifted in an assault on his senses. He knew that her closeness to his body wasn't meant to be a come-on, that it wasn't her intention to stir him. The grasp she had on him served another purpose, though he was confused as to what it was. He was the one making something sexual out of her attempt to warn him, to protect him. Bronse wasn't used to anyone outside of his team wanting to protect him. The feeling was disquieting.

Ravenna tilted her head to the side, her eyes opening and refocusing on him at last. As she came to herself again, she studied him carefully.

"I always know. I am never wrong. I do not know how it is we meet like this; I do not know what draws me to you night after night, Bronse, but I know you are in danger and I know that very soon you and I will meet in the flesh."

"We will?" An exciting thought, to say the least. All of Bronse's concerns about security and safety had fled. He was pretty much convinced that this was all a dream anyway.

"No!" she cried in despair.

Bronse woke up with a ragged gasp, sitting upright on the gravity mat in his shock. His heart was pounding hard enough to burst out of his chest. As he realized that it had indeed been a dream, he shuddered with the terribly real feeling that it had left behind. He could still feel the sweet weight of her body against his—a silhouette burned into the entire length of him. He was tense with foreboding and hard with arousal, the confusion of the two incongruous feelings twisting his gut and his brain into knots. Danger and desire clashed with mystification as he leapt to his feet, instantly feeling better once he was standing.

He had fallen asleep on the mat. He'd had a dream. That was all it was. Just a very strange dream. He had woken up the moment he had realized he was caught up in a fantasy. So why did it still feel so real? Shouldn't that feeling of realness shake off the longer he was awake?

It would, he realized. He just needed a few minutes.

Meanwhile, he also needed a cold shower and a visit to Medbay.

Ravenna woke with a stuttered gasp, sitting up on her pallet as she tore violently out of her sleep.

Curse him! He did it every single time! Him and his logical mind, disassembling and dissecting everything into neat, explainable categories; the minute he told himself he was dreaming, the dream ended. It was one of the conditions of such connections carried out in a dreamworld. That fragile state was always conditional to a being's belief system. While imagination could take a being to wild places, it would stop as soon as acceptance stopped.

Rave threw off her covers and swept to her feet. She reached to touch the thin gown she had worn to bed; she was still caught enough between sleeping and waking to need to check to see if she were wearing the nightgown she had donned at bedtime, or the wine burnoose she had worn earlier in the day. Thankfully she had a sense of modesty when she decided to visit the dreams of this strange man. He had gazed at her with more than enough obvious hunger while she was fully dressed. She could imagine his reaction if she'd shown up in the transparent Yojni silk with only its trimmings of Delran thread and Jimsu lace.

Actually, she could very easily imagine it, she admitted as she pressed cool hands to her heated cheeks. There had been no way to mistake the reactions of his body as she had leaned against him. And why was this the first detail jumping out at her, especially when there was so much danger and so little time left?

Yet she could not shake away the feeling. She moved to the small window of her chambers, ignoring the bars impeding her view so she could look up at the night sky. He was somewhere out there, this powerful man with his hard voice and even harder body. Rave shivered as she remembered the feel of all that corded sinew against her body. Gods above, but he had been so magnificently made. Did men truly come with such strength packed into their bodies? Or was he an exception, with his layers of twisting muscle? She had seen broad-shouldered men, but none so well shaped, nor so obviously powerful on sight alone. Bronse's chest had been a map of pure might; his skin heated and moist beneath her hands as she made the contact she had needed to read him. The power of his bulging biceps had been proved as his hands had found and gripped her back, the pure energy of his vigor radiating from his fingers. There was no mistaking the thick potency in his muscular thighs.

Ravenna's cheeks grew still hotter as she avoided descriptives of other thick and potent parts of his body.

She forced herself to concentrate on other things, reaching to pluck the silk of her gown away from her suddenly damp skin. She was telling him a bold truth when she had said they would be meeting soon, and it would not do for her to react in this wild manner when they did. Especially considering the danger to both of their lives she had predicted. She needed to focus on how she could possibly be of help to him.

She did not have the answer to that, though, aside from her obvious abilities, at least. It was all too vague. Would it be before or after the day looming in threat? Would this man rescue her from the awful fate of servitude that was being forced upon her, or would it be even more dangerous than that, the danger coming later, and in treacherous, foreign territory? Perhaps so. This she could not see. Damn her clarity anyway. Her clairvoyance was stubbornly capricious, picking and choosing what it would reveal. Bronse had asked her to elaborate, and she was not trying to be enigmatic when she couldn't do so. She was just as frustrated as he was. But at least she was sure now that he had gotten her warnings. She had been afraid that he would not remember the messages she had sent into his dreams. His reactions to her tonight, however, told her that he had remembered the messages, if not the messenger herself, in his waking world.

Oh, how she wondered about that world. She always met him in his immediate territory. It seemed so different, so beautiful and cold sometimes. He lived strangely, she knew. Their surroundings changed constantly in their shared dreams. One night she would sense metallic, hulking surroundings that clanged and echoed with the restless movements of others she could not see. The next night Bronse would be huddled under scraggly brush with black sand all around him. In all this time—a lunar month, as far as she could remember—he had never had a woman beside him. There had been men, however. She had never seen them, but she had sensed his awareness of their proximity. She might have thought it his preference if not for the way he reacted to her in his dreams.

That and the fact that she had come to understand that he was a soldier of some kind. A leader, actually. She had sensed that. He did not look like the warriors she was familiar with. Then again, she suspected that he came from a world that was very different from hers.

This brought her focus back to the stars. The brightest ones were planets. At certain times of the year, more or fewer of them were visible in the night sky. She had heard rumors that other beings lived on some of those planets. She had even heard stories that ships on her own homeworld left for those places constantly, that in the Citified States, such things were commonplace. These were tales told by fanciful bards and merchants who were looking to tweak some coin out of a naïve person's purse, she suspected. Still, how else would one explain a man like Bronse? She was no simple wilderness girl whose head could be turned by a charlatan's stories. She had a logical mind to go with her psionic one, and together they told her that there may be a great deal of truth in these matters.

If this were true, though, what would an off-world soldier have to do with her? How could their paths possibly cross? Even she knew how enormous Ebbany was. One man meeting up with one woman in the entire universe? It seemed impossible. And yet her heart had fluttered with excitement when she had remembered something from one of her geography lessons. Ebbany comprised mostly deserts, each different and unique. But the largest was the most unique of all.

Because of its black sand.

Did that mean Bronse had already been to Ebbany? She remembered the black sand so clearly. He had held his hands over it to warm them as the heat of the day escaped into the frigid cold of the desert night. He had talked to her so wearily, clearly tired from his disturbed nights of dreaming with her, yet still sharing innocuous facts about the desert animals at night. It had been a short lesson because he had woken up quickly. She had almost forgotten about it herself. It seemed, however, that tonight's dream had been different. It had been more like a culmination, a solidifying of the past visitations, bringing them into the forefront of memory so they were no longer vague and irresolvable.

All of this meant that time was drawing to an end.

Ravenna shivered as she cast her eyes down from the heavens and looked at the village, at her jailers, whom she had once treated with respect and honor. A deference they had more than reciprocated. The level of their betrayal burned within her like a fury. She was biding her time, though, before she let them feel it. They all would.

There was not much time, but there was enough. If Bronse came in time, she would wish to help him in every way she could imagine, so that they would meet as they were destined to and would both survive that meeting.

But if he came too late . . . ?

She would already have been sacrificed for the "good of her people," which would make any chance of saving her almost, if not completely, impossible.

CHAPTER
THREE

Lieutenant Commander Morse groaned as a high-pitched tone penetrated his sleep. He knew the tone and he knew it inevitably meant that he was not going to get his full eight hours of rack time. Not that he wouldn't survive. He had hundreds of times before. But the First Actives were on downtime, and that meant sleep, beer, and women, and hopefully lots of all three at that. If Bronse had reactivated them without telling him again, he was going to shoot him in the head first and ask questions much, much later.

Lasher gave in and reached to touch the communications pad with a light brush of a finger.

"Morse here."

"Sorry to bother you, Lieutenant, but I have a little problem and I think I'm going to need your . . . umm . . . special skills to assist me on the matter."

Masin hesitated for a beat, suddenly coming awake and processing a shipload of information at once.

"Trick?" he asked with surprise.

"Aye, sir."

"Chief, why the hell are you calling me at this hour? And don't tell me it's official when I know your ass is strapped to a bed in Medbay."

"No, sir. Actually, I'd like to keep it really unofficial . . . if you grasp my meaning."

Lasher sat up suddenly. Trick was never this vague. Not unless he had a damn good reason to be. He was practically speaking in code. A very obvious code, Lasher realized as he smacked himself in his thick head for not being quicker on the uptake the first time Trick had greeted him.

"On my way," he said shortly, punching the button to cut off the communication.

He leapt out of bed and began to jerk on his black uniform pants. His eyes dropped to his knife and gun in anticipation of dressing them on next.

Lasher had to enter a special code in order to access Medbay after hours. Luckily his rank allowed him access to that code. He was cautious as he entered the bay, not having a clue as to what he would find. The medics' station was abandoned; apparently the night medics were making rounds or doing whatever it was they did. Feeling grateful rather than suspicious, Lasher walked freely back through the halls of the huge bay to Trick's room, the location of which he already knew by heart. He passed a second medics' station and gave a smart salute to the man behind the desk, who automatically jumped up in haste and saluted back. Lasher chuckled to himself. Privilege number one in ETF was always the awe/respect factor that made it rare for the crew members' movements and actions to be questioned.

He pushed into Trick's room. He immediately stepped back to lock the door when he saw Bronse sitting on the chair near the chief's bed with a grim expression on his face, dressed in full uniform and just as armed as Lasher was.

"Have a seat," Bronse commanded politely, indicating a chair on the opposite side of Trick's bed.

Lasher did so without question or hesitation. As he drew himself into the chair, he noted the CompuVid on the table resting across Trick's lap. Apparently the chief had grown bored, and someone had plugged him into the Universal Database to amuse him or shut him up. Possibly both. There was nothing less tolerable than a high-adrenaline soldier stuck with bed rest.

"Comfy?" Bronse's sardonic tone was not lost on Lasher.

"As a babe," Masin said with a cheeky grin.

"Well, then, Trick, how about telling the lieutenant commander here a bedtime story?"

Trick grinned and saluted the commander enthusiastically, although his hand quickly recoiled to his flank as the sharp movement tugged at his healing wound. His first words came out a little strangled with pain.

"I was getting bored, you know. Almost a week down here by myself and all. So I found ways to entertain myself—"

"Let's skip the 'chasing nurses' part of the story, soldier."

"Well . . ." Trick grinned, clearly unrepentant. "The medic in charge got tired of me bugging everyone, so he jacked me into the Universal Database. So I'm flying all over the U.D. and I thought it would be funny to . . . uh . . . visit some places I'd never seen before."

"Translated—I take it—to mean that you hacked into restricted-access sectors?" Lasher queried.

"Which I am totally cleared to do, by the way," Trick argued.

"Under orders, supervision, or reasonable suspicion," Lasher retorted dryly, glancing at Bronse's impassive expression. Was the commander looking to discipline the junior officer?

"Yeah, well." Trick brushed all that aside with the careless flip of a hand. "So I thought it would make a good joke to hack into the IM database. I mean, all I was going to do was maybe issue you guys some false orders about delivering my favorite foods and an attractive woman."

Lasher glanced at Bronse, who was still playing at being impassive, but Masin could see the brief glow of humor in his eyes. Clearly something serious had happened; otherwise, the commander would have enjoyed the clever joke. They were always pulling stunts like this during downtime. Actually, it was something of a one-upmanship contest, although mostly among the junior officers.

"To issue orders, however, our young chief had to hack into the command codes in the IM database," said Bronse. "His codes of choice were those of Admiral JuJuren."

Lasher whistled low and with obvious amazement.

"Only you would pick the codes of the hardest ass in the entire IM fleet, Chief," said Lasher. "JuJuren is the one surefire way to get your rank busted down to that of a ground slug if you get caught." Lasher paused only a beat. "Tell me you did not get caught."

Trick scoffed with obvious derision at the very idea.

"But," Bronse said quietly, "our chief did catch something else of interest."

Trick turned the CompuVid screen toward Lasher. With a few light touches on the control pad, classified information from internal documents started to fly across the screen. Lasher read them quickly, trying to grasp what he was seeing and why it should be of interest. Suddenly a map in 3D with topographical color delineations exploded onto the screen, turning and pivoting on a central axis point that began to fill with names, dates, and what was clearly troop movement and military information in great detail.

"That's the Grinpar Desert. This is the data we just retrieved. North camp . . . northwest camp . . ." Lasher pointed to the camps as they rotated past him on the screen. "So what's—?"

Bronse almost smiled when Lasher broke off and frowned darkly in his confusion. He loved how quick Masin could be. One man in a million would have noticed a discrepancy that small, in such a short amount of time, even with hints to look for it. Lasher was grim and silent as he finished reading the information that Bronse had told Trick to show him.

"Why?" Lasher ground out suddenly, his anger back-building behind his pale jade eyes, the little black flecks floating in the sea of light color seeming more obvious in his outrage.

"Excellent question. According to that information, recon and PhotoVids had already been done prior to our excursion. The IM already had all of the information they needed, so why send us back out there? Which now also casts a peculiar light on why they urged me so strongly to split up the team. Now for the topper."

Bronse nodded to Trick. The young officer pulled up a file that he had recovered from the admiral's erased mail. The letter unfurled good as new on the screen, a testament to the chief's awesome skills. All the protected information on the IM database had "shredder" programs implanted to prevent anyone from doing exactly what he had done after the information was discarded.

A blank directive had been sent from IM headquarters to a receiving computer on Ebbany, divulging the coordinates of Bronse and Trick's location. Attached to that was a command to terminate them.

"That communiqué is stamped with Admiral JuJuren's personal send-code. Only he knows the code, and only his terminal can accept it and send from it like this," Trick informed Lasher quietly. "The rat-bastard sold out me and the commander. That was why that armed guard came up on us out of nowhere so suddenly. They didn't expect either of us to make it out alive, and if it weren't for Commander Chapel, we would have been bait for the sand hurricanes by now."

"They?" Lasher bit the word out. "So far I see evidence of only one traitor here."

"I know you aren't that naïve. Even an admiral couldn't justify sending the First Active ETF team on a recon that was already done. Someone had to bury the original intel and wipe the database of any information about the team that they'd sent out already. It also struck me that, with all the recon I've done for the IM, except for the major pooch-screw that happened, this was what I would've called—"

"A candy-assed assignment?" Lasher finished for him. "It wasn't an easy one, but I agree. It wasn't worthy of the First Actives. There are secondary and tertiary teams in the ETF that could've done just as well as we did. Better, apparently, because they didn't have bull's-eyes painted on their naïve asses."

"Easy does it. Who can we trust if not our superiors?" Bronse said softly.

"Commander, clearly we can't trust them," Lasher hissed, pointing to the evidence on the screen.

"We can't trust JuJuren or any of his immediate staff," Bronse corrected. "Our advantage here, thanks to Trick, is that JuJuren has no idea we're on to him. Laid up with nothing better to do, Trick can hack the old man right down to his undershorts and find out exactly how far this cancer has spread. Then we can think about how to proceed."

"What if we go active before we know the whole of it?" said Lasher. "Sir, we're grunts. Bottom line. We aren't intel officers. We have to go where the brass tells us to go, whether we like it or not. Whether we know it means certain death or not. Unless we bring this information to intel."

"Luckily we're a man down, and I took us off duty. They won't countermand my decision until Trick is operational. I say that gives us two weeks. I don't want to wait that long, though. Trick, only the Great Being knows if you'll get detected snooping around. I know . . ." Bronse held up a hand to fend off the indignant retort. "I know how good you are, kid, but there's always somebody better. Besides that, I need you to hurry. There are lives at stake here, and I don't want anyone's death on my hands any more than I wanted yours. Copy?"

"Copy, sir."

"Good. Keep low, keep cool, keep quiet," Bronse warned, as he did at the start of all their missions. "Lasher and I will rally with Jus and Ender later and do some fact sharing. For now, sign off and get some rack time under you, kid. I need you healed up fast."

"Aye, sir," Trick said with a cocky but eager attitude as he wiped away traces of his forays into the military database and shut down the system.

Lasher and Bronse rose to their feet and together they exited the infirmary. They waited until they were in regular corridors before they began to talk. The hour was still quiet, so they could talk relatively freely, though in soft voices.

"What's your plan, Commander?"

"To sleep with my knife and my laser gun."

"Mmm, I think I'll do the same, even though they targeted you and Trick. My guess is they were targeting you, and Trick was just an unfortunate bystander."

"My guess says you're right," Bronse said grimly. "But why the elaborate setup? And why now? Why me? I don't mean that in a whiny pity party way, either."

"Perish the thought," Masin said with a chuckle.

"My head is reeling with these questions. None of this adds up. I'm sure I've accumulated an enemy or two over the years, but to get an admiral to order an assassination attempt on me? I mean, do I look like I'm going to cause political trouble? I've followed orders since I was—"

"Sperm," Lasher interjected.

"Just about," Bronse agreed. "I thrive on taking orders and doing my job with little to no questions asked. What kind of threat am I to a man like that?"

"Besides being able to break his neck in forty-two different ways?"

"Besides that," Bronse agreed dryly. He sounded exasperated, but in truth he appreciated Lasher's lightening up of the grim circumstances. In the span of an hour, everything Bronse had believed in and planned on for himself had been thrown into play. His career and his life were both at risk, and he did not know why. That infuriated him almost as much as the impotent feeling that his strings were being pulled by some maniacal IM puppeteer.

"Well, there's always the big three."

"Money, power, and . . . ?"

"Sex."

"Of course," Bronse said, chuckling. "Sorry, I forgot who I was talking to."

"I'm serious. People do damn strange things for sex. Some greatly evil, some greatly good. Same goes for the other two. They are man's three most powerful motivators."

"Well, JuJuren has power."

"He could have more. There is always more. Top of the heap is . . . who? Prime Minister of the three worlds?"

"Yeah. That's definitely a good one. Or one of the overlords or emperors on the lower rung of Ebbany maybe. It's the most likely to be corruptible, as you know. And it's clear that he's buying favors already. He wouldn't send us there unless he was highly confident of his success and highly confident that he could manipulate what was happening in the territory."

"Okay. What about money?"

"Ebbany is not a rich planet, and even in the developed cities living is hostile. Tari has all the Delran platinum mines. That's where the money lies."

"Okay, what about sex?"

Sex. Bronse's mind immediately swam to the encounter he'd had in his sleep with Ravenna. He almost laughed at how quickly his body remembered every detail of that dream.

Suddenly he stopped walking.

What if the dreams of Ravenna had something to do with this? She had warned him of danger. Danger to his life and the lives of his crew. She had been warning him, it seemed, for quite some time, but it was only recently that he was able to remember that. What was worse, he understood clearly that there was still a future danger out there, somewhere, most likely on-mission. She had behaved and sounded so urgent. He had the impression that this danger was far more imminent than the two weeks that Trick would need to get fully cleared for returning to duty. It would not be unusual for them to be sent out as a foursome. They had been operating without a communications officer like Trick on and off for a full year now.

Bronse shook his head as if the movement could order his scattered thoughts. Why was he taking the portents of a dream so much to heart? Why did he believe in this warning so implicitly? He wasn't even bothering to question it. He was even less inclined to question it now that he had learned of JuJuren's betrayals. He cast a glance at Lasher, who was patiently awaiting his next thoughts. How much should he share with his second? What if Masin began to think he was losing his mind? Bronse couldn't have his second doubting his sanity or his clarity of thought or purpose. It was his job to inspire confidence in all his junior officers, and that included Lasher.

How could he even begin to explain what he himself did not clearly comprehend? If he believed this dream woman, then he would have to believe that she had an ability that was, quite frankly, inconceivable. A precognition of sorts, and a powerful one at that to be so detailed. But the military had researched and tested paranormal and psychic capabilities dozens of times and had found no foundation for them. If there had been even an ounce of reality to the idea of such abilities, the military would have been the first to exploit and incorporate them into the services.

Then again, until an hour ago, Admiral JuJuren had been the least likely corruptible admiral in the IM services. Bronse would have to be infinitely more cautious in the way he thought about things.

"We aren't just grunts, you know," he corrected Lasher belatedly. "We're all highly intelligent and well diversified. We're always given an objective and a plotting from point A to point B and then back again for extraction, but you tell me how often those best-laid plans have gone off without a hitch."

"Not too damn often," Lasher agreed.

"And we'd be dead a hundred times over if we weren't quick on our feet and able to outthink our enemies while keeping an eye on the military horizon. There's a reason why people respect us . . . and fear us."

"I know that, sir. I was just making the point that we're still subject to orders and military restrictions."

"I know."

"Why don't you just go to intel with this?" Lasher questioned Bronse further. "Why are you dropping it into Trick's lap?"

"Because I trust Trick. Normally, with him being the new guy, I wouldn't say that so easily. I mean, we're still feeling each other out and all. But Trick came to me with this and made me aware. He wouldn't have done that if he was on JuJuren's payroll."

"So that's it? You're afraid that intel has spies?"

"Aren't you? JuJuren's powerful. Spy or no spy, some-one he knows or someone who respects him sees his name come across a desk somewhere and they pick up the phone and tip him off. I don't want that to happen. I want the kid to get some better proof than what he has now. A preponderance of information. This way we get a look at what JuJuren's been doing before the bureaucrats fuck it all up."

Bronse was silent for another long minute, thinking dark and leading thoughts that he wasn't going to share. Lasher wished he could just ask him to spill whatever he was holding back. However, Lasher had known Bronse long enough to realize that he would just piss him off if he pushed him before he was ready.

"Lasher, I have a real sick feeling in my gut again," Bronse informed him gravely.

"I know, sir. I feel it too."

"I don't want Justice and Ender going another minute without being on the update. I'll take Ender. You go to Jus. Make sure everyone stays armed at all times, both day and night rotation, and that means backup and covert weapons too. Tell them to choose something non-standard for at least one hidden weapon. I want everyone to have something up their sleeve that isn't a well-known military trick. Copy?"

"Aye, loud and clear. What say we round up at mid-day meal in your quarters? I'll pay a visit to Trick right before then, so I'll have updates to share with the crew if there are any to be had."

"Good idea. I want us acting as though we're on-mission. Make it clear. But I also don't want us raising any suspicion, so everyone needs to appear relaxed and off-mission."

"Got it."

"See you at midday."

"Yup!"

Lasher jogged off and took the left corridor, heading in the direction of Justice's quarters.

When Bronse entered his quarters some time later, after his interesting informational encounter with Ender, the sound that came to his urgent attention was the steady beep that seemed to seek out his spine and wrack it with a foreboding chill. He knew the sound well. His eyes darted to the ComVid as he rapidly approached it. Sure enough, a redlined message was flashing in wait on the screen, its accompanying tone indicating that the First Active team had just been issued orders.

Bronse felt as though someone had poured molten lead into his gut. Was this merely coincidental? Or had Trick's stealthy skills been overestimated? He dreaded taking his team out on any operation without knowing if he or they would at least be safe from the resources that were supposed to be backing them up.

Bronse cursed viciously under his breath as he punched up the orders. The swearing only intensified when he saw the operational locale.

Ebbany.

They were going back to that desert hell-acre with its strangely colored sands and enemies that were plotting with the upper echelon of the IM. Oddly enough, it gave him comfort to see that it was JuJuren who had signed the orders and approved the mission. It meant he didn't have to wonder if the mission would get shot to shit. He didn't have to worry about when the next attempt would be to murder him. He had the exact date and time flashing on the screen right before his eyes. By now, Lasher, Ender, and Justice had also become aware of their orders and all their implications, and no doubt they were furious and chomping at their bits with the need to act. They were soldiers, and that was what they did—act. But what could they really do?

Bronse sighed and looked around his rooms thoughtfully. He reached for a metal bangle sitting on his nightstand and snapped it around his wrist. The handsome piece of jewelry was finely etched, the silvery metal glinting in the center so the design was highlighted, but burnished to a duller tone at the ends where they touched together in a pair of intricately woven knots. What was not so readily seen was a seam in the etching where the cuff would break easily into halves, exposing a good two feet of delicately barbed garrote wire strung between the halves. This was one of the hidden tools that were not standard military tricks. He would arm himself with others as well.

Someone was going to find him a very difficult target to terminate.

CHAPTER
FOUR

Kith flinched outwardly, though he tried his best to resist the reaction. Nevertheless, when Ravenna took the vicious blow to her back and fell to the dirt floor, no doubt skinning her knees as she landed on them, he felt the physical pain himself as it shuddered up and down her spine. That, of course, was why he was here. They knew that he would feel every moment of Rave's agony, knew that it would be torture for him to kneel there helplessly watching as they did their worst to her.

Finally, they reached for the back of her gown, tearing it roughly, their huge, mauling hands rending the Yojni silk with eager ease. One of the Banda Nomaads chuckled with that grunting way they all had when they saw the smooth copper skin of Rave's back. Then the bastard reached out with rough, short fingers to stroke her lasciviously. Kith felt Rave's sudden wash of revulsion and shame as well as blinding fury, both his own and hers, as she was violated by the common scum of this tribe. He tried to surge to his feet. The guards behind him were prepared for his reaction, though, and they easily shoved him back to his knees with their harsh hands on his shoulders. His arms were bound to a prison stick running horizontally across his back; otherwise, he would have ripped out their cursed hearts.

The guard continued his foray across Rave's skin, and

Kith could feel her embarrassment and anguish right down to his soul. He could not see her bowed face from behind the fall of her hair, but he knew she had lost her pride to slow, pained tears. The guard made free with her, stroking under the silk of the torn gown and around to her breast. Kith wanted to scream, to roar his emotions and hers to the entire universe. Surely, feelings like this had a power more useful and more potent than to shred a spirit apart!

Why did she not fight them? Gods, how he wished he could touch her mind and force her to resist. He knew she was holding back, lying in wait, biding her time for her "hero," this warrior she saw in her visions. She had made Kith promise that no matter what happened, he would not betray her secrets until she was ready. It was a promise he now despised himself for.

"Rave!"

"No!" she cried back, because as always she already knew what he was thinking.

If she could bear this humiliation, then Kith must bear it, too, she thought, squeezing her eyes tightly shut as coarse, clumsy fingers jerked at her sensitive nipple. She knew they would not, could not rape her. They couldn't lessen her sale value in that way. Though they could probably do everything but. They would do it not just to make use of her, commoners suddenly able to access a Chosen One; they would do it just for the delight of torturing Kith. She knew Kith wanted her to fight. She knew they both had the power to escape this prison chamber and these callous ruffians, but there were other lives at stake, and she could not tip her hand until the time was right. She felt it in the marrow of her bones: Bronse was coming. He was even now hurtling toward his destiny with her. If he survived the test to come, he would be her deliverer. If she left it up to herself and Kith alone, they might escape the room, might even escape the stronghold if they were extraordinarily lucky, but there were only enemies and wilderness all around them after that.

No, what they needed was a direct route off the planet. And Bronse would come with that. She knew it assuredly even though she knew so little about the method of escape she sought. Her confidence was borrowed from Bronse, she believed. His knowledge was so secure and so self-assured in these matters that she knew he would know the way. Just as she knew he was even now finding the way to her side. She let her feelings of faith and sureness in her rescue wash through her with more power than her shame and her fear, knowing that this was the only true way to communicate with, and help, her brother.

Kith felt all his empathic senses flare to life, turning in focus as Ravenna manipulated her connection with him. He wanted to be furious with her, but he could not. He could not begrudge her whatever hope or conviction she needed to make it through these next minutes. Selfishly, he could not begrudge himself, either. It would destroy him to see her abused. So he let her well-being of emotion soak into him, even though he fixed his shimmering hazel eyes on the scene before him. He would remember every moment of this, every action and every sin. Just as he would remember each of the men's faces and each of the acts they individually subjected her to. He would remember for as long as the sun and moons stroked Ebbany's back. He would remember until the blood of these men warmed his hands and their deaths warmed his tortured soul.

Ravenna wished she could command herself suddenly to sleep. It was strange that something that had troubled her for so long had suddenly become a haven and a comfort. When she slept, if Bronse slept as well, she could feel him with her. Not as powerfully as their last real communication, when she had actually felt him beneath her hands and against her body, but almost as though they somehow held each other loosely, a linking of spirits that gave them rest and peace now that they had clarified the messages they had been sharing.

But she would not seek his comfort, she knew, when all she would deliver to him would be distress and an outrage to his sense of honor. Funny, she thought, that she should know that about him. That though he was a soldier and a man of war, he had an honor that would never allow him to do to a woman what was being done to her even now.

"Bronse . . ." she whispered, not knowing why she felt compelled to say his name aloud. But hearing it gave her a measure of comfort.

The Nomaads were riled up now, calling encouragement to the one who touched her so disgracefully. Their noise brought her back to the dreadful reality of the moment as her abuser's second hand stole around to clutch her other breast in a bruising grip. She cried out with pain despite her intentions otherwise, making them roar with approval and delight. They mistook her pain for their idea of an aroused response, and she felt the Nomaad's burnoose fluttering around her as he moved to rub himself against her back. Tears welled once more, and she swallowed back all further sounds of dismay. His hard male member was pressed between her shoulders, and he pushed with increasing fervor against her in a mock of mating. She sensed his lust. She knew he wanted to force her to do terrible things, just as his friends did. There were ways of raping the Chosen One without taking her precious and coveted virginity.

"*Areste!*"

Kith caught his breath when Rave finally spoke, her bold, authoritative voice barely showing emotion as she commanded them to halt in the Banda's own tribal language. It said a lot about the lore and legends of the Chosen Ones that every guard in the room froze, even to the point of forgetting to breathe. Kith lowered his head to hide the twitch at the corner of his lips and the amusement in his eyes. He waited as his sister let the command stretch out a good minute before she continued to speak in their tongue. She had learned quickly in her captivity, he marveled. As he listened, he barely was able to translate.

"You have touched me and I have had a vision from it," she spoke over her shoulder to the one who still clutched at her body. Her announcement elicited a few cautious chuckles and some quick whispers. "Would you know your fate, Banda? Or would you prefer to live in ignorance?"

Kith gave his bowed head a little shake, letting his sandy blond and brown hair fall forward to further conceal his features. Let them think he was being submissive, when in fact Rave's ruse was making him grin. He knew what Ravenna looked like when a vision hit, and he knew she needed to touch someone in a particular manner in order to specifically read their personal future. She had definitely done neither in the past thirty minutes that they had been confined to this chamber. But during her captivity among this tribe, every one of the Nomaads had come to learn about the Chosen One Ravenna and her stunningly accurate visions.

The Banda Nomaad suddenly jumped away from Rave as if she had burned him. She sagged forward with her release, but only for an instant. Kith watched through the fall of his hair as she threw back her shoulders and her hair with incredibly regal grace, and then hoisted herself to her feet so she could turn to face her assailants. It was no simple trick for her to regain her footing from a kneeling position when her arms were tied to a prison pole against her back. But Ravenna did it with poise and made it look easy. Kith felt so proud of her then that he was close to bursting with admiration and love. She had everyone's attention, but Kith knew that it was not her intention to escape, only to buy herself a little time, and a little power while she was at it.

"What fools you are, wasting your opportunity with a Chosen One on beatings and lustful games when you could be finding out your futures. I can tell you the present and the past. I can tell you when you will die or when a family member will pass on. Would you not wish to know ways to obtain riches? No. You prefer to waste your time playing like barbarians! Pah!" she scoffed. "You wouldn't know what to do with the glory of a Chosen woman even if she drew up detailed instructions! I have a direct love with the gods!" she said feverishly. "They tell me their words and touch my mind! I am their child! They are looking down upon you even now. And what do you think the gods are feeling for you as you molest their daughter?"

Rave let that sink in as she glanced surreptitiously at Kith, checking to see if her sensitive brother was well. Through the fall of his dusty hair, she saw the shine of amusement glittering from his hazel eyes. Rave then looked boldly at the guard who had thrust himself against her. He had turned white as chalk, not easy for a swarthy-skinned Banda Nomaad. He was also sweating up a storm under his burnoose even though the climate underground in their new prison was cool and controlled. She stepped up to him and saw his Adam's apple working hard as he swallowed.

"Do you wish to know your future, foolish one? I will give you another chance if you promise never to violate a Chosen woman in such a manner again. I will speak softly to the gods about you and convince them to ease their wrath."

"Yes, angel, I beg you." He bowed at his waist, touching his fingertips to his forehead and then his heart in a traditional salaam. "We were ordered to lash you and to take the spirit from you, so you would be more docile a bride for the Shiasha of the ruling tribe."

"Yes, angel," spoke up another guard quickly. "Though you have the queenly grace and manners that the Shiasha would find valuable in his bride, and your status as a Chosen One will bring our tribe much reward, your stubborn manner and prideful attitude is most unappealing in such a role. The Shiasha would be angry with our tribe if we produced a less than suitable—and biddable—bride to him."

"So you were ordered to shame me? To mar my perfectly unblemished skin with lashing? You think the Shiasha would want a scarred bride? Idiots! Who gave such a stupid order?"

"The Shia of our tribe."

"Your king then. A minor king who thinks he knows what the Shiasha wants in a bride?" Again she scoffed with queenly derision. "And your little king would have a daughter of the gods beaten and then gifted to the Shiasha so that the curses of the gods would follow me to his household?"

Every guard, to a man, gasped in horror. The Shiasha of this area was a powerful warlord. Everyone curried favor with him and scraped and bowed to avoid his wrath in even the smallest way. Even Rave and Kith's own village had eventually betrayed them, sold them out to this higher-powered tribe, making gifts of them to the high king, the Shiasha, to help placate him and honor him. They were willing to risk the ephemeral fury of the gods they could not see in order to appease the brutal warlord breathing down their necks.

Rave and Kith had spent time in captivity in their home village, and now in this more barbaric Nomaadic one that Kith could hardly believe was called civilization.

Their village may have been small, but it had been far more educated and peaceful. At least he had thought so, until they had been sold as slaves to these barbarians. Valuable Chosen Ones to be offered like delicacies to the Shiasha—one to be a bride, one to be a personal slave to the Shiasha.

Neither position was a welcome one. Kith would spend his days chained by his ankle to the throne of the Shiasha, using his Chosen powers to tell the warlord what people were feeling, if they were lying or not, and—his special talent—touching objects to learn their historical value, their stories, and their lives.

As a bride, Ravenna would do little better. She would join an already expansive harem, no doubt. The Shiasha was a man in his fortieth year at least. He had acquired a great many "gifts" like Ravenna over the years of his sexual maturity, although it was not likely that he had been gifted with a Chosen One before. Chosen Ones tended to live in sacred temples, as priests and priestesses, just as Rave and Kith had lived before their village had bartered them away. The Shiasha would think he could gain power by bedding Rave. There were many who thought that. As if psychic ability were catching like a sexually transmitted disease. When he tired of trying, he would get her with child, forget her, or use her just as he would use Kith. In fact, Rave's powers were ten times what Kith's were. She would be the more valuable of them, if she ever let it be known.

However, Rave believed that she and Kith would never meet that terrible fate. And when Rave believed in a specific future, Kith had no choice but to follow her on faith. She had been right too many times. This time she seemed almost fanatical about it. He had never before seen her believe in her gift with such zeal. She was putting all of her bets on this warrior she saw coming. Kith could only pray that she was right. She would be crushed

if this soldier failed to show, or failed to be everything
she had envisioned him to be.

For now, Kith watched her hold the attention of the
Nomaads with the power and aplomb she had used to
keep the temple in order. As High Priestess, she had
called powerful beings into harmony. These non-Chosen
men were a puzzle hardly worthy of her mastery. They
had leapt into her palm in a single heartbeat. Now she
would spend her time slowly closing her hand and squeezing her fingers about them.

Bronse turned fitfully on his bunk, flipping onto his
back with a frustrated sigh as he tucked a hand beneath
his head and stared up at the metal plates of the ceiling
above him. They were en route to Ebbany, taking the
trip there far slower than they had when they had last
left it. They had been forced to stop at a supply depot on
one of the more distant planetside stations on Ulrike,
and it had taken two days before they were mission-
ready. He and the crew had taken the time to work out
varying strategies, but the delay had chafed at Bronse in-
terminably. Time, he felt, was slipping away.

And it was his dreams that were telling him so.

For the most part, they had become something less
defined, but comforting in their vague way. He knew she
came to him at least once during every sleep cycle. The visitation in his mind was of varying lengths of time, sometimes all too short, sometimes long spans of a cocooned
existence where her steady, calming essence seemed to
surround him, and his surrounded her and was received
as if it gave her equal depth of peace. Sleep had come
quicker and easier these past nights, his troubling insom-
nia now gone since the dream in the gym.

Until tonight.

Tonight they were spaceborne, hurtling back toward
Ebbany at a steady clip. They would reach the planet in

two more days. He wished he could attribute his sudden sleeplessness to the anxiety one would have when making a forced march to certain death. However, he had too much faith in himself and his junior officers, in spite of ominous portents and obvious plots, to truly be that worried and fatalistic.

So he was suddenly afraid that something else was amiss.

"Great Being, Chapel, when did you get so superstitious?" Bronse muttered aloud to himself.

He closed his eyes, trying to settle himself and his thoughts. He heard the treading of metal just outside his quarters and knew that it was Ender pacing the corridors just by the weight and cadence of his steps. Justice was asleep, as was Lasher. That left Ender on maintenance. Bronse smiled softly. Lasher was supposed to be on maintenance, but clearly Ender had made other plans. Bronse had no cause to object. He knew that Ender would have stayed on shift either way, even if he was ordered to his rack. The arms master did not like knowing he was on a suicide mission that someone else had plotted for him. Granted, that was probably the very definition of their jobs, but this was different. This was betrayal and treason at their most malevolent.

Bronse had given each of the crew the choice of an out. He could not in good conscience do anything less. In his quarters, after they had received their orders and while sharing the midday meal, he had given each of them the opportunity to back out of the mission. He'd almost faced a rousing mutiny at the very suggestion, and he still felt unbelievable pride in his crew when he remembered it. He had not thought they would abandon him in such a clear hour of need, but he had been obliged to give them a choice. They would likely be cut off, unable to depend on IM resources until they returned to the actual base. If he were JuJuren, Bronse thought, he would not make the same mistakes twice. This time he would see to it that Bronse was somehow cut away from his best resource—his crew—and then JuJuren would make his next attempt. The crew was a man down—their communications officer at that—and this would be viewed as an advantage for JuJuren. Normally it might be, if not for the fact that their comms officer had spiked the IM database already, giving the crew a crucial heads-up on what awaited them for this mission.

"Bronse . . ."

Bronse's breath hitched in his chest at that now familiar voice beckoning to him. His heartbeats shifted into double time. He could not help the reaction even if he wanted to. Great Being, how that silky, sultry little accent played over his senses. Did she have any idea how she sounded? For that matter, did she know how she affected him?

He opened his eyes and sat up, throwing his legs over the side of his bunk. Bronse searched for her, waiting patiently for the slow fading in of her image. It came gradually, low to the ground, little more than the sweep of her dark, unbound hair. And yes, it was just as incredibly long as he had suspected it would be. And thick. He could see the density of it clearly now that it wasn't bound into those looping braids.

It took him a moment to realize that she was kneeling on the ground, sitting back on her heels, and this was why he could see only the mantle of her hair.

"Ravenna?"

She turned her head slightly, then her chin dropped down and she turned back away.

"I did not want you here," she said. "Why did you come?"

It was not the greeting he had gotten used to. She had been far more welcoming recently. This felt like a sudden step backward, almost like the sharp stinging slap of rejection.

"I never plan these meetings," he reminded her. It was only a half-truth at this point, however. He may not plan them, but he had begun to look forward to them.

"But it is only a dream after all," she said coldly.

Bronse sucked in a breath as a ferocious chill of warning walked down his spine. Ravenna had never encouraged the breaking off of communication between them. By saying that, she had all but guaranteed the event. Even now he was surprised that he remained asleep. Perhaps he was too exhausted to be so easily put off, or too soon into the visit for such a trick to work. All he knew was that he was grateful her ploy had failed.

But something was very wrong here.

He stood up and began to walk toward her. She suddenly flung a halting hand back toward him, turning her face away.

"No! Don't come any closer!"

Her violent demand and body language made him hesitate for a second. But then her body motion also parted her hair against her back. Bronse sucked in a harsh, choking breath when the unmistakable redness of blood and swelling appeared in an angry red line. No. Many lines, he realized.

"By all that is cursed and holy!" he swore, suddenly rushing to her and falling to his knees behind her. "Ravenna, what in the Great Being's name happened?" Why did he even ask? He already knew, even before he brushed her hair away with both hands as gingerly as he could. The strands, delicate as they were, clung to the wounds, stuck to the dried blood on her back. She had been whipped. There was no mistaking such wounds. No mistaking the ragged tearing of her silken gown down its back.

"Please, don't . . ." she whispered.

Bronse could not grant her the request. In their short, vague acquaintance, he had seen a proud beauty who knew her mind and how to express her convictions. She was gentle by nature in spite of that. She was not the type to give anyone cause to do such a thing, not that anyone ever deserved it. He knew it hurt her to be seen like this by him, to be shamed and weakened before him, and he felt his throat closing with fury and sympathetic pain for her because he would feel exactly the same way. He, too, would have tried to push her away had the situation been reversed. Yet he would have secretly welcomed what he was about to do for her.

"Hush," he soothed her gently, reaching to cup her chin in his fingers, his thumb stroking her cheek from his position behind her. "There is no shame between friends, Ravenna. No shame when we are abused in ways we do not deserve."

"Bronse, please," she gasped, and he could feel her shaking with repressed emotion.

"No," he said firmly. "I will not leave you to suffer alone. Don't be so brave, that's my profession."

At last, she broke, a hard, shuddering sob wracking through her. She keened softly in her pain and despair, and Bronse slid around her so he could pull her against him in an effort to comfort her. He did so gingerly, holding her by an arm and the back of her head, knowing that she would feel agonizing pain if he touched or pulled at her back in any way.

"I was not made for this." She wept softly, her face burrowing against the fabric of his sleeping tunic. "I have been cherished most of my life. I believed that the gods would always protect me. I don't understand why it all changed!"

Bronse suspected that was not true, that she understood it all too well, but he did not expect her to be logical when she was suffering so much. There would come a time, later, when he would be able to understand everything about her with clarity. For now, he worked with instincts he hadn't even realized that a hard-core warrior like him could have. But this woman had always touched him in the strangest ways, even though they had never met.

He gently brushed her hair away from her tear-streaked cheeks, feeling the pangs of so many emotions that he hardly had time to identify them all. Bronse touched his lips to her forehead in comfort.

"No," he agreed softly, "I can tell you were not made for this. None of us is truly made for acts of war and violence."

"You are," she countered, even in her upset refusing to allow him to get away with that generalization.

"Perhaps." He chuckled softly. "But even I have my limits. I'm trained to face this kind of . . . of torture in the event of captivity, but I don't have the stomach to mete out cruelty for the sake of my own enjoyment. I have never understood those who like to toy with their victims. That's not to say I don't mete out justice, though. I'm no saint."

"I never thought you were. No saint, but destined to be a savior. Mine." She spoke with such conviction that it gave Bronse a chill that washed down through his guts.

"I hope you're right, Ravenna," he murmured softly against her skin. "I wish I had the faith of your conviction."

"Why should you when you know nothing about me, or this connection we have between us? You would be a fool to accept my word with no empirical proof or data. You are a man of logic, I know, inasmuch as you are a soldier."

"And you are a very wise woman." He drew a deep breath, the softly spiced scent she wore on her skin drifting into his lungs. "Is there no one to tend these wounds where you are?"

"No one who is allowed the opportunity," she said vaguely. "I am being left to suffer because I tried to buy myself some time and . . ."

There was something ominous to the feel of her unspoken sentence. It was reinforced when she shuddered with a feminine violence that he had felt once before. Bronse had once come upon a village in the Tari wilderness that had been decimated by a war between clans. One clan had swooped down mercilessly upon the other, slaughtering every single male in the town. As Bronse had walked through the devastation, a woman had staggered into him, gripping him wordlessly as her wide eyes reflected the horrors that had been visited upon her by her enemies. She, too, had worn a dress torn asunder, and blood had stained rivulets down her thighs as she had shuddered with that same violence.

Again, Bronse was overcome with an outrageous wrath that he could barely control. He was not one to feel so stark and wild, so he felt lost, as though he were foundering for direction as he held her tightly against him. "Did they rape you?" he asked heedlessly, knowing it was a terrible thing to ask her even as the words passed his wooden lips. But he simply could not help himself. Then, being a man and knowing what men were capable of doing, he amended the question. "Did they violate you, Ravenna?"

She had not reacted to the first question, but she crumbled at the second version of it, giving him an answer he did not have the capacity to deal with just then. He stored the outcries and rage buffeting through him for another time. And he knew that time would come. Soon. Someone would pay for every tear and every tremble ratcheting through this precious woman. He would see to that. Yet he knew that promises of vengeance and retribution meant little to her. Her needs were altogether different right now.

As carefully as he could as he sat cross-legged on the floor, he drew her into the well of his lap, cradling her gently and holding her close to the warmth and security of his body. "You will be safe with me," he promised her. It was a promise for the future and, hopefully, for the present as well. "We will find each other soon. Remember?"

"Yes. If you and your companions survive the separation that is coming."

"We will," he assured her with all the ETF superiority he could muster. He felt her smiling against his chest, and he smiled, too, in response. "Can you tell me where I will find you?"

"I don't know where anymore. I don't know where I am. I only know we are now underground."

"I keep hearing a 'we' here. Is that something I should know?"

"Perhaps. My brother, Kith, is a captive here as well. They . . . they like to make him watch . . . what they do to me."

"By all that is cursed!" he ground out, unable to suppress his furious reaction. "You're being held by Nomaads!"

"Yes. How did you—?"

"Well, telling me you were underground was a good clue. But I've seen Nomaadic torture methods before. The one you speak of is an old favorite of theirs. Forcing family to watch." He stopped, knowing she didn't need his recounting when she was obviously experiencing the facts firsthand. She and her brother.

"Bronse . . ." She suddenly turned, and her hands slid up over his chest to grasp his shoulders.

He tried. He honestly tried, but he could not repress the shudder of pleasure her touch sent through him. Furious with himself, Bronse shoved down the wayward and inappropriate reactions. He could only hope she did not sense the reason behind his response. Perhaps she had not noticed it.

"It's okay," he said with an even, soothing tone as he tried to hold her in comfort and avoid her raw back. He felt awkward, as if his hands were superfluous, because he *wanted* to touch her so badly, because he felt that instinctual urge within himself to stroke her and soothe her, feeding her disturbed psyche with the warmth of his strength and good intentions through the touch of his hands.

"Tell me," she begged softly. "How long before you come here? Do you know?"

Bronse closed his eyes tightly, suddenly feeling all the inadequacies of his situation with a great deal of pain and frustration. How could he possibly predict the unpredictable? Were it his choice, he would be liberating her even then.

But he had no choice. He had a mission to fulfill.

Whether it was a trap, lambs to the slaughter or even a legitimate operation, he must carry out his orders as instructed until he felt that other action was warranted. His team understood that, and they were prepared for it. How could he possibly prepare this serene woman for a wait that promised to be pure hell at the hands of the bastards who held her? They had whipped her today. The Great Being knew what else they had done. What would tomorrow hold for her?

"No sooner than two days," he said at last. "Beyond that, I cannot say."

She met his gaze as soon as his eyes opened. Bronse was struck by the soulful depths of her soft topaz irises, the deeply toasted gold with its starbursts of brown and their incredible bravery in the face of all the implications of his answer.

"I understand," she murmured. "It is meant to be. I don't know why I asked. Everything will unfold in its predestined way. Nothing that either of us does will change that. Or perhaps if we change it, we risk never meeting at all. Such is the danger of precognition."

Bronse felt her logic and her acceptance on what could only be described as a spiritual level. How could he not? It was so soft and simple, without hint of bitterness or resignation. It was a rare and painfully beautiful thing to behold in such close proximity. *She* was a rare and beautiful thing to behold. He finally found an acceptable locale for his hand, raising it to her soft, high cheek, brushing a calloused thumb over a perfection of smooth skin. She felt so real and so warm. He had never felt anything as supple as her skin. He had never seen eyes of such fortitude in a woman that could also be so exquisitely lovely.

Of its own accord, his gaze drifted down to the ample shape of her jewel-toned lips. Before he realized it, his thumb was brushing over the breadth of her bottom lip, feeling its lush warmth and slight dampness as her heated breath cascaded over his hand. He was breathing as if he had run an obstacle course by the time his gaze darted back up to hers with guilt, need, and other conflicts gleaming in periwinkle depths.

Bronse was shocked to realize that his other hand had found a comfortable home wrapped around the thick swath of her hair. This time, he recognized grimly, it was he who held her in the lovers' embrace. Only where her intent had been innocent of those connotations, he knew that his was not. He was fighting the urge to draw her to his kiss like he had never fought any other impulse before in his life.

"Why?" She asked the question so softly that he wasn't sure he had even heard her correctly at first.

"Why . . . what?"

"Why not follow your impulses?" she asked with painfully blatant curiosity. "Why would you think that, in the face of all I must endure here, I would not want something purer and of my own free will to sustain me?"

Bronse groaned as aching desire trebled throughout his body. His forehead fell forward to touch hers as he clenched his teeth together.

"Because you don't . . . Ravenna, you don't understand. I'm not some gentle savior. I'm afraid you have made me out to be something in your mind that I'm not. I'm not the kind of man who would treat you the way you'd want me to. Treat you as you deserve to be treated."

"And the Nomaads are? What man is it that you think I deserve? I may see you as a savior, but I have never expected gentility from you. Though you have shown it in abundance, Bronse, I have never blindly assumed you to have gentleness in your nature." She lifted her hand from his shoulder, her hot fingers spreading across his cheek, her nails scraping through the nighttime shadow along his jaw. "What will you give me that you think will be so offensive?" she asked breathlessly.

"Nothing. Everything! Hell . . ." he ground out, her invitations sending heat searing through his flesh and bones. Inch by inch he flooded with a slow, intense burn for her. It left him with negative life signs—no breath, no heartbeat, not even a coherent brain wave—for all of thirty seconds. "It's not right," he said stubbornly.

"It's not?" she asked, blinking those damnably beautiful eyes at him with utter guilelessness.

"No!" he insisted furiously, right before he dragged her mouth beneath his. Then he was kissing her, getting it out of his cursedly callous system, greedy, rotten bastard that he was turning out to be. Undeserving. He knew it even if she did not. He didn't deserve . . .

Ravenna's mouth. It felt just as full as it had looked, her warm lips spreading generously over his as if she had no reason to second-guess or hesitate. Her perfume welled up into his senses with heady perfection—flowers, spice, and the warmth of a woman all wrapped up in a potent confection. Her body gave a luscious little tremble in his lap, her breath catching and exhaling in a jolted shudder of surprise. She made a sweet sound of wonder and astonishment, as though she hadn't expected to be pleased. Bronse might have been a little insulted if her lips hadn't parted to make the little noise, leaving him with an irresistible opening. He took advantage, touching the velvet warmth of his tongue to the inside of her lower lip. Great Being, that lip suddenly seemed the most delectable thing he'd ever come across in his life. He sucked it gently, savoring it for a very long moment, making a liar of himself about his deficiencies in gentility. He silkily switched from lower lip to upper, tasting her sweetness and her surprise with a surging sense of delight and male satisfaction.

By now, both of his hands were cradling her head, his thumbs stroking over her incredibly soft cheeks again and again as he became more liberal in his exploration. He pressed his palms gently against her jaw, pulling apart her teeth, allowing him access beyond them. His tongue swept into her mouth, instantly finding hers, encouraging her into exploring with him their shared taste and textures. She made tiny little noises, short sighs of wonder and appreciation, at regular intervals. If Bronse had not been so swept up in the way she tasted, the way she made him feel, he might have teased her for her innocent vocalizations.

Bronse broke away from the addictive act of plundering her mouth with a strangled groan. He pressed his lips to the corners of hers, the grip of his hands against her face and around her head tightening reflexively. "Sweet Beyond, Ravenna, you've never been kissed before," he uttered fiercely in belated realization.

"No, never," she affirmed with short, panting breaths that spilled a fiery heat over his face. "But I want to be kissed again."

Bronse had no idea how he could possibly resist that kind of invitation. Why in hell would he even want to? Bronse couldn't think of any satisfactory answers, not that he gave himself much time for contemplation before he dragged her luscious mouth back under his own.

He was the last man in the galaxy who would find virgin territory interesting, or so he might have thought ten minutes ago. He preferred women to be experienced and skilled. Easy come, easy go, so to speak.

Ah, but there was something to be said for the sweet, slow feel of a woman who was learning to explore her own desires in a kiss for the very first time. She slipped eagerly into his mouth, her inquisitive and ambitious tongue rubbing delightfully sensuous strokes against his. Ravenna sought his taste with slow and quick curiosities, the flick and tangle of her tongue devastating in its sumptuous explorations. She wriggled imprisoning fingers into his short hair and against his scalp so she could keep him exactly where she wished him to be—sealed tight to her suddenly hungry mouth.

Unfortunately, Bronse was not as innocent as she was, and his more practiced body was responding to her allure with a hellish heat and hardness. Holding her in the encompassing cradle of his lap and arms, he shuddered roughly around her. Her ambition drove him crazy as she sucked his tongue and lips with increasing fervor and very obvious excitement. He felt the blush of her face against his own, a telltale burning heat that told him she was just as affected as he was, though she may not have as easy an understanding of it as he did. Ravenna was pressing flush against him now, her breasts thrust against the muscular wall of his chest, their delicious weight painfully tempting. He could feel the points of her taut-ened nipples prodding him teasingly. Her round, gener-ous bottom was snuggled deep in his lap.

Great Being, she was made for loving, Bronse thought fervently.

She was young, he knew, but not so young as to ex-plain why she had never known the kiss of a man. What male could look at her and resist the temptation? Surely she had been approached by *someone*.

Bronse shoved the thought aside the moment he enter-tained it, not liking the idea of it. He stopped short of identifying the sudden emotional response as jealousy, but he did acknowledge that he was intensely glad to be her first. And one kiss, he quickly found, was hardly suf-ficient. As his passion was roused to a point of frenzy, he dismissed her explorations and opted for what could only be described as ravishment. Ravenna gasped in breaths when she could as his kisses bruised her lips and scorched her tongue. Her raspy inhalations drove Bronse crazy. His hands swept down to her neck, his thumbs stroking the column of her long throat. By the Great Being, her skin was like Yojni silk! Only much, much warmer. Much more vital. Her pulses were thrumming wildly beneath his fingers.

He broke away from her mouth so he could feel that pounding cadence of her life's blood beneath his lips. He pressed his mouth to the upper pulse point just below her jaw, feeling, hearing, and tasting her response as he touched his tongue to her carotid artery. The feminine musk of arousal wafted over his senses, and he groaned with the agonizing understanding and its consequential response. He was aroused to the point of rigid steel, the evidence of it nudged up firmly against her hip, and, damn her, she kept shifting her soft bottom against him until he thought he would explode.

Bronse wanted nothing more in that moment than to

toss her beneath him on the floor and show her about two dozen other things she'd been missing in this particular venue. He was shouting for it. Roaring like a beast demanding release. By everything holy, he could slake a hundred hungers on this incredible creature!

But . . .

After all, it was only a . . .

Dream.

Ravenna woke with a cry of impassioned despair. The moment she did, all the delicious heat and liquid sensations that Bronse had sent melting through her vanished under the onslaught of incredible agony.

She was lying on her stomach on the crude pallet they forced her to sleep on. She was trapped under the stiffness and pain of her own body, the smallest movement a brutal torture. How had she ever fallen asleep in the first place with such pain? She must have passed out, she realized, the darkness of unconsciousness bridging the distance between her and Bronse. That depth of existence had no doubt also allowed for the length of time and clarity of feeling they had shared as well.

Gods, there had been such feeling!

The conflict of arousal and the excruciating throbbing from her earlier punishments brought tears to her eyes. Did she cry from pain? Or was it the sudden deprivation of those intense, skilled lips that were shockingly soft and contrastingly voracious all at once? Was she already missing those calloused hands against her skin? Ravenna swam in a sea of confusion, the brutal replacement of reality rushing back into her as the dream faded to its realm of the semi-unreal. Her skin burned, yes, but it was the fire of torn and swelling flesh and not the smoldering of a man's sensual caress.

Ravenna had spent hours manipulating the guards with her powers and promises, but it had come to a crashing end when the shift had changed and their relief had found her sitting in state and decidedly unlashed. They had rectified the error before she or Kith could even speak to protest. Kith had screamed in rage as she was beaten first with a cane until she swelled, and then with a thin lash until she was covered in dozens of cuts that bled in rivers over her skin, soaking her clothes.

In the dream, Bronse had not seen the half of it. What he had seen had been what her mind had represented to him, and somehow she had managed to make it seem less than what it truly had been. She could not have him acting rashly. She appreciated her ability to conceal the truth of her condition. Especially now that she was learning that beneath all his logic and reserve, Bronse was a man of deep passions. Awake once more, Ravenna knew that her condition was even worse than she had thought it was. Only Kith could tell her how awful the abuse had been, for only he had truly seen the whole of it. She had been given the occasional mercy of blacking out twice during the process.

But at least she had not been molested again. That was very important to her. If she had let the earlier shift of guards continue without interruption, they would have incited one another into all manner of perversions. At least she had been able to skip over that torture, sparing Kith from suffering any more of it. For all his martial arts training, for all his gruff bluster, he would always be an empath and therefore would always be truly sensitive. He would never have been able to bear watching her be defiled. He would never have survived it without permanent damage to his soul and with his psyche unscathed. As it was, she worried that the experience of watching her torture had done him a great harm already. One could never be sure. Psionics were very precarious personalities sometimes.

Ravenna wiped the sweat from her brow, then pressed

her burning face into the rolled rag that served as a pillow. The skin on her back was stiff with dried blood, and the wounds, she could feel, were weeping in places. Was she still bleeding? She did not think so, she realized with a growing sense of dread. If it was not blood, then it was likely to be something far worse.

A chill shivered sickly through her, reinforcing her fears.

CHAPTER
FIVE

Justice had no idea what had crawled up the commander's ass, but she was just this side of committing a major infraction against a senior officer. Commander Chapel had been in a raring nasty mood for the past twenty-four hours, and there wasn't a single crew member who wasn't feeling the backass side of it. Even the medic was making himself mighty scarce after daring to suggest that the commander might need something to relieve his tension. Needless to say, the suggestion wasn't well received.

Justice glared over her shoulder at the one and only member of the crew who would survive telling the commander to kindly remove said bug from said ass. Lasher cocked a brow at her in response and calmly stared her down.

"That's easy for you to say," she grumbled. "He isn't chewing nails and spitting them out at *you*."

Lasher was well aware that Bronse was in a bad mood. Frankly, as far as Masin was concerned, Chapel had as much a right as anyone else to have a decent funk now and then. Granted, the timing was poor and the cause was questionable, but Bronse was just venting. Lasher knew he would steam down after a while. Hopefully it would be before he alienated the entire crew.

Lasher finished studying his schematics for the mission.

He had done so dozens of times, and now he felt ready to present the mission parameters to the crew when they met for the midday meal. They would be touching down in nineteen hours. That gave them time for chart review, mission review, reports, rack time, and gear-up.

Lasher logged off his CompuVid and stood up. He trekked back to Medbay, and the door hissed open easily at his approach. The pneumatics of the door actually were drowned out by the compressors that misted the air with disinfectant every time someone passed through the portal. On large flight ships and on space stations, a laser shower was used instead, more efficiently zapping away all surface bacteria from visitors and doing so without their notice. Lasher brushed a hand back through his lightly dampened hair. The mist would evaporate in a few seconds.

"Jet?"

"Yeah?"

Jet popped up from behind one of the diagnostic palettes, a laser wrench in one hand and a calibrator in the other. The medic was obviously tweaking his equipment in anticipation of any possible casualties.

"I need a favor."

"A sedative for Commander Chapel?" Jet asked hopefully.

"Yeah. Right. When Hepraps fly."

Jet sighed with clear consternation. "It would last only five hours. Plenty of time to relax and refocus. He needs to focus, you know."

"I know. But where would you hide on a ship only so big after those five hours were up, Jet?" Lasher sighed softly. "I'll talk to him about this after midday. Listen, I need a specialized med kit."

"Specialized?"

"Yeah. I'll tell you exactly what I want and you tell me exactly how to use it. Okay?"

"Something I should know about?" Jet asked warily. He might be a medic, but Jet was as much IM soldier as the rest of them. Medics always stayed with the ship. They never went directly into the field. The ETF crew members had plenty of basic first-aid training to get them back to the ship. There was no need for a medic until after they reached extraction.

"Negative. Let's just call it a gut instinct, okay? C'mon, jack me up."

Jet gave him a crooked grin. "Come into my laboratory . . ."

Bronse sat in the mess hall working up a report while he waited for the rest of the crew to arrive for midday meal. He was tired, and he rubbed at his forehead and temples where a bitch of a headache was throbbing rhythmically. Focusing on the VidPad was no easy trick. Focusing on writing a mission report for a mission he was certain was bogus was even harder.

With a disgusted grunt, he tossed the VidPad on the table and set both hands to work at massaging his temples. How could he concentrate on anything? How could he work calmly through the day when every minute meant endless possibilities of torture for an exquisite, helpless woman? And for a brother she clearly was devoted to. When he thought of all the things they could do to her between that moment and the undefined moment when he would finally reach her side, he was blinded by rage and a sensation of angst that he had never known in all his life.

Why had he spent precious time manhandling her? Kissing her and slaking his lust on her when he could have been advising her on ways to avoid torture? On ways to counteract it? Tricks and methods of foiling a torturer's intents could always be learned and used. He should have been telling her those things! He should have held on to her and comforted her.

Why did he always push her away by excusing his behavior and feelings as only part of a dream? Chasing her away. Chasing himself away. He was himself in those dreams, yet somehow better than himself. Or was it the woman? By all that was cursed and holy, Bronse wanted the answers! What was worse, he could not turn to a single one of his crewmates to help him sort out this tangle of emotions, actions, and reactions. Lasher was already looking at him like he'd gone crazy, and Bronse suspected that Masin was hunting for a reason to relieve him of his command. Justice was a woman and would make for a potentially good perspective; however, Justice had the tact of a rhinoceros and couldn't keep a confidence for her life. Ender. Well, Ender was Ender. He'd sooner blow something to bits than talk about it. He wasn't going near the hyperspray-happy medic. He wished Trick was there, oddly enough. The kid was trustworthy with secrets and definitely knew about the nuances of women.

Lasher sauntered into the mess hall and threw himself into a chair with his own brand of laid-back authority. He slid a large CompuVid onto the table, along with a holographic imager and enough handheld VidPads for everyone to use during the briefing. Then he slowly, purposely, turned to look Bronse Chapel dead in his periwinkle eyes. "So what happened? Someone been pissing in your rations for the past twenty-four hours, or what?"

"Leave it go, Lasher," Chapel warned, pressing hard against his temples.

"No can do, sir. Not unless I want a mutiny before we hit planetside. You're alienating the very people you need in order to stay alive, Bronse. The very people who also need you in order to survive."

"Masin . . ." Bronse sighed.

"The meeting doesn't start for another ten minutes, Bronse. Go see Jet. Get rid of the headache at least. You've had it for over twelve hours already."

"I'm just a little—"

"Tense. And I'm this close . . ."—he held up a frighteningly tiny representation between his two fingers— "to ordering you to take a relaxant for five hours and a soma-induced nap in Medbay. And please don't tell me I wouldn't dare when you know damn well I would. Everyone is wired tight and on the very edge of their last nerves with this mission. It's a bad fucking time for you to be shredding everyone's confidence and stability. Now, I hope that your stress and that headache are all that's wrong with you, Commander, because I'm not letting one soldier in this unit trot out on a death mission when their C.O. has his head up his ass. You copy?"

Bronse let only a single heartbeat pass. "I copy. And you're right. I'll be back after Medbay. Be best to review plans without a headache in the way. And I think I'll do the soma-induced nap as well after the briefing." He exhaled a long, slow breath. "I'm sorry. I can't explain everything to you. I wish I could. I just think it wouldn't do you any more good than it's been doing me. We'll be seeing the plot unfold soon enough, right?"

"That's the plan," Lasher agreed, his tone grave but accepting. "Bronse, I don't mean to—"

"To what? To be right? Forget it, partner." He gripped his second's shoulder firmly before rising to his feet. "As you're fond of reminding me, we have known each other too long to worry about it."

Lasher gave him a half smile, his roughly handsome features lighting up with his amusement. "Does that mean I can—?"

"Don't push your luck" came the sharp retort as Bronse exited the mess.

*   *   *

Twenty minutes later and feeling a damn sight better, Bronse reentered the mess to join his crew.

"First Actives," he greeted, not realizing he sounded almost jovial compared to his recent tones and behaviors. He did become aware of it as silence fell over them, and he looked at them to see them all frozen like a snapshot in their surprise.

"Commander," Lasher greeted in a pointed prompt, his lips twitching with humor.

"Commander," Ender and Justice echoed in unison.

"Okay, Lasher. How about we skip the dinner date and cut right to the foreplay?" Bronse said in a prompt of his own, slinging himself into a chair and grabbing a piece of fruit.

"Copy that," Lasher agreed, grinning when Justice snorted out a laugh. He reached out to place the holographic generator in the center of the table, and they each drew a VidPad close for their notes. "Ladies and gentlemen, without further ado, I give you Project Pooch-Screw." He pressed a button and with a brilliant flicker a full-dimensional topographical map of a section of the Grinpar Desert burst to life. In full color, with black sand and significant rock formations in graphic detail, the section began to pivot on its central point, turning slowly so each soldier could get a good look at all perspectives of the area.

"All right, pay attention, kiddies," Lasher said. "First, we're going to take a look at the mission as it was handed to us by our friend at command. Insertion, point A. We land fifteen miles out from target range at the first hour of the next day, under cover of dark and, need I add, freezing-ass cold. From landing point we are to march along this line for fifteen miles until we reach point B—our goal point."

"My, that's a very nice straight line," Justice complimented him.

"Why, thank you," Lasher rejoined, smiling at her crookedly. "I thought you might like it. But wait, it gets better." He magnified and altered the map to draw in on their goal point—a ramshackle-looking building made of stone and mortar, with slabs of metal protruding from the foundation, evidently to reinforce it. The roof was bolted-down rusted metal plates—deck plates that had been scavenged, by the look of them.

"Hmm. A building," Ender said softly. "A lone building in a desert prone to the most torrential and repetitive natural disaster known to man."

"Aww, c'mon. It's practically on the wilderness border. How many sand hurricanes could they possibly get?" Lasher asked leadingly.

"Okay, I say we accept that," Justice piped up. "Location, location, location!" She spun her spoon around in the air with aplomb before setting it back in her pudding.

"So we agree to accept it as normal for a lone building to stand on the borders of the two most volatile land factions, the Nomaads and the western barbarians. Now, as luck would have it," Lasher went on, his sarcasm sparkling merrily in his tone as the structure began to pivot on the same central point as the other maps moved, "some very, very bad men and women have decided to camp out in and around this structure."

Justice and Ender leaned together to boo and hiss softly.

"Now, our heroes . . . that's us," Lasher clarified as a simulation of the team lit up in position on command. Justice and Ender added appropriate cheers and applause, making Bronse chuckle in spite of his attempt to remain in neutral command. "We're supposed to approach the building, surround it in a wide perimeter, and infiltrate with silent but . . . and might I say I love this part . . . *not* deadly force, and liberate a kidnapped political figure from our naughty bad guys. He's being held in the rear section of the building somewhere around here."

"Okay, wait. The orders actually said to extract the mark without killing the hostiles?" Justice asked.

"Death of hostiles is to be an absolute last resort. Only if absolutely necessary," Lasher qualified clearly.

"And did HQ happen to suggest how we're supposed to pull that particular rabbit out of our asses, Lieutenant Commander?" Bronse asked genially.

"Subdue with nonlethal tactics. Silent hand-to-hand, drugs, abduction—whatever works that's nonfatal."

"And who's the mark?" Ender asked.

"Han Abjurdoon, a high king—a Shiasha—of a powerful Nomaadic tribe from the Gurdon Nomaad sector, which as you know is friendly to peace efforts being made by IM and other international peacemakers."

"Nice." Bronse exhaled long and slow. "You see the problem here?" he asked his junior officers.

"You mean other than the fact that I don't get to kill anyone?" Ender asked dryly.

"I see that it makes no sense to keep a valuable ransom figure like a Gurdon Shiasha in such an exposed and—might I add—hostile locale," Justice interjected.

"That's not the problem. Logical or not," Lasher corrected her, "the problem is that if this is a fake—a setup meant to thrash us all and see to Commander Chapel's assassination—we can go in and kill whatever we want to, except a few key people to use as humanoid databases. Information gathering will be crucial in that case. But," he said, putting heavy emphasis on the conjunction, "what if there really is a Shiasha sitting trussed up in the back room of this dangerous and highly unlikely building on the borders? What if this isn't an attempt on the commander and is a legitimate mission operation that just happens to be signed by a scum of the universe admiral with ulterior motives that have nothing to do with this?"

"In spite of it taking place on the same planet and in the same desert as the last assassination attempt?" Justice asked archly.

"In spite of that," said Lasher. "The problem is, we can't risk making the assumption. We can't just stomp in there assuming something that could get an important innocent killed."

"No doubt it was planned this way for that reason," Ender noted.

"No doubt." Lasher nodded his agreement. "And so, let's look at Project Pooch-Screw, the director's cut." There were no cheers or laughter for the quip. Everyone was leaning forward at full attention now, knowing that this was when they had to focus. "My belief is that if this is another attempt to kill Bronse, they would want to make a mark of him somewhere in here—the fifteen-mile hike between insertion and target."

"They would have to. If any of us made it to target and found out it was a hoax, then got back to the IM alive, it could be a bad thing for he-who-signed-the-orders. If we all die, it was simply an honest mission gone awry," Justice said smartly.

"Bingo," Lasher agreed. "Though I'm sure they'll have plenty of armed, forewarned, and alert guards to see that that doesn't happen. We're ETF, after all. We're supposed to survive the unsurvivable. There are two ways I see this happening. They are either going to try to tank us all, or they are going to try to separate the commander from us and take him down separately."

"Makes no sense to do that. All they have to do is mine the route or the building and click . . . *poosh*!" Ender imitated the remote detonation with both sound and hand gestures. "Easier to take us all out."

"I agree," Lasher said, casting a quick glance at Bronse. Bronse knew he had made the alternative suggestion only because of the suspicions that Bronse had related to him earlier about them being separated. "So here's my version of the mission. We insert here, two hours earlier, at the twenty-sixth hour, and eight miles west of the original point, landing in this cover of low brush and scrub on the wilderness side of the border. Then we pull what now becomes a twelve-mile march parallel to the original, but we do it along this shale outcropping and the cover of the scrub, staying on the wilderness side the entire time. Besides moving through the hot zone earlier than expected, it will also give us two extra hours to jog across the border and shed the remaining eight miles to the building, approaching from the east rather than the south. It adds five miles onto the whole mission design, but I don't see much choice. The new approach should circumvent any ambushes."

"Okay, so that gets us to this building, for better or worse, right?" said Ender.

"Right," Lasher continued. "Only we're going to send just one man into the perimeter, not the whole squad trying to take down all the hostiles. We won't know the best point until we see the guard dispersal, but I plan to approach and eliminate all hostiles on the eastern side of the structure using silent force."

Lasher pulled out a stick and smacked it firmly down on the table, eliciting a whoop from Justice and a round of clapping from Ender. The metal stick was about eight inches long and thin enough to fit up a sleeve, and it had a dual pronged tip that could not only jab into someone but deliver a nasty, nerve-jiggling shock through the person's entire body, rendering them unconscious. The "juice sticks," as they were called, had been outlawed in the IM years ago as being inhumane, due to the sometimes permanent scrambling of their victims' brains. Although it was suspected that the prohibition was more likely because too many soldiers had gotten disarmed of them and received a jolt of their own medicine instead, ending up with valuable training hours suddenly unable to do much more than eat pudding through a straw.

"After which," Lasher went on, "I will insert myself through this door—after I introduce a Jeffon gas bomb, that is. It'll take out anyone not wearing a gas mask, and I'll use the simultaneous smoke cover to rip off the masks of any of those who might be protected. Justice, Ender—you are my backups." Lasher turned to Bronse. "Sorry, sir, but I strongly suggest that you back up the backups and leave the driving to us."

"Lieutenant, I have absolutely no problem with that. And what about extraction?"

"We truss up the unconscious Shiasha—just in case he wakes up and just in case he's not a Shiasha—and we hump him out in a reverse course as fast as our little legs can make it. I expect that an alarm will eventually go out. That's why I chose the shale outcropping. It will drop us below sight level as we trek back to the ship. The worst part will be the first five miles eastward. We'll be relatively naked until we reach the shale. There's cover here—and here—and along here—to help. Not much, but not bad, either."

"I have a thought," Ender spoke up. "Why not set out some sweat and tears on the way to the target structure? We can line up smoke and gas bombs for the entire five-mile track in intermittent bursts—like here and here—and when they follow us, it will slow *them* down but not us. I can take us around what I set. Nonfatal, sir, but effective." Ender gave them a wolfish, eager grin. The arms master did love his ordnance.

"Excellent," Bronse praised.

"Other than a few other details and surprises I've thought of, that's the plan," Lasher concluded. "If we hit any snafus, we rally back and regroup seven miles deeper into the wilderness at this cave and rock formation. Do you copy? Snafu means any segregations of troops that are unplanned, any casualties, and any other general fuckups that are otherwise undesirable. I mean it. No solo actions, no joyrides. We keep tight and together on this. The instant it goes even the littlest bad, we fall back and regroup. Anyone hard of hearing here today?"

"No, sir," Ender and Justice assured him.

"Good. Now let's talk about surprises and minor details."

Kith reached down to stroke his sister's cheek, his fingers so light that she would barely feel them. That was, actually, the idea. The gesture of comfort was more for his benefit than hers, and he did not want to wake her. When they had finally let him into her cell to see her at the break of light, he had been relieved for all of a minute before he'd gotten close enough to her to realize that the damage they had done had not stopped when the beating had stopped.

Oh, he had been foolish to think she was too precious a commodity for them to waste on carelessness, but the Banda Nomaads were little better than wilderness barbarians. In their stupidity they had let her wounds fester for an entire day before throwing him in with her in order to tend what they had inflicted. By now she burned with fever and incoherency, her lucid moments filled with tears of regret. Regret for him, of course, and that she was too weak to protect him or be of any use to him. Were she not his sister, he might have felt that as a mighty blow to his ego, but there was no time or energy to spare on such things.

They gave him reasonably clean water and rags to cleanse her wounds, but it was too late. The crisscrossing weals and ridges had swollen to the point where the original cuts of the whip could hardly be found. Still, Kith did the best he could. Mostly he used the water to cool her fevered body. He shouted demands for topical ointments, for basic antibiotics. They were a crude society in these wild places, but even the crudest of them knew ways to heal.

But clearly they did not care. Or more likely they believed that it was some form of trickery that the Chosen Ones did not die of fevers and illnesses. And that was true. But had they still been at the temple of their tribe, Ravenna would not be this ill because Ophelia would have been there. Ophelia, their youngest sister, with her delicate little hands that need only touch a person in order to use her psionic power to heal. Then again, if they had been home, Ravenna would never have been treated in such an unspeakable manner.

But Kith was not even sure of that anymore. Until a couple of months ago, he would have never thought that he or any of the Chosen Ones would be mistreated. When the Nomaads had come for Rave and him, it had all changed. He was tired of trying to figure out why. Kith kept looking for a deeper meaning than that of just power or politics or money, but he could think of none, and he had to accept that he and Rave had simply been sold into slavery on an ill-thought whim. They who were supposed to be revered above all others as children of the gods. And only the gods knew if Ophelia or Devan or Domino had met the same fates. What would they do without Rave to protect, comfort, and guide them, even if they were left to live in peace in the temple? Who would keep Vivienne's temper in line? Fallon, who had never understood Kith and had tried to shun Rave's kindnesses—would he feel anything even now that they were gone, or would he remain as impassive and seemingly composed as ever?

Kith rubbed the bridge of his nose with a long sigh.

His eyes smarted with fury and fear for both of his sisters and the others as well. Never had he felt Rave's burdens of responsibility until this very moment. He had always been so self-involved, buried in his arts and skills, just as many of the Chosen Ones were after they had been brought to the temple to live. He would trade all his studies of art and form, of centering and calming of the soul through the bodily shapes of ancient hand-to-hand-fighting skills, for but a fraction of Ophelia's healing knowledge. Young and delicate as she was, she knew more about herbology and medicines than even the wisest midwife in the village. She would know how to use the dirt and dust upon the floor to make a healing poultice, if such a thing were possible. If it weren't possible, Ophelia would find a way to make it possible.

Kith reached down to re-situate the rough brown blanket covering his sister, making sure that the filthy thing did not touch her back but still kept her legs warm. He held her in his lap, her torso across his thighs as she lay facedown, an attempt to share his warmth with her shivering body. Soon he would have to run the cloth over the raw wounds again to clean them. He bit down on his lips at the thought of it, for even in her fevered state she felt the agony of it because she cried out and screamed as if she were being flayed all over again. She had not made half so much noise of anguish when she had been tortured in the first place. Now, in her delirium, she was betraying how much she had concealed her agony. He knew that she had done so for his benefit, so he would not have to listen to her pain even as he watched it and felt it. Close to her at last, Kith could now see where the Nomaads' careless zeal had caused welts upon her cheeks and arms as their aim had strayed from the center of her back. He could see that she had bitten clean through her lip in order to force herself to stifle her outcries.

Kith had been unable to show half as much control

and courage, and he felt nothing but contempt for himself now as he recalled the furious shouts and rage that he had forced *her* to listen to. That he was an empath was no excuse. He should have found a way to deal with her pain and his. After all his lessons and all his wisdom in meditational arts, he had crumbled at the first test.

Now he must sit idly by and wait, as Ravenna had waited, for a rescue that would come only by way of faith.

All Kith could think was that he had best come soon, this warrior of hers.

And he had best bring some friends.

Each step Lasher took over the terrain was perfectly silent. He moved low and fast, but he watched through his night vision specs, carefully studying the ground in sweeps for any traps or mines, and leading his crew around any suspected dangers as they followed in his every step.

Justice followed their point man, laser rifle at the ready hanging from a strap over her shoulder and against her side, freeing up her left hand for passing on silent hand signals when communications traffic was unwise or impossible. Everyone in the crew was covered in black, their gear strapped in tight to their vests, and the many pockets and holsters lashed close to their fit bodies. Their clothing was laced with circuitry that was the latest in laser-resistant technology, meant to defray and shed as much of a laser hit as possible. Unfortunately, it never worked 100 percent and tended to short out after a few hits, but it was a damn sight better than the alternative.

Behind Justice was Bronse, and Ender brought up the rear. Bronse knew he was being sandwiched for protective purposes, but he hadn't argued about it—much. Lasher was always on point, and Ender needed to be in the rear to lay his ordnance, so it didn't leave Bronse many choices. He would have preferred his usual position at Lasher's back, but he was willing to give up those few crucial steps if it meant increasing the safety of the entire group.

They were five miles into the first hike, and so far everything was progressing as planned. The wilderness this close to the Grinpar Desert was fairly lacking in wildlife. Fighting hostile terrain sometimes could be the most deadly part of a mission. Although sand hurricanes were less frequent this close to the border, they did exist. The danger lay in the fact that the dips between the sand dunes and the trees and brush of the wilderness obscured the sandline, so forewarning was left to their instruments.

Justice was playing nav/com officer in Trick's absence, so the maps they were using were at the ready in her VidPad as she silently tracked their progress. They were following the shale outcropping as planned, so they hardly needed guidance on this leg of the trek. When she finally signaled that it was time to break away and head over the borders, there was a soundless but collective sigh of relief. They were far from being out of danger, though, leaving behind the crucial part of the trek and trading up to deadly. Bronse stepped into sand a short time later, almost feeling an affinity for its shifting familiarity now that he was about two hundred pounds lighter without Trick on his back. As they crossed into desert, Bronse felt his back become exposed as Ender began to seed their path with ordnance.

The challenge of sand dunes of any color was their visual distortion as they rolled up and down over the miles. Things seemed closer, then farther away. Each dip between dunes could hide an army, and you wouldn't know it until you were right on top of them. Then again, the dips also helped hide an army—or a four-person wrecking crew, in this case.

Bronse's adrenaline, already high, began to spike as

Justice signaled that they were close to the target structure. Lying down atop a high dune, they each crawled to a position where they could see the target through their night specs. Justice's low whistle of awe was not necessary, but it was definitely empathized with.

"I count ten on the eastern exposure alone, Lash."

"My infrared is tracking fifteen free-moving forms in the structure itself. I see no clue of a permanently seated or bound individual at this time," Lasher added.

"Can anyone say 'we're fucked'?" Justice asked with low heat.

"No kidding," Ender said softly. "Forty exterior guards for one supposed Shiasha?"

"Major overkill," Bronse agreed. "If this was legit, they would have sent more than one team for the extraction of the target. You all damn well know that the recon team would have noted all of this. And there had to be recon for them to note the locale of the prisoner. Shit!"

"Hey, Boss, you ever get the feeling that someone wants you dead a couple of times over?" Ender asked.

"Every damn day," Bronse responded. "They never expected us to get this far. JuJuren knows I would have called an abort if I saw this setup. This is a backup scenario, just in case we got through the trap on the original mission track."

"Makes you wonder what the trap looks like," Lasher speculated.

"No, it doesn't," Bronse said grimly. "Let's abort. This is insanity. Rally back to the border and be careful. We're past due on the original track by now, and they're going to come looking for us."

"Copy."

"Copy that."

"Copy."

The team reversed track, only this time with Ender on point to guide them through his mine lines. Lasher brought up Bronse's back.

They had barely gotten a mile and a half away from the threat around the target structure when Ender and Lasher both came to a sudden and tense halt. Alert, Justice and Bronse followed the reaction instantly.

"Did you see—?"

"I hear—"

"Shit!"

"Sand flays! Scatter!"

Each of the soldiers reacted with lightning-quick reflexes and bolted in four opposing directions, exactly as they had practiced the scenario hundreds of times in training. A ripple of movement wriggled through the sand where they had been standing a second ago, and suddenly the black grains were bursting upward into the night in a half-dozen sandy explosions. Small-black-and-gray-speckled balls seemed to bounce into the air, shedding sand as they gained several feet of sky. Then, with a spin, the balls began to unfurl wings, one pair each, and a frightening whining sound began to fill the air. Moonlight glinted off the wicked wings as the angry-looking creatures hovered for a moment in order to fix targets onto the predators that had disturbed their nest.

There was no way to detect or avoid a sand flay nest, whether it was night or day, no matter how sensitive your equipment. The flays absorbed the temperature of the sand around them, so they had no heat signature differentials; they moved only when hunting or, unfortunately, when disturbed by the weight and tread of a predator crossing directly over the nest. The movement in the sand and an angry chittering sound were the only warnings that a really attentive person would get, and Lasher and Ender had caught one each.

Anyone who disturbs a sand flay nest has only one re-course. To run. Very, very fast. No easy trick on the shift-ing sand. But running was the only choice because the sand flays were too small and quick to shoot down when you were standing right on top of them.

And their wings, which spanned a good three feet when fully unfurled, were as sharp as razor blades, as the whipping, whining sound of the blades cutting through the air would remind the runners as they were pursued. The sand flay would dive-bomb its targeted enemy fear-lessly, using its deadly wings to cut away at the threat until it was either far enough from the nest for forgive-ness, or it was dead.

By scattering, the soldiers split up the threat among them. Or that was how they hoped it would work in the-ory. As in training, each had a predetermined direction, and Bronse went due north. Justice and Lasher were the lightest of the four of them and made the best runners in desert conditions, so they got excellent distance as he headed west and she headed south. Ender was left with east, toward the wilderness they had been headed for. Once the flays were airborne, they hesitated as they made their choice of direction. Ender and Bronse lost the toss, and each gained an extra flay as the nest split into four directions.

"Justice!" Bronse cried, the small communications patch on his throat engaging at his touch. "Southeast! Don't run due south!" The trap that was awaiting them along their original insert path was due south. "Everyone! Screw silence. Take these things out any way you can! We'll deal with the fallout later!"

Bronse had been in a flay attack twice before. He had seen a flay buzz a soldier and amputate his arm in one sweep. The other time had resulted in a Nomaad's par-tial decapitation and another soldier getting gutted. Even a glancing blow from one of those wings could mean nicking an artery and bleeding out within a few pounding heartbeats.

"Chapel! The fire line!"

Ender's warning came two strides before Bronse reached the firing line of the ordnance that Ender had laid out as a trap. Bronse prepared to leap over the trip sensors but then suddenly thought better of it. Taking a deep breath, he purposely triggered the gas and smoke bombs in his path. He ran like hell as sand exploded in smoke and gas clouds. He was wearing goggles, so he did not need to protect his eyes, but he would need to breathe eventually. The clouds, designed to spread fast across the ground, soon overtook him. But he was already unstrapping a gas mask, only as big as his hand, from his vest, and he smacked it on over his mouth and nose. The smoke would hopefully disorient the flays from targeting him, and the gas might make them sick. It depended on whether the flays "breathed" chemicals similarly to most mammals.

As Bronse continued to run at full bolt, he heard more mines explode and assumed that Ender had liked the idea of using them for cover and done so for himself. Of course, Ender could choose from any number of toys hidden in his vest. Lasher was Bronse's main worry. Running full west would take him directly to the structure they had just left. With ordnance now announcing the crew's presence, Nomaads would be crawling all over their location. That worried the commander more than the idea of Lasher getting hit by a sand flay.

Bronse turned his attention forward and listened for the telltale whine of bladed wings. They sounded far behind him, and there was disorientation in their flight. It was a hesitant whipping sound rather than the fast cutting of the air on a sure target. Taking no chances, he kept running and would do so until he was a good mile from the nest. Hopefully, he wouldn't hit another on the way.

No sooner was that thought passing through his brain

than the desert seemed to suddenly reach up and grab him. Bronse fell in an awkward sprawl as his legs were sucked down into the sand. He roared in fury and frustration as the sinkhole opened up to take him in and sand quickly rushed down the sides of the hole to cover his head. There was a frightening black sensation of suffocation, only the mask on his face protecting him from inhaling sand. He tried to kick and claw from under the cursed black grains and their stifling heat, but the pressure was crushing him as the sand shifted and slid.

And just as suddenly he was spat out.

Like a grain of sand through an hourglass, he slid from the above world, through a bottleneck, and into the dark of the underworld. The trouble was that he was supported and buoyed up by the sand, however crushing it had been, until that point. Now he was in a free fall.

For a few seconds at least.

He crashed to a halt on his back in a huge pile of somewhat soft sand. The breath whooshed out of his body on impact; every bone and muscle was pounded by the force of deceleration. Sand was falling from above him in a heavy shower that, thankfully, began to diminish in force before it could bury him. Two full minutes seemed to pass before he could force his body to draw a breath. When he did, his body immediately kicked the gift back out in coughs and gasps of pain. Bronse hissed at the pain lancing through his right side like a spreading wildfire, and his left side was doing little better. Sand was still streaming down from above, slowly burying him. He had no choice but to move, even though he was certain that he'd cracked a few ribs. Cracked vertebrae were not an unreasonable supposition either, considering.

Groaning, he managed to sit up, sand sifting off his body and out of his hair. He'd lost his helmet and his laser rifle, and the little gas mask had been torn from his face at some point. He tried breathing again, and settled for agonizing coughs and gasps. As long as he was getting oxygen, though, he wouldn't be picky about the method. The night vision function of his goggles was still in working order, and he could see that he was sitting at the top of a very large pyramid of sand. As more sand continued to stream from above, it scattered and slowly rolled down the sides of the pile.

Bronse gave in to the inevitable and, like the fresh influx of sand, began to slide down the pile. The instant his feet touched the solid rock of the cavern floor, he staggered to them and pulled out his hand laser. He shook his head hard, sending sand flying and pain lancing across his back, but he was breathing easier, so he counted that as a plus. He reached up, yanked off his goggles, and stowed them in a pocket. He flipped on his wrist light, and a brilliant spotlight lit up the areas where he pointed his fist. He seemed to be in one of the underground caverns that were sprawled underneath the desert. The caverns were usually occupied, although this one seemed empty at the moment, probably because it was proven to be dangerous. Flashing the light above him, he saw no possibility of exiting the way he had come. Sand was still trickling in from a tightly packed hole. He had disrupted the pressure when his weight had hit the sinkhole, and now it was restoring itself. He figured that the next sand hurricanes would hide and refill the sinkhole until the sand pile he had been sitting on reached the top of the cavern.

Lowered into a ready crouch, he walked a circle of the immediate area, light and pistol pointed forward until he was positive he was alone. Only then did he lean back against one of the cool walls of the cavern and concentrate on fine-tuning his breathing and contemplating his next course of action.

He touched the communications patch on his throat.

"Honey . . . kids . . . I'm home," he said softly.

There was a nearly imperceptible crackle of static. His heart pounded with anxiety as he waited.

"Hello, dear" came Lasher's response at last.

"Hi, Dad." Justice.

"Hey, Dad." Ender.

Everyone was safe. Bronse sighed with relief.

"So how was your day, dear?" Lasher quipped softly.

"Sucked," Bronse said, coughing softly.

"Guys, this place is crawling with movement," Justice warned.

"Copy that," Bronse said quickly, straightening. "I'm in a bit of a real estate relocation situation. Need to find an exit. You all rally back to—"

Bronse broke off as a sudden chill walked his spine.

Ravenna.

"Didn't copy your last," Lasher noted over the com.

"Do not let them leave you . . . they will die without you."

The words of her prophecy suddenly rang like bells in his head. Without a single doubt, Bronse knew that this was the moment he had been dreading for so long. His choices and his decisions in this moment would determine who among them lived or died.

Now, in this harrowing moment, he must truly be a leader.

"You will die without them. You must stay together."

Now he must choose whether to believe in the unbelievable beyond a doubt, or leave his faith to the decade and more of military training that he had embedded in his very soul by act of repetitive pounding.

"Didn't copy your last," Lasher repeated, sounding as anxious as Bronse would sound if the com had gone silent on him.

"Belay my last," Bronse said suddenly. "Rally to me. Do you copy? Rally to me."

There was a noted silence.

"Copy that," Lasher said firmly.

"Copy."

"Copy you, Boss," Justice said slowly.

Bronse did not have to give them coordinates. Their instruments would bring them to him. "Be careful," he warned. "I slid down a long rabbit hole. Didn't even see it coming. And I didn't kill the flays, so you might come across them."

Aboveground, Lasher exhaled a slow, tense breath. Bronse was asking them to cross to the north, back over the explosion points that had already drawn the enemy's attention. The others could circle around, but Lasher's own position was precarious because he was close to the target building. He kicked at the dead flay he had shot when he'd gained a moment's advantage. The little bastards. They had managed to cause exactly what Bronse had been fearing would happen. They had forced them to split up. Now Bronse was drawing the whole crew toward serious danger just because some prophetic sensation was telling him that their lives would be at stake without him.

"Kids, I'm coming to you. Rally to Ender's position and wait till I get there. Copy?" Lasher said.

"Copy."

"Copy."

Justice would reach Ender first. Lasher's reading said that Ender was at the border and Justice was due south of him. They could take cover and would double their firepower if they stayed together. Now he had to risk his neck crossing east, then north, or the quicker northeast route, which would take him back over Ender's now-exposed munitions fire line. Lasher decided to go northeast, praying that he could hide in the dunes if he came across anyone. He did not like Bronse being stuck alone "down a rabbit hole." That meant he'd fallen into a pit of some kind. He could be injured, but he would not say so over the communications channel. Only the Great Being knew if the enemy had been given copies of their communications equipment by the traitor admiral. At this point, after seeing the size of the traps set for them, Lasher wouldn't put anything past JuJuren. He was already praying, as he began to hustle over the sand, that they weren't being tracked now that the explosions had given them away. If so, all they had going for them was a very small head start. Being closest to the enemy, he was in the most danger, but he was also endangering Ender and Justice by making them stand around and wait.

He also prayed that Bronse's gut instincts were up to snuff.

As for Ender and Justice, as soon as they met up at Ender's position, the look Jus gave him spoke eloquently of her confusion over the orders they were being given.

"I know." The arms master frowned as he rearranged the munitions on his vest so he had quicker access to what he wanted fast at hand. "But the boss has never let us down yet."

"There's always a first time," she muttered, stealing two spare light grenades from him. "Am I reading this right?" She showed him her VidPad screen.

"Yeah. Looks like he's underground."

"How the hell did that happen?" she wondered. "A trap?"

"Doubt it. He would've said. The thing is, I don't see an entrance near him."

"Well, he didn't just pass through solid rock!"

"Stranger things have happened," Ender said with a shrug.

Justice looked at him, aghast. "When did you become so wise and laid back?"

He just gave her an infuriatingly smug smile. "Better concentrate on finding an underground entrance and mapping a route to the commander," he told her.

"Fuck. Where the hell is Trick when we need him?" she grumbled. She picked up the VidPad and began to study the readings so she could navigate them to the commander's location.

CHAPTER

SIX

Bronse unzipped his vest, unable to bear the stricture of it as his bruised body began to swell around the back of his ribs. He needed to breathe, and that was far more important than well-groomed gear. He did not, however, relieve himself of any of the weight or equipment. A bunch of sand vacated his clothing, and he sighed as it eased away. There must have been five pounds of the stuff packed between his vest and shirt.

Breathing easier and with time on his hands, Bronse began to widen his area of exploration. He snapped off his lights and, after fishing out his goggles and allowing his eyes to readjust to the dark, he continued his search, letting the technologically lighted terrain in his lenses show him a fair picture of his surroundings. He could see only in black and white, but otherwise the picture was clear.

There was no telling whether this cavern was a rogue that had no outlet or connections to others, a highly unlikely and rare occurrence. It was far more likely that it joined up with a tunnel leading into a network that belonged to a tribe or to some of the miles of uninhabited or traveling caverns that the various tribes used. Bronse's goal was to make certain that there were no immediate surprises. Perhaps, if he were lucky, he might find a quick exit to the surface where he could meet up with his crew.

Moving on silent feet, keeping to the cool curve of the walls, he began to follow the readings on his VidPad. Justice and Ender were to his south and awaiting Lasher. Lasher was a quick-moving blip on his screen. Through the rock, Bronse could not read any other life-forms. His crew's transponders were the only thing allowing him to follow their progress and movement. It was how they would find him as well. There was no way for him to tell what kinds of threats were awaiting his second, or if Ender and Justice were being closed in on. He would have to trust them to take care of themselves. There was nothing he could do from his current position. They were coming to him, and that was all he could manage.

Well, almost.

Just as he could not read life through the rock, neither could they. He would serve them best by getting above-ground, negotiating any underground sentients. Carefully he began to move southward. Because readings tended to bounce and echo in caves and caverns, he was best off abandoning the tech and working with his own senses. His pistol at the ready, and with goggles to guide him, he moved onward, keeping alert for any echoes.

He had gone barely a hundred feet before he heard signs of life. It was a conversation in a guttural tribal language that Bronse was not familiar with. He could make out very few of the more universal references, but none of it was in any useful context. Waiting with bated breath, he pressed against the wall around the corner from the speakers. He quietly reached up and slid off his goggles. Sure enough, the corridor was lighted, a detail that his black-and-white tech did not differentiate.

Dim as the light was, Bronse preferred to use his own eyes to guide him. The conversation began to fade away as the speakers moved off, and he slowly peered around the corner. The passage was lighted in only one direction, telling him what he already knew—that he had come from a dead end. If he walked into populated areas, he put himself at risk, but he could also follow the light and quickly find an exit. Besides, as long as there were only a few Nomaads, he could handle them. Even with cracked ribs, he assured himself. Just to be safe, he reached into his vest and pulled out a narc patch. He peeled it off and pressed it into the palm of his glove on his free hand. Now if he simply touched someone's bare skin, they would be out in five seconds flat.

He set the laser pistol to a very strong stun. He wasn't out to kill any innocents—and he had to assume that they were innocent, despite their proximity to the trouble aboveground. The upper and lower worlds were like two different planets, and they often had little to do with each other in any given moment.

But strangers were not welcome in either world, and a stranger he definitely was. Plus, Bronse's equipment alone held a value for these people that would outdo Delran platinum. So, with trepidation and a slow, fortifying breath, he eased into the dimly lit passage. There were plenty of shadows, and he stuck to them as he began to pass doors—leather and wood bound, some solid metal—that closed off sectioned parts of the cave formations. In the upper world it was still night. It appeared that this tribe followed the day of that world, so there was almost no one about, although Bronse dodged a few close calls as he edged deeper into the lighted areas and cross corridors.

After a left turn, he began to pass nothing but bolted metal doors. Bolted from the outside, he realized after he'd eased past a couple. That was when he saw the first guard. Swearing softly under his breath, he began to back away. The last place he needed to be was in a prison section! Heart pounding, ribs aching under the onslaught of his rapid breath, he flattened and crouched back into a curve of the cavern wall. Wearing black, he blended in with the dark shadows of the worn hollow. He managed to regulate his breathing into silence just as the guard swept past him, his burnoose fluttering and snapping in his wake. After the guard rounded a turn, Bronse straightened, then glanced at his VidPad. Lasher had finally reached the others. They were already headed in his direction, he realized with relief.

Wanting to distance himself from the guarded section, Bronze began to move.

Then he froze.

It struck him softly, almost imperceptibly—a combination of awareness and sensory memory. Yet even so gentle a stimulus as it was, it impacted him like a blow to his spine that shuddered through his entire nervous system.

The unmistakable uniqueness of the scent of exotic flowers combined with Ayalya spice.

That and the sensation that he was balanced on a spear point of knowledge. Of need. It was a draw that demanded all of his attention, all of his senses, wiping away his military-trained skills that told him to focus on more important things.

But his very essence told him that nothing was more important than this.

There would never be anything more important than this.

He moved forward quickly, as if in a trance, his movement instinctually careful and quiet even though he put no thought into it. He came around the bend in the tunnel and picked up speed. He saw the two guards standing at attention by the door, but he made no attempt to slow or hide himself. Neither did he speak and give them any warning. Like a silent whirlwind he struck them. The nearest he cold-cocked with the crush of a swinging elbow.

The Nomaad was out cold before he even crumpled to the floor. The second was reaching for his weapon, but Bronse was already there. He kneed him with powerful momentum in his belly. When he doubled over, Bronse cracked him in the back of his neck.

Once both were in heaps on the floor, he reached to flatten his hand against the bare skin of their cheeks, dosing each with the narc patch. Then he glanced at the door they had been guarding. His heart was racing madly, and it had nothing to do with the brief battle and the ache in his ribs.

He knew.

He just knew.

He searched the guards for keys, cursing softly when he realized they didn't have them. Taking a moment to think and to wish Ender was there, he ran through his inventory in his mind. Studying the lock, he knew that his lock picks would do him no good. It was a strange multi-slatted tumbler that would require two sets of hands to pick. If he used plastique explosive he would attract attention, and he could not cut off his final chance at exiting this messed-up mission in one piece.

But leaving without her was not an option.

He touched his com patch.

"ETA kids?"

"Just looking for an inroad, honey," Lasher informed him. "Give us ten more minutes."

"Listen, I'm in a civilized section. Be careful. And hurry."

"Copy that," his second assured.

Ten minutes were too long for him to sit exposed in the corridor. Ravenna had been right. He would get himself killed without his team to back him up.

Then he remembered the small can of flash-freeze. He reached for it more quickly than his ribs would have liked, and yanked it free of his vest. He quickly attached the small tube to the can and turned to insert it in the metal lock. As he depressed the canister nozzle, gel began to ooze into the tumblers. Bronse felt the sudden cold flash across the entire metal surface of the door. Leaning so close to it, he could see his breath when he exhaled against it. Then, stopping the gel, he waited only ten seconds before standing up and body-slamming the door. The lock and catch shattered under the force of his weight.

The clang of the metal was louder than he would have liked, but as soon as the door swung open, he couldn't have cared less.

She was real.

He would have known her anywhere. The hair alone, spread out in a stream of chocolaty brown, like a rich decadence.

The fist came out of nowhere. Bronse caught it less than an inch from his throat, back-stepping under the surprising force of it. The second strike came at his now unprotected side, and it hit, sending the soldier careening into the near wall, slamming him against his cracked ribs. Winded, Bronse had to regroup quickly. He met a series of wickedly fast movements, a form of hand-to-hand artistry he was not familiar with, but he still managed to counteract enough to earn himself an opening. The kid, and he realized—with a bit of consternation—that it was a very young man, was damn fast and made sure he did not let Bronse touch his bare skin. But Bronse did finally grab him by his soiled tunic front and shoved him into the stone wall with force enough to stun him, his forearm pressed firmly against the kid's windpipe.

"Relax, kid! I'm not here to hurt you!" he hissed, realizing that the young man was certainly not a guard, dressed the way he was. Bronse looked past strands of sand-and-gold blond hair as they hung over defiant hazel eyes. After a beat, those eyes went wide with shock, and then, strangely, a desperate relief.

"Great gods, it's you," he rasped against the pressure of Bronse's arm. "I was . . . I should have known she was right! It just took you so long! Where the hell have you been?"

Bronse blinked at the angry, accusatory tone. He noted that the fight had left the kid's body, in spite of his very obvious fury for Bronse's supposed tardiness. The commander stepped back and carefully let the young man go. Then he completely dismissed him and swung around to the sole focus that had brought him there.

Ravenna.

He strode across the room to the pallet lying on the floor and quickly knelt beside her.

And that was when the full impact of what she was suffering hit him.

"What the hell happened to her?" he growled in rough demand, setting down his weapon and yanking off his gloves as he turned on the other man with fury blazing in his eyes.

"They beat her!"

"I know that!" Bronse barked, laying the back of his hand against her burning face. His distressed gaze raked down her swollen back, the wounds oozing blood and pus. "No one tended her after?" he demanded.

"This is a prison! They don't give a damn about those things!"

Bronse's response was to swear, making the younger man's eyes go wide in awe. Kith, having been raised in the sanctity of a temple, would never have dared say a single one of those words, never mind link them together.

"She didn't look this bad when I saw her. I had no idea," Bronse said, confusing Kith with the strange statement. "Ravenna?" Bronse leaned over her, his breath brushing her perspiring cheek, her fevered heat striking him like a desert wind. "Ravenna, I'm here." He reached out and stroked his fingers through her wet hair. "Ravenna?"

Bronse couldn't believe she was real, that he was actually touching her. He was almost afraid it was a dream and he would wake up. But as the thought struck him and she yet remained, he knew it wasn't a dream. The fact that she was gravely ill was no illusion, either. His eyes swept the cell, the scant water in a bowl, and the bloodied cloths.

"You're her brother." He wasn't asking, and he did not turn to face Kith. "My name is Commander Bronse Chapel. I'm with the Interplanetary Militia, and I'm here to lend assistance. How long has she been this way?"

"I think it started soon after they did it. They kept me from her until they thought to use me to tend her. The ignorant bastards didn't give me anything to help."

"You did your best. She'll be all right. We'll see to that."

"We?"

"Yup, we."

Kith and Bronse both swung around to see Justice leaning with saucy aplomb in the door frame, wiggling fingers of greeting at him. Ender and Lasher were squeezing past her and entering the cell.

"What's up, sir?" Lasher asked quickly, settling onto a knee beside him.

"Got your kit?"

"Aye."

Lasher fished out the first-aid kit and Bronse opened it. He hesitated long enough to send Lasher a puzzled look when he saw the contents. Lasher just shrugged. "I had a gut feeling," he said dismissively. He took back the enhanced kit and began to load the first hyperspray.

He reached to touch it to Ravenna's neck. "Jet said this should be compatible with most of Ebbany's species. It's a cocktail of antibiotics and a vitals stabilizer." Lasher's jade eyes swept over the raw exposed back of the woman before he finally injected her, a deep frown playing over his features. "That's a topical desensitizer," he said with a nod toward a spray. "Hold it three inches above the wounds and spray her liberally. She'll need it if you plan on taking her with us."

Bronse's lips quirked. Lasher hadn't even bothered to ask. He'd simply known that Ravenna was not to be left behind, even though it was highly irregular and against standing orders to rescue civilians during a mission unless specified. Bronse reached for the spray and applied it.

"The kid's coming too," he said simply.

"Figured" was the even simpler reply.

"I'm not a kid" came the disgruntled protest from behind them. But when Bronse looked over his shoulder, Ravenna's brother had eyes only for his sick sister and the care she was finally getting.

Ravenna moaned softly, and Bronse's head whipped around. He leaned over, pushing Lasher out of the way, and brushed his fingers over her cheek.

"Ravenna?"

Her eyes cracked slightly, and then they fluttered open, revealing weary topaz and fevered browns. But when she saw him, her beautiful mouth spread into a generous smile.

"Hello," she said, her voice dry and rasping.

"Hey," he greeted in return, smiling himself.

"You made it," she noted.

"More or less," he said with a chuckle.

She looked up and around, taking in his crew.

"You stayed together," she said, sighing with relief. "I'm so glad."

"Yeah. All alive and well so far, though it was close a

couple of times," Bronse told her, ignoring Lasher's gaze as it narrowed on him in suspicion. "Ravenna, sweetheart, we're going to have to move you now. We can't stay here any longer. There's danger."

"Okay," she whispered.

"Honey"—he gritted his teeth together an instant—"it's going to hurt like a bitch. Worse even. But we've numbed you. Just . . . tell us if you need to stop, because we can't have you crying out, okay? Do you want me to knock you out? We could carry you, but you'd be dead-weight and—"

"No. I want to stay awake. I want to walk."

Bronse doubted that was possible. Not over so many miles when she was so sick. He looked to Lasher with his indecision. His second shook his head once sharply.

"You have to narc her, Bronse. She won't be able to take it. Hell, I'm not sure I would be able to take it. I'd say maybe if she didn't have the fever and all that swelling, but there's no way to carry her without putting pressure on the wounds, and she'll be screaming."

"No! I need to help you!" Ravenna begged him, reaching to grasp his hand. "I can help you."

"Rave." Kith came around to kneel by her head, whispering in her ear. "Rave, let them do it. You can't help when you're this sick. You'd never be strong enough."

"There is danger," she argued hoarsely. "Soon. Don't put me to sleep."

"What about a nerve blocker?" Bronse asked suddenly. "On the back of her neck. Numb her from the neck down. We'll help her and she'll stay aware. That's what you need, right, Ravenna? You want to stay aware? To warn us if you need to?"

"Yes," she said with a sigh. "Yes. And to help."

"Do it," Bronse commanded Lasher. He grabbed his gloves and jerked them on. He disposed of the narc patch on the palm of his glove, clicked his sidearm into its holster. "What's your name, kid?" he demanded of the boy.

"Kith."

"Well, Kith, are you strong enough to help me carry your sister?"

"Of course," he scoffed.

"Over fifteen miles?"

"Sure," the younger man said stubbornly. "No problem."

"Fine. Same rules for you. Not a sound. If you need to stop, you say so and we trade off. No heroics."

"Okay," he agreed.

"Sir," Lasher interrupted, "we could move faster if you and Ender—"

"Ender needs his hands free for munitions. I need you on point and Justice watching our backs. Final orders, Lieutenant Commander," Bronse said shortly when Lasher looked like he was going to protest. "Ender, dump those guards in here. Go down the corridor and take out the guard making rounds. Maybe if we can keep the alarm from being raised, it'll make it easier for us."

"Gotchya, Boss."

Ender faded back down the hall a minute later and Justice watched him go. She also watched the corridor for movement as Lasher moved behind Ravenna and helped Bronse and Kith pull her to her feet.

"You can't feel your legs, but you can move them if you focus," Lasher told her. "But let the guys do most of the work." Lasher looked at Bronse, concern in his eyes. "She's in bad shape, and we got some seriously bad miles to go. The wilderness and desert are crawling with activity."

"Any suggestions?"

"I have one, sir." Justice stepped up. "We can remote-pilot the ship, making them think we left. We can then bring it down deep into the wilderness due east from here. It'll be a longer, rougher trek, though. We'd have to make it a good fifty miles in if we expect the ship's return to go unnoticed by the enemy." She paused a beat. "Or I could go back to the ship alone and pilot to a rendezvous poi—"

"No!"

Bronse and Ravenna chorused the countermand harshly, shocking the others in the room.

"No separation," Ravenna insisted.

"Ravenna's right. We stick together," said Bronse.

Ravenna gasped then, lifting her head.

"Ophelia," she croaked. "We can't leave her, Kith! Vivienne and Devan . . . all the others! If we escape, they will—" she gasped in breathless panic.

"Ravenna, take it easy!" Bronse tried to soothe her, reaching to cup her face as she swayed on her feet.

"No! No separation!" she gasped. "Don't you see? They sold us! If we escape, they will sell the others to replace us!"

Kith sucked in a sharp breath and spat out a curse recently acquired from Bronse.

"She's right! We need to get the others."

"Listen, kid, this isn't a rescue mission," Lasher argued sharply.

Bronse gave his second a look, reminding him that it actually was a rescue mission, or it was supposed to have been. Lasher had the scruples to look sheepish.

"But, sir, they're civilians."

"We're Chosen Ones! Priests and priestesses!" Kith snapped. "Sold and defiled, our temple desecrated by greed! They were selling Ravenna to be a Shiasha's bride so he could rape her for the powers she has. They were selling me to be his chained pet and gods only know what else. Rave is right. We have a baby sister. The temple will be ransacked for the powerful Chosen Ones who are still virgins. That would be our sixteen-year-old sister,

Ophelia. And there's fourteen-year-old Devan. But then again, there's Fallon, who's seventeen if the Shiasha likes boys."

"What the hell is a Chosen One?" Lasher barked.

"No time. No time," Ravenna murmured.

"She's right. Let's solve this later. Let's just get out of here and head east into the wilderness. We'll figure the rest as we go."

"Good. Our temple is in the wilderness," Kith said darkly.

"I didn't make any promises, kid," Bronse snapped. "And while I'm at it, I'm in charge of this mission. What I say goes. If men like these can accept that, then so can you. You copy?"

"Yeah," Kith agreed after a wide-eyed moment resembling respect. But then again, everyone respected Bronse when he used that tone.

CHAPTER
SEVEN

Ravenna was only partly conscious and even less aware than that when the next part of her prophecy came roaring out of a dark corridor. An unexpected troop of guards dropped right on top of them. Had Bronse been alone helping Kith and Ravenna, he would have been outnumbered ten to one and likely slaughtered in a heartbeat. Instead, the speed and violent skill of his team burst to life all around him, and he and Kith drew Rave out of the way of danger.

After leaning Rave against Kith, Bronse joined the melee. His team, however, had rallied with splendid efficiency. They did a fine job of silently dispatching the threat, with a little help from Ender's more stealthy tricks of his trade. Not a single whine of laser fire was to be heard. The guards lay sagged against the walls—all of them unconscious because Bronse had ordered a "no kill" until they were aboveground, when the rules would change significantly. Breathless, Bronse took a minute to lean against a wall, wiping sweat from his brow.

A moment later he heard a sharp intake of breath from Kith and turned to see what was wrong. He found the younger man glaring at him with accusation.

"What?" Bronse asked impatiently.

"You're injured!" Kith snapped.

Bronse felt the attention of his entire crew swinging

toward him, three pairs of sharp eyes assessing him quickly.

"I'm fine," Bronse dismissed their concern gruffly. He straightened from the wall and took half of Ravenna's weight onto himself again, ending any argument.

At least with his crew.

"He's lying!" Kith blustered. "He's in agony!"

"Let's get moving, kid," Bronse commanded.

"But—"

"Move or let Ender take your place!" Bronse barked.

Ender didn't give the kid a choice. The huge munitions officer plucked Kith out from under his sister's arm, yanking him back in Justice's direction, and then swept up Ravenna's weight on the left side as if she were a paper doll. Bronse secretly took a breath of relief as Ender bore his half of her weight far better than Kith had.

Kith, meanwhile, was cussing and grumbling under his breath about Bronse. "He's hurt," he groused to Justice, "and he's lying about it."

"He's a soldier," Justice responded with a shrug, clearly the end of the discussion on the matter.

When they finally exited the tunnel entrance his crew had found in their efforts to reach Bronse, the commander never thought he would be so glad to see the black sands of the Grinpar Desert again. But one look at the lightening sky sent his mind reeling. He hadn't realized how much time had passed. Dawn came early on Ebbany, and it was already upon them.

"We have to get to the wilderness, fast," he said, shifting Ravenna's weight entirely onto Ender so he could quickly shrug out of his gear vest. He stripped off his double holster, then his long-sleeved black shirt. This exposed a short-sleeved Skintex T-shirt, also black, which he left on. He reached to slide the discarded shirt onto Ravenna, covering her exposed arms and back, buttoning it over the ragged remains of her gown in the front.

"This will protect your skin in case we don't make it to cover before the sun is high enough to burn."

"Thank you," she murmured. "I am used to the sun."

"I know. But it's different when you're injured."

"Okay," she accepted.

Bronse reached to redress his gear, his keen eyes sweeping around the terrain as he tried to think of an advanced course of action.

"Ender, how many miles could you carry her on your own if you had to?"

"How many do you need?" the giant rejoined without humor or ego.

"Kith, how many miles to your temple from here?"

Kith stepped forward eagerly. "This is Banda territory. I don't know exactly how far in we are, but I guess about thirty miles. Northeast," he clarified before Bronse could ask, refusing to let the commander have any more opportunity to treat him like a simplistic kid. He was twenty-one years old, making him more than a man in many cultures, and he was quickly getting tired of the way this stranger treated him.

"They'll expect them to run straight home," Lasher offered warily. "They'd try to reacquire them there."

"If their villagers sold them out, I wouldn't call it a safe haven," Justice added.

"The temple is set deep in the forest, away from the village," said Kith. "They wouldn't even know we were there. The Banda don't know where the temple is, only the village. It would take them time to catch up to us." Kith was trying not to sound as anxious as he felt, but he had too much at stake to manage the same cool contemplation of their tones.

"Frankly, I don't see that we have much choice," said Bronse. "The temple will provide shelter and a temporary safe haven. We need somewhere to hide from the larger threat of the trap closing in around us." Bronse placed his hands on his hips for a minute as he surveyed the dawn coming over the terrain. "We can handle the Banda better than the other threat. Agreed?"

"Sir, the ship has medical care. I don't see logic in going in the opposite direction," Justice complained softly. As a pilot, she inherently craved having a ship at hand. Being without it was like amputating a major skill.

"Ophelia is a healer," Kith countered. "And far better at it than anything you can come up with."

"I doubt that," Bronse said dryly. "Okay. The bottom line is that everything to the south is hot with danger and enemies. We can't risk it with an injured woman and a civilian. Northeast it is."

"Aye, sir," Lasher said smartly, putting an end to any further debates.

Bronse swept Ravenna back up against him, again sharing her weight with Ender. They linked arms beneath her bottom, fashioning a perch for her as they each pulled an arm across their shoulders. It drew her feet off the ground without putting any stress on her injured back other than the outstretching of her arms. The nerve block and topical were doing their job, though, and she didn't seem to feel a thing.

As they began to trek toward the wilderness, Bronse contemplated Kith and things he had said and done that began to make him speculate. He had to accept that Ravenna was a very special creature. Now that he was positive that she was real, he had to accept that she had some odd abilities. Appearing to him in dreams, for one—although she had seemed just as surprised as he on several of those occasions. However, there had been no mistaking her ability to see future occurrences. Even if all the rest could be put down to good guesses and logical explanation, he couldn't explain away her assurances that they would meet. He also couldn't explain the feelings and senses that had guided him right to her, and his ability to sense the distinctive smell of her perfume. Especially when he'd sensed it only in dreams. How could he have noted such a thing when she'd been behind sealed and locked doors? And there had been that strange inner pull . . .

Now he had to wonder about Kith as well. How had this kid known so assuredly that he was injured? He'd managed to keep it hidden even from his pack of highly trained men. Did Kith have perceptions like those of his sister? Why was it that this kid was investing trust in someone he clearly didn't like? Despite his personal clashes with Bronse, Kith seemed to have no doubts that Bronse would be the one to guide him and Ravenna out of trouble.

Chosen Ones.

Sold for their power.

Kith had said Ravenna would have been sold and raped in an attempt to gain her power. A backwater belief if ever he had heard one, but unsurprising in these primitive cultures. Yet even the most primitive beliefs had births attached to truths. It appeared that the truth here was that Ravenna did, indeed, have power. It wasn't too far of a stretch to see how her siblings would also have gifts.

The problem was, Bronse's crew wasn't stupid. As things progressed, they'd be picking up on this information as well. How would they feel once they knew that Bronse had been making decisions based on "visions" of this woman? Even Lasher didn't know, or hadn't known, that Bronse's anticipatory feelings had come from dreams and an outside source. By all rights, his crew should depose him of his authority immediately and pack him off to Psyche Services as soon as they docked to station. By the rules, they would have ample cause. He had certainly behaved far out of his norm during this entire mission. Even now he was leading his crew to step over bounds that were not to be crossed. Picking up civilians?

Treating Rave would have been acceptable, but rescuing her and taking her brother? Even now Bronse was heading deeper into troubled waters because he was actually contemplating picking up a temple full of these Chosen Ones and giving them transport.

Just what did he think he was going to do with them? He couldn't very well bring them onto a military installation.

Bronse stumbled in the sand and brush of the leading edge of the wilderness, making him aware that they were crossing the border. Catching himself sent a jerk of agony through his abused body, and he came to a halt as he fought the reflexive sound of pain welling up from his chest. Ender stopped, silently keeping his eyes skimming the terrain as he allowed his commander to collect himself. Without a word, they both started off in step again.

Ender didn't bother to ask the commander if he was okay, if he needed to slow down or take a break. Bronse would do one or all of the above when and if it was necessary. However, if anyone asked Arms Master Rush "Ender" Blakely his opinion on the matter, he'd say that the nearest hell-acre would freeze over before that happened.

Ender did spare a glance for the disheveled female civilian, though, unable to help his curiosity over her and the commander's behavior toward her. She was tall, dusky skinned, and pleasantly weighty for a female. Certainly not unattractive, and Rush could understand how Bronse could be quickly drawn by her. Her beauty was strong, and yet she seemed vulnerable in both appearance and physicality to many things, not the least of which had been her captors.

Frankly, he was glad the commander had broken with protocol and taken her along for the ride. Ender had seen some gruesome methods of flagellation in the Tari wilderness where he had grown up, and he knew that this woman's festering wounds could easily mean her death. No. Since no one had properly tended her, it would definitely mean her death, unless the Great Being touched her with a miracle. Even now, he knew that if it were not for medical technology helping her, she would be out cold from agony. He should know. He himself had the scars across his back to remind him of the feeling . . . and the infections.

So maybe he was a little personally involved in his need to help rescue the appealing woman, and maybe she and the boy were added dangers that the crew could have done without, but far be it from Ender or any of his companions to shy away from diminishing odds. The only one who seemed unhappy with the choice was Justice, but Rush knew that was because she just wanted to get her flight stick between her knees. They all had their security blankets when they were in danger. For Justice, it was yanking and banking. For himself, it was a gear vest full of ordnance. For Lasher? He turned to Bronse for steadying on the rare occasion of feeling insecure.

Ender hadn't ever figured out what Bronse's crutch was. He had once thought that leaders didn't have crutches. He knew better now. Perhaps one day he would figure it out, although after four years under Bronse Chapel's command, he highly doubted that he was going to be enlightened if he hadn't been already.

Bronse didn't call for a break in their increasingly difficult hike over rough terrain until sometime later, when Ravenna made a soft, almost imperceptible sound of pain.

"Halt!"

The crew did so instantly, and Kith rushed to his sister as she was set on a large boulder with a rough but flat surface. All of the surrounding rock, shale, and soil were black, but the vegetation was becoming greener, denser, and taller the deeper into the wilderness they went. Justice and Ender automatically began to circle and secure a perimeter as Lasher slung up his rifle and trekked back to his patient. He had the most field medical training of the quartet, so they always deferred to his judgment. Bronse was just thankful Masin had had the forethought to expand the standard first-aid kit. It was another anomaly that he would have to examine at a better time, he thought. They were all trained to avoid carrying even the smallest amount of undue extraneous weight. It simply didn't make sense that Masin had suddenly made an exception.

Lasher pushed Kith out of his way, sending the kid back a few steps and unwittingly pissing off the little hothead, though his only intention had been efficiency. Lasher was used to dealing with soldiers who scattered on command and without question. Kith was a vision of outrage, although Masin's attention was all for Ravenna.

"Pain?" he asked gently, looking into her eyes and seeing his answer even without her nod and the telltale gnawing of her bottom lip. Brave little thing, he thought with admiration. She had been bearing it longer than she had allowed them to think. He gently bent her head forward and checked the flashing node he'd attached to the back of her neck. It was glowing yellow, indicating that the neural medication was almost depleted.

He didn't have a replacement. It wasn't meant to last for such a long hike. He glanced up at Bronse, sending a clear message to his commander though he didn't speak aloud.

"How far?" Bronse asked Kith, taking brief note of the kid's tense lips and clenched fists.

"Fifteen miles at least."

Bronse didn't have to swear out loud for his crew to hear it in their heads when his lavender eyes flashed angrily. But he kept silent, unwilling to broadcast his upset to the woman trying so valiantly to be stoic.

"Then we better make them fast ones," Bronse said

with firm determination. "Give her some topical. It should help. We'll take it as far as we can. Then, if we have to, we'll narc her."

"No!" she protested quickly, forcing her body to straighten, as if to convince them of the impossible. "I'm fine. I'm fine. Let's just go."

Lasher ignored her and obeyed his commander, gently sweeping her hair into his hands and dropping it over her shoulder out of his way. He didn't notice the fine tensing of Bronse's body as his eyes fell covetously on Lasher's hands in the soft mass of Ravenna's dark hair. Masin inspected the back of the shirt she wore, and it took only an instant to see that the material gleamed with wetness. Very gently he peeled away the cloth from Rave's back and off her arms. His teeth made a small gritting sound as they clenched. Laying the shirt aside, he glanced up at Bronse, and the commander instantly read the silent message and came around to look at Ravenna's back.

Their movement had torn open every last lash. The welts were bleeding freely.

"Bandages?" he asked, the muscle ticking in his jaw the only giveaway as to his feelings on seeing the woman's ravaged skin.

"Unwise. What goes on must come off."

Kith watched the commander with surprise as the violence of Chapel's emotion struck him like a relentless riptide. Why would this stranger feel so strongly about his sister's pain, he wondered. Kith had been puzzled by it from the outset, but it came stronger and stronger, it seemed, with every passing mile. Why would this strange warrior care so much for a woman he no doubt considered little better than a savage? All of the men, in fact, displayed a great level of concern for her well-being. Men in Kith's world gave very little consideration to females. It was different in the temple, of course, because

the women tended to be more powerful than the men;
but in the village, women were meant for breeding, sex,
and household management. One woman was as good
as another, and emotions were rarely a factor. Living in
a wilderness village was a hard existence, and there was
little time for soft emotions. It made Kith wonder what
kind of world these men came from. What kind of world
used women as soldiers? What was truly startling was
that the woman soldier seemed the least inclined of them
all to care for the pain of another. It confused Kith because all the women he knew were extraordinarily compelled to be nurturing. This anomaly mystified him.

"Ravenna," Bronse whispered as he leaned over her
shoulder from behind to speak softly to her. It was an instant intimacy, one that flew in the faces of the onlook-
ers around them, narrowing the world to just the two of
them. Her pain, his concern. Her gratitude, his empathy.
"The choice is yours," he said quietly, his fingertips tenderly sliding over her silky hair, wishing it could soothe
her somehow. "You are bleeding. We can bandage you
to stop the bleeding, but it will mean a great deal of pain
later on when the bandages have to come off. I cannot
guarantee that our medic will be able to use any more pain
medication by the time we get to him. Even as advanced
as our medicaments are, too much can cause harm."

"And if we don't bandage them?"

"Blood loss. The shirt will stick to your skin. Dirt and
debris might further the infection."

"Bandages then. Ophelia will take care of the rest. We
just need to get there."

Bronse didn't waste her energy or fortitude with arguments. He accepted her choice and nodded to Lasher to
proceed. But even as he began to unfurl reams of sterile
cloth and hold it over her back, Lasher hesitated.

"Bronse, I need . . . I won't get the pressure I need to
staunch the bleeding unless I wrap her full around."

"Ender, Justice, Kith . . . take a walk," Bronse ordered instantly without looking up at them. "Kith, help them find fresh water and edible plants. We could use something to eat, and I'd rather save rations if there are natural resources close by."

"Hey, she's my sister," Kith argued, not liking the idea of leaving her alone with them.

"And I'm sure she'd rather not be stripped in front of her younger brother," Bronse retorted.

"Oh, and strangers are okay?" Kith snapped.

"Kith." Ravenna spoke up gently before Bronse could escalate the argument. "Please do as he asks. I'll be fine. Stop arguing. Learn to trust what you feel."

Kith flushed, lowering his face as his ears turned pink. She was right. His empathy would tell him if they meant her harm, and it was obvious that they didn't. Bronse had anticipated Ravenna's feelings about being stripped in front of him, and it bothered Kith that, after so short an acquaintance, this stranger could know her better than he did.

Everything about these soldiers, especially their leader, disoriented Kith. He knew they honestly wished to help them survive, but he felt an elemental fear every time he looked at or into Bronse. Something about this man alarmed him. Kith was bewildered not just by the strangeness of Chapel's feelings toward Ravenna, but her equally strange impulses toward him. Being an empath all of his life had taught Kith a great deal about listening to the feelings from within. Within himself and within others. Emotions shifted fast and often, and for an empath, the targets emitting them shifted just as fast. Kith had learned that he was inherently able to sift through all of that and focus on what was important. It was a skill that he had consciously refined as he had grown and mastered himself. Kith believed that it was safe to say he'd fallen into a very comfortable state of being, where things ebbed and flowed around him in a specific way that he was used to.

Until now.

When Bronse and Ravenna came close to each other, it was as though the miasma of emotions that always swam around Kith was swept back by a torrential rain of feelings that were demanding someone's—anyone's—attention. It left Kith raw with intensity and confusion, and he could not understand why, or why he should feel so desperately worried about leaving this hard warrior alone with his sister. She was everything opposite to what he was. Too gentle and too naïve in certain respects to be trusted in the hands of a man who bit off orders and decisions about people's lives based on some logical formula that he seemed to have stored in his head.

But Kith had never countermanded Rave's wishes, and he would not start now. She was the eldest in the family and by far the wisest. With his tense hands closed into fists, he turned and led the other two soldiers toward the sound of water.

Bronse slowly walked around the boulder that Rave was seated on and unhurriedly crouched down in front of her until they were eye to eye.

"Hey," he greeted with a smile that was enigmatic but warmed his periwinkle eyes.

"You keep saying that," she told him, her smile far more tremulous. She blinked and tried to turn her face away when the gleam of tears filled her topaz eyes.

"Hey, hey now," he soothed sympathetically, reaching to cup her cheek and turn her face back to look at him. "It will be okay. I promise you. I will keep you safe."

"I know," she said with absolute faith in her gentle voice. "Please. Let's just hurry."

He nodded. He reached forward to touch her shoulders, which were swelled and red from the secondary infection, and caught what remained of the small sleeves of her gown in his fingers. Gingerly, keeping his eyes on hers, he inched the tattered material down her arms. She slid her wrists and forearms free when the material fell to her waist. Shyly, she raised awkward arms to cover her bared breasts. Her cheeks flushed, and she couldn't keep his gaze.

"Ravenna, I need you to hold your hair and raise your arms," Lasher instructed, "if you can. Bronse, if you take the roll when I pass it forward, it will keep me from having to reach around her and bumping into her raw skin."

"Okay," Bronse said with far more efficient neutrality than he actually felt. It infuriated him that she was so injured and so in need of him, and yet all he could do was think about how damn attractive she was, how smooth and soft her skin looked. She seemed fragile, and he saw her trembling. Why did he want so badly to sweep her into his arms and kiss her into comfort, gently and with care? He would serve her better helping Lasher bind her, not smearing her with . . . with useless physical affections.

Ravenna wrapped the tousled sheaf of her hair twice around her wrist before grasping it in her fingers. The rising sun shimmered through the mussed mass, giving it golden lights as well as deeper amber ones. Again a surging need to touch it washed through Bronse. *To touch it, to touch her, any kind of contact,* his mind and body cried desperately. Why? Damn it all, why was he so plagued by this need? Disgusted with himself for his mental fancies, Bronse strove for competence as Ravenna raised her arms and the secured hair over her head and Lasher began to pass the sterile fabric to him. Bronse made it through three revolutions of winding fabric before he actually allowed himself to look at her breasts as he laid the fabric over the swells of feminine flesh.

The vicious curse exploded out of him before he even knew it was forming.

His eyes widened with outrage and unspeakable fury when he saw the mean fingerprints bruised onto her precious skin. Both breasts were marred with these bruises, as well as angry scratches flared with inflammation because the nails on the ends of the offending fingers had been sharp and dirty. She had been callously manhandled, and the evidence of it was stamped into her skin for him to see.

"By all that is cursed and holy," he swore vehemently, reaching out to brush his knuckles over the blue and black marks near her areola. "Is there much pain?" he asked hoarsely.

He wanted to ask who had done it. Oh, he knew it was the guards, but he would elicit a description if he could and go back to hunt the specific bastards for himself, and damn the danger. Still, he knew he could not. He would have to satisfy himself knowing he had gotten her away from them, that she'd be safe with him from now on.

When she didn't answer, he looked up at her. Her face was flushed a furious rose color, and she wasn't looking at him. He searched for tears, but her averted eyes were clear and dry, only her rapid breath giving him any hint of her emotion.

"Lasher, she has some angry bruising," he said softly, running his thumb ever so gently across the marks. "Do you have a reabsorption patch? Tight bandages will hurt if we—"

"Absolutely. Just a sec," Lasher said, turning to rummage in his kit.

But Bronse was not paying him any attention. He had suddenly become aware of the soft, breathless gasp that Ravenna uttered, and the immediate reaction to follow.

The nipple close to his caressing thumb tightened and formed itself into a thrusting point, and a ripple of goose-flesh prickled beneath his fingertips and palm where they rested artlessly against her. Bronse watched the reaction with the same fascination as one would watch the inevitable rush of an approaching avalanche. Awe at the sheer magnificence of how natural and beautiful it was sent a thrill of body-rocking excitement completely through him. Then came the realization that if he didn't move, and move fast, all hell would break loose and sheer survival would become an issue.

Bronse jerked away from her as if he'd been stabbed through his hand, awkwardly staggering back as he gained his feet, which, for some reason, refused to work with their usual dexterity. He was dimly aware of Lasher looking at him in surprise and confusion from over her shoulder, and he almost laughed at how well his second's expression reflected his own feelings of the moment.

"I need to—"

It was all he said before executing an about-face and walking off. Lasher watched him go with a sense of disbelief and consternation. "Now what the hell got into him?" he asked aloud. His patient didn't answer, keeping her arms raised and her face averted as he moved around her to apply the reabsorption patch to the space just under the first bandage wrapping. Then with her help he finished covering the bleeding wounds. It was awkward and would have been far easier with Bronse's help. Shaking his head, Lasher grimly noted the bruises on Ravenna's breasts and wondered if Bronse had left to cover a bout of temper. His commander had a well-defined sense of honor, and evidence of defilement such as this would be just the sort of thing to piss him off beyond control for a moment.

Lasher helped Ravenna tie off her dress at her waist so

the skirt remained in place, and then he helped her ease back into Bronse's shirt. He took a deep breath and met her troubled gaze firmly as he buttoned it for her.

"There is only about sixty minutes' worth of medication in the block. The topical and bandages will help, but not much. I'm going to be watching you. Please . . . please let us narc you when it gets to be too much. If for nothing else than your brother will have an apoplexy if he sees you hurting. Trust us, we can take care of whatever comes up. Besides, I think you know that you . . . you have an effect on my commander. Don't be a distraction for him. He needs to focus on keeping everyone safe, not on worrying about your pain."

"How long will I be out?"

"I'll give you a patch. It will let me be able to take it off you at whim, and you'll wake in fifteen to twenty minutes max. Or sooner, if I'm guessing your pain level right."

"Okay. Lasher . . . I . . ."

She broke off and looked dead and deep into his very light jade eyes, their unusual specks of black an instant fascination. Ravenna had only meant to express her thanks to him. She was so grateful for all of his care and all of his acceptance. She knew how far above and beyond they were all going strictly for her benefit and to see her safe. She was a stranger. They cared because they cared about Bronse's wishes, but she sensed that for Lasher and Ender it meant more to them than just orders. Lasher's concern went beyond his love for his commander. It was touching and a rare blessing in her life and she wished to acknowledge that.

But the words suddenly wouldn't come. She looked up into his eyes and was swept into that sensation of chill that washed down the back of her neck and demanded her attention. She suddenly reached out for him. Lasher jolted, grabbing her forearms as she seized him by the back of his neck and laid a hand over his heart, physically fishing past the weight of his vest in order to find the flat span of his pectoral muscle through his shirt. She drew him forward with surprising strength, and he went to pry her hands off his chest in discomfited reflex.

Her eyes flashed open, the topaz glowing with fierce purpose as they looked up at him through her lashes, and he found himself paralyzed by her gaze. She looked like a hunting cat fixed on a target, and he felt like he had just become lunch. Then her whole body jerked and she gasped. Her focus blurred, then softened, and she seemed to mentally disappear from the close clutch they shared.

"Masin," she said quietly, using his given name and chilling him to the bone because he couldn't remember anyone having used it in front of her. "Masin, you must be careful. Bronse needs you. There are those who plot against him and wish him dead."

"I . . . I know," he found himself saying in spite of himself. But how did *she* know?

"A woman will come to you," she continued as if he'd never spoken. "She comes under the guise of neutrality or friendship. But be warned, she seeks to remove you from the equation. She will strip Bronse of his armor. You, Masin. You are his armor."

And just as suddenly, Ravenna released him, sagging back as she shook from head to toe, as if she had exerted herself mightily. Lasher instinctively surged away, up to his feet, bracing his legs and body defensively as his eyes widened with a dozen rushing emotions and ten times as many thoughts.

"What the hell was that?" he demanded fiercely.

"A gift," she said shakily, shivering. "My gift to you.

Do not ignore it. Please . . ." The plain fear in her tone grabbed at Lasher's guts with icy fingers of dread and foreboding.

And Lasher suddenly knew where Bronse's premonitions had come from.

CHAPTER
EIGHT

Lasher waited until the others came back before he marched off in search of their wayward commander. After ordering the crew to eat and rest, he followed Bronse's path with a quick, determined stride. He didn't know exactly what was going on around here, but he was about to find out. Bronse Chapel never held out on him. *Never.* Lasher had functioned smoothly for ten years based on that single belief. Granted, Bronse wasn't required to share everything. As commander he often received orders meant only for him. Bronse simply chose to share them with his second.

But Lasher had begun to suspect that there were two different missions on Bronse's mind. It was the only explanation for what they were trying to juggle. Four soldiers in a massive hostile environment with not one but *two* enemies searching them out. Not only that, they were trekking around with civilians, one of whom was severely wounded.

Lasher followed Bronse's faint track until it took him to the edge of a small creek. His commander was crouched down on his haunches, pulling water over his head. He swept his fingers through his hair, spiking it up, and then reached for more water to throw against his face, washing away sand and dust, something they didn't usually do until they were safe at base. Dirt coating the skin helped with camouflage.

Shaking his head, Lasher approached Chapel with a clear bite in his step. "You want to tell me what the hell is going on around here?" he snapped.

Bronse paused, shook water off his hands, and then slowly rose to his full height. "I'm sorry," he said coldly, "but would you care to repeat that question?"

Lasher felt the whip in those flatly spoken words, and he winced inwardly.

"Do you want to tell me what the hell is going on around here, *sir*?" Lasher corrected himself, adding respect to his frustration but refusing to completely play games of rank. "Bronse, I need to know what you're thinking. I know you know I'll follow any order you give me short of dancing naked on the IM tarmac at midmorning, but I need to understand those orders and their motivations. That's how we've always worked. After ten years, that's what I need in order to function at my best. And let me tell ya, functioning below par is not a good thing in this situation, if you hadn't noticed.

"Bronse, that woman just grabbed hold of me and . . . and told me my fortune! And it was a bloody frightening one at that. Why do I think that she's responsible for all these gut feelings you've had over the past few days? Why do I feel like you knew she was going to be here on this planet? She and the kid aren't acting the least surprised that a troop of ETF soldiers just broke them out of prison. You've never treated me like an idiot before, and you damn well better not start now, *sir*!"

Bronse waited for several beats while Lasher caught his breath and calmed down enough to hear past what was no doubt the massive roaring of his blood pressure in his ears.

"I have never and will never treat you like an idiot. I wanted to explain, but we've been pressed for time,"

Bronse said efficiently. "As far as what Ravenna can do, you now know as much as I do. She seems to see the future. She told me mine too; that was how I knew we needed to stick together."

"But you'd never met—"

"In a dream. I met her in a dream. Several of them, I think. I don't remember all of them. I would dream her telling me the prophecy, and it would sublimate into those gut feelings I was plagued with. I didn't know until after we talked about it that night. I was a little afraid to tell you any more than that. I wasn't sure I wasn't going nuts, and I didn't want you or the crew feeling that you couldn't trust me.

"Don't ask me to make sense of it because neither one of us will be able to. We have no experience in this. It wasn't till I busted into that cell that I was sure she was real and not a figment of my imagination. Not until then did I realize I *wasn't* going out of my mind. I'm sorry, but after that I couldn't leave her behind to suffer. I felt her suffering before we got here. I knew they'd whipped the hell out of her." Bronse swore softly, brushing his hand through his hair in agitation. "That's it. That's all I know. You know everything else. I'm learning as I go just like you are. I . . . I'm sorry I took her out of there for personal reasons. It was . . . I know it was wrong, and it was worse not to tell you."

"If you're going to endanger the crew for your personal reasons, Bronse, don't you think they deserve to know that? Hell, don't you think *I* need to know? I mean, I could guess just by the way you look at her, for the Great Being's sake!"

"I don't . . . I can't . . . ," Bronse protested helplessly.

"Oh, please!" Lasher chuckled and shook his head with amazement. "Chapel, I don't need any more explanations, but you better not sit there and deny you look at that woman like a catabee looks at pole cherries. You would gorge yourself on her until you popped, too, and it's written all over you."

"Lasher, damn you," Bronse grumbled without enthusiasm, "you're a real bastard sometimes."

"An intuitive bastard."

"An intuitive pain in my ass," Bronse corrected harshly. "Now, are you done grilling me? I don't like leaving them alone like this."

"I'll be done when you promise me no more secrets on this trip."

"I can promise you that I will make my best effort to keep you fully apprised of our situation at all times. How's that?"

"Good enough."

They calmed for several beats, each man silent as they began to walk back toward the others.

"Do you want to tell me why you took off before?" Lasher asked him.

Bronse laughed in a short, sharp burst. "That, my friend, is a discussion we will never have. But I am curious about what Ravenna told you. She had a premonition?"

"If that was what that was. She grabbed hold of my neck and chest. She's lucky I didn't clock her," Lasher said with a grin. "For a minute there, though, I thought she was coming on to me, so I decided hitting her would be contrary to promoting romance."

"Nice. Cut to the chase, smart-ass," Bronse said dryly. But then, all lightness flew from Lasher's expression, and Bronze had a sick feeling in his gut that he wouldn't like what he was about to hear.

"She talked about the attempts on your life. That they aren't over. That I'm meant to protect you. She said that someone . . . some woman I might ordinarily trust, will try to take me out so I can't be there for you."

"Well . . . that really sucks," the commander understated. "What the hell is going on around here? I want to know just exactly what I did to deserve this. There must be something. Maybe some information I have that I don't realize I have."

"I think we'd better find out. Fast would be nice. I'd hate to think I'd be afraid to get laid until we do." Lasher smirked at Bronse.

"You know, I'm so glad my impending homicide is such a source of humor for you," Bronse said.

"Hey, it's *my* impending homicide I'm talking about. But seriously," Lasher's tone switched to suit, "do you think the others are in danger in the same way?"

"I think we are all expendable. JuJuren has more than proven that. I also think the team has figured that out by now."

"You're talking in the field. I have a feeling I'm looking at danger during downtime. Off-mission. It will be the next step. If they can't kill us on-mission, they'll try for off."

"Then we better hope that Trick has some information when we get back. I have no intention of dodging any laser fire that I'm not already being paid to dodge."

"Copy that," Lasher agreed enthusiastically.

"But you're right. Tell the others to consider themselves targets until otherwise noted."

When Bronse stepped into the makeshift rest stop, his eyes tracked to Ravenna like magnets to metal. She was already looking at him, but it didn't last long. Color stained her cheeks, and she turned her face away. Bronse felt a surge of excitement in response. He'd almost convinced himself that he had been mistaken; that he had, through some perversion of his own desert-baked brain, turned an innocently caught chill into some kind of reaction of arousal because of the touch of his hand. But her blushing innocence told him she had indeed felt much more than a chill in that moment.

The very concept baffled the hell out of him. He had meant nothing by the touch, he was certain. Not only that, he'd been tending her for bruises left by cruel, abusive men. How could she possibly find the touch of any man anything but repulsive at this point? And how was he going to keep his hands off her when her blushes and blatantly curious topaz eyes kept following him as he moved? By all that was holy, she could tempt a saint to reconsider.

She was leaning a shoulder against her brother, nibbling at a piece of local fruit, but she was all eyes for him. And he for her, he realized, as he caught himself staring at her.

He realized then that he couldn't carry her again. He could not be that close and concentrate on their lives and safety. The entire trek had been spent in a daze of thoughts that had no place in his mind during such a dangerous situation. Thankfully, everyone else was on guard, but it was an untenable state of mind for him to be in. Too many lives were at stake.

"Ender, Lasher," he broadcasted as he strode firmly into their midst. "Carry the girl. Justice, take point. I'll take the rear. Kith, stay between us and keep your eyes peeled. Tell Justice where she's going. Let's move. We're working against the clock."

His eyes drifted to Ravenna before he could help it. Less than an hour of pain block. Then what? A litter, he supposed, would be best. He would have to keep his eyes peeled for materials to improvise with. Damn it all, why did he want to go over there and touch her so badly? Brush back that infernally glorious hair; touch just one fingertip to the creamy soft cheek and its perfect smooth tan.

Bronse reached blindly for the rifle that Lasher handed off to him. He automatically checked the weapon, the routine soothing him and refocusing his attention. Within five minutes they were off again. He concentrated on the terrain, ignoring the back of the girl riding between the men in front of him.

Ravenna was swimming in a sea of misery. She had pulled Kith aside earlier and told him that, no matter how much he felt her pain, he was not to betray her. If she could bear it, so could he. He had gotten that stubborn tilt to his chin and said of course *he* could bear it, but why should *she*? It was simple. They would move faster, and she would be aware enough to help them if they needed it. The danger had not passed. She was sure of it. Oh, danger was following them, of course. Searching for them. She knew that. But that was behind them. Pretty far behind them if she was sensing it right. No. This danger lay before them.

The forest had become thick and blindingly dense around them. She knew they were headed the right way, just as Kith did, but nothing was yet familiar to them. It was exhausting to look for just one familiar branch or path that would indicate that home could not be too much farther ahead. The only thing that these branches seemed to do was hide unknown dangers. Great beasts lived in the wild places of the wilderness. Even the villages weren't always safe, though the forest creatures tended to stay clear of settled places.

So she gritted her teeth, breathed as evenly as possible, and forced down any and all sounds of pain. She used her hair to shade her face from the grimaces she could not resist, keeping Lasher, at least, unaware. Ender had already caught her silent agony twice, but he seemed to understand her determination to stay in charge of herself. Sweat was soaking through her clothes, and the terrain was beginning to blur, but she had made it well past the time that Lasher had given her for the block to wear off. He had asked after her health several times, and by some miracle she had convinced him that the topical and bandages had made all the difference.

She was infinitely pleased with herself right up to the very moment she passed out.

Ender and Lasher both made a misstep as all of the weight of their burden was flung suddenly forward. Only their grip on her arms over their necks kept her from taking a full header onto the forest floor.

"Shit!" Lasher exclaimed, dropping to a knee when Ender did in order to ease her gently into the ferns and leaf litter. Bronse was rushing up with a loud crush of underbrush as Lasher rolled her onto her side. She was deathly pale, and her hair was soaked in sweat. Lasher repeated his curse, realizing that she had lied to him, that he should have forced a stop and checked her more thoroughly.

"Lash!" Bronse commanded.

"Out cold, sir. From the pain. The fever is back too. And before you yell at me, she kept telling me she was fine."

"Do you have another shot for the fever?"

"No. I'm going to narc her and break a chill pack. It should keep her fever down. Jeez, she's a mess." Lasher lifted the back of the shirt to show the soaked and bloody bandages.

"How far?" Bronse demanded, turning to Kith.

"Not far now. Four miles max."

"We could take turns piggybacking her," Ender suggested.

"Not Bronse. He cracked some ribs," Lasher said, giving a smug sideways look to his commander.

"Me and you then. It's only a few miles."

"And you're already exhausted from the last twenty-four," Lasher dismissed him. "Maybe we ought to camp here."

"Not a good idea," Kith warned. "The Fromegs are in

rut. See the marks on the trees? That's from rubbing their horn against the bark to mark territory. Fromegs are mighty territorial and awful big."

"Then we fashion a litter. Jus, Lash, Ender—strip your outer shirts. Kid, find me two man-sized limbs fallen from trees. Strong, no dry rot. Justice, gather up some of this bracken."

With quick efficiency, Bronse had fashioned, and cushioned, a litter for Ravenna. They carefully laid her onto it after Lasher stuck the narc patch on her. Bronse switched off with Ender, and Kith replaced Lasher. They were back on their way in no time.

Bronse was leading the litter right behind Lasher, who was on point. They hadn't gone but half a mile when a crash in the brush brought everyone's attention swinging left. Out of the dense, dark vegetation sprang a lightning-fast body. A giant wall of fur, it crashed through the ranks of the humanoids and struck a random target.

Bronse was plucked out of line so fast that the litter didn't even drop on its end before he and the beast hit the forest floor ten feet away. They rolled. Or the beast rolled with Bronse caught between its four massive paws. The pounce ended with Bronse slamming hard onto his back and the snarling forest creature pinning him by his hips with its hind legs and paws, and his shoulders by the front paws. The animal was some sort of cat; Lasher had never seen anything so enormous in his life. The paws alone were twice the size of those on a Turba tiger.

"What the fuck is that?" Ender was screaming as they all drew laser weapons on it.

"It's a Hutha lion!" yelled Kith.

Lasher didn't care what it was. He was already firing on it.

The first stun didn't even seem to phase it. Lasher heard Bronse shout out as he flipped over to a kill setting. The laser whined loud and sharp through the air and struck hard enough to send the cat rolling to the left. It sprang up instantly, though, wounded and seriously pissed off. It roared, an ear-shattering sound that sent chills down their spines. The next shot came in a trio as Justice and Ender fired with Lasher. The smell of roasting flesh surrounded them as they aborted the cat's second pounce on Bronse. The animal hit the dirt mid-stride, mid-roar, kicking up leaf debris and bracken as it slid to a halt with its muzzle in the soil. It released a horrible shudder, its breath rattling loudly out of its enormous body.

Jus and Ender both rushed up to the beast, their weapons still fully trained on it. Lasher went in the other direction, heading for Bronse now that the threat was neutralized. Lasher dreaded what he was going to see, and he was right to feel that way. Bronse lay sprawled on the ground, gasping for breath, and Lasher could smell fresh blood. The animal's claws had torn through his vest and the Skintex shirt over his shoulders, exposing large, deep furrows in his skin. Looking farther down, Lasher saw that Bronse's pants across his thighs were in similar shape, only the wounds were deeper, having borne the brunt of the weight of the attacking animal.

"Great Being," Lasher whispered, his voice failing him as he dropped his rifle and flung himself down to his commander's side. "Bronse!" Bronse turned dark blue-violet eyes on Lasher, his expression stark and horrifying. Bronse was struggling for every breath and could not speak, but he reached out with strength to grab Lasher's forearm. "Bronse, relax. I think one of the ribs you cracked earlier may have hit a lung." Lasher tried to reassure his friend that he knew what was wrong, though fixing the problem was not going to be so easy. He whipped out the first-aid kit as the others finally arrived to kneel beside them.

"What can I do?" Justice demanded.

"Give me something to stop the bleeding," Ender commanded Lasher as he pressed a hand to the free-flowing blood on Bronse's right thigh.

"Justice, get up and maintain a guard," Lasher barked. "For all we know, there's more of these things. Cats can hunt in prides. Ender, forget the blood. He needs to breathe before we worry about that. Close ranks and bring the kid and his sister close over."

"Got it."

Lasher looked down into a desperate periwinkle gaze. Bronse's skin was turning dusky and tinged with blue around his lips. "Easy does it, my friend. I'm going to take excellent care of you." Lasher pulled out a breathing assist disc and ripped it out of its sterile packing. He reached to tear open Bronse's shirt—the task made easy by the rending left by the beast—and exposed his chest. Then he placed the disc along the breastbone, beneath the heart and between both lungs. The device blinked to life almost instantly, and Lasher watched carefully for the readout and diagnostic.

Sure enough, with a petulant beep, the disc warned that Bronse had punctured his left lung, and the technology would now be inserting tubules into the healthy lung so it could enrich the oxygen intake enough on the functioning side in order to sustain the patient until advanced medical services were reached. Bronse did not feel the invasion because the tubes were smaller than needles, but the difference in his coloring and the urgency of his breathing was immediate. The commander was breathing far easier by the time Ravenna was set down beside him.

"Okay, now let's stop the bleeding. The worst is the legs."

Ender and Lasher worked quickly and with little need for instruction as they prepared the commander for stasis until they could reach help. Bronse hardly made a sound outside of the odd groan of pain. Lasher gave him blood fortifiers and, without even bothering to ask, a medium-dose narc patch. It didn't put him out, but in a few minutes there was clearly no focus to his light eyes.

"All right, I'm open to suggestions," Lasher bit out as he continued to tend their newest patient. He tore into a pressure bandage with his teeth, shucking off the packaging.

"We can't remote the ship this deep in," Jus said. "It's too dense here. Nowhere to land."

"I can get help."

They looked at Kith as a trio, giving him a chill at the synchronized effect. "I'm light and fast and I know where I'm going. I can fetch Ophelia and one or two of the others to help us bring them back to the temple."

Lasher didn't know what a sixteen-year-old healer could possibly do that he couldn't, but Kith had been itching to get his sister to Ophelia from the get-go, so it was more than worth thinking about. If it was good enough for Ravenna, it would have to be good enough for the commander.

"That doubles the travel," Ender said. "There and back."

"And halves the time," Kith retorted. "Trust me, it'll be easier to travel to the temple after Ophelia tends to them and the others come to help."

"I don't see any other choices. Can this little sister of yours run as fast as you do? Can she travel this kind of terrain?" Lasher asked.

"In her sleep. We were born here, remember? You have to trust me. The longer we argue—"

"Right. Jus, go with him."

"Hey . . . ," Kith protested.

"You're no help dead. Justice is light and fast, too, but a crack shot besides."

"Fine." Clearly Kith was not fine with it, but he was anxious to get home now that it seemed imminently in his future. "Let's go."

They went crashing off at a run through the underbrush, making Lasher wince visibly. "Well, I think all of Ebbany can hear them coming."

"No doubt. How's he doing?" Ender asked, nodding to their leader.

"Breathing easier, stoned to the gills, bleeding like a stuck pig on that left thigh. Improvement on the right. The shoulder wounds are shallower, but I think one joint is dislocated, and there's a good chance that the bruising you see there is a broken clavicle."

Ender released a low whistle and shook his head.

"That thing had to weigh at least nine hundred pounds. More, I'm sure. No wonder it kicked the shit out of him."

"Envision if we'd been five seconds slower on the draw."

"No, thank you. Imagine it. After all of this—assassination by Hutha lion."

Lasher laughed sardonically, the sound decompressing in its relief as he understood that the most immediate danger had passed. However, there were still others to consider. It was already midday, and Lasher didn't want to be in the woods come nightfall. "What time is nightfall on this forsaken hunk of planet?"

"I think we have five to six hours tops."

"Yeah? You don't happen to remember Justice's cross-country times from last season's IM games, do you?"

Ender chuckled, reaching to help Lasher bind one of Bronse's wounds.

Lasher heard footfalls long before he could see the source. He was checking Bronse's dry skin by touch, knowing that he needed blood among other things, but he had traded saline supplements in order to make room for some of his last-minute medical changes. Since the benefits had far outweighed the detriment so far, he didn't kick himself over it at all.

Not willing to take any chances and assume that the approach was friendly, Lasher and Ender drew weapons and took aim where the noise was coming from. Ender was closer to the sounds, so Lasher got the benefit of a forewarning when the arms master shot him a look across the distance. Curious, he watched the trees.

The small troop that came through the foliage was exactly that—small. Or, rather, young. There were four of them, including Kith. One was a tiny girl, her features elfin and as fragile as a pixie's. Most outstanding was a cape of white and ash blond hair that nearly reached her knees, and this even though it was braided. Lasher could see it swinging behind her with her forward progress, and several thin, long braids with blue beads worked into them were swinging free from the rest of it. She clutched a bundle that was nearly as big as her entire torso; both arms were wrapped tightly around it. Lasher could make out little else about her. He had never seen anyone so petite—five feet tall at most and looking as though she could use some of Lasher's mother's Uhauh stew to put some meat on her. It wasn't until she was a bit closer that he was able to see the angelic baby blue of her large eyes, their color announced by the backdrop of mocha-colored skin and the accents of the blue beads in her hair.

Lasher couldn't explain it, but he had the strangest sensation of familiarity as he looked at her. He knew it was impossible, knew for certain that they had never met, but he couldn't shake the feeling.

He realized then that Kith had chosen to fortify himself with males, in addition to the single girl child. Lasher's lips twitched in amusement. Did Kith think that these young ones could fight against even their diminished ranks? Had he learned nothing in his short time with ETF officers? Although it wasn't until then that Lasher realized that Justice was not with them, and he wondered what had happened to the pilot.

The taller of the two new males was also clearly the eldest—older even than Ravenna, Lasher realized upon closer inspection. He was a full-grown man, broad in the shoulder though tending toward the same lean athletic build that seemed to characterize their people. He was firm and healthy, evidently used to exercise and—Lasher guessed—hardship. There was something about the roughness of his features that announced this to the worlds. He was about the same height as Kith, but what truly stood out was the shocking contrast of his black and white hair. There was no rhyme or reason to it, it seemed. It was long in back and shorter in front, and the hanks of color were in random blocks of white and black, each distinct and not blending in with the other even where they met.

The other male was younger than Kith. He was a bit shorter than the other boys, but he was broader in his frame. He was also heavier, although Lasher couldn't call him fat. He seemed densely built, solid, and perhaps even strong. Lasher couldn't tell right off. His hair was an intriguing rust and gold color, the gleam of the loose curls brightly catching the sunlight. His light brown eyes appeared gold as well, probably because of the highlights of his hair and the swarthy tan of his skin.

They each wore a tunic and trousers that were neat and well made. The garments were trimmed in expensive threads and decorated with Delran platinum discs and chains. They wore these with the comfort of dismissive experience, as though they thought little to nothing of the valuable baubles. Even Kith had changed from the soiled tunic he'd worn since the escape from the prison.

Only the girl wore anything else. She was adorned in a multi-tiered necklace made up of many flat blue speckled stones. The stones had been smoothed into glossy squares, but they didn't seem to have the glow of precious gems. Delran platinum linked the stones in an upside-down pyramid, from wide around her throat to a single dangling chip between her breasts. The platinum had to be the most valuable part of the entire ornament. It was unique and beautiful, if a little gaudy to Lasher's eye.

But she wasn't here to be judged for her fashion sense, he acknowledged as they broke into the small area that had become increasingly trampled by their activity.

"Where is Justice?" Lasher asked.

He didn't miss that the girl nearly jumped out of her skin when he spoke. The reaction made him suspicious. What did she have to hide? Was Justice okay?

"She remained behind," Kith said quickly. "She wished to guard the girls, since all of the men were coming to help."

"This is all of the men in your temple?" Ender asked with surprise.

"Of course. Men don't have much power," the girl said with a matter-of-fact shrug.

The statement, so clearly innocent and misinformed, made Ender laugh in a loud guffaw. The girl rapidly blushed to the roots of her fair hair and beyond. Charmed enough to take pity on her, Lasher waved Ender to silence.

"Greetings to you all. I am Lieutenant Commander Masin Morse, but everyone calls me Lasher. You can take your pick of whatever name suits you—I answer to most of them. This is Arms Master Rush Blakely, but we call him Ender."

"This is my sister and our healer, Ophelia," Kith returned graciously. "This is Domino." He gestured to the obvious choice of the black-and-white-haired man, making Lasher wonder if that strange hair coloring had been just as obvious at birth. "This is Fallon," Kith finished.

"Thank you all for your assistance. Please, Ophelia, your patients await you," Lasher invited warmly, holding out an arm and gesturing her forward. He smiled at her when two spots of color burned her cheeks, but her eyes had already fallen to her upcoming duty. It allowed her to overcome her shyness and move forward into his care.

Lasher led her directly to Bronse.

Ophelia saw her patients lying together, and she couldn't suppress her cry of dismay. Her sister lying lifeless and wounded was a shock, and it took all of her will to turn away from her to the one who was obviously more in need of her attention. She kneeled hurriedly beside the large male, dropping her pack into the soft bed of leaves and ferns on the forest floor. Nibbling anxiously on her nail as she looked over the soldier, she took in a soft, sniffing breath through her nose. She leaned cautiously closer and repeated the sniff, this time taking in a deep breath. She jerked back, her nose wrinkling with obvious distaste.

"There are pollutants in this man's body," she accused. Then her china blue eyes widened to the size of large coins. "And in my sister!"

"The drugs," Kith clarified when Lasher looked at her with puzzlement.

"Yes. Narcotics. For pain."

"I see. They must be removed."

"I can take off the patches and they will be diluted within a half hour," Lasher said. "But they will be in tremendous pain once I do. Why can't you just—?"

"Masin, correct?" she interrupted, her big eyes taking him in as her head tilted to the side.

"Yes . . ."

"Healer, correct?" she asked, pointing to herself simply.

Put delightfully in his place, Lasher chuckled and nodded. "That would be correct. Might I suggest we work on one at a time though? Just in case things take longer than expected, I wouldn't wish Ravenna to suffer." It was the perfect way to phrase it to get her to think very carefully. Finally, she nodded acquiescence.

Lasher peeled off Bronse's narc patch. He glanced up at the sky, betraying his nervousness at the low angle of the sun, because Ophelia looked at him as she folded her prim little hands into her lap.

"Looking at it will not slow it down," she mused. "Darkness comes of her own will and no one else's. Only Daylight may push his sister around, as brothers are wont to do with sisters."

"Indeed, we're very guilty of that," he agreed, amused by her wisely proposed advice. "Does your brother push you around, honey?"

"Incessantly." She sighed, rolling her big blues with drama. "But he does so out of love and concern. It makes me happy to know he cares. Have you a sister?"

Lasher did not answer straightaway. He looked at her bundle, then at Bronse, and wondered why she didn't begin to work. The narc would wear off soon enough, and Bronse would be in brutal pain.

"I have many sisters. Ten, actually."

"Ten!" she exclaimed breathlessly. "How blessed your mother is. Are any of them Chosen?"

"Uh . . ." Lasher glanced up at Kith briefly, but then thought better of it. Since Kith wished his sister and the rest of the Chosen Ones to go off-world, he was about to quickly learn how it would affect his innocent sibling. "No. We don't have Chosen Ones where we come from."

"That is unfortunate," she said, actually reaching to

pat his hand in sympathy. "But it is common. Only, imagine all those girls! Are you the only boy?" she asked curiously.

Lasher smiled, trying to remember the last time he had been referred to as a boy. "I am one of three brothers."

"My. A magnificent family!" The soldier didn't miss the wistfulness in her tone as she sighed gustily and smiled with a delight that must have made her cheek muscles ache.

"Umm . . . is there anything I can help you with here?" Lasher hinted, gesturing to Bronse hopefully.

Ophelia held her index finger out to him.

"Masin?"

"Yes?"

She then cocked a questioning brow and pointed to herself, a small smile tugging at her lips. Lasher almost fell over in the dirt. She had gotten him once again, the sly little minx! Had he thought her shy?

"Healer," he responded obediently, feeling she deserved her full victory. He did burst out laughing, feeling far easier than he had the entire day. "My apologies. You will let me know though?" She nodded with a smile. "How old are you?" he asked, realizing that she was no child, but a young woman at least, for all she looked like a child with that fine bone structure.

"I am sixteen years."

Yes. Kith had said as much. Lasher frowned, worrying suddenly about other things Kith had said about what would happen to this girl if they were left unprotected in the temple.

He was silenced by that grim thought for several minutes, but roused himself when Ophelia finally moved from her delicate kneeling pose. She leaned forward and sniffed daintily over Bronse. She nodded, seeming satisfied, just as a low sound roused out of the commander. Lasher watched carefully as the blond girl reached out to gently brush her hand over Bronse's face, a soothing gesture that made him stir all the more.

"Ravenna . . ." Bronse said with a harsh rasp.

"She is safe," Ophelia said softly, beating Lasher to the punch. Ophelia's hand drifted down to her patient's chest. She looked with consternation at the device assisting the commander's breathing, and then tried to pull it off. Lasher's hand shot out to grab her wrist, stopping her. The action elicited a simultaneous forward movement from the young males, but Masin ignored them. He did gentle his touch, though, realizing that he had scared her.

"Don't. It's helping him breathe. You can't take it off that way."

"Remove it for me then," she said, using a haughty tone to cover her disquiet. It was a poor attempt because he felt her shaking right through her delicate little wrist.

Lasher wanted to argue the wisdom, but, as she had tried to pound into his head rather gently on two occasions now, she was the healer here. Besides, the device could be replaced if she found herself in over her head. He turned off the assist and it popped easily into his hand.

Bronse immediately began to labor for breath.

The pixie was calm as she moved her wrist back, only to lay her palm along the length of Bronse's breastbone. Slowly she moved her hand over his skin, sliding it to the left, seeking slowly. Then, just at the curve around to his back, she stopped.

She took a breath and closed her eyes.

Lasher didn't know what he had expected, but it wasn't the sudden flare of blue light erupting from the small hand. "What the hell?" he exclaimed, hearing the sentiment echoed by Ender, who hurried over to see and possibly protect their commander. She ignored their reactions and kept her eyes closed.

Ophelia turned all of her thoughts toward the injury

she had sensed inside this man. There were many injuries, but this was by far the worst. She let the light of her soul escape her body through her palm, and it entered the severe wound. It was, she acknowledged, a wound he had sustained while rescuing her beloved sister and brother. This meant the world to her, and she allowed her gratitude to flow out of her heart so it could add to the energy of her power. An umbilical formed between herself and her patient, a link between spiritual selves. Bronse stopped struggling for breath, stopped feeling pain, and no longer thrashed with worry for Ravenna and his men. The men were, she recognized, his most serious responsibility. Their safety meant everything to him. He was a very foreign being, she realized as they shared spiritual space, but in this regard they were similar.

She had not known many men, and certainly not men like this. She had been brought to the temple at a very young age. She had hardly known her father. Kith, Domino, and Fallon were the only males whom she knew with any form of intimacy. The men who came for healing . . . well, it was a brief visitation, and their souls all seemed very much the same.

She liked Bronse's spirit. He was strong and sure. He had a sense of responsibility and determination that reminded her of Ravenna's. He had a large appetite for things that were wild and exciting, and had heavy expectations of those around him. He was not one to settle for less. He was kinder and gentler than he realized, and he was not afraid to feel fear. He embraced it, learned from it, and felt that it made him grow. There was so much richness to his personality and being that Ophelia wished she could lose herself within him. But that, she knew, was not her place.

It was, she thought with pleasant surprise, Ravenna's place.

Or at least it had a great potential to be. This soldier felt very strongly for her elder sister, though he was not yet reconciled to the feelings. Since he was inherently a good man, Ophelia approved heartily. He was quite compatible with Ravenna in essentials.

His violent lifestyle would be an issue, however.

Lasher watched with awe as the magical little creature sighed so deeply that he felt the warmth of her breath even across Bronse's prone body. He had followed the progress of the electric blue light that had spread out from the contact point of Ophelia's hand until it had encompassed every inch of Bronse's skin. Now that blue light was retracting back, rolling up Bronse's body like a reeled-in fishing line, until only her hand glowed once more. Then a smaller sigh, and she let go of him.

"Just give him a—"

She broke off, and only Lasher's quick reflexes kept her from taking a header across Bronse's body. He grabbed her up by both forearms as she weaved and wobbled on her knees. She was shaking like a Kanji puff-junkie.

"—minute," she finished breathlessly.

Lasher's eyes darted up to the three men who knew her, the beginnings of irritation settling along the ridge of his spine for some reason, and he wished he could figure out why.

"That happens to her when someone is hurting really bad. He'll be up real soon now, though," Fallon said, giving a shrug of careless explanation.

Yes, Lasher thought, that's all well and good, but what about Ophelia? They didn't seem to care that she was falling over like a drunkard. None had even twitched to help her. It made no sense. They didn't like it when he touched her, flaring up protectively, but they were willing to let her drop exhausted to the ground?

"You should take away Rave's drugs," Ophelia informed him, sounding tired and exceedingly weak.

"Maybe you ought to rest for a little while," he argued, swinging himself over Bronse so he was on her side of him, leaning her against his chest.

"No. I only need the time it will take for the drugs to wear off."

And just like that a puzzle piece clicked into place. Ophelia couldn't heal someone who was drugged. Was it because she would be affected by the drugs, he wondered. It was hard to tell, but it was very clear that she had to avoid the "pollution" of narcotics in order to perform her magic.

And magic it was, he realized a minute later.

Bronse Chapel flew awake and sat up at full alert.

And, it seemed, full health.

Almost.

"You must be easy," Ophelia warned. "Your healed tissues are still young and therefore vulnerable. It will take time to fully strengthen them. You will also experience a little weakness for the next two days."

Bronse looked at the small woman who sat practically in his second's lap. He was feeling perplexed and disoriented. The last thing he remembered was a devastating impact, and that was the end of it. Looking down at his clothes and the bloody bandages still covering him, it looked like he should be grateful for that lack of memory. Then the young girl in Lasher's care reached over and gently took away the bandages that were apparently no longer needed. As noted, the skin that had filled in the wounds was sensitive pink tissue. Long furrows of newly healed claw marks glared back at him through his torn pants and over his bare shoulders and chest. He shucked off what remained of his Skintex shirt and then turned to lean over Ravenna when he noticed that she was lying by his side.

She quickly began to stir after her narc patch was removed, but Lasher left her to Bronse. He resisted letting

Ophelia go to her right away. Lasher explained that it would take a few minutes for the drugs to be fully purged, and she was better off resting. Ophelia seemed satisfied with that and laid her head against his shoulder, her cheek against his heart. She was so small, so light, Lasher marveled, that he wondered if she was even really there.

When Ravenna opened her eyes, it was to see Bronse leaning over her with an off-kilter smile and a broadly bare chest that was as darkly tanned as she was. The sight was enough to keep her pain at bay, a narcotic all its own. She smiled at him, allowing her eyes to roam over him slowly. He had the lightest dusting of dark curls on his chest in a soft swath between two dark nipples, the curls drawing to a faint point by the time they reached his solar plexus. After that a light line led to his navel. Below that the hairs curled a little darker and thicker as they guided her eyes down to the waistband of his pants, a mysterious tease to points beyond.

He also had quite a few scars, she realized as she backtracked to the strange array of white markings that stood out from his tan. Then she recognized the familiar pink of newly healed flesh as only Ophelia could manage it, and she gasped when it registered that the markings came together to make deep gouges that were clearly claw marks. She sat up into his arms, her hands flying to his shoulders and chest, covering the wounds in the exact position they had been received.

Even though her contact was a stroke of dismay, her touch sparked instant awareness. Bronse was getting used to it happening, but he would never overcome the sheer power of it. No matter how simple, the brush of her hands had the capacity to floor him. The sleeves of his shirt were so big on her that they had shimmied down to her elbows, baring her forearms. As her hands and forearms lay against his bare skin, he could feel her heat and softness.

"Bronse," she whispered with shock, the narcotics in her system making her voice low and husky. "What happened?"

"I honestly couldn't tell you. An accident that is over now."

"But . . ." She looked him over more closely, warm topaz eyes drifting down his body with what felt like unending thoroughness before she cried out with horrified dismay. "Great gods, your legs!" Her hands fell to the rents in the fabric of his pants, her warm fingers unerringly slipping into them to touch the newly healed gouges. Her fingers slid against his new and sensitive skin with the smoothness of silk on silk. Bronse felt every nerve in his body suddenly firing to attention, the fine hairs on his legs prickling with greed, yearning to be the next to bask beneath her touch. The sensation shivered up his legs and settled hot and low in his tightening groin. Just like that, like magic, he'd woken to confusion and a blur of memory, only to be plunged into a clarity of consciousness reserved only for her, and his reaction to her.

Bronse turned his head to the right, away from the audience watching them, as he bore her unwittingly intimate caresses. She searched his skin with concern so thoroughly that he thought he would crush her elbows where he'd caught them in his hands. She certainly didn't act as though she felt the increasing pressure of his squeezing. Then again, she was only half roused from sleep herself, drugs still swimming within her. Great Being, if he had any sense, any decency, he would remind himself of that fact and a thousand other reasons why he should stop acting like a hormonal teenager around her.

But oh, to be eighteen years again, if this fast and ferocious firing of the nerves and speeding of the heart were part and parcel of it. However, he remembered eighteen, and as wild a ride as it had been, he had never experienced anything like this. Of that much he was entirely certain. If it had all felt like this, he'd never have done a single useful thing in his whole damn life. Heaven knows he hadn't taken a clear step since the first time he'd come into contact with the breathtaking Ravenna.

Finally, Bronse turned his head to brush a kiss against her near cheek, and then let his lips brush her ear.

"Ravenna, sweet, I am well. But . . ." He exhaled harshly, his breath hot against her ear. "Ravenna, your touch, as innocently meant as it is, is driving me crazy," he confessed.

Ravenna's fingers stilled suddenly, and he had to smile when he felt her cheek flare with heat against his.

"I—I'm so sorry," she stammered, a tremble traveling the length of her arms to her fingers and into his skin. He bit back a groan as her fingers curled up and slid slowly away. She self-consciously tucked her clasped hands between her knees, which she clutched together with equal tightness.

"Don't apologize. It's simply neither the time nor the place for me to enjoy what you do to me. It will be different when we're safe and alone, okay?"

He heard her breath catch, then release with an excited shudder. She nodded eagerly, and he closed his eyes as he realized that she'd just admitted to being as aware of him as he was of her. He'd suspected as much. He had felt it in that dream. But reality . . . oh, it was so different. So much better. Reality made his heart pound with the thrill of anticipation, made his arms and legs flush with life and heat, and made him throb with a deep sexual pulse that spoke of cravings for surcease in a hot, wet haven that would draw him in tight and sweet.

Ravenna released a gasping breath as her weakened barriers and dizzying heartbeat opened her up to a sudden premonition. Instead of fading gently into the images as usual, she was sucked in, slammed against them. She was thrown down, her rich hair flying loose back over sheets and pillows, hair still damp from a recent washing because she could smell the scent of her shampoo.

Hands. Roughly calloused but sliding gently over her skin in spite of their need. Her naked skin. She was begging. Pleading with tears of agonizing need.

Hold on to me, sweetheart, and then let go.

She heard wanton cries and recognized them as her own. Felt her hands gliding over steely muscle, hardened flesh. The taste of salt and musk swept over her tongue.

Ravenna came back to Bronse's arms and the forest around them with a shuddering breath, her topaz eyes disappearing under the black dilation of her pupils even as she met his gaze and realized that she had never actually left his arms. Those calloused hands held her even now, his muscled body resting like unyielding steel against her. She was breathing so fast that she was panting, and she felt and heard a soft, wild sound vibrating out of him as he shook her.

"Stop!" he hissed hotly. "Stop looking at me like that or I swear to the Great Being I will forget everything and answer the pleas I see in those bewitching eyes of yours!"

"I . . ."

"And don't you apologize to me again, damn it!"

"No. I wasn't. I saw . . . a vision."

Bronse sighed raggedly. "I don't think I can handle any more doom and gloom right now, Ravenna."

"No. It was not . . . it was not a bad vision," she said breathlessly, her fingers scrabbling up absently to grasp his shoulders. "It was about us. It was you . . . and me. You were touching me. Bronse . . ."

"Sweet holy heaven," Bronse uttered achingly when he suddenly realized what she was saying to him.

A vision. The future.

About us, she had said.

Farther off, Domino snorted in disgust.

"What?" Kith asked.

"You don't want to know," Domino countered.

"I asked, didn't I?"

Domino gave Kith an appraising look. Kith was five years Domino's junior, and it made all the difference in the world, in his opinion. Who could suspect that five years made the difference between a young male and an adult man. He suspected that Kith would react all wrong if he told him what he wanted to know.

Domino shrugged. It wasn't his problem, he supposed.

"That one . . . the one whispering to Rave?" Domino indicated.

"Chapel," Kith said with clear derision. "Yeah?"

"He wants her, you know. So badly he can barely think straight. Right now, all he can think about is getting her alone so he can explore their chemistry."

"Is that true?" Kith demanded of Fallon, turning sharply to the younger man.

"How should I know? I don't read people's minds all the time and stick my nose in their business," Fallon said pointedly, giving Domino a disdainful look.

"I didn't nose in. He's so hot for her right now, he's projecting. I can feel his lust without even trying. And hers, too, I might add," he said, trying not to grin as he waited for Kith's explosion.

Kith whipped to face Domino, a low sound much like a growl rumbling out of him with the buildup of his rage. "How dare you talk about her like that!"

"Relax, Kith," Domino said dryly, sighing as if he was bored. "Your sister is a grown woman. If she wants to have sex with *all* of these guys, who are we to say anything about it?"

"I'm her brother!" he roared.

"And I'm her cousin. What the hell does that have to do with it? You think that gives you rights in her life choices? I knew I shouldn't have told you. I knew you were too immature to handle it."

"Hey, is there a problem here?"

Ender's towering presence ended it if there was. They all gave solemn shakes of their heads and made as though they were calm and companionable—until he moved back along his perimeter.

"I am not immature," Kith spat as soon as Ender was out of earshot.

"Mmm. Then leave your sister alone. Your older sister, I might add."

"I don't like Chapel," Kith confided, trying a different tack to get Domino to rally to his cause. "I mean, he's okay as a soldier, and I trust him to help us, but I think he's just doing it because of Rave. Maybe he's just doing this to get at her."

"Uh, Kith, does he look to you like the kind of guy who has to go through this much crap just to get a woman to spread her legs for him?" Domino laughed with his infamously jaded humor. "And if this keeps up," he pointed to the superheated clutch that Bronse and Ravenna were sharing, "he's going to get some really sweet wishes granted before we even get away from the temple. Maybe you should pull Rave aside, share your theory, and tell her to hold off until after we're safe."

With that final word and a mockingly jolly laugh, Domino turned his back on the young fool and walked away. Let him chew on that idea for a while, he thought bitterly. The sooner Kith got over his delusions of grandeur, the better off they all would be. If Kith messed up this opportunity, now that change finally seemed imminent—and change for the better at that—Domino would brave Ravenna's wrath and strangle the brat himself.

CHAPTER
NINE

Bronse decided to forget where he was for exactly one minute. The choice made, he dragged Ravenna beneath his mouth and kissed her with a burn to rival the heat of hell. Again it was reality versus dreams, and reality ran away with the gold medal. Her lips were soft and sweet, her mouth so full of promise that it could make a stone weep.

Ravenna had learned one thing from the dream, however, that she hadn't known in reality, and now she applied the winning knowledge. She parted her lips in an achingly precious tremble of need and invitation. Rave felt his hands sinking suddenly into the depths of her hair, even as his tongue slid deep into the fathoms of her wet mouth.

He tasted wonderfully robust to her, replete with masculine flavor.

Bronse realized that this was her first kiss all over again, but he couldn't measure himself down to the task this time. He needed to devour the luscious, honeyed taste of her, and he swirled his tongue deep into her mouth in order to achieve his goal. She released a pleasured moan, the sound bursting into his mouth beautifully, followed by the thrust of her hungry little tongue. She changed the field of play into *his* mouth, and he welcomed her with a sigh.

It was that moment, as she rose up into his body, that restrictions began to make themselves known. He became aware in the nick of time that he should curb the impulse he had to slide his hands onto her back. She felt the flesh between her shoulders resist tautly as she tried to circle her arms around his shoulders.

And then she felt the pain.

She cried out, her anguish filling his mouth and piercing his soul.

He broke from her quickly, his hands flying to cup her face apologetically and tenderly.

"I'm sorry!" he said low and fierce, kissing the corners of her mouth soothingly. "I'm sorry. Damn, I'm a selfish bastard! I am so sorry, beauty." He whipped his head around and narrowed his eyes on the young girl in Lasher's care. "Are you Ophelia? The healer?"

"My little sister," Ravenna corrected him gently when his tone came out abrupt and commandeering.

"Can you heal her?" he asked more softly of the small young woman.

"Yes. It is why I am here."

Ophelia slid away from Lasher and eagerly picked up her sister's hands. Bronse saw tears form in the younger woman's eyes, and he was forced to remember that they had been torn away from each other and kept apart for an amount of time he was not privy to. Ravenna wept just as freely, twisting his heart into knots as she hugged the little sister who couldn't hug her back just yet. He watched, though, as Ophelia laid the most ginger of touches across Ravenna's horribly disfigured and infected back.

Blue light exploded over them both, setting Bronse and Lasher back on their asses about a foot in opposite directions. This was nothing like the slow, easing healing Masin had seen Ophelia perform on Bronse. The light was all-consuming and blinding. For a moment it looked like the women were locked in a hug of death, like what might happen if someone tried to hug someone who was in the process of being electrocuted.

Then, suddenly, someone turned off the juice.

Lasher and Bronse shot forward, each catching a female as she staggered back. Ophelia fainted dead away in Lasher's arms. Ravenna shook her head and recovered in Bronse's arms after a dazed moment. Unable to help himself, Bronse swept up the shirt she wore in the back and reached to pull away a strip of bandage. The skin beneath it was pink and tender.

"That is the damndest thing I've ever seen!" he exclaimed, pulling more strips of bandage free to reveal perfectly healed skin. It was as new as a baby's, but it was perfect. He finished removing her bindings and then ran an eager, flat palm over the entirety of her soft back. "Great Being, Ravenna, I had no idea things like this existed!"

"Bronse, please," she said, laughing and trying to pull away as his touch turned her cheeks as pink as her back. "Let me tend to Ophelia."

"Of course," he said hastily, letting her go after a long moment.

Rave went to kneel beside Lasher, touching her baby sister's sweating brow.

"What the hell was that? That didn't happen when she healed Bronse."

"She was at full strength when she healed him. She was tired when she healed me, and it makes control of the power nearly impossible. She is young yet and it's hard for her to stress herself. Yet she does it all the time because she does not have the heart to turn away anyone who needs her. It makes her so frail."

"Then I'd say it's damn well time that someone make her turn them away," Lasher growled irritably. "This isn't right! She's still a kid!"

"A young woman with a very big heart and a deep conscience. I am her high priestess, and I do restrict her whenever possible, but I wish you luck if you think you can do better at getting her to listen to reason, because gods know I have tried again and again."

Lasher frowned ominously, his dark scowl like a storm on his normally laid-back features.

"Not to fear," Rave soothed him with a gentle hand on the arm that cradled her sister's head so tenderly. "She will sleep now and will awaken refreshed in the morning."

"Speaking of which, it's getting on to dusk. We had best make tracks. We've been sitting still too long as it is," Bronse said.

"I'll carry Ophelia," Lasher said, his tone dismissing any arguments. He handed his rifle to Bronse as Ender rounded up the others. After brief introductions to Bronse, followed by the commander's crash course in who exactly was in charge, Bronse took point, pulling Rave behind him as she guided him toward the temple.

Bronse was pacing the chamber he'd been shown to, his impatience radiating into the room in wide, kinetic eddies that seemed to bounce off the walls and vibrate back against his skin, further agitating him. It was a perception, he knew, but he couldn't escape it.

The temple was a magnificent place. To say it was old would be an understatement. It had clearly been there since close to the dawn of the planet's earliest civilizations. Situated half in and half out of the side of an earthen steppe, it towered above the tree line.

They had been readily greeted by the other Chosen Ones. There had been a small-boned sassy little thing named Vivienne, whose brilliant flame red hair was so very different from that of the others, and whose cool blue eyes danced with easy merriment. Certainly she and the others had been brimming with delight to see Ravenna safely returned to them. There was also a girl of only fourteen years or so named Devan, who, with long black hair that hung in silky coils, and emerald eyes with jade suns radiating from their centers, had the promise of being an amazing beauty as a woman. Her peculiar eye color was almost unnerving and Bronse supposed it was a genetic anomaly, perhaps one that was attached to whatever gene it was that made her psionic like the rest of the Chosen Ones. It struck him that there seemed to be a hand-in-hand sort of connection between their abilities and their looks. Or perhaps being Chosen had not been a matter of mere ability.

There were also servants in the temple. This had upset Bronse greatly because he knew that if there was one untrustworthy aspect to any dwelling, it was to be found in the servants. He had infiltrated enough places to know that using servants as spies was a classic, effective method that would never go out of style. The crew's presence there would, no doubt, be as good as reported by now, even though Justice had done her best to contain the household. But in a structure as old and as large as this, there were usually as many hidden chambers and passages as there were visible ones. Plenty of ways to escape in and out without being noticed. He had known it the minute he had seen the twisting, turning labyrinth of stone embedded half in the forest, half in the bedrock of the earth. The natural world had been incorporated into the complex design. Only those who lived in the temple for their entire lives would ever know all of its secrets. Considering how young all the Chosen Ones appeared to be, with none over the age of twenty-six, it seemed unlikely that they would know even a third of what a longtime servant might know.

It had not escaped Bronse's notice that there were no elderly Chosen Ones. Not even middle-aged Chosen

Ones. He had thought, mistakenly, that age and virginity might have had something to do with that, some temples finding only the young and pure to be holy, but Bronse had discovered during dinner that the priests and priestesses were not required to be chaste. That explained why Ravenna hadn't had any qualms when she'd asked him so enthusiastically for his kiss. At supper, Vivienne had made cracks about how hard it had been to get laid since she'd become a Chosen One. He'd even seen Kith eyeing a serving girl, no doubt with more than wine on his mind after being imprisoned for so long.

The clincher had been Domino. The outspoken man had run Bronse down in the corridor earlier and pulled him to a stop. After a moment of debate that went on behind his cool, silvery eyes, the eldest Chosen One had decided to impart his brand of wisdom. "I guess you've figured out we all have special talents," he supplied. "I think you have also figured out that Kith's special talent is being a bit of an ass. He means well, though. Looking out for his big and little sis being at the heart of it."

"I sense a point," Bronse had encouraged.

"The point is that I know Kith. He's feeling threatened by you. Especially after you laid that scorcher of a kiss on his big sis earlier. He near popped a vessel. Some jealousy I imagine, more likely some fear—the usual motivators in these things."

"I know them well," Bronse had agreed.

"I think I may have inadvertently handed Kith a way of trying to mess up you and Ravenna, and I don't like the idea of my abilities being twisted around like that—at least not unless I'm doing the twisting." Domino gave Bronse a capricious little grin, then shifted his weight and met Bronse's eyes without hesitation. "I'm what's known as a psychosexual empath. It's a long name that means I'm highly attuned to all things sexual—past, present, and future. Believe me, it's not as much fun as it sounds," Domino joked when Bronse arched a curious brow. "Sure, it's nice being able to rewind and replay the hot bit of loving that went on up against that wall over there earlier today," he indicated the spot with a casual flip of a hand, "between a chambermaid and a cook's apprentice, but try blocking out or filtering through all the bits of loving that ever happened in all the existing years of this hall being in place. Considering that humanoids are a right randy bunch, it gets a bit noisy, a lot uncomfortable, and damn overwhelming.

"But about my point," he had hurried on when Bronse seemed to patiently grasp his explanation of his ability. "Don't put it past Kith to lie to you about Rave's motivation toward you. And don't put it past him to lie to Rave about yours. She's sensitive, but not always when she's too close to a matter to see straight. I don't think I need to tell you she's innocent in her way, for all her power and her ability to lead us little Chosen lambs. The lessons she's learned about men and sex have come only recently, and only from two quarters. You and that bastard at the prison. For her, that's a lot of unexpected information to sort through all at once. I can tell right off that you're honorable enough, but Kith could twist pure snow until it looked like piss."

"Kith's games won't bother me or Ravenna," Bronse had told him surely, surprised at just how confident he was speaking for a woman who, for all intents and purposes, he'd just met. "He's a little man who's grown up in a sheltered world. I, however, am not. But thank you for the heads-up. I appreciate it."

The sentiment was genuine.

"Just so long as your appreciation includes a cubbyhole on that ship of yours. As long as you can take us out of here, my favors get stacked outside your door, my new friend."

At least Domino had been balls-out up front about his

mercenary motivations. Bronse had a powerful appreciation for the honesty, and it made him more inclined to trust what Domino was telling him.

But now, in the present, Bronse had a headache. He rubbed at the knotted muscles in the back of his neck as he paced some more.

Damn. He hated sitting still in hostile territory, but there was little he could do in the dark with these untrained children suddenly attached to his hip holsters. Departure had to wait until tomorrow at dawn, when Justice could be led to a clearing that would allow her to remote-land the flyer.

Luckily Bronse had picked something bigger and faster for her to fly for this mission. It looked like he would be taking on about seven refugees, and he would need the space. Not to mention the speed if he was going to pull off a passenger dump and manage to keep IM ignorant of it in official logs on both the ship and whatever station or port they hesitated at in order to drop them off.

Great Being, he was tired. Worried. Aggravated. Stressed. In danger.

Horny as hell.

Damn, damn, damn.

Now that he'd confessed the true crux of the problem to himself, he couldn't pawn it off on anything else. Every cell in his body, right down to the tired, stressed and endangered ones, beat with a very singular need that only a very singular woman could ease.

Bronse plucked absently at the superfine silk material of the tunic he had been given to replace his torn shirt. It was a bit snug, these people clearly not used to seeing men of his stature and physical development, which made him chuckle and wonder what they made of Ender, who was much bigger than he was. The close-fitting material seemed to chafe at Bronse, for all its infinitely pristine softness. He felt he couldn't breathe.

In truth, he could not *understand*.

What would bar the woman from coming to his quarters?

Tricky question. With thousands of answers. She had been warm, friendly, and as open as ever at the banquet-style meal they had been served, even seating him beside her and flirtatiously feeding him an occasional taste of her culture's cuisine from her own plate. He hadn't even allowed the presence of his crew and the fact that they were still very much on-mission to interfere with the desire to give and receive affection. He'd already crossed that line earlier when he'd kissed her right out of her drug-induced stupor in front of all the spirits in heaven.

When they'd finished eating, she had slowly walked him through the temple gardens, and he had immediately smelled the overwhelming sweep of Ayalya spice. He realized then that the mixture of a garden in bloom and Ayalya spice would probably get him rock solid hard for the rest of his natural life.

Then she'd been called away on a temple matter and, despite his resistance, she had asked him to go to his chambers. She had said she would speak to him later.

Well, it was later. Much later.

Had Kith butted in and scared her off? Was she frightened of him enough on her own without anyone else's help? Hell, he knew what he looked like; so big and imposing and reeking of military command. He had already botched things up with her dozens of times, that thoughtless kiss this afternoon being a good example.

For that matter, she had been away from here for at least a month, having been held captive in the village, then having slipped into the Banda's clutches. There must be hundreds of things a high priestess would be in demand for this first night back. But it wasn't as though all of that mattered anymore. She would be leaving here for good anyway.

He knew he was being selfish and self-centered along with everything else. Not a good thing in general, but definitely a huge mistake in a building where the residents can just about sense your every thought, mood, and intention. Actually, Kith was the only true empath. Domino was only sexually empathic, but that definitely applied to Bronse's situation of the moment. Fallon, it turned out, was the one and only actual telepath, although he was quite voluble about the fact that he hated reading minds. He viewed it like a dental rerouting procedure.

Vivienne. Now, to Bronse, Vivienne was a fascinating mystery. She had a fierce power—one that Bronse suspected was strongly aggressive by the way she was deferred to, but he had yet to obtain a single telling clue as to what it was. The commander had learned that potential determined rank among the Chosen Ones, and Vivienne was second to his Ravenna. That left Devan and Ophelia. Ophelia healed, he knew, but little Devan—she was so quiet. He had no idea she was even there half the time, so it hardly seemed to matter what her abilities were.

That was neither here nor there, he thought impatiently. He was not a sit-and-wait kind of guy. He was a go-and-get-her kind of guy. Well, okay, maybe he was both. The ETF had taught him patience *and* aggression. It had taught him how to apply both and how to determine when each was called for. So why was waiting for her now so damn difficult? Bronse growled out a sound of frustration between his gritted teeth.

It wasn't as though he would make Ravenna do things she wasn't ready for. She could come here and feel as safe as she needed to feel.

Patience. He was an expert sometimes. When he had

kissed that delectable mouth of hers and she had started to drive him crazy, he'd still managed to withdraw and keep his wits about him. He would just have to convince her how much she wanted him.

That was aggression, and he was definitely an expert there. Of course, he would understand if she didn't show up at all tonight. Perhaps for her last night here in her home territory, a place where she felt safe and secure, she didn't want to disturb the image of her childhood home with such a clear transition into womanhood.

Patience would absolutely be called for in that case. So he needed to quash his urge to storm out of this room and drag her beneath him so he could teach her about the feel of his deeply thrusting body transitioning in and out of hers.

Or perhaps such aggression would be a needed spark in this case?

That does it! There was only one thing he could possibly do. Bronse burst out of his room and went to find Lasher so he could either get some advice or have his longtime friend help him find a way to get moderately drunk. Masin had provided both services since officers' college, and he would hardly fail Bronse now.

Bronse made it as far as the antechamber that served as a sort of crossroads to the four distinct wings of the temple, where they intersected and could be most easily traveled between.

There stood Ravenna, pacing just as energetically as he had been doing, the train and skirt of the bright red-orange gown she wore skimming back away from her legs at the thighs. Long sleeves dropped to the floor from her wrists and were cuffed in a beautiful white fur, and they too swept the stone mosaic laid so intricately and patiently a great many centuries ago. Her shoulders were almost bare, the neckline cocked at the very edges of her shoulder joints. Around her neck she wore a single bloodstone teardrop on a Delran platinum chain, the metal spun into a twisted rope that caught the light with every shift her body made.

She was a vision. A confection floating just out of his reach. He could see her every curve, her thrusting nipples against thin Yojni silk attesting to the chill in the night air, the silhouette of her navel evident, and the tempting shadow of dark curls just beneath that. She cleaned up magnificently, he realized, feeling the understanding clawing through him with physical pain. Her face and body were glowing from a fresh bath, and her hair, no doubt still damp from that bath, was twisted into a single roping braid to keep it managed. She wore three thin bands of platinum on her right hand, one ring to a finger among the center fingers, the elegance of the metal sparkling as she slid that restless hand up over her breastbone and throat with agitation, finally ending up at her neck, where she rubbed at it with a grimace.

Watching her, knowing that she struggled just as much as he had struggled, gave him a measured sense of calm and security. As that sensation of restfulness fell over him, he abruptly understood the single most important factor about his need for Ravenna. As physical as it was, it was nothing compared to the swirl of emotional upheaval he was being swept into. He recognized it simply by its strangeness and its absence from his life to date. It was probably why he had such a hard time controlling it, he realized. What experience did he truly have with feeling emotions of any real depth toward a woman? This idea disturbed him in just the same way that the approach of an unknown opponent would disturb him. The questions were the same, actually, in both instances. Would he measure up to the challenge? Did he have the skills he needed? Was it a friend or a foe? When he persevered, what were the advantages to be had?

Bronse's adrenaline oozed through him as he considered

all these questions. Ravenna was not an opponent to be battled. She was a precious, remarkable woman, and he would never find anyone like her anywhere else in the entire galaxy.

He knew. He had been just about everywhere in the galaxy.

There simply was no one he would ever consider her equal. To him, she was that extraordinary. And for all his confidence, he still feared that he wouldn't deserve her. She was everything he wanted and so much more than he would have ever considered for himself. Surprisingly, though, he found that he wasn't inclined to balk at the idea of an intensive attachment. This in spite of his scars at Liely's hands. It was a potentially intimidating realization for a man whose only real attachments in life were his outwardly untouchable crew.

Bronse was admittedly daunted by his and Ravenna's individual responsibilities. They were both highly positioned and crucial to their own specific societies. Where and how would these things ever mesh? It would be easier to bring their bodies together, he thought, than to enjoin their worlds.

He knew what she was thinking as she paced into yet another circuit.

If I begin this, I will risk everything. I will risk family, friends, love, pain—everything. Why? Why should I walk into his arms when my eyes are so wide open to the enormous hurt that could be awaiting me?

He knew what she was thinking because he wanted to know the answer as well. There were a great many answers he wanted. But none of them, he realized, would ever change the one answer he simply could not escape.

The answer to the question *Why?*

Because he wanted her with all of his heart and soul, and never before in his life had he known such a perfect need. Never had his very spirit sparked as if it had been touched by lightning, as it did when it recognized that her spirit was close by.

He could only wonder if the answer was the same for her, and if she thought it was important enough to lay the rest aside to be worked out in its own time.

Bronse pushed away from the wall that he had used for shadow and concealment.

"Ravenna."

Ravenna's pacing braked to a halt as the object of her obsessive worrying seemed suddenly to be conjured to life by the intensity of her own mind. Oh, but he looked real enough, she thought, her tongue darting out nervously to moisten suddenly dry lips. He was so tall, so robustly healthy, she marveled as he began to cross the mosaic toward her. He was so real, and it was overwhelming how his presence filled even this enormous stone intersection. She trembled visibly, quickly clasping her hands together to try to hide it. To try to hide from him how her very blood sang with joy when he came close, as he was doing now. It reveled and danced in her veins as if in the midst of a wild carnival. More! More! Always wanting more. Wanting him closer. She was looking for satiation, and she knew it with instincts as inherently feminine as giving birth.

Bronse closed the distance between them until he stood an arm's length away. She twisted one hand in the other as she realized that all of her courage had fled her, and she couldn't make herself so much as lift a single eyelash toward raising her gaze to his. Then that infernal burning on the rises of her cheeks began, and she knew she was fully flushed with color, the tide of it creeping toward her hairline.

"Are you afraid to look at me?" he asked, his whisper reverent in this place that was built to worship her gods, created to make her the child of a deity, as she no doubt deserved to be. Bronse could easily believe her to be divine in that moment, for all her submissive shyness.

"I don't think I could ever be afraid of you," she told him breathlessly.

"Then look at me, Ravenna," he beckoned softly.

She did so, but by the time her eyes finally touched on his, her breasts were heaving with wild breaths and her fingers had squeezed each other to whiteness. Now he could see her body trembling in entirety, and he couldn't fathom why it made him smile. Perhaps it was because she had no concept of her power over him. She had no idea of how she took his breath away, made him shudder just as much as she did in anticipation, turned his knuckles white on the crests of his fists as they clenched in order to strive for a control that he feared had abandoned him. The difference was, he'd been trained to appear calm in the face of a storm, and she had not.

She didn't know the tempest that she was.

But he would show her.

"You're so incredibly beautiful," he said gruffly, his hand reaching for her face and closing the distance between them at least that much. He swept her chin in hand, making sure she kept her eyes on his as he stepped closer to her. It brought them nose to nose, breast to breast, and thigh to thigh. At last. A collective sigh seemed to shudder through their bodies, and he tilted up her chin so her mouth grazed his very lightly.

"I . . . I had my first real kiss today," she told him softly.

Bronse closed his eyes briefly, remembering far too keenly for sanity how he'd been driven to devour her with that kiss. Her first real kiss. A budding young woman in this way alone, for she was already "mother" to a brood beneath her. Cloistered. Sheltered. Far too pristine for the likes of him. He would have to do something miraculous in his future to make up for such a gift.

"I was so very glad to give it to you," he said, rubbing his mouth over hers and thrilling in the way her lips parted and pouted so eagerly for him. "Should I give you another? You seem to like them."

"Yes. Yes, you should, and yes, I do!"

He chuckled at her enthusiasm, and her blush heightened, but she smiled beneath his lips just before she added to her invitation the stroke of her tongue across his lower lip, sealing the deal as far as he was concerned. He caught her up and unleashed his hunger. He hadn't intended to. He'd meant to treasure this time with her and savor it, but he couldn't help himself. The taste of her flowed like premium wine over his tongue, the warmth of her mouth mulling her flavor perfectly. She was so receptive, so welcoming as she coaxed him into her mouth with her sweet little tongue that he groaned with deeply surging need.

Ravenna felt him shudder and knew a rush of fabulous understanding. She was only half certain of the details, but the feelings were clear as crystal. Her hands slid up to rest against his chest, and she could unexpectedly feel everything. The pounding of his heart as it crashed madly against his rib cage, the fine shimmers that coursed through him with ever-increasing intensity to match the increasing lust of their kiss, and—she thought with sly satisfaction as she leaned just a little more forward, settling her hips against his—the incredibly evident thrust of an erection that made no mistake of his desire for her.

Her little wriggle in search of telltale signs caused a sudden rigidity throughout his entire body. There was a heartbeat of utter stillness, even his mouth freezing in its lock against hers. Then his hands were snaking around her, grasping her tightly by her bottom and dragging her in an enthusiastic grinding of his hips against her. She gasped, and a shiver of pure excitement swiveled madly around inside of her, a dollop of melted fire splashing into the core of her body and sending a slick invitation into the very heart of the expectant place between her thighs.

"Interesting," he murmured against her stunned lips.

"How so?" she managed to squeak out.

"Oh, just taking a few personalized notes, sweet. I'm learning all kinds of things about you with every passing second."

"Can I learn things about you?"

She didn't wait for an answer and went right for what she wanted to know most. Her hands slid over his hips, her fingers curving over the taut musculature of his backside and thighs, her sweeping touch fondling him thoroughly until she could feel the burn of his skin right through his clothing. All the while he was alternately kissing her and breaking away to catch his breath. Her hands swept forward over the frame of his hips and both slid directly to the huge swell of his arousal, as if she'd done it a hundred times before.

The widening of her eyes as she touched him tattled on her. She hadn't done so even once before. He wanted to speak, say something to ease her into the familiarity she was achieving wickedly quick, but he could barely keep his legs under him, never mind form coherent sentences. She was so curious and thorough, and she was going to kill him, he thought madly. Either that or he was going to come like a rocket right then and there.

Since this wasn't at all how he wanted it to go, he fell back on training and knew that it was time to regroup.

He reached out to grasp her by her upper arms as tightly as he dared and dragged her the full distance of his reach away from his maddened body. Surprise lit her eyes, and she had the temerity to pout, damn her, as she was forced to relinquish her task of intimate exploration. It took a very long minute, but he finally was able to find his speech.

"This is not . . ." He had to stop and clear the growling pitch from his voice so she wouldn't mistake arousal for displeasure. "I need to take you somewhere more private than this," he explained roughly. "I'm not about to make love to you in the middle of the most public hall in the temple, Ravenna."

There it was, he thought with ridiculously instant delight. That hot little blush that was everything innocent about her and everything passionate as well. He was dying to explore these contradictions, and she would never know what this walk toward privacy was going to cost him in sheer levels of torture.

Ravenna couldn't understand what had come over her. It was, she sighed to herself, what always came over her when Bronse came into her sight. Responsibility and propriety simply melted away, and the world would narrow only to the two of them. Privacy would become complete, even if it was only in their two minds. At least it felt that way to her. She decided it must be true for him as well.

"Of course," she murmured, honestly grateful that at least one of them was showing a sense of self-preservation. Living in the temple made it nearly impossible to have any life one could call truly private, but she was used to that. And she suspected that a military lifestyle would have made Bronse just as easily able to dismiss exterior disturbances. However, maintaining as much of an illusion of privacy as possible was essential and, of course, wise.

Bronse reached for her hand and grabbed it tightly by lacing his fingers with hers and pressing their palms snugly together. Then he led her back toward the guest quarters where he and his crew had been situated. She had known all along which room was his, had honestly made a great deal of progress toward it, but as she had reached the crossroads she had panicked.

Now, as he led her inside and released her hand in order to draw the door closed, she tried to remember why she had hesitated. Hearing the slide of the privacy bolt clicking soundly into place, she felt her heart jump with a thrill. How long, she thought in a rush, had she been longing for this moment of being alone with him? It felt like a lifetime, yet it had been no time at all in reality— and out of reality. She suspected that they had been in contact through dreams even longer than she had been recalling it, building a bridge between them. But how and when it all started had not mattered and would never matter. She pressed a hand to her breast, trying to keep her savagely throbbing heart from bursting out of her. She had known him forever. She knew that now. And, one day, so would he. He sensed it deeply, reacted to it strongly, but he hadn't accepted the real truth of it because he was rooted in the logical, not the spiritual.

But he was learning.

Feeling more secure in their privacy, Bronse turned from the door and faced her with a ready smile, unaware of the wolfish tilt that the grin acquired when he coupled it with a long, thorough perusal of her. She was flushed and breathless, pressing an elegant hand to the rapid rise and fall of her chest. He smiled a little more broadly, unable to help himself even though it was caddish of him to be tickled by her heightened nerves. This was an extraordinary adventure for her, he realized. Something she had never done before, had never chosen to indulge in for whatever reasons, though he suspected that the most likely of causes would be too much responsibility, not enough time to explore her own needs, and a highly limited selection of men from which to choose. A brother, a cousin, and a youth were her most intimate male acquaintances. There were the servants, but someone who couldn't meet her on an intellectual level would never suit a woman like Ravenna.

It had occurred to him that possibly he was a man of infinitely lucky convenience, but that didn't suit this woman, either. He pushed away from the door and stepped across to her, his eyes trained steadily on her ravishing face, all of its sweeps and hollows coming together to make her so exquisite. Some might find her coloring simplistic, but he saw richness in her hair and gorgeous glitter in her eyes that could never be plain, or ever be described as merely brown. When he neared her, he reached to stroke her face, along the line of her jaw from her chin to the soft, sensitive spot just before her ear. The way she was looking at him, her eyes so wide and her breath so wild, told him she could plainly see the hunger in his expression. Afraid she was going to hyperventilate, he smiled again and leaned forward to place a simple, gentle kiss on her burning cheek.

"Shh," he soothed her softly. "Listen to me, Ravenna," he murmured as he pushed her hair back to expose her ear. "I want you to listen and know something that's very important to me."

He had her full attention, her gears shifting from a frightened and overexcited little bird to an attentive mother hen, so that her breathing slowed down as he pulled away to meet her eyes.

"Most of my crew came from very difficult backgrounds," he said quietly, touching her cheek briefly before letting his hand fall away to catch hers in his grasp. "No details, but needless to say they bear the scars and, though they have all risen above it, it shaped what they are . . . who they became."

"This is true of all of us," she said, her head tilting, curiosity evident in her eyes. He smiled, knowing she was trying to figure out this choice of topic and the seeming shift in his mood.

"Mmm," he agreed. "Don't you want to know how I

grew up? What influenced my life?" He raised her fingertips to his lips, rubbing them softly, placing occasional slow kisses on the pads as he spoke.

"O—Of course," she breathed, a shiver shuddering up her arm and through her body. He acted as if he didn't notice it. "I would like to know anything about you."

"Ah, but this is of very specific importance," he assured her, turning her palm to his toying lips. "I came from a family that is secure, simple, hardworking, and very independent thinking. My parents have been married for . . . umm . . ." He paused as if counting, but he was just drawing her in, and he felt her leaning closer with her interest. "I'm pretty sure it's been forty-four years now. And though I don't have a dozen brothers and sisters like my friend Lasher does, my father had six brothers, and that gave me more uncles than I knew what to do with." He watched her smile, her topaz eyes laughing. He slowly touched his tongue to the center of her palm. This time the shiver was accompanied by a sharp indrawn breath that accented the tremor's path across her nipples, hardening them into delectable points beneath that thin, brightly colored silk.

"I mention this because each of my uncles had a hand in raising me. They ranged greatly in age, so some were married and some were not. Consequently, I got a lot of experience in how a man should treat a woman long before I even realized I was supposed to like girls." His eyes twinkled with mischief, and she laughed at him. "I was fixated on being a soldier from a young age, so that actually took a little longer than was usual."

"One might find that hard to believe," she mused, her tone absolutely sarcastic despite its delicacy.

"One might think so," he said with a dramatic sigh, his lips moving to the sensitive interior of her wrist, "but alas it was true. I was a late bloomer."

"Well, you are clearly in full bloom now," she noted with that sexy breathlessness in her voice that drove him wild.

He chuckled at her wit. "And thus we come to the point."

"Ah, there's a point." She laughed.

"Yes. The point is, my father and my uncles were the most honorable, respectful men I have ever and will ever know. There is no higher standard, in my opinion. And it was a standard I was molded into meeting. Especially when it came to the treatment and care of women. And don't you know that when they all settled down, which they all eventually did, they all remained married to the same woman. This, in my society, is a rare and remarkable thing."

"The villagers trade mates very often," she said with a frown. "They commit, and then have relations with others against their vows to the gods. Children are born confused about their families. The most violent of their crimes are crimes of passion and vengeance. I can appreciate the value in what you speak."

"Good. I'm glad." He kissed the inside of her elbow, and then stepped closer to bypass her sleeve and touch his mouth to her round shoulder where it peeked out of her neckline. "Because this is my point," he said softly, brushing over her collarbone briefly before touching a kiss to her cheek and then whispering into her ear. "To the best of my knowledge, I have never knowingly and with malice mistreated a woman. Every fiber of my being abhors the idea of it. I have no need of cruelty and deception to bolster my own ego. What I need is the beauty of a woman who trusts me. I need to know she feels respected and treasured because that *is* what soothes my ego. I relish every smile, every laugh, every sigh, every soft, husky little moan." Bronse nibbled at the sensitive line of her neck, his tongue touching hot and wet to her pulse, flicking gently up toward her ear until he got his soft, husky little moan.

Her hands came up to cling to his upper arms and she shuddered once more, only this time he felt it with his entire body. His composure was rocked, a renewed surge of desire rushing through him, sending a painful upwelling of blood to an already taut erection. Bronse gritted his teeth quietly. It was not her fault that he had been walking around in an aroused state for all the hours since that kiss in the forest. Well, okay, so it *was* her fault. But he wouldn't rush her or skip over a single nicety just because his body couldn't stop screaming demands at him.

"Is this . . . your point?" she whispered against his cheek.

One day, he would know her well enough to make a naughty joke of that question. One involving a strategic shift of his hips. For the moment, the gentleman took rein.

"My point is, don't be afraid of me, beauty. Neither of us knows where this will take us, but I will treat you like the precious creature I feel you are until we figure it out, and after as well. I won't hurt you. If you're afraid, tell me so and I will help you become unafraid. If you are overwhelmed, tell me so and I will stop. Nothing will ever happen between us that I feel you do not want to happen with the whole of your heart," he said in a fierce, rumbling tone. "I *demand* that, Ravenna. I won't be satisfied if you compromise your needs and desires for the sake of mine.

"You are my need and desire," he told her heatedly, drawing her flush against his obviously aching body. She released one of those little gasps that had more delight than shock to it, and her eyes lit with golden fire. "Heaven help me, you have power over me like nothing I have ever known! I can't think or see straight, and I may not notice subtle signs of fear or distress in my passion for you. I need you to promise me you will tell me . . ." He swallowed hard as he realized that he was shaking hard enough to send the vibration through her. "Don't let me give you any reason to think badly of me. Promise me you'll tell me what you need."

She reached up to touch his lips with soft, stroking fingers, her eyes lifting slowly to his, smoky sensuality lacing her irises. "I promise, I will always tell you what I want. And I will never think badly of you. I know your soul, Bronse Chapel. You're a good and honorable man."

"I try," he murmured with a smile that quickly turned into a trap for her fingertips. He drew her two fingers into his mouth for a brief suckle and a teasing flick of his tongue. He could tell by her expression and her rosy cheeks that she was thinking decidedly naughty thoughts about the possible applications of his eager mouth. He released her and swooped down on the already well-kissed lips that had been taunting him with their pouting fullness all of this time. He was amazed by his own restraint thus far, and mentally thanked each of his uncles by name, because more than anything he didn't want to screw this up.

Ravenna had been very surprised when Bronse didn't just pick up where they had left off in the corridor the minute the door was secured. Then she had been a little confused and possibly a tiny bit insecure about whether he still wanted her. Her relief and gratitude were profound when she finally realized what he was trying to do. She knew he was right for her, but she never guessed it would be such a fine attunement. He seemed to read her as though he had an instruction manual on her. He sensed her fear, her anxiety mostly, and even secured her confidence that she could always share her doubts with him, while wiping away that smidge of insecurity when he confessed how affected by her he really was.

Oh, and it showed! His kiss was something wild and voracious. She might still be learning the basics, but she could feel that intensity with mind-blowing certainty. His hands were bracketing her waist, clutching her soft sides as he held her fully and snugly against his hard body. The muscles beneath her hands as she clung to his arms were like solid stone, although she fathomed that stone didn't twitch with excitement the way he tended to. Especially as she swept her touch along his arms and shoulders and the back of his neck. There, his hair was short and crisp and she loved the feel of it under her fingers. Before she knew it, she was holding him firmly to a zealously reciprocated chain of kisses that robbed them both of sense and breath.

Suddenly he broke away from the kiss and grabbed her by the shoulders. His breathing ragged and harsh, he twisted her in his grasp until she was facing fully away from him. His breath fell hotly on her bare neck as she felt a tug on her hair. She gasped when she realized he was unraveling her braid. He caught her hand when she tried to stop him with a protest.

"Uh-uh," he denied her. "This is a game of fair play. I want to touch your hair just like you touch mine."

"But it's so long . . ."

"And I can't wait until we're both covered in it," he told her vehemently, the blunt eroticism of the statement making her entire insides flush with liquid anticipation. Sensing his hands rapidly unraveling her braid made her feel like they were rushing toward the image he had painted. Finally she was freed, the still-damp mass releasing the scent of her shampoo all around them, and he leaned in to breathe deeply of it. "You always smell so good. This is how I found you. I could suddenly smell you . . ."

He brushed aside the mass of chocolaty tendrils and worked his mouth with wicked sensuality over the back of her neck and the slopes into her collarbone. She felt his lips, tongue, teeth, and even his breath as he spoke softly to her.

She felt him touch her back and then felt the tug of the laces that held the gown closed. She closed her eyes, breathing heavily in anticipation and crossing her arms over her breasts as the dress loosened enough to fall completely off her body if she but slid out of her sleeves. The laces snaked free, and he slowly parted the fabric covering her back. The first touch of his fingers was so light and skimming, she shivered as it gave her goose bumps from the back of her neck to the backs of her thighs.

"Any pain?" he asked huskily, making her aware that there was a pattern to his traces. He could still see the lash marks.

"I honestly wouldn't know if there was," she said, breathless and direct.

He laughed, and both palms slid over her back, the touch firmer, less nurturing and far more sensual. His stroke became a very purposeful dance over her eager, quivering skin. He teased her spine all the way down to its last curve before her bottom, and he brushed very close to the sides of her breasts, though never truly touching her there. It was shockingly effective, making her yearn for his hands to be everywhere, almost to the point of dropping the dress, turning around, and demanding it flat out. But though she had her share of courage, she couldn't bring herself to be so bold.

"Turn to me," he beckoned her with a low, throaty command.

She obeyed, shaking and shivering the entire time with excitement and anticipation and a thousand other emotions. She looked into his eyes and released a noise of exclamation. Gone was the light color she had known, a deep purple that was so intense and erotically full of hunger taking its place. His brow was dotted with perspiration, and tension lines had appeared near the sides of his mouth and eyes. Then his hands were grasping hers and placing them against his chest.

"Touch me, Ravenna. Just a little," he pleaded softly.

She didn't need any further encouragement. She also didn't bother with any patience for the silk tunic. She pulled the snug shirt off him, sighing in appreciation as the garment fell forgotten to the floor.

"Thank you," he chuckled, flattered by her wordless compliment.

Ravenna smiled and reached to touch him. A slow, purposeful spreading of her hands and fingers over his rigid wall of muscle and strength. Those soft curls of hair tickled her fingers, and her smile faded as her eyes became smoky dark with sensual pleasure. She touched him over every inch of exposed skin, front and back, that she could reach, uttering small sounds of contented pleasure that made him a little dizzy when added to the unbelievable bliss of her touch on his body.

Then her mouth touched him, and he groaned at the power of how she could make him feel. Fire burst like impacting laser blasts in a path that was forged by her lips and tongue. His hands had long since locked into her luscious hair, one kneading her scalp convulsively, trying not to crush her precious little skull when the sensations overwhelmed him.

Her mouth took just as much delight as her hands had, with the energy and enthusiasm of a child tasting candy for the first time. When she found enchantment with his nipples, Bronse knew he had to get her in bed fast. He drew her away from her ambitions and stood her straight.

"Lower your arms, Rave," he instructed roughly.

She did and, with a tug on her sleeves, he sent the dress sheeting off her body. She gasped, feeling every inch as naked as she suddenly was. Bronse tried not to smile when that blush burned in just about every blushable place on her entire body. But smiling was a foregone conclusion. She was extraordinary. He caught her hands before she could make any self-conscious concealing gestures, and he spread her arms wide. He took his time looking at her, making sure she knew that he was enjoying everything he saw.

"Bronse . . . ," she said, her breath coming in soft little pants.

And just like that, sanity disappeared.

Bronse grabbed her up good and tight, her feet flying off the floor as he drew her with him. He flung her onto the bed, the sweep of her hair flying, then sprawling out behind her head just as she was laid out on the plush bedding like a naked offering. Then his hands slid onto her skin, starting up her arms, over her shoulders, and, as he knelt over her, a single knee nudging up between her thighs, she felt those huge, callused palms sweeping down to envelop her breasts. The dizzying excitement of his sudden urgency was one thing, but when he added his touch to her like that, she nearly exploded off the mattress with her pleasure. He stayed with her, moving his body over her to ease her back down as he continued to shape and stroke her with those incredible hands. Half the time it was like he held precious treasure, then he would pluck up a nipple and roll it tightly between insistent fingers while his pressure intensified until she was crying out with the extreme stimulation.

When he traded a hand for his mouth, Ravenna felt a hot flood of wet anticipation preparing her body for him. She moaned wildly as he sucked her and licked her as though she were a feast, trading sides so there could be no neglect and so he could gorge himself. His hands were moving over her skin, his palms burning hot and

damp as he slipped them down her belly and hips,
stroking her thighs and calves. He relinquished the
sweet weight of her breast, his lips trailing away until he
was pressing his forehead against her breastbone and
gasping hard for breath.

"Mercy, Ravenna, what you do to me," he ground out.

He had to be overwhelming her, Bronse thought
wildly as he tried to scale back from his red haze of lust
and desire. Heaven help him, he could smell her. Her excitement, musky and warm and pure Ravenna. His heart
pounded relentlessly, and his brain warred between ci-
vility and . . . and whatever beast this was she touched
in him and caused him to give rein to.

No. No. No. Damn it. I am better than this!

"Ravenna, raise your knees, and open for me, sweetheart."

Okay, so he wasn't better than this, he thought with
resignation. He pulled away from her so she could obey
his instructions, and she did so instantly, without reser-
vation, shyness, or hesitation. It nearly gave him a heart
attack.

"Ravenna," he croaked, "you are so fucking beautiful."

In the heat of that moment, Bronse had no other way
of expressing himself, and he looked up quickly to see if
he had offended her. He hadn't. She was smiling shyly,
that sexy blush burning on her skin like wildfire. Bronse
reached out and stroked gentle fingers down the inside
of her thigh. She quivered, and he could hardly breathe.
His fingers skimmed softly and briefly over the feminine
heart of her, through the glistening moisture that was
announcing to him that he was more than welcome. Oh,
how he wanted to be inside her in that moment! His
entire body was raging. His mind as well. It wanted
everything all at once. Taste, touch, and thrust, and he

couldn't accommodate the demands fast enough. He was a reasonably skilled lover, but he wouldn't have known it by listening to his own impulses.

Touch. He could do touch. He needed to do that, to help ease his way and to keep from hurting her. She was a virgin, and he was not a small man in any sense.

Ah, but she was so beautiful, he thought, deep need riding him hard as he slipped his fingertips over her once more, teasing her and making her breath catch in fabulous little anticipatory hitches. He shifted his position, stretching out alongside her, delighting in the way her eager hands groped for him the moment he began to move back within her reach. The slickness of her body let him part the folds of feminine flesh. He bent to kiss her even as she made a low sound of pleasure at his advancing and seeking touch.

"Ravenna," he whispered against her mouth, "you are so wet, sweetheart . . . you feel like heaven."

His heaven. And his eventual haven, he knew. But first . . .

He found her clitoris, and it took barely a stroke of his finger over her sweet, swollen bud for her reaction to bolt visually through her highly responsive body. Ravenna cried out his name, and he bowed his head to her breast as her desperate hands clutched madly at his hair.

The combination of sucking and touching filled Rave with ecstasy, two paths from different quarters that somehow met and melded in the center of her womb. She became mad with desire, her head swimming as tension shimmered beneath her skin. Tears sprang into her eyes as a frustration she didn't understand began to blanket her body.

Then he slid a finger inside of her, slowly and gently. But his gentleness was more sinuous than anything, and she writhed beneath the magic he was working on her.

"Bronse . . . please . . . ," she begged him, dragging him up to look into her pleading eyes. "Please . . ."

Bronse knew what she wanted, felt it in her shifting legs and seeking hips, but she was so tight. Too tight. He kissed her apologetically as he eased a second finger inside of her, stretching her, stimulating her beyond all reason. He knew she was close to coming, and he wanted that more than anything, even if it killed him to watch her take pleasure without him. It would be a miracle if the sight of her alone didn't throw him past his own breaking point—he was that close to the edge. He felt her muscles tensing from head to toe, her pelvis reaching for the press of his hand. Her face flushed with perspiration and fiery blushes. Her eyes were locked to his, wide and shocked. She gasped—husky, chained rasps of breath punctuated by her desperate whispers of his name.

Then she flew.

Her entire being convulsed, physically and spiritually, and she was flung away from herself and off into all those mysterious "other" places, swirling among them like a star in the universe. Bright light burst behind her suddenly clenched eyelids, and she shouted out in a long, rough cry of female pleasure. She fell back onto the bed, not even realizing she'd arched so high off of it, gasping for breath and the smallest point of focus.

It came in the form of watching Bronse slide to the edge of the bed, working his belt free and quickly removing the rest of his clothing. He was climbing up the center of her body moments later, wrenching her mouth beneath his for a wild and brutal kiss.

"I need you," he rasped, tension vibrating through his entire frame as he gingerly lowered his body flush to hers. She felt the rigid length of his sex sliding between the saturated folds of her own, and she shuddered with the sensation as it clashed with the micro-tremors still twitching through her.

Bronse swore on a groan as he was bathed in the honey of her. He was convinced that he had never been so aroused, so hard that it was utter agony. She was relaxed and opened to him; it was the perfect opportunity to transition her to his invasion. He slid to her entrance, edging the head of his engorged penis into her as carefully as he could possibly manage.

He wanted to tell her to stop him if it hurt. He wanted to go slow and easy. He wanted to savor every inch and be savored in return.

"Mercy, Ravenna . . . I can't . . ." he gasped in a strangled voice. "I . . . forgive me, but I can't . . ."

He did not rend into her, but neither did he ease slowly forward. He thrust into her in two elongated strokes. He wanted to curse himself for his lack of control, but that flew from his mind when he hilted deep into her, her heat clutching him like a hot, pulsating vise. If he could die of pleasure, they would be scraping him off the damn ceiling come morning. He was in ecstasies beyond all imagining—until she surged up toward him with a tilt of her hips and an instinctive clutch of her thighs against his hips. Then his imagination was forced to expand.

He made some kind of animalistic sound of satisfaction and managed to withdraw enough to make for a decent return thrust. She answered him, higher in pitch but just as untamed and uncontrolled. He fought himself as long as he could, stroking into her two or three times more before the inevitable crashed over him like a tsunami. His entire body was turned inside out by the force of his pulsing climax, and he heard himself make another savage male sound that echoed loudly into the room as he poured relentlessly into her.

He was lucky that she was a strong, sturdy girl, because all chivalry abandoned him right along with his strength, and he collapsed weak and gasping on top of her. She didn't mind though. She merely wrapped her arms around him and stroked her hands through his hair, waiting with a smile for him to regain his composure.

"If your crew could see you now," she teased him softly.

He laughed in breathless acknowledgment, finally drawing himself onto his elbows, his forearms framing her shoulders as he looked down into her pretty face. "My crew...hmm...we're still technically on-mission. Do you know what I would do to one of my crew who dared to do something like this while on-mission?"

She swiped a deadly finger across her throat.

"Yup." He chuckled. "It is highly against regulations. A soldier could get busted down quite a few ranks for this."

"Obviously you don't practice what you preach."

"No," he said thoughtfully, reaching to toy with a strand of hair beneath her ear, "actually I do. Except, for some reason, it doesn't matter with you. I mean risking my rank. You're worth it. Even if I got caught and was reported, which I highly doubt anyone in my crew would do, I'd probably welcome the demotion. Maybe that will get me out of the sights of—"

He broke off, realizing that he was about to make the blunder that was the main reason why sleeping with a girl while on-mission was such a big mistake. Pillow talk. Satiation loosening the tongue. He didn't want Ravenna worrying about him. He still needed to keep this assassination business close to the vest. He didn't even know if it was safe for her people to come with them, or if they would be safer on the planet rather than a ship with a cosmic bull's-eye on it. But he was afraid he had little choice. The cities on Ebbany were uncivilized and loaded with unsavory types who would eat up naïve people like them. Plus, as he understood it, most of the Chosen Ones wouldn't survive the psychic input of a city-sized population.

"Anyway," he sighed softly, "the point is, if I gave a damn about being caught, I wouldn't be here. Or you wouldn't be here." He shrugged when she laughed. "You get my point."

"I believe I do," she mused, giving her hips a saucy little wriggle that caused him to stir to life inside of her. "Hmm." She released a delicious sigh. "You felt good. You *feel* good," she amended when he smiled and bent to kiss her.

"Good seems like such a mild descriptive," he remarked. "You do nothing for my confidence."

"Good. You don't need any more confidence."

"Tell me, though, are you okay? I . . ." He hesitated, and she felt her heart tighten with warmth. "I didn't mean to go so fast." He released an invective that told her how uncomfortable he was with his behavior, though, in truth, she had seen nothing wrong with it. She had liked how he had made her feel. Physical sensations aside, he'd made her feel like an irresistibly desirable woman, as though she, with her minimum experience, had shown him something new as well. "Did I hurt you?" he asked, shifting his weight as though he would leave her body.

Her hands flew out to grasp him by his hips, keeping him firmly where he was, making him look at her with surprise and a slow smile.

"Don't leave me," she murmured, sliding her hands up the length of his sweat-dampened body until she could draw him back down to her mouth.

"Hmm. One of my uncles' favorite rules," he said before sweeping her up in a deep sensual kiss that instantly kicked up breaths and heartbeats.

"Oh?"

"Yes. Always give a woman what she wants."

"Hmm," she hummed appreciatively, "I like that one."

"You know what? So do I."

CHAPTER
TEN

Masin was just coming off his turn at sentry duty, exhausted after a long day. Ender had just relieved him, and Lasher was looking forward to some rack time, even if he didn't agree with Bronse about taking the opportunity to rest. At least one of the enemies out to get them would be able to deduce exactly where their escaped prisoners might go, and that would lead them straight to the temple doors.

On the other hand, there was very little that the crew could do in the dark with what amounted to a group of kids. And, frankly, all of them were worn out. Oh, the soldiers among them had toughed out worse things than this for longer periods of time, but trying to figure out who was out to kill them next could really wear a body out.

On the way to his room, Lasher passed by Bronse's. He entertained doing a situation evaluation with his boss for all of ten seconds, but the soft feminine cry that eddied past the door quickly brought him up short with surprised and outright disbelief. He'd known the commander for a long time. He'd seen the unusual way he was taken with the high priestess of the temple, and had found that baffling enough on its own, but this . . . this was something totally different. This proved just how much Bronse's head was not in the game.

Masin couldn't help the bemused smile that toyed at his lips. As a soldier, he supposed that Bronse's activities should really disturb him. For one, it was a huge violation of on-mission behavior expectation. Second, this kind of distraction could really affect the commander's motivations when making decisions.

But the fact of the matter was that this was a mission unlike any other. This was a woman unlike any other. Her abilities alone were simply astounding. All of the psionics they had seen displayed by the Chosen Ones were far out of the scope of anyone's experience. It did change the rules a bit. Especially when one of them could see things coming in a way that no soldier ever could.

Then there was Masin's viewpoint as Bronse's friend. He'd never before seen the man show such partiality toward a woman. Even when he'd stumbled onto Liely, Bronse had never been swept up in what he was feeling to the point where he'd forgotten himself. As a soldier this should scare the shit out of Lasher, but as a friend it was refreshing to experience it. And now, by the sound of it, Bronse had taken things with Rave to a whole new level. It was baffling, amusing, and frightening all at once. In the span of a single day, this woman had managed to get under Chapel's skin. On the one hand, Lasher couldn't understand how that was even possible. On the other hand, it was nice to see Bronse acting like a human being for a change.

Lasher was giving himself a headache as he stood there thinking himself into nice concentric circles, so he moved on to the room he'd been assigned. It was a functional and even cozy twelve by twelve space with a roomy bed covered with soft furs to keep out the cold wilderness air. It was ten times as luxurious as what he was used to while on-mission, and it looked like a little slice of heaven. He undressed his vest and his weapons belt, the anticipation of his bed making him more tired.

He had just begun to crawl onto his bed when a rapid, panicked sounding, two-fisted knock banged against his door. He was wide awake and hurrying across the room in an instant, yanking open the door.

He was surprised to find Ophelia there and not Justice or Ender. Then again, neither of them would have bothered to knock. The delicate little blonde was wide-eyed and frantic, fear written starkly over her features. The minute he opened the door to her, she threw herself against him in a clinching hug that squeezed the breath right out of him. Stunned but still alert, he grabbed hold of her arms and demanded, "What is it? What's happened?"

"I can't find Ravenna!" The girl was bordering on hysteria, her eyes brimming with tears. "Not anywhere!"

Masin winced when he recalled why that was and wondered if it was his place to tell a sixteen-year-old girl about her sister's sexual business.

"Why do you need Ravenna? Did something happen?"

"I had such a horrible dream! So terrible! People were sick and dying all around me and they kept clawing at me, grabbing me, demanding I help heal them. But I couldn't. I was so exhausted and there was no way for me to save them all."

A nightmare? Masin exhaled with some relief. As far as he knew, Ophelia was just a healer. There was nothing prophetic about her. And it didn't take a shrink to understand that Ophelia was always afraid of not being able to do enough for those in need. In fact, she had no sense of self-regulation. She would probably burn herself out if given half the chance. And, in a certain light, he could understand the feeling. It was hard not to help when you knew how but your body just didn't have it to follow through. It was something that men in his profession had to face all the time.

"Honey, it was just a dream," he tried to reassure her,

feeling like he was failing when she began sobbing. Still, he didn't want to send her off crying to others, like maybe her hotheaded brother Kith, about how she could not find Rave. Worse would be if she did find her and then proved not to have any discretion. He didn't think she would be that way, but he wasn't willing to risk any altercations between Bronse and the other men in the temple. It was clear how protective they were of one another, and Kith at least would burst a vessel if he caught the two of them together. Luckily for Bronse, the kid had been preoccupied with one of the serving girls earlier and wouldn't likely be looking for Rave.

With protecting his commander on his mind, Masin drew Ophelia into his room and shut the door. He sat her on his bed, taking a moment to wipe away her tears with his fingertips and cradle that frightened elfin face in his hands.

"It's all right," he reassured her. "I won't let anything bad happen to you tonight."

She looked up at him with those incredibly huge eyes of hers, and he felt a knee-jerk response of anger over her vulnerability. Ravenna was the only one he had seen behave protectively of her. The boys in the temple had treated her much more matter-of-factly, as if she were required to do their bidding and fulfill the healing needs of those around her regardless of what it might cost her. On some level, she had to be aware of that. She had to know there was little to no protection for her in this place. What had it been like for her without Rave to shield her? To care for her? No wonder she had sought her sister for comfort on her first night back at the temple.

"Really?" she asked, looking so starkly in need of reassurance. "You have no idea what it's been like here without Rave."

But he could easily imagine.

"What has it been like without Rave?"

"Well," she sniffled, "so many people came to her seeking something, some kind of reassurances about their future or help counseling them about their lives. She can see the past, present, and future, you know."

"No, I didn't know."

"She helps people with their marriages, their family relationships. She helps them understand the difference between the right and wrong of what they are doing. She brings them so much clarity, and they depend on her greatly. I think that's one reason why it was so shocking that they would betray her. They were so shortsighted about it. They didn't realize just how much she did for them. All they wanted was to ensure that the Shiasha would not raid the village. They thought they could placate the warlord by gifting him with Kith and Rave. It might have worked, but it really was terribly shortsighted, don't you think? It would be only a matter of time before the Shiasha would reconsider. Or after tasting the powers of the Chosen Ones, he might then want the rest of us. As it is, there is no way for us to ever live here safely again. If you had not come along, I don't know what we would have done. When I think of what could have become of us . . ." She trailed off and shuddered delicately.

"If Ravenna can see so much, how did she not know about them coming to take her and Kith?" he found himself asking.

"She sensed that something was going to happen, but without reading someone directly for the clearest vision, she really is limited in what she knows. It's a capricious ability sometimes. It's always hard to read one's own future."

"I see."

"And when she was gone, everyone was coming to me and Vivienne, trying to replace their need for her with us. People come to me with all manner of illness, and I know how to fix that. But I cannot heal a broken heart or shattered trust. When they come to me for that, I have to turn them away. I don't know what to do, so I have to turn them away!"

Ophelia was so upset by her perceived failure that she began to cry again. It tore at Lasher to see her beating herself up for things she couldn't control. Wanting to comfort her, he drew her into his arms and hugged her close to his chest. He had a sister close to her age, one who had the luxury of a concerned and caring big brother, whom she often took advantage of in their communiqués. Because he was rarely at home and traveled out of touch so much, he would often come back to base and find a long list of letters from her. She would write to him about everything; he was a distant confidant she could always count on even if he wasn't immediately able to respond.

Ophelia's older brother was far too self-centered a little bastard for her to turn to. Lasher wanted to excuse him just by virtue of his immaturity, but it went deeper than that. Kith was as spoiled as they came.

Masin waited until Ophelia grew quiet. He simply sat there and enjoyed the flowery smell of her hair and the way the young had of being able to hug someone to within an inch of their life. Then, after a while, he pulled back.

"You should get back to bed. We're going to have a long day tomorrow."

"Oh! No! Please don't make me," she begged him. She crawled all the way onto the bed, nearly sitting on the pillow beside him and clinging to the headboard. He tried not to smile when he realized that she intended to force her way into staying, as if her slender little arms could hold on against him if the two of them went in a head-to-head contest of strength. "I'll never be able to sleep anyway. And if I did, I'd just have another terrible dream. I want to stay here with you."

She punctuated the point by pulling up a corner of the cover and drawing it over herself. "I'll go to sleep and I won't be any bother. You won't even know I'm here."

He doubted that. Ophelia was one of those people who, as small as she was, would always have a dynamic presence. She would always leave a mark wherever she went.

"I don't think that's a very good idea," he told her. "Your family would pitch a fit if they caught you in here." Not to mention what Bronse would do.

"They won't care," she said, the bitterness in her voice telling him just how aware she was of the callousness of the men around her. "They never care about me. Only Rave cares about me, and I know she wouldn't mind. She likes you. All of you."

"That isn't the point," Masin hedged, finding it difficult to look into those big, liquid eyes of hers and think clearly about what was the right thing for him to do.

After all, it wasn't as though he was taking advantage of her. Sure, she was sixteen, a beautiful young woman by anyone's standards, but she was much too young to ever interest him. The idea was preposterous. But she damn well reminded him of his sister too much for him to resist her fearful vulnerability for long.

"Look, I'll sit up and keep an eye out. You can sleep. But I'm going to wake you in a few hours so you can go back to your own bed, got it?"

"Oh, yes. I understand. Thank you!" She hugged him around his neck fast and tight, and then snuggled down beneath the covers. Masin leaned back against the headboard and watched her as she drifted off to sleep.

Ravenna stirred. Bronse was very unused to sleeping with someone, so she woke him with her restlessness for the third time. She was sprawled over his body, her cheek pressed to his heart, her arms flung out in opposite directions, and a leg insinuated around one of his. He touched his hand to her back, instinctively trying to soothe her with his touch. It seemed that every time she fell asleep, she began to dream fitfully. It worried him, considering all she had been through lately.

He tucked a hand into her hair, fondling the strands absently as he stared up at the ceiling through the darkness. It had probably been wrong for him to take her to bed in the face of all the trauma and life changes she'd been pushed through recently, but in his heart he couldn't make himself feel guilt or regret or even the smallest flash of conscience. She belonged in his arms.

Bronse held his breath at the possessive thought. He consciously controlled his breathing—since his chest was currently fulfilling the role of her pillow—not wanting her disturbed any more than she already was. He had learned long ago that he had no right to make any demands on a woman, and to be honest he'd never had any trouble with that. His one exception, his marriage, had turned out to be a disaster, and he wasn't willing to go through that again. He'd been devastated on a personal level by that failure. Not because he'd been attached to Liely, though. He'd felt as if he'd failed the code of the exceptional men in his family by ruining their track record of long, fulfilling marriages.

His father had been quick to point out that one failed marriage and the future ability to have a relationship were not exclusive to each other. His mother had agreed. They felt that he had settled with Liely because he hadn't thought he'd do better, and he hadn't expected better. A strange realization, considering his penchant for perfectionism, Bronse thought. But Masin had told Bronse his own theories about that as well. Although the brain, Masin had said, looks for perfection, the heart is what actually finds it. Bronse had used his brain when selecting Liely, using rationale and balancing pros and cons. Love had never entered the equation.

It was odd that Bronse, of all people, should make such a mistake. He'd had something that a great many people never had. Perfect examples of love and its enduring qualities. And friends like Justice and Ender, who had grown up so cruelly in worlds so lacking in love, had shown him how fortunate he was. As hard as Bronse had worked for his calling, he had been given the luxury of being perfectly nurtured and groomed for it. Jus and Rush had struggled every inch of the way, making themselves their only source of support. It was what made them so close to one another. Bronse knew that he and Masin with their experience in love and close family, and Justice and Rush and their family deprivation, all combined to make a new family with a mesh of loyalty that couldn't be broken.

Where would Ravenna fit into such a family?

That was another shock to Bronse's system. These were very personal, intimate thoughts, and his mind told him that it was far too soon to consider these questions.

Ravenna moaned softly in her sleep, her arm twitching until her hand dropped onto his chest next to her nose. It brought his attention back to her. The previous two times this had happened, his comforting had woken her, and they had ended up making love again. Knowing already that he wanted her still, he refused to wake her. He had gone well beyond all chivalrous intentions tonight as it was. She was too new to this intimacy to take his passion so often without repercussions. She was going to be sore come the morning, and that was bad enough on its own. He didn't want to compound her discomfort any more than he already had.

So much for all his proclamations of honor and integrity. He'd behaved like an adolescent, completely lacking in self-control. Even as an adolescent, he had actually shown more discretion. Ravenna simply blew his mind.

She was beyond even *his* experiences, both in and out of bed.

She shifted restlessly against him, making a distressed sound that tore at his heart. Her opposite hand drew in as well, sliding beneath his neck and grasping him lightly in her sleep.

Suddenly she jerked, and he looked quickly at her face. Her eyes moved rapidly behind her lids. She seemed to be dreaming, only something was wrong. It felt different, felt wrong and distressing to him somehow. She jerked harder, crying out in a sound of terror that chilled him. He brought both hands to her shoulders, determined to stop this torture, when she suddenly jolted awake on her own.

Ravenna scrambled to her knees, pushing against him as she swayed in disorientation and her eyes shifted in panic.

"Ravenna! It's okay, sweetheart, it was just a dream," he said quickly, sitting up to draw her into his embrace. But she only let him take her partially close.

"No! No," she cried, her breathing ragged. "It was no dream!"

"A premonition?" Bronse's entire body tensed at the understanding.

"They're coming. They will be here by dawn! I saw them," she gasped. "I saw them! Nomaads armed like soldiers, so many of them! I saw the slaughter of the village! Hundreds of people will die! The temple will be desecrated with our blood! I saw . . ." She was panting and in tears, hardly able to speak. "I saw your death! Everyone will die if . . . if . . ."

"If we're here when they get here," he finished for her, swinging himself out of bed like lightning. "When is dawn, Ravenna?"

"A few hours . . ." She glanced at the clock on the table, then at him. "Four hours exactly."

"Damn! I should have known better than to rest here. I did know better. Rave, I need you to fetch your family and the others. Tell them to pack light and only the essentials. Tell them we'll be running and to keep that in mind. Try not to panic the young ones, but make it clear that they have to be ready to go in twenty minutes and not an instant longer. Do not tell a single servant until the moment we leave. Then tell them to run and get as far away as they can. Go, Ravenna!"

They both flew into their clothes, Ravenna finishing quicker because she did not have to gear up like Bronse did. But he was not far behind. He also had a shorter distance to go to rouse his companions. He reached Lasher's quarters first, not even bothering to knock as he burst in. Masin jerked awake, and Bronse ducked when he fell into a laser pistol's sights.

"Whoa!" he called out. "Masin!"

Lasher recognized him instantly, but he lunged out of bed, knowing something was wrong.

"We're leaving. And I mean yesterday. Get—"

Bronse broke off in absolute shock when he realized that there was someone else in Masin's bed. A woman.

No . . . a girl.

"Wait, it's not what you think." Lasher said hastily as Ophelia stirred and raised her sleepy blond head, beaded braids sliding together with several clicks.

Bronse silently let his eyes shift from the girl to his best friend.

"If it were anyone else, Lieutenant, I'm sure it would be what I think. But a time constraint gives you the benefit of the doubt. Explain later. And don't let anyone catch her in here, Masin, or I swear—"

"Done." The agreement was swift and sharp. "I'll be geared to go in five."

"Less. I'll wake Mulettere and Blakely." Bronse made sure he took one last picture of what he was seeing, so that later when he'd have time to go over it he would be sure to remember the clues that would exonerate his friend of what—on the surface—appeared to be a highly unconscionable act.

Then he went to wake Justice and Ender.

"Jet says the ship is okay and prepped for flight," said Justice. "As soon as we get to a suitable field, it will take me twenty minutes, give or take, to get it here and another ten for the remote landing."

"That doesn't give us much time," Bronse said, rubbing a hand over his tired eyes. "They aren't more than two hours behind us. They'll realize right away that the temple is abandoned." He lowered his voice as he paused between swigs of water. "The fact is that the little ones are slowing us down. Devan is already exhausted, and Ophelia . . ." Bronse glanced at Lasher, who didn't bother to look away from the assessing eyes of his commander. "She's very fragile and was weak to begin with because she didn't get to fully rest up from her healing exertions yesterday."

"I can carry her. Ender can take Devan," Lasher said.

"We'll be just as slow. We need a field," said Bronse.

"Hard to do in a forest this dense," Justice said. "Kith knows a suitable one six to seven miles north."

"Not good enough," said Bronse. "We'll take an unsuitable one if we have to. Ask him again. This time I want you to give him bare minimum requirements. Screw the safety parameters, Jus. I trust you."

"Aye, sir," she said smartly, about-facing and jogging toward Kith.

"Ender, make sure the kids are well hydrated and understand we won't be stopping again."

"Got it, sir."

Ender left Lasher and Bronse alone, the two of them turning to the issue at hand.

"I have to say, Morse, it's a hell of a time for me to be dealing with something like this, so please ease my mind and do it quick."

"Bronse, I would never—"

"I don't give a damn what you would never do. And I'm not your friend right now; I think you know that."

"Sorry, sir," Lasher corrected himself sharply, doing only a partial job of hiding his tension and irritation as he linked his hands behind his back and stood at attention. "Commander, I was in my quarters sleeping when the girl showed up. She was in distress, sir, crying hysterically, and unable to find her brother . . . ," Lasher's mouth twitched slightly, "or her sister," he drawled, daring to give Bronse a direct and pointed look, "in their own beds. I guess we formed a bond during the ordeal earlier, and she trusted me to make her feel safe." Lasher eased out of attention and crossed his arms over his chest. "Look, she was barely able to breathe from a nightmare she'd had, so I watched over her until she fell asleep. I knew she wasn't going to find Rave or Kith until the morning. Unless you would have preferred I disturb you . . . sir?" he asked archly.

Bronse grinned, finally easing his side of the situation. He took a swig of water, not bothering to dignify the question with an answer.

"I put her to bed and sat back, above the covers and as fully clothed as she was, mind you, and I guess I fell asleep because it was dark and I was tired. That tends to happen, I hear."

"Smart-ass," Bronse shot at him. He recalled his mental picture of how he'd found Lasher and Ophelia, and it suited everything his friend was claiming. Adding that to what he understood about the other man, he knew it was the truth. "Still, it wasn't very wise. What if that hothead brother of hers had gone looking for her?"

"Before or after he was done screwing the servant girl?"

"That's not the point," Bronse retorted sharply.

"I'm sorry. You're right. I just . . ." Masin made a sound of frustration. "Have you seen the way they treat her? Not Ravenna, but the others?"

"I thought they were very protective of her," Bronse said with surprise.

"To a point. Because she's a precious commodity. No one, except Ravenna, not even her big brother, pays her the slightest bit of attention unless it's to make her work or protect their investment. Did you see her brother give her any affection? Ravenna is the only one who touches her. None of these people touch. I knew the minute I held Ophelia in the forest after she healed you. She was hugging me like she was starved for affection. I bet that's because no one here has even looked at her as anything but a healer since Rave was kidnapped from the temple. She's a child badly in need of an adult's love. Even Rave can't give her all she clearly craves. Frankly, sir, it pisses me off and I can't seem to help it."

"Having four little sisters will do that to a man," Bronse taunted him gently. "But be more careful, please. It would have been bad enough if Kith had come looking for Rave. But at least she is a consenting adult, and as much as he'd have kicked up a fuss, she would have put him in his place—right before I would have put him in it even harder."

Lasher chuckled. "No doubt. Surely you didn't think . . . ?"

"Of course I didn't, Masin, but that's not my point."

"I know what your point is. And it's right. I made a mistake, and I won't repeat it. Next time I'll search for Ravenna."

"That or comfort her in a highly public place, not in your bed."

"Good point," Lasher said with a grimace as he rubbed at the tension in his temple. "Honestly, I didn't even think about it like that."

"I know you didn't. Be careful, Masin. Not just because of Kith and the others, either. She's already got a crush on you."

"Now you're delusional." His second laughed. "She's a good kid."

"Yeah. The women of the family are quite exceptional," Bronse noted absently, his gaze drifting to Ravenna as she sat with Devan, rubbing the youngest girl's back in comfort. Rave had to be exhausted. She hadn't slept either, really, and that was entirely his fault.

Well, partially my fault, he thought with an irrepressible grin.

"Wow, that is some goofy grin you got going on," Lasher mused.

"Shut up. You're lucky I don't discipline you."

"I won't if you won't," Lasher countered.

"Pervert," Bronse retorted.

"Deflowerer." Lasher laughed.

"Shut up and get them ready to go. You're giving me an ulcer."

"Aye, sir!" Lasher said cheerfully.

Kith was fuming.

It hadn't taken him long to feel the massive waves of connection that had developed between his sister and the commander. The sexual attraction between them had more than tripled overnight, it seemed, and the way they kept looking at each other was sending off huge bursts of erotic emotional energy between them.

It didn't take a rocket scientist to figure it out.

Appalled by his sister's behavior and downright infuriated by the commander's, Kith took out his anger on the easier of the two targets. As they marched through the wilderness in a line, Kith hurried to catch up with Ravenna.

"You slept with him!" he hissed at her in introduction.

Ravenna was startled by the accusation for all of a second, then she flashed angry eyes at him, whispering, "Keep your voice down!" She glanced back at Ender who was following up the rear of the line.

"Why? Are you ashamed?" Kith sneered.

"Hardly that," she snapped. "I just don't want my business announced to the whole world! And that is what it is, you know. *My* business. Not yours!" Ravenna punctuated every word with the cadence of her marching feet as she followed Bronse's back with enthusiasm.

The problem with empaths, she thought, was that they were entirely too nosey and too sensitive. Male empaths were by far the worst, she was sure. Males were horrible when it came to handling their own emotions. Imagine that *and* the emotions of others! Add to it Kith's emotional immaturity and his persistent need to see himself as the man in charge of their family, and it made for a serious ego problem.

And once again it forced Rave into the position of having to set him down a few pegs. Every time Kith flared up like this, acting too big for his own good, he left her no choice. Not only was she the eldest and the head of their sectioned-off little family, she was also the high priestess of the temple. Just because they were abandoning that temple did not mean that sovereignty was going to alter between them.

"I think it *is* my business when it affects all of us here! If he's spending all of his time chasing your skirts, just how good will he be at keeping us alive and getting us the hell out of here?"

She stopped and turned on him, her face aflame with fury. "If Bronse was having the worst day of his life and was plagued with twenty different distractions, he'd still have a better chance of getting us all out of here than you would! I swear to the gods, Kith, if you don't quit this puffed-up attitude, you're going to force me to pop that big head of yours like a balloon! You mistakenly think you're in charge around here when you most certainly are not. I'm in charge of the Chosen Ones. They are my responsibility. Not yours!"

"Don't you know he's using you?" Kith railed back at her. "Men like him pick up girls everywhere they go. You're just another port to park it in, Sis."

That remark compelled Rave to do something she'd never done. She whipped out her hand and slapped him hard across the face. The sound of the strike cracked through the forest like a shot, and the entire line jolted to a halt. Ender, however, had seen the source of the sound, so he cut his fingers over his throat and shook his head at the others.

"How dare you!" Rave spat, not caring that they had drawn everyone's attention, including Bronse's. Kith was nursing a hand to his abused cheek and he recoiled, looking at her with utter shock. For all his empathy, he had not seen that coming. "You who tosses up the skirts of any comely servant girl! After I expressly asked you to be more discreet and caring of your choices! Think you I don't know what occurs in my own temple? You foolish, arrogant boy! Think you there are no repercussions to what you do so casually? So carelessly? You puff and preen and think to make yourself the man among us. No true man would spill his seed left and right with no thought or qualm as to what may become of it. Do you know what it does to those girls when they have to beg Ophelia, a mere child herself, to give them the herbs that will purge your bastards from their wombs? Do you think about what it does to Ophelia—when all she wants in the world is to save and protect life—to be the method by which they must destroy a life?

"No! You never think," she answered for him. "I love you dearly, Kith, but sometimes you disgust me! How I shudder with agony some nights when I see you all, my children, growing to become less than what you are capable of. Domino and his jaded heart are not my burden because it happened before he came to us, but you . . . and now Fallon, who refuses to use his gifts. Ophelia who overuses hers. Poor Devan, who looks up at all of you in confusion, seeking a path to follow, and none of you can satisfy her. Her temper notwithstanding, the only one who gives me no grief is Vivienne. She, thank the gods, is a woman of strength and independence and has a heart made of Delran platinum. If anything happened to me, Kith, she is the one who would step into my place. Certainly not you! So you take a moment, just this once, and *think* before you stand there trying to dress me down!

"You are an empath, but you are the least in touch with true emotion of anyone I know. At least Domino's jading comes from his heart being hurt by the deceptions he sees day in and day out. He is sensitive, despite what he would have the rest of us believe, and that is why his power hardens him. I thought, for a moment when we were in prison, that there was hope for you. I had not seen Kith my brother in so long, and I had missed him sorely. But that moment of agony and torture for me was almost worth it because I felt him again! The child I had once known who is lost to me now! Go! Leave my sight! I have other things to deal with that are much more important than the self-centered acts of a boy!"

By the time Kith stormed off in high temper and low shame, Bronse had come to Rave's side. Without hesitation he enfolded her in his embrace. He hushed and soothed her.

"Easy," he said. "Pay him no mind. He's no more or less a cocky bastard than any boy his age. What is he?

Twenty? It's all hormones and thinking they know everything at that age."

"I know." She turned and began walking again at his urging, both of them keenly aware that they did not have time for internal squabbling. "It's like suddenly having a stranger in your house. I mean, he has always been moody. His empathy is very difficult to manage and very hard on his psyche, but there's no excuse for his callousness. He has had a good life in the temple. Perhaps too good a life. Perhaps some of the hardships of this outside world will temper him. But I do fear that it might make matters worse. This could be an issue for all of us. We have been relatively isolated for all of our lives. To be thrust into heavily civilized worlds may be too harsh for the young ones to handle. Especially Ophelia. She cannot bear even the smallest suffering without wanting to fix it. She would heal the world if she could. But we have no choice, and it's up to me to take them safely through this change." She bit her lip. "And things have been changing for me as well."

"Wow. That makes me feel like shit," he said grimly. "You have so much on your plate and I—"

"No!" she cut him off quickly, grabbing hold of his arm with both her hands and sliding down it until she had his hand in hers. "You've done nothing wrong. You've saved all of our lives and we are grateful for it."

"I haven't saved anything yet. We're still in danger." That said, he hurried her on a little faster. "But I will get you out of here. My problem becomes what to do with you afterward. I can't show up at base with a ship full of civilians. Especially not a military base. If they found out about you and what you could do—"

"What? What would they do?" she asked curiously.

"Find a way to harness you. A way to use you for military purposes."

"And that's a bad thing? But you are military. They have harnessed you."

"Well," he hesitated, not knowing how to best explain it to someone as naïve as she was, "being part of the militia is something a person should be allowed to volunteer for, not be forced to do. The military can be a little too coersive when it comes to certain things."

"You mean abusive? Like the Nomaads?"

"No! Not at all like that. But there are ways to make a person do things without being physically abusive."

"Like using the children against me."

Bronse looked at her with surprise. Maybe he was not giving her enough credit. "The militia is a hard life. You certainly wouldn't want Ophelia exposed to the things we do to keep peace on all three of our planets, not to mention all the space in between. She doesn't seem like the type who could bear that."

"Ophelia has borne more than you realize," she said sagely. "She has had to heal violence on many, many occasions, ever since she was a child. And Kith . . . Kith might do well to have such structure and discipline as you seem to have."

Bronse could see she was thinking, her mind churning over possibilities.

"Let me be clear about something else though," he said softly to her, keeping his voice low enough for her ears only. "The military has its flaws. One in particular is part of the reason there has been so much danger for me and my crew. Someone . . . someone has been trying to kill me. My last two missions have been traps set just for that purpose. We were running from one of those traps when I found you."

"But why?" she demanded to know. "What could you have done to warrant such a thing? Your own people are trying to hurt you? How can you possibly go back there?"

"Because it's not 'people.' It's one person in particular. He's working hard to make it look like a failed mission, which means he doesn't want it to trace back to him. He doesn't want to get caught with my blood on his hands."

"What did you do to anger him so?"

"Nothing that I know of. It's one of many questions I need to answer, and yet another reason why I wouldn't want to bring you onto the base. I wouldn't feel that you were safe until after I see this man brought to justice. And for me to see that done, I need to think clearly and find evidence."

"And I keep you from thinking clearly?" she asked.

Bronse didn't want to lie to her, but neither did he want to upset her. Still, he was truthful. "In a way, yes. You make me do things I never thought I would do. Things that could be costly mistakes. But at the same time, if it weren't for you, we'd all be dead right now. And to tell you the truth, I'd rather have you close by where I can protect you and keep an eye on you. If I drop you off somewhere, I won't be able to control what happens to you. It's a damn untenable position I find myself in."

"I don't know why," she said baldly. "It seems very clear to me what you have to do."

He looked at her and raised a brow. "Oh?"

"You need to bring us with you. You need to tell them who we are and what we can do. That will give you and me the power to keep all of us on the base together where we can keep an eye on one another. I can see to it that the children are well protected even against the pushier tactics the military might want to try. There are things I can do that you don't even know about yet. Trust me, we are very capable of taking care of ourselves." She nodded her head. "Yes. That's what we should do. The Chosen Ones should be brought to the militia. It seems to me you would be rewarded for bringing us to them."

He would be. A great deal, in fact. The intelligence division would go crazy for the things Ravenna alone could do. But he wasn't looking for rewards. And certainly not at her expense.

"I would never forgive myself if we did this and you became unhappy."

"This isn't about you, Bronse," she said, her tone very matter of fact. "This is about me trying to find a place for my brood that will be best for them. Can you think of a place where we would be better protected than on a military installation?"

No. He really couldn't. "But you realize I'm an active soldier," he hedged. "I'm off the station just as much as I'm on. I wouldn't always be there to protect you."

"I don't need you to protect me. I've already told you, we're quite capable of protecting ourselves."

"Is that how you ended up getting whipped by the Banda?" he shot out harshly.

She turned her pretty face to him and gave him the most unusually enigmatic smile. "That happened because I made a choice to wait for you. I knew it would mean the least amount of injury and death to those who were holding me captive. They may have wished harm on me and Kith, but I did not wish the same on them. But believe me, had I wanted to, I could have found the opportunity to free us. I simply was not willing to pay the price it would have cost while knowing that there was an alternative."

"But you did pay a high price. They really hurt you."

"They did. But they are victims of their own ignorance."

Bronse shook his head. "I don't know if you're disgustingly noble or just plain out of your mind."

"Think what you will. Just do not mistake me for a victim."

"I'll be sure not to do that. I have to go catch up to

Justice and take care of a few things. Let me know if you need anything."

She already had everything she needed from him, she thought as she watched him leave her and hustle up to the front of the line they made. Kith's audacity in treating her like she had been a whore to Bronse—a man who had treated her more preciously than any other when Kith himself was infamous for using women and discarding them as easily—had galled her, but she considered the source. Kith hadn't even bothered to search beyond the sexual desire she had felt for Bronse. Had he thought to dig further, he would have found the deeper emotions. He may even have found them in Bronse, too, if he had bothered to look. She was not certain yet, but she suspected that Bronse was coming to care for her deeply and quickly.

It was Bronse's acts of uncanny tenderness and thoughtfulness that told her she was more than a bed partner to him. He watched, sensed, and acted, always considering her best interests. She was confident that she was first in his mind at all times because he proved it with incessant consistency.

She did look on herself with criticism though. She shouldn't have lost her temper with Kith to the point of violence. She was a much better person than that. She simply did not like herself much when she lost control. Violence should always be used with complete control of thought and total lack of raw emotions, she felt. It was a concept that she believed Bronse epitomized. Even when he had been emotionally distraught over her captivity and the violence that had been done to her, he had never used it as an excuse to get out of hand and commit uncontrolled mayhem. He was trained to think with his head and not his heart. It was a quality she found commendable in situations like this.

After Bronse had consulted with Justice, he drifted

back down the line again and walked beside Ravenna. They broke through the brush, and he occasionally took her hand to help her over a rock or a fallen tree, but he kept his attention and his rifle trained before him. Everyone was silent as they moved toward the pasture that they were looking for.

They broke into it all of a sudden. It was not flat—it was rough and littered with fallen trees—but it was just big enough to suit Bronse's needs.

"That's going to be one tight squeeze," Lasher mused as he surveyed the area.

"And a bumpy landing," Ender remarked.

"But both are doable," Justice said confidently, whipping out her remote pilot pad and seating herself on a boulder at the edge of the glade.

"Okay, Lasher, Ender, cut a perimeter around the glade twice. I don't want any surprises today."

"No more dances with Hutha lions?"

"Exactly," Bronse said grimly. "Domino, Kith, take these." He held out two pistols to them. "Do not fire unless you're staring an enemy in the eye. You got me?"

"What, no guns for the girls?" Justice asked with a smirk. But what looked like chauvinism to her was just keen thinking to him. Rave and the females under her care would not resort to violence if it could be avoided, and if someone came up on them, it would no longer be a matter of avoidance. Despite Rave's statements of confidence, he didn't see that she had it in her to do what was necessary. These females had been raised with a different sort of deference than Justice had been.

Bronse saw Kith's surprise that he had been handed a loaded weapon and trusted to use it. Kith *should* look that way. Given a decent choice, Bronse would have done neither. But he needed to reconnoiter behind them and see how close the enemy was, how many there were, and if he could learn their intentions. So, leaving Justice to maintain order until Lasher and Ender returned from scouting out the perimeter, he moved to backtrack their progress.

"Wait." Ravenna made the command softly, but there was power in her grip as she clasped Bronse's biceps and pulled him to a halt. "I know you do not have to answer to me, but I would feel better if you told me where you were going."

He hesitated long enough to give the request serious thought. She was as much a part of this mission as any of them now. But he couldn't escape the urge he had to protect her from the starker truths of their situation.

"Bronse, I have a family at stake here," she reminded him.

"Of course. You're right. I'm sorry. I'm scouting back to see how far behind us our pursuit is."

"Alone?"

"One man traveling fast and silent. Trust me, this is my job. I'll go out only as far as I need to and will be back before the ship lands. I need to reassure myself that they are far enough behind and that we're protected long enough."

"Okay. I understand. I'm sorry to sound as though I'm questioning you."

"It's okay." He smiled, giving her cheek a sweep with a single finger. "Stay with the girls. I'll be right back."

Ravenna reached up suddenly, flinging herself against him as she wrapped her left hand around his neck and laid her right on his heart. She dragged him down for a deep, desperate kiss that she refused to relinquish until she was satisfied. She stepped back at last, wiping her finger over her moist lips and meeting his eyes. She saw him narrowing his thoughtful periwinkle gaze on her, and she flushed.

"We're going to talk about that later," he chided her. He turned and ran into the woodlands.

Feeling at ease, despite his warning, Ravenna returned to the others.

Bronse gritted his teeth at what he saw. The enemy was much closer than comfort would allow. He should have sent Ender to recon, but he was the faster runner. Ender would have strung out some nice tricks for this bunch to run into. And it was a bunch. Fifty strong and far too well armed for mere Nomaads in a backwater world. Ravenna had seen them loud and clear in her sleeping vision. Bronse could also tell that their rambunctious attitude was that of soldiers who had had a recent victory, and a lot of fun pulling it off. Their morale was sky-high.

The village.

He couldn't let himself worry about the villagers. Hopefully the warned servants had been able to get some villagers to safety, but he doubted it would have been very many. There was nothing his crew could have done to help them. They would all be prisoners by now, or worse if they had tried to defend the indefensible.

Bronse slunk out of range of contact and then ran light and silent back to the makeshift landing field.

"Justice, we're out of time!" he shouted as he ran into the glen.

"Two minutes tops, Commander."

"Make it thirty seconds. The minute they hear the ship fly overhead, they'll be after us."

"Coming in now, sir."

They could hear the scream of the ship's engines as she brought it in fast and heavy. Bronse and the men pulled the kids to their feet and corralled them together. Ender and Lasher kept their eyes on the forest where Bronse had come from.

Justice landed the ship in the bracken with a loud and awkward thunk. They didn't wait for Jet to open the bay doors before they went running for it. Bronse hauled Ophelia off her feet, and Lasher grabbed Devan, tossing the girls aboard before the ramp had even touched down. They all raced on board, and Justice threw herself into her seat. The ramp was closing when the whine of laser fire could be heard. Bronse shoved everyone deeper into the ship.

"Now, Justice, now!"

She yanked and banked so hard that the gravity plating couldn't compensate, and they all went flying over the deck, save Bronse, who grabbed onto his seat.

Then they were up and away.

Bronse threw himself into his seat, gripping the armrests tightly and staring hard at the forward screen until they were safely out of the atmosphere. With no sign of any kind of pursuit, he finally exhaled and sat back, taking the time to visually check on the passengers. The lot of them had picked themselves up and were huddled together, clinging to one another the way only family would do. In the center of it all was Ravenna, and all of her attention was fixed on his face as she held her flock close.

"All right, we're safe now," she said softly to them.

It was like casting a spell to animate them. As she touched a hand of comfort to each of them, they began to draw away from her, their confidence in her statement quite the thing to behold. Ravenna had grown up just as sheltered as they had, but she didn't look the least bit frightened of the things she was seeing and doing. Quite the opposite, in fact. She looked strong and secure and very much like a true leader.

Bronse stood up and walked over to her, helping Devan to her feet as he did so. He then stood barely a foot away from Rave and found himself staring into her rich topaz eyes. He suddenly reached out to ring her neck with one hand, and then he pulled her up to the hard fall of his mouth against hers. He kissed her as if he had nothing else to worry about, as if it wasn't highly inappropriate behavior for the commander of the crew, and as if he was not interested in stopping. Finally he broke away for a breath.

"You're right," he said fiercely. "You're safe now."

The promise made in that single statement was clear. She was safe, and as long as he was alive in this universe, she was going to stay that way. He would see to it personally, no matter what.

It was so strange to think he'd known her for barely a day. And yet she'd had such a tremendous impact on him. On everything. He had no idea what the future held for any of them, but he did know that he was not going to let her go.

CHAPTER
ELEVEN

"Justice, stay at the stick," Bronse instructed. "You're not to leave that seat unless something blows you out of it. Ender, find these kids some quarters. It's going to be a while before we get anywhere, and I want them out from underfoot. Lasher, you and I have to start talking about what our reports will say."

Lasher gave him the same grim nod that the others did. He took up a position at Bronse's elbow and watched as Ender herded the Chosen Ones deeper into the ship.

"You know there are only six cabins on this thing," said Lasher.

"It'll be tight, but it'll be enough," said Bronse. "Surely the crew won't mind sharing their quarters."

"Some of us less than others," Masin said with a smirk. Sitting with her back to them, Justice muffled a snort of laughter, but not well enough.

"Can we talk about the mission, please?" Bronse said sternly. He shifted with discomfort in his chair. It wasn't that he minded being the butt of the occasional joke, but he was feeling bad enough that it was over his own questionable behavior. He wished he could somehow excuse it or explain it, but the truth was that he was just as baffled by it as his crew was.

"As I see it, the mission is over," Lasher said. "It's what

will happen when we go in for debriefing that I'm sweating."

"Me too," Bronse said honestly. "I have to confess I'm at a loss here. We clearly know who we can't trust; we know he isn't afraid to be blatant in his attempts to get rid of me; and we know that as soon as we check in and debrief, he has the power to send us right back out, again and again, until we finally come up dead or die later from sheer exhaustion." Bronse rubbed wearily at his eyes. "To compound the problem, I have to figure out what to do about Rave and the others. She's actually talking about letting them be turned over to IM, but until I know that the corruption we've seen begins and ends with JuJuren, I'm really leery about the idea. She doesn't understand . . . anything."

"First of all, you can't get paranoid just because someone's out to get you," Lasher advised, speaking lightly but making it clear how seriously he was actually taking it. "Caution is warranted, but you've made your life in the IM just as I have. This is a good outfit. A strong one. One corrupt bastard is not going to ruin it for me, and the same should go for you."

"I just wish I knew what the hell it is that I know or did to earn JuJuren's sweet attentions. It would help me make some sense out of this, and I really need it to make sense."

"Men like JuJuren don't have to make sense. They just have to be stopped. Why don't you focus on that?"

Bronse tapped his fingers on the armrest of his chair, drumming them steadily as he thought. "I think I have an idea. But I'm going to need a crew briefing before I take any action. We do this like we do everything, as a whole. As a team. I'm not going to stretch our necks any further until we agree on a game plan."

"Fine. We'll brief in twenty minutes. I'll let Jet and

Ender know. As to the problem of our Chosen Ones, let's start with them getting physicals and inoculations, so wherever they end up going, they don't drop dead of the Tarian flu or something like that."

"Good idea." Bronse frowned. "Twenty minutes," he said. "Right here. I don't want Justice out of that chair."

"Feeling antsy?" Lasher queried, his tone flat serious.

"I don't think I'll stop feeling antsy until I get this all set straight."

Ravenna waited until Ender left to go to his meeting with the others, then she called her Chosen Ones around her, bringing the boys and the girls together in one of the cabins they'd been assigned to. There weren't enough bunks for them, even with them split by sex between this and another cabin, but that was the least of her worries for the moment. Right now, she had to make some hard choices, and needed all of the Chosen Ones on the same page that she was on.

"I've been forced to think very quickly about what we should do from here," she began, walking a winding path among them as she spoke. "I know I can see the future, but even I can't predict the long-term outcomes of the choices we are going to be making. So I have to do what I feel is best for us all. But I have never made a unilateral decision for you unless I was absolutely forced to, so I need to talk to you all about this."

"What are you thinking, Rave?" Domino asked, as blunt as he always was. "And don't coddle us."

Ravenna looked at young Devan and Ophelia and wished she could coddle them. They were too young to be making such dramatic choices in their lives. They ought to have been cherished and protected from this until they were ready.

But that was not to be. She had to face it. And so did they.

"As I see this, we have two choices before us." She linked her hands together at the fingers, squeezing tightly to keep them from shaking and showing her nervousness. She had to project confidence to them. It was so important that they come to the right decisions. "We can settle somewhere out there, out there anywhere, and try to live in peace together, try to adapt to no longer being in the temple and no longer having the protections that it afforded . . . when they were still in place. But we face many problems if we do. One, we will have to learn and adapt to an alien way of living. And two, we will run the risk of the exact same thing that just happened to us happening again. If our own people were willing to sell us out to the highest bidders, imagine what total strangers will do to us when they learn how different we are."

"Then we hide our differences," Kith spoke up. "No one has to know anything about us. We just won't tell."

"That will not happen," Ravenna said gravely. "We all know that all it will take is Ophelia seeing one small injury or one very sick person and she will not be able to help herself. No more than I will be able to resist acting on any visions I might have. Besides, it goes against everything I believe in. We have these gifts for a reason. We're not meant to keep them selfishly to ourselves."

"And what's your alternative suggestion?" Kith nearly sneered the remark, his taut body language telling her that he already had an inkling of where she was going to go, and he was preparing to do battle with her over it.

"We choose a champion."

"I knew it. You mean Chapel." Kith spat the name like an invective.

"No. I mean a body of people who are powerful as a whole with a trustworthy track record who will hire us to work for them and, in trade, they will protect us. Preferably we will work for a greater good. It will be up to us to locate such a group. Frankly, we know nothing of the worlds out here or how to go about finding any-one of note or of trust. We need to learn. We need a stepping-stone. A place to exist while we learn the things we need to learn."

"I'll bet she has a suggestion," Kith said darkly.

"I do," she countered, not at all swayed by his behav-ior. "The Interplanetary Militia. The people Bronse works for. They are the peacekeepers in this galaxy. They strive to make these worlds peaceful places. Even as sheltered as we were, we have heard of them. They are well mean-ing if nothing else. But the truth is, this will be a blind al-ley. All we have to base our choice on is the example we have seen set by Bronse and his crew. Now I don't know about you, but they have proven to me that they are honorable and well minded and strive to make morally right choices."

"Is that what Bronse was proving to you last night?" Kith's derisive tone was cutting. "You can't listen to her," her brother said to the others. "She's been com-pletely taken in by him. Listen, Sis, you're new at the whole sex thing, so let me clue you in. He's a soldier and you're just the flavor of the minute."

Ravenna had to control her urge to slap him again, no matter how much her palm itched to do it. Acting wildly would do nothing but prove him right, and prove that her normally staid judgment was impaired by Bronse somehow. She refused to give him the satisfaction.

"Just because that is how you treat women does not make it so for everyone else," she said as calmly and qui-etly as she could, her entire body tight with her emo-tions. "And my private relationship with Bronse is a separate matter from this. I am merely trying to find us the best possible home, if only for the moment. If we get to the militia and we show them who and what we are, they will covet us. Prize us even. They will want to use us as tools to achieving their peaceful goals, and we will make them compensate us with things we need, like food, shelter, and safety."

"And if they turn on us?" This time it was Domino who spoke. "What if they decide to force us to do whatever they want, whether we want to or not?"

"If they prove themselves dishonorable, we will leave. And I think you know that we are more than capable of doing so." She reached out to touch Vivienne's cheek lovingly. "Right?"

"Yes. We can do anything," Vivienne said. She bit her lip. "And this time you'd let me? You'd let me help us this time?"

The last time, Ravenna had called Vivienne off. She had known that if Vivi showed her power, it could come back to haunt them. Rave had feared that they'd all be taken, instead of just her and Kith. But should push come to shove, she and Vivi could do a great deal of damage together.

"I would. What's more, I will suggest that we keep my other power to ourselves until such time as we all agree we can trust the militia. Vivi, you can show yours, but downplay just how strong you are. We should all take care to measure what we show at first. I won't have us losing control again. And I won't let us be separated. Temple or no, I am the leader of the Chosen Ones. I am your priestess. But I am also your sister and your friend, and I believe that this is the best thing we can do."

"You know," Kith laughed without humor, "I think you want to join the IM just so you can keep close to your new man. If you think you guys are going to actually make something of this thing going on between you, then you're out of your mind, Rave."

"Kith," she said, forcing his name through her teeth, "you are an empath and yet you have no clue to my emotions. If you would stop balking like a spoiled child for one second and open your power to me, you would see that my motivations are to keep this family safe, fed, and well balanced."

"He doesn't need to see," Fallon spoke up, stepping forward. "I can read your every thought, Rave, and I can assure everyone here that you have no ulterior motives. She never does," he added. "And if you accuse her of it one more time, Kith, I'm going to knock your teeth down your throat."

"Thank you, Fallon," Rave said pointedly, appreciating him coming to her defense but not wanting to provoke any violence on behalf of her temperamental brother. "So I need to know what you all are thinking. Ask me anything. I will listen to all opinions, good or bad. Even yours," she said to Kith, "if they're not motivated by your own selfish jealousies."

"You already have my answer," he shot back angrily. "I'd rather we take our chances on our own."

"I think Rave is right," Vivienne said. "We need protection. As strong as we are, we have our weaknesses, and they could be exploited again. We could find ourselves doing nothing more than running away for the rest of our lives."

"I'm with you, Rave," Fallon said. "We have to trust someone while we get our feet wet. The IM is as good as any. Better because it isn't as much of an unknown."

"I think I speak for everyone," Domino said carefully, "even Kith, when I say that you are our leader and always will be. You have taken care of us every moment since we were first brought to the temple, and you have yet to make a bad decision."

"Except when it came to letting them take you prisoner," Vivi said. "I know you think it would have been wrong to hurt the villagers, but it was wrong for them to separate you from us. Whatever we do, now and in the future, we do it together. This won't work otherwise."

With that, they all turned expectant looks to the dissenter among them. Ravenna had to give Kith credit for one thing: he knew when he was outnumbered and he knew that no manner of game he tried to play would work to make them doubt Rave's choices. In truth, he knew that she had never once made a selfish decision in all of her life. Everything she had ever done had been for them all. Including taking a beating that she hadn't deserved and could easily have avoided.

"Do what you want," he said at last. "But don't expect me to be happy about it."

That said, he marched out of the room.

Several minutes later, Jet and Ender were on the bridge of the ship, allowing Justice to turn in her chair and join in. Bronse could no longer sit still, so he was pacing the deck before them.

"I have a few ideas, but I need to run them past you guys first. I know I've asked a lot of you all this trip, that I've done things I wasn't supposed to, acted out of the norm, made choices that weren't by the book. Until now, I've swept you all along with me. I don't want to do that anymore."

"Damn. And it was such a fun ride," Ender joked.

"I mean it. I should have been more up-front with you all. I can't change the past, but I can start being more forthright. Justice, can you make it so that we come in during the middle of night cycle on the station?"

"Sure." She did a quick calculation in her head. "All I have to do is slow us down a little. Why the night cycle?"

"Fewer witnesses for one. For another, it helps me put the debriefing on a different footing. I'm thinking of calling in a favor. I'm going to call my old commander, Chaser Abingdon. He's an admiral now, in the justice department. It's time we clued IM Justice in on JuJuren's activities. If we come in at night, JuJuren will be asleep. We can arrange a debrief without him and with Abingdon

present. As I see it, it's the only way we can keep ourselves on that station and not chasing after JuJuren's
next death trap."

"And the downside to this is . . . ?" Justice asked leadingly.

"It could blow up in our faces. Or we could end up
docked for a good long time while IM Justice court-
martials JuJuren. You know how IMJ hates to lose its
prime witnesses."

"Ugh. I hate being mollycoddled," Lasher groaned.

"So do I," Bronse said. "But it's important to expose
the admiral for the backstabbing bastard he is. Our mission reports are the only thing we have so far to prove it."

"Hopefully Trick has found more while he's been on
bed rest," Lasher said.

"We can't count on 'hopefully.' I have to act on what
I have at hand. And that leads me to the next point."
Bronse cleared his throat. "We're not hiding anything
from our reports. Nothing. Am I clear? That includes
whatever you have to say about . . . about my behavior
as far as Ravenna is concerned."

Justice snorted. "Look, Boss, as far as we're concerned,
you've been a perfect gentleman. Besides, it would all be
conjecture anyway. The only thing I've seen is a kiss or
two. I don't see how that fits into our report."

"It fits if it affected my decision making," Bronse
pointed out quietly. "Staying at the temple last night was
a bad choice. Any admiral worth his salt will see that.
He'll wonder why. Hell, I wonder why."

Lasher was dismissive. "It's not the first bad choice
you've made. At least this was for a good reason. But
how are you proposing to introduce the subject of Rave
and the others?"

"I think Ravenna has plans to introduce herself. She
wants to protect her family, and she's willing to let the
IM do it in trade for what the Chosen Ones can do for

the IM. But I'm not comfortable with JuJuren ever finding out about what they can do. I don't even think she should approach IM until he's been excised."

"But there's the time factor," Jet mused knowingly. "They're on board here and now, and they got here during a mission that you're about to be debriefed on."

"Exactly. So I don't see how I have much choice in the matter," said Bronse. "None of us seems to have a real choice here. Not until we take care of this problem with JuJuren."

"So make the call. After these past few days, I'll enjoy the downtime," Ender said.

Bronse appreciated the gesture for what it was. If there was one thing that Ender despised, it was downtime.

"Okay, so I make the call." Bronse looked at them all. "One other thing. We need to share bunks. Justice, you can double up with Vivienne. Ender, you can have Fallon. Ophelia and Devan get one of the spare rooms, and Kith and Domino get the other."

"And Ravenna?" Lasher asked with a troublemaking sparkle in his eyes. "Is she sharing with you?"

Bronse didn't dignify the question with a response.

He didn't even know the answer.

It was nearly ten hours later before Bronse got up the nerve to leave the bridge. Damn it all, he'd faced down some of the scariest shit that the three worlds had to offer, but one woman had somehow managed to tie him into knots to the point where he was afraid to run into her. He didn't know what to make of her. She was a peaceful, nonviolent person, but she was willing to embed herself in the military? Just like a lot of things about Ravenna, it just didn't make any sense. It was as confusing as her naïve fearlessness and as baffling as her effect on him.

Bronse stepped into his rooms but stopped immediately

short after the threshold. The lights were on and there, sitting in the middle of his bed in a rather peaceful, cross-legged position, was Ravenna. She looked like she was waiting for him, as if they had prearranged to meet there.

"How did you get in here?" he asked as the doors slid automatically shut at his back. "It has a secure lock."

"Let's call that my little secret," she said with a winsome smile that just about sucked the breath right out of him.

No, damn it, no! He had to keep his head on straight these next few hours! He couldn't afford to be so easily distracted by her smiles and the exotic warmth of her scent as it filled his quarters.

"Ravenna, I have work to do," he said dismissively, walking over to his workstation and sitting down as if he was going to start right then. But the truth was, he'd already written all of his reports. In fact, he'd been pretty impressed at how easy it was to avoid any mention of having been intimate with a civilian while on-mission. Too easy.

Too tempting, he thought as she unfolded her long legs from beneath her and pushed off the bed. She walked over to him in distinctly placed steps. If he didn't know any better, he'd say she was being coy. There was an almost blatant flirtation in the way she moved, oh so slowly, toward him.

"I thought you were working all this time on the bridge. What will you do here that you could not do there?"

Never lie to a Chosen One, Bronse advised himself. They were too hard to trick.

"That's not your business," he said sharply, suddenly surging to his feet because he simply could not be sitting down while she sidled up to him. It made him feel completely off his mark. Almost subordinate. Like she was the one with all the power.

But she didn't have power and neither did he. Didn't she see that? Didn't she appreciate how much danger the worlds had to offer?

"Very well." She paused for only a beat. "I spoke with the Chosen Ones. We have all agreed that, for now, we will offer our services to the Interplanetary Militia. This solves both the problem of what to do with us and how to explain our presence on this ship. You found an excellent resource for the IM to use and brought it to them."

It sounded so perfunctory, so coldly matter of fact. So simple when it was anything but.

"It also allows you and me to remain close so you can satisfy your desire to protect me," she added.

That wasn't the only desire he wanted to satisfy, damn it, and he'd bet big money that she knew it. Well, he had to shake that notion out of her head straight off.

"See, that just proves how naïve you really are," he said in hard bursts. "I won't be around. I'm never around. I'm either on-mission or I'm training my troops for being on-mission or I'm being briefed on my next mission. I'm never, ever around. If you think we're going to play house together and have romantic dinners every night, you're sorely mistaken."

Bronse reached out to grab her by her shoulders and shake her when she gave him a serene smile. Wasn't she listening to him? Didn't she understand? He was an ETF First Active soldier. The best of the best when it came to soldiering and the worst of the worst when it came to relationships.

"I don't recall ever asking for romantic dinners," she mused blithely.

Bronse snapped. Maybe it was anger, maybe it was frustration, but whatever it was it was powerful and unstoppable. He spun her around hard and shoved her across the room toward the door.

"Do yourself a favor and get out!" he barked at her.

"I'm not leaving."

"Why the hell not?"

"Well, you just said you're never around."

Bronse tried not to growl out in frustration. "You're not making any sense!"

"No. I make perfect sense. If you are never around, that means I should take advantage of every moment that you *are* around. But I think my being here is making you very uncomfortable, and I am curious as to why that is."

"Maybe it's because you're in my fucking bedroom when my crew is marching watch in the corridor only a few sheets of metal away! I've compromised the integrity of this ship and this crew enough for one mission, Ravenna. I'm not going to compound the issue!"

He grabbed hold of her arm and tried to march her toward the door, but she ducked and slipped right out of his hand, moving back toward his bed. Bronse had to stop her. He didn't think he could stand the sight of her in his bed again. It would play tawdry tricks with his imagination—more so than the scent of her perfume was already doing. That intoxicating Ayalya spice was just about killing him. Just breathing it in was making him hard. He had to get her out of his room. He refused to force his crew to "pretend" to not see or know any of this. He'd disgraced them enough. He needed to take back control. He needed to prove to himself that he could.

"I want you to leave. Can I make it any clearer? Are you going to make me use force?"

"Hmm." She hummed that as if contemplating the possibilities, and abruptly he was contemplating them too.

Then suddenly he wasn't just contemplating. He all but pounced on her, grabbing her by both arms and slamming her up hard against his chest and body. So hard that the air left her lungs in a sudden gust.

"You're doing this on purpose," he gritted out between his teeth, trying not to notice how her body heat seemed to burn so much fiercer than his own. She was so hot in so many ways.

"I never made a secret of that," she said. "Do you want to know what I see?"

As she asked the question, she reached to place one hand over his heart and the other around his neck. He squeezed her hard between his hands.

"Is it the same thing you saw when you read me before I went back to find out where the Nomaads were?" he asked. "Don't you see? You're afraid of me. Afraid of what I do. You can't read my fortune every time I go off on a mission just to see if it will turn out okay!"

"Why not?" she asked simply. "I have a power and I'm going to use it. If it benefits you, I see no wrong in it."

"It's the fear that I see is wrong," he said with intensity. "You're afraid of what I do. By the Being, could you see yourself if this ever really went anywhere? You'd be a basket case, afraid of what I might be doing or how I might be trying to get myself killed!"

"Think that if you must. If it gives you comfort. But you don't look comforted, Bronse," she said softly. "You look like you're the one who's scared."

Bronse's brain hazed over with emotion, more than he could identify right then all at once.

"You have no idea what you're getting into," he hissed softly. He lurched forward, just a single hard step, and she hit the side of his bed and fell down onto it.

No. He actually threw her onto it, he confessed to himself as he flipped her hard onto her belly and followed her down with a fierce caging of his body over hers. He pressed down over her, his whole body screaming with the relief of feeling her beneath him again. There was a way, he realized, of making his point to her *and* satisfying this unholy craving he had for her. As he yanked her onto her knees and against his chest, he groaned with uncontrolled pleasure when her bottom rose up against the fly of his uniform pants. He rubbed up hard against her, trying to relieve the pressure of his swiftly growing erection and serving only to make it worse. His hands were nothing less than harsh on her as they swept to embrace both her breasts through the fabric of the shirt she was wearing.

That was when he realized that it was his shirt. She wore only his shirt. Like some kind of brand he'd stamped there himself, his mind swam with a possessive fury that rushed through him. She looked incredible like this. So curvaceous and feminine in an article of clothing meant for war in the desert. The blackness of it was stark against her soft skin, making it seem paler than it was. Making her seem somehow more vulnerable and more womanly all at once. No wonder the sight of her had been driving him crazy ever since he'd walked in the door.

Normally he'd have been more considerate, more patient. He'd have preferred to shower to wash away the long hike they'd taken to get to the ship. But he didn't care about niceties. In fact, lack of gentility was his very goal. She needed to learn more about him than just the gentleman she had seen last night. She needed to know just what she was getting herself into.

He shoved the hem of the shirt up over the round curve of her backside, baring her creamy smooth skin and that delightfully naughty curve of flesh that he was stroking in stronger and stronger passes of his hand. He wanted her to feel the rough calluses of a soldier's hands, to feel how uncivilized and coarse he could be even in the smallest details.

The problem was the way she pressed back against

him, teasing his cock with the curve of her butt and taunting his sense of smell with the sudden wash of aroused female scent that drifted up between them. Unable to help himself against even the slightest impulse, he stroked her down between the split of her cheeks and straight into the hot and ready wetness waiting for him. His fingers were working inside of her an instant after that, testing her heat and tightness for what would come next.

Then he was ripping at the front of his trousers with growling impatience, freeing himself in just a few temperamental tugs until his swollen cock was lying hot against her. Without any preamble or anything even remotely resembling foreplay or gentlemanly behavior, he thrust himself into her, shoving into the dark liquid fist of her body and sinking deep and true to the hilt.

She gasped in a staggered breath, but at the same time she pushed back against him to make certain that she had him as deeply as she could. Bronse rose up to balance on his knees, digging them into the mattress even as he dug a bruising grip into her hips. With a surge of power he undulated into a deep, body-crashing thrust that sent an impact completely through her body. The next thrust was harder still, the sound he made raw and savage. But as rough as he was, as brutish as was his technique, she reached back to grab him by his shirt, fisting her fingers in deeply, holding him to her and telling him she wanted exactly what he was giving her.

But all he had for her was savagery, one blind and banging thrust after another until he finally heard her moan in an attractive breath of pleasure. He had meant to give her nothing, meant only to take, but that changed as he vented his frustration in passionate thrusts. Now he chased her. Chased her satisfaction down, fucked her to the very edge until she was forced to press her face down into the mattress and muffle the shouts ejecting from her body. He felt the very instant she broke into orgasm, felt it because he'd never known anything so tight and wrenching to his soul. Then he was just blindly thrusting, taking her up off her knees with every impact until his chest was on fire for oxygen and his gut was clenched forever in anticipation. He finished with a ripping roar, the ejaculation streaking out of him in vicious pulses that were pain and pleasure combined. Only the clench of his teeth kept him from shouting down the ship, and only the sudden brace of his hand kept him from falling down over her and crushing her flat beneath him.

Bronse kneeled there, propped over her, for several long minutes as he sucked hard for breath and tried to focus. He'd never felt anything so incredible in all his life, and had never done anything so damning. His behavior had been appalling, had gone against everything he'd ever trained himself to be when it came to women. The worst part was that he couldn't see what she had done to deserve it. What had seemed to have logic in the heat of the moment was now lost on him. It was one of the most horrific moments of realization he'd ever had.

Drawing himself from her, he fell back onto the bed, his hands scrubbing up to cover his face as waves of shameful guilt rode over him. Why had he done this? Why had he been such a bastard to her?

"Bronse."

She said his name, still breathless with her exertions, and then slid herself over him. She straddled his body, her hot, wet core slipping over his relaxed penis and lower belly. He looked at her, the sight of her astride him so painfully wonderful that he could hardly stand it. She was driving him insane. He'd utterly lost his mind. And yet she had the sweetest little smile playing at her lips as if he weren't the worst kind of jerk on the planet.

"Bronse, you don't have to be afraid of me," she said

softly to him, bending forward to give his lips a kiss too warm and affectionate for him to have deserved. "You don't have to be afraid I'm going to ask for too much. Take too much. Be too much of a liability. That isn't what I want."

"It's too late for that," he said hoarsely. "You're already a liability. I haven't made a single right step since the moment I first laid eyes on you."

"That's not true," she soothed him softly, kissing him again until he was compelled to kiss her back. He started it off with confusion and compulsion, but by the time his tongue swept in to touch hers, he was starting to settle, starting to concede to the inevitability he saw before him. "You are doing much better than you think you are. But tell me," she coaxed him, "why you are so afraid of me."

Not of her, he realized, but of himself when he was with her. He was overwhelmed by how quickly she was getting under his skin. When he looked up into her beautiful face, he started to see cravings in himself that had no place in his life. He had already proved to himself that he wouldn't be able to have what his father and his uncles had had. His career choice had made it impossible. And he was afraid she would get too attached to him too quickly and would be hurt badly when he inevitably failed to satisfy her needs.

"Why," she breathed softly against his mouth before kissing him, "are you assuming that what you feel for me is wrong?"

Put like that, Bronse felt his heart hiccup in his chest. What he felt for her? How could he feel anything for her? He hardly knew her! And she hardly knew him. Wasn't that what he was trying to prove just now as he had taken her so roughly and crudely?

And yet she had accepted it. Every minute of it. Hell, she'd even taken her pleasure in it. She'd kept pace with him every single step of the way. How could someone so new to these sorts of things take to them so easily and with so little confusion? How was it that she always seemed to be thinking so clearly when he was a jumble of disorganized thoughts and feelings? He was supposed to have the coolest head in the business.

At least, that was true when it came to his work.

This was something else entirely.

But he kept confusing the issues because at the moment the issues were lying on top of one another just as surely as she was lying on top of him. Of course, they weren't reaching to strip off her shirt the way she was right then.

And just like that he was distracted from the turmoil of his thoughts by the creamy perfection of her skin and the startling dark points of her gorgeous nipples in full thrust and in full reach of his hands. Like metal to magnet, he stroked bold hands over her breasts, catching the nipples between his knuckles and tugging on them again and again as he kneaded her in leisurely pulls of his fingers and palms. She fit him so well like this, filling even his very big hands. As with everything else, it was as though she'd been made to match him perfectly.

"I don't think it's wrong," he said at last, speaking the words aloud and realizing that he believed them. She was anything but wrong for him. "It's just that I know how hard it is to be part of my life. I'm not sure someone who is so strongly centered in home and family could ever find happiness waiting for me to show up." Leaving her breasts, he stroked down over her ribs. "Ravenna, you need a strong partner. Someone who can help you raise those kids and keep Kith and the others in line. That means someone who will be there for you."

"And you think you are not strong? That you could not help to raise these kids? That you could not keep Kith in line?"

That wasn't true, he realized as she reached to push his shirt up his body. Distracted by his thoughts, he had lifted up for her without even thinking about it and helped her free it. Now she was at liberty to slide her hands up and down his bare chest and was able to scrape teasing nails over the flat disks of his nipples. The sensation shimmered right through him, both clouding and clearing his mind as he talked with her.

"I could do all of those things," he conceded, but then added his caveat, "if I were around. But—"

"You're never around," she supplied for him helpfully. "I see. But did it never occur to you that I have done just fine ruling my roost all on my own, long before you came into the picture? I'm used to fending for myself. I'm used to defending my Chosen Ones. You continually mistake me for having need of you in a way that is heavily dependent. I had need of you in this particular situation, yes, but this was once in many years. Don't you think having you available to me only once in many days would not be anything but an improvement?"

It was far too logical and making far too much sense for him to be staggered by the spell of her touch. Bronse reached out and caught her hands, stilling them against himself.

"You say this now," he said warily, "but how do I know that it will not change once you've gotten a real dose of what it's like to be involved with me?"

"You *don't* know. No more than I do. But I can tell you a very certain way of finding out." Her smile was teasing and went straight to her eyes. "If you want empirical evidence, Bronse Chapel, you must carry out the experiment."

Bronse caught his breath at the very idea of what she was suggesting. She was saying that she wanted to try out a relationship between them. Like dating. Like normal people. The idea made him nervous, but he quickly realized that it wasn't because he was afraid of the experimentation; it was because he was afraid he would fail at it. Fail miserably. Just like he had once before.

But Liely had been a very different kind of woman. One who had been less than honest with him about her expectations. How could he be certain that Ravenna was telling him the truth? Once again, the answer was as she had said. The only way to know would be to throw himself into the situation and find out the hard way. What he couldn't believe was how strongly his psyche balked at the idea. Perhaps, he thought, he had been more damaged by his ex wife than he had given himself credit for.

The idea left a sour taste in his mouth. Would he really pass up a woman as incredible and unique as Ravenna just because of his failure with one messed-up female?

The answer was no. And just as soon as he realized that, he also realized that Ravenna had already understood this. She'd understood everything. His confusion, his fear, even what had bordered on barbaric behavior.

"Rave," he whispered softly, reaching to cup her whole head in his hands as regret filled his eyes. "I didn't mean to be so crude with you."

She had the temerity to shrug a single shoulder, as if it meant nothing at all to her. "I rather liked it, to be honest." And Bronse could tell by the excited lilt in her voice and the shiver that shimmied down her spine that there was no way she was lying to him. She really had liked seeing that coarser and ungentle side of him. "I like every single aspect of you I discover, each in their turn"—she suddenly scooted back onto his thighs, exposing him to the cold refined air in the cabin as she pulled his pants down over his hips—"each one slowly coming to light as I uncover them."

Ravenna slowly bent forward to kiss his half attentive cock, then she slid back up into position over him, enjoying the hardening of the shaft as she wriggled herself down into place.

Bronse sat up suddenly, sending her sinking deep into his lap, the position spreading her legs wide open. He reached to rapidly unlace his boots, then shucked off his pants and socks. Suddenly he wanted more than anything to simply be there, naked with her. He drew her in tight to his chest and ran his hands up her long, lean back, bending his nose to her sweet, clean skin and the enchantingly spicy scent of her.

"I'm an idiot," he confessed to her. "I'm not normally so dense or so boorish, but I think this situation strikes closer to me than anything else ever has." He reached to kiss her mouth in a lingering clinging of lips. "I think I might be afraid to fail you because I don't *want* to fail you. And I'm not certain I know how to avoid it."

"Perhaps you should stop thinking so hard about it and start seeking more practical experiences to prove to yourself that you might succeed, that you will not fail."

Bronse smiled beneath her lips as she nibbled kisses across his mouth.

"Perhaps I should," he agreed with her, suddenly feeling the lightest he had felt in hours. He turned her and rolled her beneath him, settling himself comfortably up the center of her body and between her thighs. Feeling suddenly ravenous for the temptations of her bare skin, he began to kiss and lick a path of exploration down her throat, along her breastbone and breasts, and over the taut line of her tummy. He swirled his tongue over her as he went lower and lower. But just as he reached the damp curls protecting her sex, she seemed to balk. She reached to grab hold of him by both ears and pulled against his effort to touch his mouth to her most private places. He looked up in curiosity.

"What are you doing?" she wanted to know.

"I'm kissing you. Everywhere." The way the quantification rumbled out of him was nothing short of sinful. But she was suddenly covered nearly head to toe in a body blush.

"Why would you want to do that?" she asked him as if he was out of his mind. "No. Please don't. Let's just make love."

"That's what I'm trying to do," he countered. "I'm trying to give you such a healthy dose of pleasure that you'll try to fly right out of my arms." His smile was wicked and hot. "Now, let go of me."

"No. This isn't how it works," she insisted breathlessly.

"Oh, it will work. Trust me."

He pulled out of her staying grasp and lowered his head between her thighs. He could see the fine anticipatory tremors running through them, as well as the resistant tension. Her naïveté was showing itself again, and it made him chuckle softly to himself. With the lightest touch of his fingers, he spread her open, taking in the sight of her and breathing in the raw, uncensored smell of their earlier frantic sex. She smelled of excitement and of him, as if she were now deeply marked as his very own. Now he wanted to leave yet another mark, an indelible memory on her that she wouldn't soon forget. What's more, he wanted to know what their combined flavors would taste like on his working tongue.

He started by kissing her firmly at the far upper cleft of her pussy, his tongue flicking down only briefly to flirt against her untried clit. He absorbed her shocked gasp greedily, but ignored the unsure clutch of her fingers fisting into his hair. He knew she was in for a very big surprise, and he was of a mind to bring it to her with teasing slowness. Very carefully he began to kiss and lick at the richly damp folds before him, and his fingers painted her in teasing touches, but both they and his mouth stayed very clear of her fattening clit. He could tell by her breathing that she had gone from cautious and uncertain to curious and then craving. She relaxed back with a purring little moan, lifting her pelvis from the bed and seeking his mouth blindly. She might not know exactly what it was she was looking for, but she was beginning to want it very badly.

"Bronse," she begged him softly as her nails scraped over his scalp.

But Bronse was already more than busy enough drawing her against his palate again and again with ever-broadening strokes of his tongue. He even tried to thrust his tongue inside of her, but she was too tightly tensed for it. Another time, he thought, as he drew a long, slow line up her pussy with his tongue until it led him straight to her clitoris. As he washed up flatly against her sensitive nerves, Ravenna cried out in a combination of shock, surprise, and need. But that was nothing compared to what she was going to feel very soon, he thought, when he began swirling his tongue against her in long, slow-turning strokes.

Ravenna gasped with every stroke, the pitch of it climbing just as her swaying pelvis tried to climb closer and deeper into his mouth. He wasn't very gentle as he introduced the shocking thrust of two fingers deep into her hot center. Out of her mind with climbing pleasure, Ravenna felt herself detonate under his skilled manipulations. The orgasm was tremendous, blacking out her vision entirely as her head and neck arched back into the crest of it. She had never felt anything so shocking and so glorious all at once. She fell from the crest with a crash, sucking for breath, trying to get away from the overwhelming continuation of his attentions. But he held her down to the bed tightly and began all over again, determined to start anew and not taking no for an answer. He wasn't going to trade away hearing her abandoned groans of pleasure or the erotic undulations of a body going wild for the things he was doing to her. The second crest she hit was of a keener pitch, almost more painful and infinitely more pleasurable because of it. She had never dreamed of such things. She had thought herself learned in the ways of sex, even though until now she had never taken part in them, but this was something she hadn't ever been able to conceive of on her own, and none of her experiences had led to the explanation of the act.

Bronse was surging up over the center of her body, and it was clear by the passionate violet of his eyes that he was nowhere near done with her. His mouth was wet with his sinful work. Suddenly and boldly she wanted to kiss him, so she grabbed hold of him and did so. Taking the alien taste of her own pleasure onto her tongue, at first she thought it so very strange. She tried to seek the appeal for him in this salty, musky flavor, and as he deepened his kiss and the play of his tongue against hers, she realized the erotic power of it. She instantly wondered what he tasted like. Her teasing kiss of earlier had allowed her only a sample of the rich musk of his scent, but not of anything resembling this exotic tang she was savoring.

She broke from his kiss and breathed, "I want to taste you too. Do you taste like this?"

"I'm not nearly as delicious as you are, but that's from my perspective. You might feel very differently." The idea of her mouth on him, exploring him as thoroughly as he had her, made his already heavy cock ache with fresh interest. He rolled aside, lying on his back and trying for all he was worth to adopt a note of control and calm. Waiting for her to approach him was sheer torture, and it pulsed through him over and over again as she reached out with tentative fingertips. The pads of her first two fingers slowly rode his length from tip to base, her breath buffeting against him over and over as her excitement climbed. He reached down to close his hand around himself, the thickness weighing heavy in his hand as he squeezed a little patience into himself. But he was also showing her that he could tolerate a very strong touch and she need not be afraid she'd do something wrong and hurt him.

"Just do what I did. Use all the soft parts of your mouth against me. You can take me into your mouth and suck on me." He was amazed he got the instruction out coherently. Just the thought had his cock drooling for her attentions. The appearance of the wet liquid at the tip instantly caught her attention and her fascination. She bent over him and reached out to take it onto her tongue, giving him a tentative little tasting.

"But it's so different," she marveled in a whisper. "The same in some ways, but so very different from me. And you're wrong; I think you taste much better than I do."

Bronse groaned as she pushed his hands away from her field of interest and took him in her hand as he had done. She squeezed him every so lightly, sending flames of white fire burning over him. She wasted no time in exploring him further, her tongue licking over him again and again until he had to shut his eyes and grit his teeth to keep from screaming. Then she pursed her lips around him and tried her hand at sucking him into her mouth. The unguarded scrape of her teeth nearly broke him, nearly had him shouting out with the pleasure of it.

"You're holding back," she noted with a pout. The plushness of her lips kissed against his straining cock.

"Bad enough to have a psychosexual and your brother the damn empath in my business," he hissed. "I'll not give any more food for ship gossip. This is private. Between you and me and—Great Being, you're driving me mad!" The last was a clenched whisper as his hands dove deep into her hair. He made her pay full attention to the things her mouth was doing, and the more focused she was, the more unfocused he became.

He knew she had no idea what she was doing, but he also knew that when she got the hang of it, she'd be a natural killer. Right now, though, it seemed to be everything to him that each of her first steps, first explorations, were with *him*. They were taking place against *his* skin. Testing *his* sanity.

The roll of possessive emotion that followed every roll of pleasure that buffeted through him was breathtaking and intimidating. He had never felt anything so fierce and strong as he was feeling right then. Not for any woman. Not even close. It was like being introduced to a part of himself he'd never met before. A different and powerful part. A potentially dangerous part.

And just the knowledge of that made the next stroke of her tongue against him seem like she had poured acidic pleasure across him. As inexperienced as she was, as awkward and seeking as her discovery was, he was positive that all it would take was just one more sinful second inside of her mouth and he would come apart. His mind and his emotions had made him a hair trigger.

And, of course, with that uncanny instinct she always seemed to have, she did exactly that. She used her tongue to draw him into the hot haven of her mouth, and then she began to test him in increasingly strong sucking draws.

But not nearly strong enough.

"You won't hurt me," he choked out. "I'm so hard right now that nothing could hurt me. Suck me harder. Just a little—ah! Heaven help me, you're going to—"

Oh yes. One day soon she'd be giving the most skilled head in the universe, but today was about firsts and about onlys. It was about him being her choice and her being his.

It was everything.

"Ravenna, I'm going to come," he warned her, trying to draw her away because he knew how shocking it would be to her inexperienced tastes. "Ravenna!" he cried when she wouldn't give way, "I'll fill your mouth and then some and—and—"

He was in no space to properly explain or make even the remotest kind of sense. The urge to release was ripping out of him like a violent storm, and his whole being shook with the power of it. He began to ejaculate into her mouth, the hard spurts like spasms as they shot from his body. She drew back in surprise, releasing him about halfway through and letting herself get shot with pearly strings of the stuff against her cheek and lips and then down over the fingers that still had hold of him.

Bronse had all he could do to suck in breath after breath and keep himself from yelling out for the universe to hear.

CHAPTER
TWELVE

The proximity alarm went off, jolting Bronse out of the deepest sleep he'd had in years. He felt Ravenna startle awake where she lay in the crook of his arm. He should have bolted out of bed and started gearing up, but he knew that Justice wouldn't park them until he gave her the go-ahead to dock. It gave him just enough of an excuse to spend time breathing in the smell of his shampoo in her hair. It wasn't Ayalya spice, but it was yet another stamp of himself on her that gave him a deeply grounding sense of rightness and satisfaction. By then he had stopped trying to understand it and was simply embracing it. It was right for him. It felt right on every level. That was all that mattered to a man like him who lived by his gut instincts.

"What is it?" she asked sleepily, her beautiful eyes confused in the dim light of the panel that was flashing the alert just to the left of the bed.

"We've reached the IM station. We're home."

"Oh." She closed her eyes and sighed. "I guess I better go wake up the others."

But she wasn't moving any faster than he was to get to her feet. And it was no wonder. They were extremely comfortable as they lay there snuggled together beneath the warmth of their blanket. It would be hard for any-one to want to leave such a safe haven and leap forward into unknown dangers ahead. It was a moment of reckoning for both of them. Things were about to get really crazy, and it could all go very smoothly or it could get shot to hell.

They simply didn't know which.

But they both realized, in that moment, that they would find comfort in each other over the next few days and weeks. No matter what the days threw at them, there could be nights of respite, just like last night, waiting for them.

"I'm going to be right with you," he promised her softly, gently brushing her mussed hair from her cheek. "I'll fight like hell for it. I won't let anyone hurt you or your Chosen Ones."

"I've always believed that," she told him. "If I didn't, I wouldn't be here."

He gave her a kiss, something warm and passionate to remember him by as they worked their way through the next hours, and then he broke away from her, finally sitting up and climbing over her to get out of the bed. She was very quiet as she watched him dress in his entire uniform, absently re-dressing herself in the shirt she had borrowed from his belongings. Bronse got the distinct feeling she was gearing up just as he was, but hers was a mental process instead of the actual strapping on of a knife and the cinching of a belt.

They left the room together but immediately went their separate ways. Bronse headed straight for the bridge and his weary pilot.

"Hey, Commander," Justice greeted him. "We're approaching base and it's right in the middle of night cycle as planned. Most of them are snoozing away."

"Hopefully not Chaser. He said he'd greet us at landing. I'm counting on that."

"I'm with you on that one, sir." Justice kept her eyes glued to the space station looming large on the front screens. She passed chatter with the landing dock for a brief minute, then guided the ship smoothly into port.

By the time the docking was finished, the deck was swarming with Bronse's crew and Rave's Chosen Ones. Bronse walked up to her, his mouth grimly set and keeping his hands and everything else firmly to himself. He was nervous for her, and he knew it showed to his crew, who knew him well. He only hoped he wasn't showing it to her and that it wouldn't be apparent to anyone else.

"Stay on board until I call for you. Okay?"

"I want to come with you. I should make a strong approach to these leaders of yours who will want to use us. I want them to know I am not afraid and I am not hiding behind anyone."

"In this case," he said quietly, "I think it's best you appear to be hiding behind me. I want them to know you have a protector. I want them to know that everything they want out of you has to go through me first." He cut her off before she could voice a protest. "At least at first. It's the best way to keep us from getting separated right off the bat. If you have no guide into this place, you will end up lost and floundering. That will ruin your image of strength very quickly."

She thought about it for a long minute, then finally nodded. "All right. I see your logic. For now," she stipulated.

"Just for now," he assured her.

The ramp and hatch opened when Bronse touched the button, and he felt the Chosen Ones move back out of sight almost as a single entity. His crew did the opposite, the lot of them strong at his back as he stood at the top of the ramp. He waited until he saw the group of high-ranking men moving toward their ship.

Bronse had never been so glad to see Chaser in his whole life. They'd been part of a crack team back in the days before he'd gotten his own command. He'd worked his way from a position similar to Ender's all the way up to Lasher's. He'd been Chaser's second a good two years before Bronse had been promoted. He knew there was no better man in the militia and no one he could trust more, other than his own crew.

Bronse strode down the ramp and offered a ready hand to his superior. Chaser smiled with just one corner of his mouth, as always, and turned to introduce the men at his side.

"Commander Chapel, this is Admiral Hural, commander of Spec Ops, and this is Admiral Greays, from tactical."

"I've met you before, Admiral," he said to Greays as he shook his hand. Then he turned to the man who deserved his more focused attention. He had all of sixty seconds to get a feel for the Special Operations admiral before he would have to introduce his passengers to him. He needed to know what he was dealing with.

"Commander. I hear you've had an unusual mission."

"More than you'll realize," Bronse assured him. "I need to know, sir, if I have a guarantee that nothing about what you're going to see will go beyond you and the highest levels of Spec Ops. I have reason to believe that there's a viper in our nest, sir, and believe me when I tell you that this is the last thing you want a viper to know about."

"I'm intrigued, Commander," the admiral said. "But why don't you let me decide what's worthy of a lock-down in Spec Ops."

That made Bronse want to smile. These people had no idea what they were about to get into. It was inconceivable really. No one had ever seen anything like the Chosen Ones before.

"Then join us for debriefing, sir. You're in for a treat." He checked the decks of the landing bay for extraneous personnel, then glanced up at the video surveillance equipment that was standard in all the bays. "I'm going to need a blackout, sir. Those two cameras. Just for this initial arrival. I don't want anyone looking up the video files and seeing what you're about to see."

"Commander, you're beginning to sound paranoid," Greays said gruffly.

"Trust me. If you knew what I knew, you'd be ordering it yourself. Just humor me until you're up to speed. Then if you want, you can send me to Psyche Services."

After a moment of sizing up Bronse, the admiral turned to his aide and ordered the blackout. It took only a single call and then they were ready.

"Ravenna, could you come here, please?" Bronse called back to the ship.

The Chosen Ones emerged.

"Well," Greays said after a long minute, sitting back in his seat to eye Bronse, his crew, and the Chosen Ones, "you spin a hell of a story, Commander."

They had all gone to one of the security rooms for the debriefing, the camera that was recording the session something only the top brass of the IM could watch. Even JuJuren would be denied access. Only if he had been there for the session would he have a clue as to what was being said. And Bronse had laid it all out in the open. Everything. Both of their failed missions, Trick's findings, all of the double crosses and mayhem. Then he had very bluntly told them about Ravenna visiting him in his dreams and everything that followed, with a few personal exclusions. Now his words hung on the minds of these superior officers, who would have to pursue his accusations and his claims to their bitter ends, whatever that may be.

"Well, young woman, all I have to go on is the reports I've heard from this crew," Greays said to Ravenna. "What I need now is some empirical proof that they're not all out of their minds."

Rave stepped forward, her long, proud bearing a breathtaking sight as she walked up to the table that the three admirals sat behind. She reached out to put her hand over Admiral Hural's. Her eyes closed briefly as she turned her attention to the influx of information she was getting from just that simple touch. Then she opened her eyes and stared hard and cool into his.

"Last night your wife became angry with you and lost her temper. She threw one of your medals at your head. It had a ribbon with a blue and gold stripe."

"For Great Being's sake!" the admiral gasped.

Chaser chuckled. "Trudy always was a firebrand," he said to the other man.

"She's right then?" Greays asked. "Have you told Chaser about it already?" He still seemed suspicious, and Rave knew immediately that her intangible power would not be the one to convince him.

"Vivi, come here, please."

Vivienne moved quickly to Rave's side, ready to do anything she asked. The dynamic was not lost on the men before them.

"And what is it you're going to show me, young lady?" Greays wanted to know in his brusque manner. Vivi looked to Rave for guidance.

"Vivienne, shut down all the power in this section of the station," Rave instructed quietly.

The admiral guffawed as if she had told a ridiculous joke. "This station has too many redundant systems. A power failure is impossible." Just the same, he turned a CompuVid screen toward Vivi, a silent dare to see if she could hack her way to her goal.

But instead of trying to type instructions or commands into the system, Vivienne simply laid her hand on the equipment itself. With only a small flicker to warn them, there was a sudden slamming sound, the sound of generators and turbines and hundreds of little bits of

electronic gadgets all shutting down at once. The room
went black, and then the gravity plating failed. Anyone
who wasn't holding on to something began to float off
the ground. It took only fifteen seconds for Greays to
shout uncle.

"Holy shit! Make her stop!"

"Vivi," Ravenna said softly.

Vivienne lifted her hand away from the terminal. The
sudden whine of everything powering back up was followed by the sound of bodies crashing back to the floor.

Bronse had managed to land on his feet and was quick
to turn to the admiral.

"Convinced?"

Greays stood up, straightening his uniform.

"Commander, let's find some quarters for your special
friends."

Bronse sat back with a sigh, rubbing his tired eyes for
the hundredth time that day. It had been a week since
they'd been debriefed about the Ebbany mission, and
since then his crew had been reassigned to Spec Ops for
the sole purpose of watching over the IM's newest hot
commodity.

And if he was exhausted just *watching* the gauntlet of
tests they were subjecting the Chosen Ones to, he could
imagine how Ravenna and the others felt.

Ravenna. He hadn't had a moment alone with her in a
week. The quarters they had been given were behind
lockdown, and no one had access in or out unless they
had very specific clearance. He could have come to see
her, he supposed, since he was one of those few, but he
would have been seen by at least four sentries as he
passed by, and he didn't think it was such a good idea to
let people know that he and Ravenna had a personal
connection. Not at that point, anyway. If he let it be

known that he had a personal stake in any part of these events, he'd be snatched out of Spec Ops so fast that his head would be missing. Then it would be months before he saw her again, if he was lucky.

No. It was best to keep things cool and professional for now. He and his team were there to protect the Chosen Ones. That had to be enough.

But watching them wear her out with their endless testing was starting to get on his nerves. And she would protest on behalf of everyone else, but never on behalf of herself. Instead, whenever she forced the IM to back off on testing one of the others, she always placated them by offering herself in their stead.

Maybe that was the sign of a true leader, of a damn good one, but it was killing him to keep quiet while she did this. She had asked him not to undermine her position, and he was trying his best not to, but it was getting beyond ridiculous at this point.

It didn't help that she was always there, through the glass partition and just out of his reach, and just as irresistibly seductive as ever. Sometimes she would look up from what she was doing and fix her eyes on him. It was keenly obvious to him that she was thinking something decidedly illicit the moment he caught her glance, and she would blush a beautiful shade of pink right before his eyes.

Those were probably the hardest times of all.

"She needs a break," he heard himself saying suddenly as his gaze stayed trained on Ravenna in the next room. Every day he stood there in the observation room watching test after test and feeling more and more out of touch with her. For some reason, today he'd had enough.

The doctors and admirals in the observation room all turned as one to look at him, surprise written clearly on their features.

"She needs a break," he reiterated, not in the least bit cowed by their stares. "You've had her reading this subject for over an hour. Can't you see how tired she is?"

"That's the point, Commander. We're doing this testing to see just what her limitations are," one of the doctors said.

"To what end? So you can burn out her brain and make her a zombie?" he demanded to know. "This isn't a machine you can test until it breaks or pops a circuit, then repair and move on. If you wait until something pops in her, she might not be able to recover from that. They came here for protection and to help us do some good. Not to be prisoners and guinea pigs for the rest of their lives! They haven't even been out of these labs since they got here."

"We can't let them out in the general population!" The doctor was horrified at the idea.

"Why not?" Bronse wanted to know. "No one knows what they're capable of. They look just like any of the other thousands of soldiers walking these halls. They aren't prisoners and they have rights. The same rights as any other soldier here."

"Weren't you the one who was so paranoid that you had me shutting off cameras?" Greays wanted to know.

"That was because of JuJuren, not because of them. Keep their abilities top secret, but not them. If you don't treat them like any other normal soldier, they'll start to rebel and then you'll lose them altogether. Admiral, this lockdown and rabid testing has to stop."

The doctors protested in tandem, talking over one another as they listed all the reasons why they felt they should keep their guinea pigs in cages, but Bronse had gotten through to Greays. He could see the man thinking hard on it.

"Every soldier has to earn the IM's trust," Greays said after a long minute. "They do that by subjecting themselves to tests and training of every nature, by letting us mold them into the soldiers we need. We expect the same from the Chosen Ones."

"And in return they expect you to treat them with humanity," said Bronse. "They get things like downtime and freedom to socialize. You'll get your tests and they'll submit to training—they've already proven as much. But you have to loosen it up just a little bit. Admiral, you've seen Kith getting more and more defiant each day. Soon even Ravenna won't be able to control him. That boy needs to steam off or he's going to explode."

The truth was that a huge part of Bronse wanted them locked down and hyper protected. He was afraid of what they'd run into in the common corridors. But he couldn't let fear rule him.

"The adults would blend in," Greays was musing, "but the children . . ."

"There are enough families on this base that they wouldn't be questioned," said Bronse. "You just have to put them up in family housing. I don't think they'd want to be separated anyhow. Not just yet. And if it makes you feel any better, my team and I will move into quarters with them and watch over them. That's six trained pairs of eyes. Best of the best, no less." He stepped closer to the admiral, eager to send his point home. "They need normalcy. They need to learn how to live their lives in our world. Those kids need schooling. This is what Ravenna wants from you but is too tired to ask for. They aren't going anywhere. They just need a little more freedom than this and a little more compassion from all of you."

The admiral nodded slowly, ignoring any further protests from the doctors. He turned to the others who had been watching the testing with him. "We'll move them today. No muss and no fuss. But a crew of ETF officers in the house will draw attention. Give me an alternative, Commander."

"Let me go in undercover. I could be . . ." He searched his tired brain.

"Ravenna's husband maybe?" Greays prompted. "You're too young for the children to be yours, but you could be raising your brothers and sisters after your parents' deaths. We'll put Justice and Fallon right next door as another couple. Domino could live with them. Then put Ender and Lasher in quarters across the way." The admiral quirked up a brow. "But you're ETF First Actives. This is long-term undercover work we're talking. This would take you out of the field for months. Your crew would be replaced. Maybe you should consult with them before making any offers."

Maybe he should. They hadn't seemed to mind the downtime so far because they'd been busy keeping watch over the Chosen Ones, but to be permanently transferred was something else entirely.

And was that something he himself wanted? He'd fought long and hard to become an ETF First Active squad leader. Was he willing to give that up all of a sudden? And for what? Special Ops? What he and the others liked to call spook work?

But one day it could end up being something even more. On the horizon the IM would want to use the Chosen Ones in the field, for practical purposes, once they'd been trained of course. Then they would need a crack military team backing them up. That kind of future prospect might just be appealing to some of his adrenaline-junkie crew, especially Lasher, even though it might mean resignations and transfers out of being First Active. Justice and Ender, however, might want to stay ETF.

There was only one way to find out. And while he was at it, he might ask himself what *he* wanted.

"I'll do that," he said aloud to the room. "But I need to know what to offer them as a carrot, sir. I mean, I assume you plan to use these people in the field one day."

"Ah, I see. Chaser warned me you could be ambitious as hell. You want to make your team the one that helps us utilize the Chosen Ones in the field."

"We're the best," Bronse said with a simple shrug. "And we're already briefed and cleared. Can you think of anyone better?"

"No. In fact I just might insist," Greays warned him. "Talk to your team. Feel them out on this. If they agree to it, then we'll set you all up to play house."

"And the testing for today?" he asked, glancing at Ravenna and her wearily drooping head as she caught it in her palm. She looked like she was ready to fall asleep right there on the table that sat between her and her subject.

"Finished."

Bronse nodded, feeling satisfied that he'd done the right thing.

Now he just had to fight the urge to break into the next room and hold her until her exhaustion took over and she could sleep. He hoped she didn't mind him taking charge. But if he was in the position to do the most good for the sake of the Chosen Ones, then why not take advantage of it?

She looked up just then and met his eyes through the observation glass. The way she suddenly lit up was damning and telling, but Bronse realized in that moment that he no longer cared. All that mattered to him was making her happy and seeing that she was taken care of. So he smiled at her, with much stronger emotions than he dared to name just then.

"Sir, do you mind if I have a minute with her?" he heard himself asking before he could curb the impulse.

Damn it, what had happened to all of his infamous control? Ever since she'd drifted into his dreams, he'd been lost to one unthinking impulse after another. Even worse was that he was enjoying it more than half the time. Enjoying the benefits of it.

Like his impulse to speak up on her behalf just now. The admiral's proposed setup was everything he could have asked for, even to the point where he'd be behind closed doors with Ravenna again. He'd be able to touch her again. To taste her.

He knew his thoughts were transparent to her the moment she blushed and turned her face down. Bronse could only hope that her thoughts weren't as easily readable by the commanding officers and medics in the room.

"I don't see why not. You can propose the whole idea to her and see what she thinks."

He nodded, his feet already carrying him to the door between the rooms. "I'll take her for a walk." Bronse walked into the testing room, and the soldier who had been Rave's subject stood up at attention at his approach. Bronse ignored the younger man and reached out to take one of Rave's warm, smooth hands into his, pulling her up to her feet. "You're done for today," he told her gently. "And we need to have a talk about some things."

Ravenna nodded and followed him from the room without argument. It took only a few moments before they were walking through the nearly abandoned bays and corridors of the lockdown section. They avoided the sentry checkpoints and soon had relative privacy, except for the cameras that were covering every inch of the secured area.

Just the same, he turned her into his arms, gave her a strong hug of strength and support, and tried his damndest to make it look ten times more platonic than it was. It didn't help that she ran hungry hands up his back and seemed to be absorbing him via the nerves of her fingertips. But as wonderful as it felt, he made himself step away from her. He knew they were being watched. He just had to hold out a little while longer and he'd have her any way he wanted her.

"Rave, I don't want you to think that I'm trying to

usurp your authority over the Chosen Ones," he prefaced before he explained what was potentially in the works for her and her powerful little family. Then he gave her his caveat. "This, of course, will all depend on whether the team wants to come off of First Active duty."

"Do you think they'll want to?"

"It's hard to say. They live for the ETF like I do."

"But you . . ." She hesitated and looked deeply into his eyes, as if she were searching for something. "You want this? You want to help give us more freedom and . . . and play house?"

Bronse couldn't count how many times he'd berated himself for how awkwardly and how badly he'd managed his emotions the last time they'd been together, and hearing her toss his snidely spoken words back up between them only made him feel like more of an ass.

"I see the potential," he explained to her. "I can see me and mine training you and yours and one day making a unit out of us that would be close to unstoppable. Vivienne could break into any electronic lock, could shut down power to installations we needed to penetrate, or could cripple malignant computing systems. Ophelia, once she's old enough, would save lives in a way that Jet never could. Kith could read ready status and enemy intentions before we breached a structure. And you. We would know what could go wrong on a mission long before it even happened. It all makes for an edge that any soldier would kill for."

"And Devan?"

Devan perhaps had more potential than any of them. She had proven herself to have the power of charming any person or animal she came into contact with. She could coax them into thinking anything, into doing anything, just with the power of her mind and voice. Her only limitation was that it wore her out considerably, and she was very young and frail. But she would grow stronger with age and could be groomed to be the soldier that the IM desperately wanted her to be. Whether her shy nature made it right for her would be another story entirely. There were still a lot of open-ended questions, but it was the infinite possibilities of application that so intrigued Bronse and his superiors.

"We have years before we have to worry about Devan being in the field. Right now, I'm worried about her getting a chance to be a kid. To go to school and make friends. To feel normal as much as she can while being above the norm."

Rave sighed and closed her weary eyes, leaning toward him but realizing she couldn't risk touching him. Any hint of the personal between them and Bronse could be yanked away from her. She hated the idea of that more than she hated not being able to touch him. He was protecting her Chosen Ones much better than she was. He had all their best interests at heart—that much was clear. And he had been so right when he told her she would be like a fish out of water in this environment. She was so out of place, so off her mark here, that she hadn't been able to think the way he had. Bronse had forced the IM to stop looking at them as lab rats and remember that they were people. It was something she should have done herself but had been too overwhelmed to think of on her own.

"I can't tell you how grateful I am," she whispered to him soft and fast. "I can't tell you how it's killing me that I can't touch you and show you my gratitude."

The heated statement made Bronse swallow visibly, and his fingers slowly curled into fists. It was so damn hard not to touch her! There she stood, looking pale and tired and all the more alluring and irresistible for it. His gaze fell to her full mouth, the one he wanted so badly to taste just then, and his fists became all the tighter.

"Soon," he promised her.

"You hope," she countered. "You have to see if your team will do this."

"I'm going to do that now. But I know my team, Ravenna. I know how much they love a challenge. How excited they are when things get hairy and scary. I also know they got attached to you and yours very quickly. They don't want to see anything happen to any of you."

"Then go talk to them. If you want to put my mind at ease, come back to me with their answer to all of this. The sooner I know we're going to be protected by you, the better I will feel. The sooner they let us free of this laboratory environment, the better it will be for the children. Especially for Kith. I think he might like the idea of living free of me and the others. It might give him the sense of adulthood he's always biting and clawing for."

"I hope you're right. The IM isn't going to put up with his attitude much longer."

"I'll have a talk with him."

"Maybe it shouldn't be you," Bronse countered. "Maybe Lasher or Ender would be the better choice."

"Maybe you're right." They both knew that Kith wasn't in any humor to listen to Bronse, so neither of them suggested it. "Tell me, whatever happened to the admiral who was trying to kill you? Did he ever explain why? Is he incarcerated for his crimes?"

Bronse's mouth thinned to a compressed line. Just the look on his face gave her the answer to her question. "No. Someone tipped him off. As careful as we were, someone leaked a warning to him and now he's off the grid, out there in space somewhere doing who knows what. But the IM is hot on his heels, I assure you. They'll catch him and then they'll lock him away for a good long time while they pick his brain for the names of any co-conspirators."

"Meanwhile those who conspired with him could be right here," she conjectured. "Anywhere. Looking for a moment when your back is open to them." She bit her lip right before her hands reached out for his neck and heart, but he caught her by her wrists and stopped her.

"No," he said firmly. "You've done enough for one day. You'll have to trust that I can take care of myself without any warning from you. We talked about this, remember? My life is always in danger. Trust me to know how to protect what is precious to me." He drew the knuckles of one captured hand to the brief touch of his lips. "That includes protecting you and those you care about."

"You've already done that," she noted. "You've gotten us a normal home. You have no idea what it means to me that you've done this for us."

But as soon as she could, as soon as there were no cameras watching them and waiting for them to expose themselves, she would show him a great many things. And she made certain that the promise of that was clear in her eyes.

"Okay," he breathed in a voice no better than a growl, "I need you to stop looking at me that way or this will all go to hell right here and now."

"I'm sorry," she whispered fast and hot as they both tried to get closer to each other without moving an inch. "I cannot help myself. I find myself missing you. Missing your warmth against me. Missing the feel of you inside me."

And just like that, in a flash of inner fire, he was hard for her. She couldn't possibly know, he thought heatedly, just how much self-control it was taking to keep from touching her. The smell of her, those gentle drifts of Ayalya spice, were intoxicating to a belly empty of the feel and taste of her.

"I feel the same," he said hoarsely. But it wasn't until he saw the relief in her expression that he realized she hadn't been sure of that. As separation had stretched between them, she had doubted the continuation of his passions for her.

Of course. He had worked very hard at trying to cut her away, reminding her that his life allowed no place for a relationship with a woman. There had been no real reassurances. All she had had was her own confidence. And now that she was worn out, that confidence had also become worn.

"Don't you doubt that," he said swiftly and heatedly as he bent his forehead to hers, nearly touching them together. "Never doubt the power of how much I crave you. Both physically and . . . and emotionally."

The confession brought her eyes swiftly to his. She was searching him again to see if he was telling her the truth. Or perhaps she didn't trust her own perceptions. It didn't help that he couldn't follow any of it with a physical demonstration. The frustration of that was gnawing at his stomach and his patience, so he shook his head at her.

"I'll explain once we're out of lockdown. Okay? Let me go find the crew and get a handle on the way they feel about all of this. I can't do this without them. I don't think I can trust anyone else to be that close to you all. I have to convince the crew that the wait will be worth it in the long run."

"I know you can do it," she said with confidence. "You're one of the strongest leaders I have ever met, and I have a great deal of faith in you."

As Bronse forced himself to leave without kissing her the way he wanted to, he hoped like hell that she was right.

CHAPTER
THIRTEEN

Bronse didn't bother going to Lasher first. Of all of his crew, he knew that Lasher would be able to see the long term best. Plus, Masin had developed a real soft spot for little Ophelia. He was always in the observation booth when they were testing her, and he always made sure that she was in his sight line when they were simply hanging around and playing their bodyguards. While in lockdown, the danger was minimal, but once the Chosen Ones were put in the general population, things would become infinitely more edgy. Especially where Ophelia was concerned. She wasn't any good at hiding what she could do. She couldn't bear to see someone hurt and then just stand around pretending there was nothing she could do about it. No doubt Lasher would take strong point when it came to her protection. Even more so when she eventually worked her way into doing field assignments. Seeing her as a little sister in need of looking after, Lasher would gladly take the downtime and the transfer out of being First Active.

Bronse's problem would come from his pilot and his ordnance man. Justice was least happy when she was grounded. She liked to have a stick in her hands and craved flying in and out of tight spots. There would be little of that at first if she took on this new detail. Frankly, Bronse couldn't see any reason why she would want to purposely ground herself. No more than he could see Ender being happy with nothing or no one to blow up.

He decided to speak with them together, alone.

They met in Ender's quarters. When Bronse arrived, his type A team was pacing the floor trying to suss out why they'd been selected for a chat with the boss.

"I'll get straight to the point," Bronse said as soon as the doors hissed shut at his back. "I want to resign the team from First Active status."

"What?" the exclamation was twofold, Justice and Ender equally shocked and bordering on indignant.

"Hear me out," Bronse requested. "At any time, no matter what I want to do or your superiors want to do, keep in mind that this is strictly volunteer. If you don't want to do this, you can resign from my team and hook on to another." The suggestion drew frowns across both their faces. They'd been a team for a very long time now. They worked together as smooth as glass, trusted one another implicitly, and knew one another inside and out. It was hard to conceive of breaking up something that worked that well. "We've been offered a very unique opportunity," Bronse continued. "Spec Ops is going to need a crack team to work in conjunction with the Chosen Ones in the field, and we're the ones they want. Missions will be way out there on the edge, just like we've always done, but this time we might be tackling objectives that will not succeed unless we have a Chosen One with us. When I say we'll be working out on the edge, I mean that—as of right now—even command has no idea just how far all of this can go. The possibilities are endless.

"That being said, you know how raw and untrained the Chosen Ones are. They aren't truly militia yet. There's a lot of work to be done before they reach that point. If we take this gig, we'd be responsible for getting them to mission-ready status, and we'd be responsible for their day-to-day well-being. That means we'll be down, possibly for months. You might say we'll be some hard-core, glorified babysitters. And that means both on and off duty. We'll be living, breathing, and saturated with Chosen Ones each and every cycle that goes by."

Bronse shifted his shoulders, shrugging back the weight of the tension he was carrying as he tried to gauge their faces. "You don't have to tell me your answer right now, but I expect one by next cycle. I want you to think on it, to truly understand just how boring this could be from time to time for people like us. But I also hope you consider the long haul, when boring will go out the window and we'll be cranking missions again like never before. Everything will change, and I want us to be at the front of it."

There. He'd said his piece. The rest would be up to them.

"Any questions?" he offered up.

"Just one," Justice said, her strong hands settling on her hips, and her feet braced hard apart. "Are you sure you're not doing this because you're hot for Ravenna? Because I don't want to be dragged along if this is all about chasing a pretty face, sir."

It was a fair question, Bronse thought. One he had been asking himself over and over again lately. Would he be doing any of this if he hadn't gotten swept away by the way Rave made him feel? Was he making clear and proper choices for his team, or were they shaded by cravings that had no place in military decisions?

"Ravenna is a very special woman who has, I admit, a very powerful effect on me," he said slowly and carefully. "I won't stand here and tell you that my desires where she is concerned are not coloring my choices, because I know that they are. But what drives me is less about sex and lust and more about who she is and what she and the others can do. She's a strong leader with control over the most powerful people I have ever met, but she needs help. She needs us to protect them and guide them into this way of living that we take so much pleasure in. They need us. The brass needs us. I don't know about you, but as long as I get to do my job, all the rest of it is just gravy." He sighed. "I hope that's some kind of answer for you. It's the best one I have."

Justice pursed her lips as she mulled that over. "Well, at least you didn't try to convince me that one had nothing to do with the other. The day my commander starts to lie to himself is the day I find a new commander."

"I'm in."

Ender said it so suddenly and so casually that Bronse didn't think he'd heard him right. That must have been reflected in his expression because Ender chuckled and repeated himself. "I said I'm in. I'm always down for some training and teaching. And I can see what our future missions are going to be like. First Active will no longer be first on the toughest jobs, as I see it. Sticking with the Chosen Ones now is how we get to be the real deal and don't find ourselves suddenly obsolete."

"Well, I don't think ETF will ever be obsolete, but I do see it changing," Bronse agreed. "Are you sure you don't want to think about it?"

"No," Justice spoke up. "Ender's right. I'm not convinced that those kids have it in them to run with the big boys, but I'd be stupid not to take the time to find out only to end up getting left behind. Just make sure I get some stick time every now and then though."

"I'm sure we can work that out," Bronse said with a grin that he couldn't suppress. He hadn't expected this. Granted, he knew how strong the team was, but adrenaline junkies faced with not getting their fix? It was a tough call to make. "All right. I'm going to talk to Lasher and Jet, but I have a feeling they'll be on board too."

"Are you kidding?" Justice teased with a laugh. "You and Lasher have boy crushes on each other. I don't think you'll ever do anything apart."

"That'll be enough of that," Bronse warned.

But he was grinning ear to ear.

"Here's how I see this," Lasher said as they looked down at the schematic of the housing level. "Four living units, two on one side of the corridor and two directly across. That gives us this entire corridor to ourselves here on a dead end. It puts us in the general population but keeps us separated enough that we can watch one another's backs. Bronse and Rave will live here with Devan. Ender will live here with Kith and Fallon. I'm going to be here with Ophelia and Vivienne, and Justice will be here with Domino."

Ravenna smiled and coyly hip-checked Lasher. "Ophelia wouldn't let you stick her with Justice, huh?"

Masin smiled, well aware that he deserved teasing for caving to Ophelia's big teary eyes and incessant begging. It was no secret by now that Ophelia had a terrible crush on him, idolizing him to the stars. But that was okay, he thought. Let her have a crush. It was a normal thing for a girl her age, and the Great Being knew she needed a good dose of normal. Besides, he wanted Ophelia where he could keep a very close eye on her. Everyone knew that she would be the hardest to control when it came to concealing her abilities.

The other weak point in this setup was Kith. He'd grown more and more sullen as time had ticked on, even the news of coming out of lockdown having no effect on his mood. The kid was in serious need of direction and discipline, and Ender was just the soldier to give it to him.

"Ready to become a father figure to the biggest pain in the ass on the station?" Masin asked Ender over the table.

"I'm ready. I'd like to see him try to start his crap with

me. I'll rig his door with a paint grenade." The harmless grenades were used in training exercises and blew out paint in a wide circle to represent explosive force and shrapnel discharge. They made a huge mess but would get the message across. "Besides, we're going to start him in base training tomorrow. He'll be too worn out at the end of the day to cause much trouble."

"Good," Bronse said. "We'll work in a shift schedule. One of us will have to sacrifice their day cycle and be awake during the night to keep an ear out on the hallways."

"I'll do it," Justice said. "You'll be busy watching over the group during the day. Besides, you have a kid on school scheduling. Leave me to do night shift. Domino can take care of himself during the day when he's with his trainers or the docs. Ender needs to be on deck when Kith is out of training to keep the kid in check, so I'm the best choice."

"Sounds like a plan. So," Bronse turned to Ravenna and grinned, "wanna go play in the real world?"

"Very much so! I'll get the others!"

They left lockdown as a group and made it to their new quarters without a single incident. Everyone split up to settle in, leaving Bronse alone with Devan and, for the first time in nearly three weeks, Ravenna.

"Devan, go find your room," he encouraged her, pointing through the front room to the back hallway. The young girl squeaked with excitement and ran for her room. Bronse waited until he heard the door hiss shut, and then he shot across the room to grab hold of Rave.

They were in a clinch instantly, each desperately grasping at the other as they kissed. It was as though they'd been drowning for a long time, and the moment their lips touched, it was like coming up for a much-needed gasp of air.

Ravenna felt more needed in that moment than she

had ever been needed by her collection of Chosen Ones. Her heart pounded beneath her breast as his hands ran fast and hungry up the long length of her back, leaving chills of satisfaction in their wake. How had she ever managed not to touch him for all of this time? How had she survived those brutally long nights outside of his bed? She'd barely had time to be with him to start with, but she had become a fast and thorough addict.

"Bronse," she murmured over and over again, wishing she could climb inside of him and, even more, wishing he would climb inside of her. But they knew that Devan would soon be back, and what they really wanted would have to wait until the young girl was in bed and asleep.

"How could I see you every single day and yet feel like I was missing you?" he demanded of her. "It was making me crazy." He brushed hot fingers down the side of her neck, turning them over her shoulder and stroking through the thin material of her militia uniform shirt. Every one of the Chosen Ones of majority age was now required to wear one. Not just because it helped them to blend in, but because they were official members of the militia and it was the required dress. "Have I told you how sexy you look in uniform?" he asked her with a low, predatory growl.

"I can't look half as good as you do," she countered, drawing him down for an even deeper kiss.

"Wow. Guys, you're burning my impressionable brain!"

They broke apart at Devan's tease, each of them coloring guiltily. But she waved it off with a bouncing hug for each of them.

"That's okay. I'll get used to it," she said happily. "I love my room! It's much bigger than the one at the temple, and the bed is great. There are clothes in there and everything!" She made a face. "And there's a VidPad that has the name of a school etched into it."

"Ah. Your schoolbooks have arrived. You have a bit of catching up to do, so you might want to start reading tonight. You'll start attending classes tomorrow," Bronse said.

Devan shuddered delicately. "I'm not looking forward to this. I was always schooled with the village children. I grew up with them. I don't know anything about how to make new friends."

"You'll learn," Bronse assured her. "Don't worry about it. You're a bright and funny girl. People are going to love that about you. You'll have new friends in no time."

"Just because you say it doesn't always make it true," the young girl said gravely, the pearl of wisdom telling him that her trust for him had grown, but she wasn't yet willing to believe his word as law. Bronse didn't mind. It just made her more clever than before in his eyes.

"We'll just have to wait and see then, won't we?"

She shrugged. "Sure." Then she hopped back off to her bedroom. Just before she stepped through the door, she said, "Oh, I'm going to try a bunch of clothes on in here. Then do some reading. I don't expect I'll come out for a good long while."

Then she disappeared through the door. Bronse and Rave looked at each other.

"Did she just give us permission to have sex?" he asked.

"Yes." Ravenna giggled. "She thinks she's being clever."

Bronse narrowed darkening eyes on Ravenna. "I think she's brilliant."

Rave stepped back when he stepped forward. "It's the middle of the day cycle!"

"So?" His look was positively predatory. He reached out to snag her wrist in his hand and continued to advance for every step she retreated.

"But Devan—"

"You heard her. She'll be busy." He grinned, teeth gleaming between his lips.

"What if one of the others comes to the door?" she persisted.

"If any of them are less savvy than a fourteen-year-old girl, they deserve to be ignored." He leapt forward and grabbed her, making her squeal as he scooped her up over his shoulder and began to march for the hallway.

"Bronse! Put me down!" She laughed, squirming under the hand that patted her upturned bottom.

"Just as soon as I get my bed underneath you."

It was three nights after that when Ravenna woke to a noise in the outer room. Devan had taken to getting up for nighttime snacks, so she didn't think anything of it as she slid out from under Bronse's arm and slipped on a robe. She left their bedroom and walked through the darkness to the living area. She thought it odd that no lights were on—until she reached for the panel that would turn them on and felt someone grab her wrist.

She was spun around so hard that her arm was shoved up her back as she was pushed into a wall. Every tendon protested as they resisted the impossible position. She opened her mouth to yell for Bronse, but the muzzle of a laser pistol shoved up under the point of her chin made the scream die in her throat.

"One sound," she heard a man whisper between the tight clench of teeth, "and I'll kill everyone I find in this house."

Afraid for Devan and Bronse, she nodded her acquiescence.

"Good girl," he said softly. "Now tell me where I can find Chapel and I'll leave you be."

Ravenna knew instantly that it was a lie. Whether she was reading him or not, she didn't know, but every instinct screamed a warning that she could not and should not believe a single word that came out of his mouth.

Who was this person? Was there random crime on a space station like this?

No. Not random at all. He was looking specifically for Bronse.

That was when she knew he was an assassin and this was yet another attempt to kill the man who had defied death again and again despite the powerful hands trying to wield it. This was JuJuren's work.

Ravenna panicked. Not because she was afraid for herself or Bronse, but because she was afraid for the freedom of the Chosen Ones. If something like this got back to the higher-ups, they might jerk them all back into lockdown.

The idea made her angry. It made her bold.

"He isn't here. He's on a mission," she said, knowing it was the most plausible excuse.

"You're a liar. I saw him come home with you earlier." The pistol became so insistent under her chin that she had to stretch her neck to accommodate it. "If I have to start searching rooms, I can't take you with me. That means you're dead. Tell me where he is right now."

"Behind you."

The snap and whip of the garrote bracelet Bronse always wore was as fast as lightning. Ravenna bolted to the right as Bronse looped the wire around the assassin's neck and yanked him back off balance. Taken so off guard, the would-be killer squeezed the trigger. The shot was so close that it singed Ravenna's hair. But within an instant the man dropped the weapon and grasped for the wire that was embedded in his throat and cutting off his air supply.

Still afraid, still needing to feel safe, Ravenna reached out her hand and called the weapon to her. It came up from the floor and flew straight into her palm. She was hoping that the darkness would hide the trick as she turned to point the pistol at the chest of the intruder.

Even in the dimness, she could see the light periwinkle eyes of her lover, as well as the shock and accusation that now emanated from them.

So much for hiding tricks, she thought.

Bronse turned all of his attention on the man he was struggling with. He was big, rather like Ender, and had a decent muscle mass. Strong. But without oxygen he was nothing. Less than nothing. And the intruder knew it. He stopped struggling to win and focused solely on making the effort to breathe against the incredible power of Bronse's grip.

"Who sent you?" Bronse demanded. He was not about to just turn him over to the justice branch and let them handle this incessant breach in security and the threats to his personal safety.

"You know who!" The man gagged. Bronse eased up only enough to give him air for his next sentence.

"I want to know why that miserable fuck is out to get me! What the hell did I do?"

"I don't know!" the assailant squeaked. "But he knows you have a woman and child now!"

The implication was clear. JuJuren would stop at nothing to get to Bronse. Even going through Ravenna and Devan to get to him.

Bronse and Rave's gazes clashed. They both knew instantly what that would mean. Rave and Devan and the other Chosen Ones were too hot a commodity to allow any kind of danger near them.

The IM would pull Bronse off their detail if they found out about this.

Unable to stomach the idea, his rage and frustration taking over, Bronse strangled the bastard to within an inch of his life. It was only because Ravenna jumped in to stop him that the intruder was left to drop to the floor in an unconscious heap instead of a dead one.

Bronse whipped the garrote free of the assassin's neck, and it retracted back into the whole bracelet again with a deadly snap. Breathing hard from exertion and the bushel of pure fear that had been dumped into his system when he had come out of the bedroom to find Rave with a gun to her face, Bronse leaned back against a near wall and let Ravenna come up to him with concern.

"It's over," he said, his voice dead and cold. "They'll separate us and I won't be allowed within a mile of you as long as JuJuren's at large."

"Then we have to see to it that he isn't at large," Rave shot back, the equally wintry nature of her voice telling him just how serious she was.

Anger snapped through him instantly. "What do you suggest? I take you with me and we go hunt him down? Spec Ops would just love that! I'd be court-martialed so fast—" He broke off and glared at her. "You've been lying to me."

"It wasn't a lie," she insisted. "I told you I could take care of myself if I wanted to!"

"What was that?" he wanted to know. "Some kind of telekinesis? You can move shit with your mind, Ravenna!"

"Shh!" she hushed him worriedly, looking toward the front door and knowing that Justice was awake and alert across the hall. "Yes, I can move things with my mind. A great many things. I can do things you probably can't even imagine—that's how strong it is! But I won't give that kind of weapon to just anyone, now will I? I can't show it to anyone! I didn't even want to show it to you! I didn't want to put you in the position of having to decide between keeping a secret I have and reporting honestly to your superiors. Once I know I can trust the people around me, then maybe I'll tell them about it. I'm hoping I can trust you not to say anything."

"Fuck!" he swore violently, running agitated hands through his hair. "It doesn't matter. As soon as he talks to anyone else, they're going to yank me out of here."

"I won't let them. I won't let that happen!" She reached out and smacked her hand against the panel, lighting the room. "Stay here with him. I'll be right back."

"Where are you going?" he demanded.

"Just let me handle this!"

Rave marched out of their quarters and headed straight for Ender and Fallon's room. The last thing she wanted was to wake up her testy brother and bring him in on this, but she doubted that she was going to get that lucky. She waited impatiently for Ender to answer the door call, and wasn't surprised when Justice came out of her quarters as well.

"What's going on?" she asked.

"Not here," Rave silenced her as the door finally opened to reveal a tousled Ender with a pistol in his hand. "I need Fallon. Right now."

Ender didn't bother to question her. He hurried back to where the boys' rooms were and came back with Fallon. As expected, Kith was also awake, his empathic senses too keen to miss the emotional uproar going on right outside his door. Rave turned to Justice. "You might as well get Lasher and the others and have them come to our quarters. We have trouble and I have the solution."

She grabbed up Fallon's hand and marched him back across the hall.

Minutes later, everyone was awake and staring down at the assassin who had come for Bronse. He was still out cold as he lay there on the floor, but that would change.

"Fallon, wake him up." She reached out a hand, spreading a palm wide, using her power to hold the turncoat down to the floor. They all knew they were looking at an IM soldier. Possibly even ETF by the look of him and if the stealth he had used to get past Justice was anything to go by. He probably hadn't even really made a noise in the outer room. Rave had probably been awakened by her own abilities, the warning coming to her in the most likely way to prompt her to get up and act.

Fallon reached deep into the darkness of the man's unconscious brain, rerouting disturbed and protective wiring until he was forcing him awake. The intruder gasped hard for breath through his swollen throat, trying to grab at it but finding his arms pinned to the floor along with every other part of him.

"I am going to ask you some very simple questions," Ravenna announced to him, "and you are going to answer whether you want to or not. If you resist, it will hurt you. I really, *really* hope you resist," she said darkly.

She didn't acknowledge Ender's grin across the way from her. He might think this was something to be laughed off, but she didn't. She'd be damned if she'd see her Chosen Ones lose what they had worked so hard for these past few weeks. And there was no way she would let them take Bronse away from her, either. This JuJuren had come after him for the last time. Now he would pay the price for what he'd been doing. This, she thought, was about to be the very first mission that the Chosen Ones would engage in.

"What's your name?" she asked first.

"Drumm Easley," Fallon answered for him as soon as the thought ripped through the man's mind.

"Drumm, did former Admiral JuJuren hire you?" Rave asked him.

"Yes," Fallon replied, "they planned it a week ago."

"What the hell is this?" Easley demanded in a panic as Fallon spoke the answers he was trying to hide.

"Where is JuJuren now?" Rave asked coldly.

"Tari." Fallon lifted two fingers to his temple, a telling sign that the headache he got when he read resistant minds was quickly starting. "Not the stations, but on the planet itself."

"The old hometown," Justice said to Ender dryly. "Good thing Ender and I know our way around." She gave the arms master a wolfish grin.

"Where on Tari?"

"I'm not telling!" Easley squawked, his frantic eyes jolting up to Fallon's. "He'll kill me!"

"Not if we kill him first," Bronse said.

Ravenna looked up to meet his eyes, seeing the determination that had settled there. She knew in that very instant that they were on exactly the same page.

They were all going to go and stop JuJuren once and for all.

"He's at a place called Prime and Lights. Or that's where they met up anyway. Several times, in fact," Fallon informed them.

"Prime and Lights is the name of a bar in one of the higher-end hotels on the upper territory coastline," Ender said. "Hot damn, I'll bet he's staying at the hotel."

"He doesn't know a room number," Fallon said wearily.

"We don't need one," Bronse remarked. "We can flash his picture to the desk or we can stake out the place."

"Or we can spring Trick from downtime and he can hack into the guest records," Justice suggested.

"Better idea," Bronse agreed.

"I'm game!" Vivi piped up. "Let's kick his ass!"

"It's not going to be that easy," Lasher said wisely. "If JuJuren can get someone in here, knowing in only three days where Bronse moved to, it means he still has a network here in the IM. Do you have any idea how hard it is to make an unauthorized access into this station? This man's a soldier." He indicated their prisoner. "There's no telling how many more of these types JuJuren has surrounded himself with. There are too many variables. We just don't know enough."

"We have no choice," Bronse said. "If we call in security before JuJuren is brought to justice, this whole setup is blown. We all know that no one can protect these kids like we can. No one is better for this job. I won't let JuJuren rob me of—"

He looked up and met Ravenna's eyes.

The understanding that he would do anything, go to any lengths to stay with her, hit him like a sucker punch. The time for excuses and outside explanations had just come to a crashing halt. As he stared into those expressive and knowing eyes of hers, he realized that nothing else mattered to him more than she did. As angry as he was at her for holding out on him, as betrayed as he had felt in that moment, it was all insignificant.

"I agree." Lasher filled in the unspoken moment for him. "Whatever it is you did to rivet his attention onto you, the only way to shut it off is to get JuJuren. But we can't walk up on the situation thinking it's going to be easy. That's how people get themselves killed."

"All we need is one shot," Ravenna said, her voice so strangely dispassionate that it was making everyone else uncomfortable. "We follow every lead to the next and then the next, and we won't come back until he's captured or dead." She clenched her fist, tipping her chin down just slightly. The prisoner on the floor suddenly soared into the air. He let out a hoarse screech of pure fear, his eyes wide as he faced a truly awesome power that he would never be able to understand. With a mere thought, she sent him flying across the room and crashing into the rear wall. She held him pinned there, only the finesse of her well-practiced ability keeping her from crushing the life out of him.

"Holy shit," Justice said with impressed awe.

"I didn't know she could do that," Ender whispered none too softly to the pilot.

"It's news to me too."

Ravenna didn't notice the byplay. She was focused on the man trapped against her living room wall. "You would have killed Bronse and every person in this house to get what you wanted," she pointed out. "But know this. One word from me and Fallon could erase your mind of everything you know yourself to be. He could steal it all away, leave you as numb and stupid as a newborn baby. It would serve you right."

"Rave . . . ," Fallon said with obvious discomfort.

"Don't worry," she absently calmed him, though it was clear that the tenderhearted Ravenna was nowhere to be found in that moment. "I'll let him remain whole. For now." She turned to glare at her victim. "But if you make so much as a single sound, blink so much as a crooked eye, he'll wipe you clean. Do you understand me?"

Easley nodded, sheer terror etched deep into his every feature.

Just like that, she shut her power off and let him come crashing down to the floor in a limp, shuddering heap. Ender didn't need direction from her or from Bronse to go up to the soldier and begin to tie him up. But Ravenna wasn't through. She turned to Vivienne.

"Scramble him."

Vivienne was used to obeying every order that Ravenna gave, so she didn't hesitate to move forward.

"Wait!" Bronse stepped into her path, looking at Ravenna and trying to find the woman he knew in the cold masque that her face wore. "What does that mean?"

"The brain is nothing but electrical impulses," Vivi said. "I control anything and everything that works with a current. If I scramble him, it means I send his whole brain out of whack. It lasts a few days. Basically makes him harmless."

"If Fallon can erase memories and thoughts, why not simply erase what he knows about his mission?" Lasher asked. "Then nothing will be at risk."

"Fallon cannot control it like that. Erasure happens in huge gaps, not specific details," Ravenna explained. "Perhaps one day, when he's older and stronger, it will be different, but for now it's our limitation. Consider it an all or nothing option."

"It's not an option I care for," Bronse said firmly. "Scrambling is more temporary and less harmful. Right, Vivi?"

"Right."

"You know there's a good chance that the IM will throw your ass in jail if you take the Chosen Ones off the station," Masin reminded his friend as he saw the inevitable washing up on the group.

Bronse thought about it for a long serious moment.

"Only if we fail," he said.

"Bronse, they're trusting us to take care of these people. If you break that trust, you risk everything for all of us. Aren't you at least going to ask us what we want to do?"

"Fine. You all can stay behind and I'll go alone with Ravenna. Clearly she can kick ass all over the place just fine by herself."

"Enough! Get your head out of your ass, Chapel!" Lasher barked at his commander. "Can't you see that she's not right?" He gestured to Ravenna and her dispassionate demeanor. "Don't let this get out of control when you can still do it the right way!"

"It's the telekinesis," Kith spoke up at last. "It takes a huge part of her to use it, and it leaves behind a residual chemical in her brain. Almost like a drug. It cuts away at her ability to feel emotions and make moral choices."

"Stop talking about me like I'm not standing right here!" Ravenna lashed out at her brother.

"Is it true?" Bronse demanded of her. "Is that what's happening to you?"

"I want JuJuren! I want this threat to your life over with! Isn't that moral enough for you?" she demanded.

Bronse walked up to her, never even hesitating in spite of what he had seen her do. He didn't know much about her powers, but he did know Ravenna. He knew that this flat affect laced liberally with bursts of rage was nothing like her.

He reached to touch her, ignoring her when she tried to shake him off. Slowly he pulled her into his embrace, hugging her resistant body close as he looked around the room at the others and tried to think more calmly.

"Let's just think a minute," he told himself as well as the others.

"There's always Chaser," Lasher suggested.

Chaser. He was with the justice department and he was someone Bronse could trust. He could call him and have him sit on the assassin without letting Spec Ops know there had been an intruder. But then what? Ju-Juren would just send someone else, and right now he had information that could let him catch Bronse once and for all.

"Chaser can connect with tactical and Spec Ops," Bronse said suddenly. "They can create a mission together. We can get them to assign us a real mission." He found himself talking to Ravenna, looking down into her immobile face. "We can get them to officially send us and the Chosen Ones out after JuJuren."

"No. They won't let us go when we're so new," she said. "I won't let you take this chance away from me. I want him gone."

"It's the perfect test run," Bronse argued. "We don't even need any special powers or abilities to get him at this point. This team could take down JuJuren doing what it has always done long before you all came into the picture. If we get Chaser to create this mission and design it specifically for us, then we won't be burning any bridges here and we'll still get what we want."

"No. They'll just take you away. They'll separate us." Finally emotion crept into her voice, her despair creasing across her face as she reached out to touch his bare chest with shaking fingertips. The tremors were like something he would expect to see on someone withdrawing from a drug. Now he could see why she hadn't wanted to use her powers to save herself. With such a strong chemical flooding her brain, interfering with her judgment of right and wrong, she could spiral into committing any number of acts that went against everything she believed in.

"We won't let that happen. Even if it takes using Devan to charm them into thinking our way, that's what we'll do," Bronse said softly. "But let's get Chaser to try first. He's much more convincing and much better placed than you might think. But we have to do this quickly. The minute JuJuren realizes he failed, he's going to bolt. We have to call Chaser now."

"And they'd put together an operation that fast?" she asked doubtfully. "They won't let JuJuren get away?"

"Have faith," Bronse told her, leaning in to kiss her cheek. "There's a reason why I've thought that the IM was the best of the best. Let me prove it to you."

"And if you can't? If it doesn't work?" she said doubtfully.

"It will work," Lasher spoke up. "Instead of letting this incident tear us all apart, we'll make it work in our favor and prove how cohesive we can really be. Granted, I'd rather you all went through all of your training before taking you out on a mission, but we've already proven we can work together. We'll go in and do our thing, and you guys can come along as a sort of safety net. We'll have you there to track and catch JuJuren if he somehow manages to get away from the initial action."

"The only thing is, the kids will have to stay home," said Bronse.

"I know that," Ravenna said quietly, searching his face, then Lasher's. "Okay," she said at last. "I'll trust you."

CHAPTER
FOURTEEN

"It's irresponsible to send them out on a mission when they haven't even been trained," Greays was saying, his aged face creased with disapproval. "What are you thinking, Abingdon?"

"I'm thinking we have one of our own out there turned against us. This new source that dropped in my lap last night is as fresh as they get. Last night he infiltrated this station with orders to kill one of us." Chase very smoothly omitted saying who the target had been. "If JuJuren can still get that close inside of this outfit, then he's even more of a danger than we first thought. He has a lot of top-secret information in his head, and he's going to start using it if we give him half a chance. With my new intel I know exactly where he is. All I need is the best of the best to extract and bring him back here, where he won't do any more harm. That means involving Bronse and his crew."

"There are other ETF teams," Greays argued. "I need Bronse's crew here protecting our assets."

"Chapel's crew is the best, as I said. But if we let them take Kith, Ravenna, and Vivienne with them, it will be the first practical application of the Chosen Ones in the field. It will go a long way to proving just how powerful an asset they'll be."

"And if we put them out there too soon, they could fail and prove just the opposite," the other admiral balked.

"Are you saying you're afraid the Chosen Ones won't succeed in the field?" Chaser asked archly, leading the other man into a well-laid trap.

"Ridiculous! You've seen the testing. These people will be unstoppable one day."

"There's no such thing," Abingdon argued. "They all have enough weaknesses in one way or another to make defeat possible. Hell, Fallon gets a migraine just about every time he uses his ability. Ophelia grows frail and weak if she overextends herself. Ravenna is strong, but her visions can be just vague enough at times to cause confusion and trouble."

"If you think they're so inferior, then why are you trying to send them out on a mission?"

"Because they'll be going with ETF. They'll be out there with Chapel. And they'll be there just as backup. It's not like I want them front and center doing infiltration and capture. I just need Kith and Fallon to monitor the thoughts and emotions of the target, and I need Vivienne to short out any security that JuJuren might have rigged up around himself. Ravenna obviously is self-explanatory."

"Fallon is only seventeen years old. Kith's not much older. Are you sure you want kids out there?"

Chaser smiled. It was the break in total resistance that he had been waiting for from Greays. Once the other man got that contemplative tone in his voice, Chaser knew he'd gone from full against the idea to starting to work the logistics. Bronse, Chaser thought with a small smile, was going to owe him big-time for this. Not that he was putting his neck on the line or anything. Liaising and helping to create missions like this one was part of his job, part of how he brought criminals in the IM and elsewhere to justice. And to be frank, he wanted to get his hands on the corrupting influence of JuJuren just as much as Bronse did. The former admiral was like a poison in what was, at heart, a good outfit. They had to stop him before it went any further. They had to stop him before Chapel's luck ran out and one of the bastard's assassination attempts finally hit the mark.

Chaser for one was really damn curious about why Ju-Juren had a hard-on for his friend, and he knew that Bronse wanted to know the same thing. Maybe it wasn't a good idea to send in someone who had such a personal stake in seeing the admiral brought in, but, on the other hand, no one would work harder toward the goal than Bronse. If he didn't come home with JuJuren or JuJuren's body, he'd send in his resignation.

"Time's a wasting, Admiral," Chaser coaxed Greays. "I need a decision."

"You can have Ravenna, Fallon, and Vivienne," Greays relented at last. "Kith isn't to be trusted yet. He's too volatile and temperamental. I'll reconsider after he has some discipline under his belt."

Like any good negotiator, Abingdon knew when to back off.

"Deal."

"This is bullshit!" Kith exploded, his face mottling with his outrage. "What the hell am I doing in this place if they won't let me do things like this?"

"You're going to train and earn some trust, so the next time they will let you do it," Bronse shot back, not letting Ravenna have the chance to soft-touch the spoiled young man. "You've done nothing but fight and gripe and act like a sullen son of a bitch in the three weeks you've been here. The only thing you've proven to the brass is just how immature you are and how much you can't be trusted to listen and follow instructions. They're taking a huge risk sending us after JuJuren; they aren't going to compound that risk by sending you with us."

Kith's hands fisted, the muscles in his jaws jumping as

he fought the urge to tell off Bronse, or yell and scream or whatever it was he was feeling. But he did none of it. For the first time since the commander had known the kid, he managed to control himself and back down. Bronse actually saw a glimmer of hope for the young man with whom he faced off.

He could feel Ravenna's absolute shock as she watched her brother wordlessly back away from the argument, watched him accept the consequences of his actions. Kith's feelings about Bronse had always been clear, but now he was listening to the other man and feeling the impact of his words. Ravenna tasted a dose of the same hope that Bronse was experiencing.

"I just wanted to help," Kith said. But all the punch had left his words, if not the whole of his body language.

"And you will. I think that, one day, with a lot of hard work and training, you'll be a hell of a soldier, Kith. You're proficient in martial arts already, and your ability to read intention from emotion is truly invaluable. If you keep working in the right direction, you'll be the best damn thing the Interplanetary Militia has seen in a long time. Better even than me."

Kith was utterly shocked by the admission, and the expression on his face was just shy of comical. Despite all of the younger man's bluster and unfocused temper, he'd come to appreciate just how skilled and impressive Bronse Chapel really was. To be told that he could be even better than that made a significant impact.

It was all Ravenna could do to keep from kissing Bronse right there in the open where everyone could see. But it certainly would be counterproductive to their goal if she were to expose her and Bronse's relationship right then, so she controlled herself with a silent, steady exhale of breath.

"I'll need you to keep a close eye on the others," Ravenna told her brother. "They'll be vulnerable without the team to watch over them. And I'm not talking about guarding their lives, either." She stepped up to him and made certain that he was meeting her eyes. "You need to keep Ophelia from using her abilities in the open, and you need to make certain that Devan isn't scared without us. Also, you can't let Spec Ops overwork them. There's no telling how long this will take, and someone needs to keep watch."

"But Domino is older," Kith said with confusion, the suspicion in his voice telling her that he thought she was humoring him.

"Domino is focused on Domino. He's more fixated on looking out for himself than he would be looking out for others. Ophelia is your sister, and I know you care about Devan, so I trust you to do right by them."

Ravenna made a mental apology to Domino for selling him short, but giving Kith this kind of responsibility in reward for controlling himself was essential to conditioning out the selfish streak that had been so prevalent in his makeup of late.

"All right," Kith said carefully. Then he squared his shoulders and nodded. "All right. I'll look out for them. You can count on me."

"Are you sure?" Ravenna pressed, knowing she had to add just a touch of doubt if she wanted him to believe her.

"Yes, of course. I'll show you that you can trust me."

Ravenna smiled at him and reached out to squeeze his hand. "I know I can." Then she turned her attention back to Bronse. "So how will we do this?"

First, we'll approach through the back of the building. Minimal exposure. Trick will hack in from the kitchens and get the room number from the guest book.

"Guys, we have a problem," Trick said softly as he sat crouched in a dark corner of the kitchen prep area, his handheld VidPad plugged into the interface port around the corner.

"You couldn't hack in?" The surprise in Lasher's voice was more than evident.

"No, that's not it." Trick double-checked his data. "JuJuren has bought out every room on his floor with his cover name's accounts. What does one man need with a whole floor of rooms?"

"Privacy?" Ender suggested.

"More like troops," Bronse realized.

Lasher, Ravenna, and I will enter the hotel straight on, as if we were guests.

"This sucks," Lasher murmured through his microphone as he sat himself down across from the elevators and crossed his legs, as if he wasn't keeping his eyes trained on the lifts and the lobby entrances all at the same time. His coat hid the laser pistol on his hip as well as the collapsible rifle slung against his spine.

He glanced over at Ravenna and Bronse just as she wound her arms around his neck and whispered to him as if they were sharing a lover's secret.

"How are we going to approach if he has a whole floor cordoned off?" she asked softly.

"Ender?"

"Yeah, Boss?"

"Position?"

Ender and Justice will be in full gear, landing a light craft on the roof as soon as the pad is clear. We'll come up from the ground and they'll drop down from above.

"Approaching the southwest corner of the roof. No sign of any guards or lookouts. Either he's really cocky or we're missing something." Ender reached the southern rail of the roof and looked down the long distance to the ground. The wind was high at that height, buffeting both soldiers strongly. "We're going to get knocked around up here," he warned Bronse. Rappelling down the side of the building would be tricky at best. With a high wind, it would be a fight.

"Copy that," Bronse said. He looked at Ravenna. "I want to have Fallon come in and ride the elevator past the twenty-third floor. I don't want him to stop on that floor, though, because they are bound to have lookouts and will see him as a threat. I just want him to ride past the floor and get as much of a read as he can from whoever is just outside the elevator door."

"How are you going to search a whole floor?" Rave asked.

If JuJuren is half the soldier he used to be, he has a corner room. They tend to have exits into two separate corridors, and the emergency stairs are located the shortest distance away.

"We need to search only four rooms," Trick said.

"That's three too many," Bronse retorted. "We have to figure out which one he's in. That's why I need Fallon."

"I won't send him alone," Rave warned him.

"I'll ride the elevator with him," Lasher spoke up.

"No. It should be me," Ravenna argued. "JuJuren knows your faces. He doesn't know mine. If something happens and we run into someone accidentally, we're not the ones they'll be looking for. And you know I can protect Fallon if need be."

Bronse knew it was the truth, but he didn't like the idea of the price she had to pay for using her telekinesis. This was too volatile a situation for her to start losing judgment. But he knew she was right. If JuJuren was wise, he'd have shown Bronse's face to every single man working for him. With so many people milling in and out of the hotel, the longer the crew stayed there, even in the lobby, the higher the risk of them getting made. Bronse had to be satisfied, for the moment, that with teams above and below the former admiral, he would run into trouble either way if he tried to escape.

*Fallon and Vivienne will wait in the van in the street.
We won't use them unless absolutely necessary.*

"Fallon, are you copying all of this?" Bronse asked.

"He's already on his way in," Vivi's voice came in over
their earpieces.

Fallon walked through the front doors of the hotel,
spying Ravenna and Bronse instantly and walking right
over to them. They greeted each other at normal vol-
ume, Ravenna reaching to kiss his cheek as she might do
for any friend who suddenly appeared before her. Then
she and Fallon left Bronse behind and walked directly to
the elevators. There was no time for any instructions
other than the ones that were spoken into their ears as
they crossed the expansive floor.

"Go in the lift and press the button for the twenty-
fourth and the twenty-second floors. That will slow you
down enough so Fallon should be able to grab something. If the elevator stops on the twenty-third floor for
any reason, you just remember to act like any other passenger and then get off on the twenty-fourth floor. Otherwise, just ride the lift back down to the lobby."

"Got it," Ravenna said softly as the lift doors opened
to let off a slew of hotel guests. She walked into the elevator and pressed the button for the twenty-second
floor. Fallon pressed the twenty-fourth floor button.

Fallon took a deep breath and closed his eyes, trying
to clear his mind for what promised to be a very difficult
trick. He would start to be able to get into the minds of
the people on the twenty-third floor from as much as a
floor away, but no matter how slow they made the elevator go, it would still be a random grab for minds that
might or might not be there.

The floors came racing up, and the elevator stopped at
twenty-two. No one came or went, and the passengers
in the car grumbled at the delay. Then the doors closed
and the lift moved on. Ravenna was so focused on

watching Fallon concentrate that she didn't realize that the elevator had stopped again until Fallon's eyes flew open with an expression of utter fear dilating them.

Ravenna looked up to see the former admiral they were chasing as he stepped onto the lift. He was about Bronse's height but clearly much older. A distinguished older. His close-cut white hair was as neat as every stitch of clothing he wore. He held one hand in the other and turned to calmly face the front of the lift. He was accompanied by two large and very obviously armed men. Bodyguards.

Ravenna couldn't believe this was happening. She was standing right behind the man who had tried on at least three occasions to kill Bronse. This monster had sent a killer into her home, a beast with a gun who would have killed her and an innocent child as well as Bronse—and for what? For what possible reason?

She wanted to grab him and demand the answers. She wanted to use her mind and throw the lot of them down the elevator shaft and be done with them once and for all. Her anger was so hot and so consuming that she had to struggle to control herself. Especially because Fallon was there, white as a sheet, afraid for his life and hers.

No doubt afraid for Bronse's and Lasher's lives as well. The minute JuJuren stepped out of the elevator and into the lobby, the risk of his identifying Bronse and Lasher was high and dangerous. The armed men he had with him didn't look like the type to care about their targets. Laser fire would start to fly, and innocent people would get hurt.

But Rave couldn't speak to warn the men. JuJuren was practically on top of her and would hear her.

"Rave? What's going on?" Bronse asked in her ear for what she realized was the second time. "Ravenna? Answer me, damn it."

"Excuse me, do you have the time?" she blurted out

suddenly, touching the former admiral on his sleeve to get his attention. It earned her dirty looks from the guards, but JuJuren lifted a hand to call them off.

"It's just about half cycle," JuJuren replied, looking her over slowly and carefully. Ravenna suppressed a chill as she realized that it was a very male appraisal. She could imagine the thoughts going through JuJuren's head based on Fallon's angry expression alone.

"Something's wrong, she's not answering," she heard Bronse direct to the team.

"But she's clearly not in trouble," Lasher returned.

"Or in trouble but can't speak up about it," said Bronse. "Damn it, someone got on the elevator with them!"

She loved him. Oh, what an insane moment to realize it, but Ravenna knew in that moment of uncanny insight that she was simply mad about Bronse Chapel. Everything about him thrilled her, from the sublime to the sexual, and right now it was the keenness of his intellect that she truly adored. With a passion. Her relief that he understood was profound, even as her epiphany about what she felt for him was shockingly overwhelming. She'd never been in a relationship before, never mind found herself in love. And she knew there were dozens of complications involved, and that she didn't have the luxury of thinking about a single one of them in that moment.

"You're not from Tari, are you?" JuJuren asked as he eyed her strange coloring and exotic features. Tarins were much more rugged, and a lot less likely to be as poised and graceful as she came across even when she was standing in a resting stance.

"Shit! That's JuJuren!" she heard Bronse hiss in her ear.

"No. I'm from Ebbany," she said with as much casual ease as she could muster. She glanced at the indicator and saw the floor numbers rapidly dwindling as the elevator headed for the lobby. They should have gotten off on the twenty-fourth floor as instructed, but she and Fallon had been taken completely off guard by JuJuren's sudden appearance.

"A hard place to grow up. But I like it there," JuJuren mentioned.

"It's a beautiful and dangerous world," she replied.

His smile was smug, but his eyes had a glint of temper in them. "Not dangerous enough," he muttered.

He had no idea that she understood the reference. Nor did she care. All she wanted to know was what she and Fallon were going to do.

"What floor are they going to?" Bronse demanded.

Ravenna turned to Fallon with a smile. "How about that lobby downstairs? Have you ever seen anything so big in your life?"

Fallon mutely shook his head, knowing the remark wasn't meant for him.

"Vivi! Get your ass in here double time!" said Bronse.

Through his earpiece Bronse could hear the sound of someone fumbling, and then he saw Vivi running and breathing heavily as she raced into the lobby.

Bronse grabbed her by her arm and led her to the elevators.

"Stop the elevators. Right now. We need to buy some time."

Vivi reached out and pressed the call button, closing her eyes as she wrapped her power around all the thousands of electrical impulses and currents in the building that were connected to that one single point. Nervous and panicked as she was, her finesse went straight out the window, and the entire hotel went suddenly black.

The elevator slammed to a halt, jolting everyone inside and making two of the passengers cry out. Now Fallon and Rave were trapped in an elevator with two, possibly three armed men and a murdering son of a bitch besides.

"Power outage," one of the bodyguards said with a shrug. "Should come back soon."

"Strange, the emergency lights aren't on," JuJuren said. Rave didn't need Fallon to grab her hand to be made aware of the suspicion lacing JuJuren's voice.

"First floor! First floor!" Bronse commanded into his mike as he yanked Vivi after him and headed for the stairs. "Trick, the minute the electricity comes back on, you override the elevators. Make the one that Rave is on stop at the first floor. I won't do this with a crowd behind me. We're going to have zero body count. You got that?"

"Copy that," Ender and Justice chimed in.

"Pulling the program up now. How much time before the electricity comes back on?" Trick demanded.

"It's recharging as we speak," Vivi said breathlessly.

Bronse ran up the stairs two and three at a time, Lasher and Vivi hot on his heels as the men both drew their weapons and kept them low against their bodies. The stairwell was pitch-black, but they used the rails to guide them straight to the door to the first floor. Once there, Bronse pulled Vivi to a halt.

"Now, you stay right here and do not move," he ordered her, gently moving her into a corner surrounded by laser-proof stone walls and metal. Vivi nodded enthusiastically, having no desire to do anything but stay way out of trouble. By the same turn, Bronse needed her close at hand in case he needed one more delay if Trick couldn't override the elevator in time.

Bronse and Lasher left Vivi there just as fluorescent lights flickered on one by one, starting with the emergency lighting.

There was a collective sigh of relief in the elevator when they came on and then a common shout as a sudden surge in power sent the lift jolting back into motion. Out of the corner of her eye, Rave saw the first-floor button suddenly light up as if an invisible hand had pushed it. Trick had worked his magic and now the elevator would stop and there would be a confrontation on the first floor instead of in the lobby. The only problem was the other people in the lift; Fallon and Rave were standing right behind their would-be target.

Ravenna stood ready.

"Ravenna, you let us handle this, you hear me?" Bronse ordered over the earpiece. "I don't want you using your telekinesis unless you absolutely have no choice. The last thing I need is three armed men and a woman with no moral compass to boot. You got it?"

There was no way she could reply and Bronse knew it, but he sensed she'd heard him loud and clear. He and Lasher stood to the sides of the elevator doors, waiting for the lift to arrive and the doors to fully open before they would drop on JuJuren and his men.

"We're coming to you, Commander," Ender said in staccato breaths. He and Justice had raced across the roof to the access door and were now running flat out down twenty-nine flights of stairs.

Ding.

The doors to the elevator opened, and Bronse and Lasher leapt forward in tandem, each pointing a gun in the face of the very startled admiral.

"Stay very still," Bronse warned the men as he eyed them down his sights. He was forced to ease forward, to put a foot in the way of the doors so they wouldn't shut and let their quarry escape.

It was hard to stare at the face of the man who had tried so hard to kill him yet somehow manage to keep from pulling the trigger. But he did it just the same, looking forward to JuJuren's long, hard road to justice. Bronse wanted to see Rave, to pull her out from behind the men, but the squirrelly and halfhearted way the men raised their open hands toward him was making him nervous. Instinct told him that these were desperate men about to try desperate measures to get free. But first he wanted them out of the elevator and away from Fallon and Ravenna.

"Come on. Out," he said, nodding to the two frightened passengers to JuJuren's right. "Now run away." They did, not bothering to look back. "Stop twitching," he warned the bodyguard on the right, "and get your fucking hands in the air where I can see them."

The guard obeyed. But the three men kept sharing shifting looks, which gave Bronse a sick feeling in his intuitive gut.

"Chapel," JuJuren drawled suddenly, "you've been nothing but a pain in my ass since the day I met you. You're lucky your promotions weren't up to me or you'd still be a half-baked sergeant somewhere in grunt land."

"I'm lucky a lot of things weren't up to you," Bronse retorted sharply. "Now step out of the elevator." Frankly, he didn't give a damn about the two guards. But the last thing he needed was hired guns running loose on JuJuren's side. And where the hell were Justice and Ender?

"You know," JuJuren said slowly as he took a step in the slowest of strides, "it's really hard to believe that some stupid grunt like you was responsible for fucking up my whole life."

"Oh, I think you took care of that all on your own," Bronse replied as he stepped back away from JuJuren as far as he could while still keeping the elevator doors ajar. He handed off the covering of JuJuren to Lasher and then turned back to focus on the men in the elevator. Now that JuJuren was out, he could see Ravenna standing still and quiet against the back wall of the lift, her body shielding Fallon's protectively. But the last thing he wanted to do was let the armed men know that he had people he cared about within their reach. "Now you." He indicated the bigger of the two. Unfortunately, keeping his attention in the elevator meant turning his back on Lasher and his prisoner.

"I want to know how someone as dumb as you managed to figure out what I was doing."

Bronse unwittingly rose to the bait, but not the way JuJuren intended.

"And I want to know what I did that makes you want to kill me so badly." Bronse took his eyes off his target for one split second to look back at the admiral, and that was all it took.

The beefier of the two guards reached out to grab Ravenna by the throat, nearly yanking her off her feet as he dragged her body across his front, protecting himself with her.

Pandemonium broke loose in the form of yells and shouts. A round of swearing bolted through them and then the anticipated threat.

"You drop those guns or I'll break her fucking neck like the little delicate twig it is." The guard yanked back hard on Rave, dragging her up his chest and off her feet until she gagged beneath his strangling hand.

"Hey!" Bronse could barely think even as he shouted the word at the guard. "If you hurt her, I swear I'll blow your head off!"

"If you don't drop those guns, I'll rip off hers."

Ravenna was choking, trying to suck in what little air she could, her feet flailing almost a foot from the floor by then. She knew she didn't have time to waste. Lasher and Bronse would never be able to choose between her life and taking JuJuren to justice. They would eventually concede to his demands and let him go—an idea she simply could not stomach. She wasn't going to let this golden opportunity slip away, and she wouldn't let anyone get hurt. But if she was going to act, she had to do it now. She couldn't afford to waste time and precious oxygen debating the matter.

With a flicker of her lashes, she met Bronse's eyes. She could see the paralyzing fear that laced their periwinkle depths, and with it she could see so much more. She could see everything he was feeling for her, right out in the open where JuJuren could see it too.

"Let her go!"

"Don't let her go," JuJuren countered hastily. "He cares about her. She's probably one of his teammates. You want her back, Chapel? All you have to do is drop your guns. Otherwise I'll tell him to rip her head off!"

"Rave," Bronse rasped, his hands around his weapon starting to shake as adrenaline coursed through his body.

Ravenna knew what he wanted from her. It was the same thing she'd already been thinking.

Her mind hit the interior of the elevator like a bomb striking at ground zero. The percussive force of the explosion sent both guards flying apart, one slamming into the left wall, the other to the right. At the same time, JuJuren was ripped off his feet. His body slammed into the floor as if he'd been tackled by a powerful, invisible player. Ravenna fell to the floor on her palms and knees, and she tried to breathe and focus on the men she held in place all at the same time. Then she got to her feet and walked out of the elevator until she was standing over JuJuren. The two guards were yanked out of the elevator with her, like kites tagging along on invisible strings that were somehow tethered to her body. They struggled against the unseen force that held them, but they couldn't move so much as an eyelash with her holding on to them.

"We have them, Rave. Let them down." Bronse had

his weapon trained on the guards as Rave saw Ender and Justice burst out of the stairwell at the end of the hall.

"Stop," Rave said.

And they did. Everyone around her found themselves suddenly frozen in place. Mid-step, mid-run, mid-blink— every last action was seized in the power of her extraordinary mind. She walked up to Bronse, whose eyes were wide with the understanding that she had lashed him in place along with the criminals he was trying to apprehend. He didn't understand it until she reached to take his weapon.

"Ravenna, no!" he croaked out of his nearly paralyzed throat.

But there was nothing he could do to stop her. It was child's play for her to make him hand her the weapon, his fingers peeling back away from the grip and trigger just as easily as she would peel a piece of fruit. The gun was in her hand now as she walked up to JuJuren.

The sweep of a finger lifted him from the ground and held him suspended in the air above her in a messiah position, the dangling helplessness of his body only accentuated by the shock and fearful understanding that washed over his face. She pointed the weapon at him. If she could have felt satisfaction right then, she would have smiled with it.

"You're a curse on my family as much as you were a blessing. If not for you, Bronse and I would never have met. Does that mean I have to be grateful to such a hateful creature?" She shook her head. "But what I know is what Bronse refuses to see and understand. You are relentless. Whatever your reasons are for hunting him down, you are the kind of hunter who will never stop. Nothing will ever get in your way. That includes military prison."

"Rave, no!"

"Ravenna, stop!"

The shouts and demands of her teammates fell on deaf ears. All of her attention and focus was on JuJuren.

"You think you have the right to make these choices. But you don't. Evil people don't have the right to destroy good people. I won't let you destroy Bronse."

Rave reached out and held the muzzle of the weapon directly against the former admiral's chest, right over his heart.

"Are you saying you have the right to say if I live or die?" JuJuren demanded in a panic. "That makes you as bad as I am."

"No, it doesn't. You see, normally I would care very much about deciding to take the life of another, but because you forced me to take control like this, I no longer give a damn. I could take your life and not feel a moment's guilt. It will merely be a means to an end."

"Until the chemical in your brain fades away, Ravenna," Bronse said in rapid gasps of breath, needing badly to get through to her before she did something she would always regret. Now he could very much see why she did not and could not use this telekinesis power of hers. The complete obliteration of her moral standards had been wickedly quick, almost violent. But when she awakened from the numbing effect on her emotions, it would be something quite different. His peaceful, gentle Ravenna would be crushed and devastated. She would be ashamed of what she had done and would think herself as evil as the man she now stood before. "When the chemical in your brain goes away, you will regret what you have done here today. You'll be hurting yourself, the children, and everything you care about."

"But I'm not making this choice in anger," she argued calmly. "The dispassion works both ways, Bronse. It makes my motives in doing this really quite pure. More a matter of cause and effect than anything else. He has caused damage and pain. The effect should be an action that puts an end to that."

"It doesn't work that way," he warned her, "and somewhere in your head you know that. You know that you can't make summary judgment. You don't have the right! You may not even have all the information you need to make a proper decision."

"But I have his own admission of guilt." She gave a little shrug. "The solution is obvious."

"Are you sure?" he asked her, trying for all he was worth to find the angle he needed to make her see reason. How was he supposed to influence a mind void of all guilt, all conscience, all measurable emotion?

Logic. Logic was the only way. And it had to be sound logic at that. She was far too smart for tricks.

"What if he isn't the one behind everything?" Bronse posited. "Oh, I know he gave orders and he orchestrated specific crimes, but what if he's not the top of the chain? What if he gets his orders from someone else?"

"Then that person should be punished as well."

"But how will we know who that person is if you kill the only person with the answer?"

She hesitated, thinking for a moment. But only a moment. "There will be evidence. We will find out in other ways."

"Are you really willing to take that chance? What if you're risking other lives by making that choice so unilaterally?" Bronse prayed that there was enough of a conscience in her that she would care about the other lives.

"Fallon, you will read his mind and make certain that there are no others above him," she commanded the Chosen One at her back.

"No, Rave, I won't."

Bronse could have kissed him. Fallon was devoted to Rave. He did whatever she asked. For him to tell her "no" had to be against everything in his nature.

"Why not?" she wanted to know, the curious tilt to her head making her seem so innocent in such a deeply macabre way.

"Because I won't help you do something that's wrong. Something *you* taught me was wrong. Because Bronse is right. As soon as you stop expending yourself, all of your conscience and guilt will return, and it will destroy you to know you'd done something so wrong. I won't be a part of that. I don't care how much this man deserves it, Rave."

"Ravenna, let us go. We have enough people to keep control of the situation," Bronse told her. "Let us do our job and let the penal system do theirs. And if you still feel like this later, if you still feel that he deserves to die like this, then you can always go back and do it. You know you're more powerful than all of us put together. You can do anything you want."

"That includes killing him now," she pointed out.

"You could," he agreed. "But don't. I don't want you to do it now. I want you to let us go so we can take these men off your hands."

"And why should I do what you want?" she genuinely wanted to know. It was almost like talking to a child, except a child didn't have the knowledge that she did, and a child was easier to reason with than she was right then.

"Because . . . because at any other time, you love me and respect me enough to know when I'm right about something. Just like I love you so much that I won't let you do this."

The gun lowered, and there was finally the registration of a fleeting emotion. It was surprise.

"What did you say?" she asked, her hand rubbing at her temple. Her head was starting to hurt. She didn't realize she was overextending herself with every minute she stood there holding them all at bay. "You love me?"

"Yes. Very much. It's something I've never felt before. I don't think you have, either. But it's important to us both, isn't it?"

"That . . . that has nothing to do with this," she insisted, turning the weapon back up toward JuJuren.

"Yes, it does. Because I'm going to find it really hard to love someone who would kill a man in cold blood, Ravenna. Think about it. You know me."

"Yes," she said hesitantly, "you always do the right thing. You wouldn't kill without cause. But I have cause. What he does is wrong."

"There are other ways to punish him for those wrongs. Take away his freedom. Take away his power. There are other ways. Ways that won't cause damage between me and you."

The weapon lowered again, and this time two sets of fingertips went to massage her temples. As he watched, small blood vessels were bursting in the whites of her eyes. She was going to burn herself out or have a stroke if she didn't let up.

"That pain means you're in danger," he warned her. "You're going to mess up your brain if you keep this up. Let us go right now, Ravenna. Right now!"

"Ravenna, listen to him," Fallon spoke up. "He's right. You can see he cares about you. You're going to get hurt if you don't listen to him."

Ravenna's chocolate dark eyes met Bronse's, the puzzlement in her gaze growing.

"Okay," she said at last.

She let go of her hold on the team so suddenly that they

had to fight to keep their feet. Bronse grabbed the laser pistol from her, then jerked her against him, his strong body holding hers as she grew increasingly unsteady.

"Now," he murmured softly into her hair, "let go of the others."

He would never know if she let go because she was listening to him or because she passed out in the very next instant.

CHAPTER
FIFTEEN

Bronse was pacing outside of the infirmary room when Admiral Greays came up on him, his gait officious and his expression grimly stern.

"What happened?" he demanded.

"I don't know," Bronse said honestly. "She was using her power and just collapsed."

"Damn. Sounds like you were right about being careful not to break her. We've been working them all too hard."

Bronse wasn't about to disabuse the admiral of his theory. Whether or not it was the cause of Ravenna's collapse, it was the truth. All of the Chosen Ones had been worked beyond their capacity. It may very well have had a hand in Ravenna's collapse. But Bronse didn't kid himself about the more serious cause of it. The telekinetic power she wielded was dangerous and poisonous. The side effects of its use were not worth even the smallest benefit it might provide. But others might not see it that way, so it was best they never know about it.

That was why he had been forced to ask Fallon to erase the memories of the men they had captured. Just the information in JuJuren's hands alone was a dangerous prospect, never mind the other two prisoners who could blab it out to anyone who'd listen. Rave's secret would stay a secret, and he no longer felt any anger and betrayal against her for keeping it to herself. He just hoped like hell that she could recover from this last display of it. What was more, he hoped she never had cause to use it again. As long as he was alive and breathing in the universe, he would see to it that she never did.

If only she survived this.

It didn't even matter to him that Fallon's memory rip had probably cost them valuable information that would lead to other names of other people who might be party to JuJuren's crimes. It didn't matter that he would never know why he'd been singled out for death by the man. All that mattered was that Rave would be all right. The Chosen Ones needed her. The Interplanetary Militia needed her. But more than all of that, he needed her.

He hadn't been lying or telling stories to get his way when he had told her that he loved her. And it meant everything to him that in a mind where all conscience had been erased, that one statement had been able to take hold of her. It meant that it was important to her and that she felt the same way. He didn't need to hear her say it to him. Just that single moment of hesitation had told him everything.

"Well, your mission was a success," said Greays. "JuJuren is pretending he doesn't know what we're talking about, but we don't need a confession. We have more than enough evidence to see him court-martialed. I'm glad you got him. He was an ugly bruise on the good name of this militia."

"Thank you, sir," Bronse replied absently, pausing in his frenetic pacing to try to see past the hazed-over glass of Rave's treatment room. They wouldn't let him in there. They wouldn't come out to talk to him until they knew for certain whether or not her brain was permanently damaged. They'd told him she could have collapsed from a stroke. Or a lot of strokes. They wouldn't know until the scans were done.

He felt like he was going to drown. Every minute was clawing the breath out of his body. He didn't care what he had to do, he was going to see that they made her better. He would force them to fix her. Or he would do it himself.

"You're not as smart as you think you are, you know," Greays said to him.

Bronse stopped short and stared at the admiral as Greays folded his arms over his chest and leaned back against the wall. "Sir?" was all Bronse could think to say. Had they found out? Did they know what Ravenna could do? Vivienne had scrambled all the security footage with just the touch of a hand, and there had been no other witnesses. Had the erasure not been enough? Had JuJuren said something?

"Oh, you're very careful not to show it," Greays mused, "but there are times when you can't hide it no matter how hard you try." The admiral cocked half a smile at Bronse's blank stare. "The girl and you, Commander. You've got that kind of energy where you can touch each other without touching each other. The closer you get, the stronger the attraction. Why do you think I put you and Ravenna in housing together? It's less of a distraction to have you close to each other than to have you separated."

"And . . . you don't object?" Bronse asked with surprise. "The way you treat her, I thought I'd end up in the brig for even thinking about touching her."

"Not that that stopped you."

"No, sir. Nothing would have stopped me," Bronse agreed.

"I don't approve of couples going out on-mission together."

"I understand, sir."

"But in this case I don't see how I have much choice. Only your team knows about the Chosen Ones, and that's the way it's going to stay. I don't need this becoming the worst-kept secret on the station."

"No, sir. We don't want that, either."

"Good. And if she makes it through this, I'll need to see some real dedication and professionalism from both of you or I *will* split you up."

"Admiral Greays," Bronse said, "if she makes it out of this, I'll give everyone anything they want."

As if on cue, the door behind Bronse opened and a senior-level medic came out of the room. He saw the drawn tension in the face of the man before him and quickly took pity on him.

"She's awake. Speech is normal and—" But he was already talking to an empty doorway. The doctor chuckled and turned to the admiral. "Motor function is a little sluggish but otherwise normal. She has a hell of a headache, and she's lucky she's not a vegetable. I don't know what went on in the field, but I've never seen a brain scan like that in my life. It was like she had hundreds of tiny strokes all at once all over her brain. How does that happen to a person?"

The admiral shrugged. "You're the doctor, you tell me."

Bronse walked into the room and saw two technicians fussing over Ravenna and the equipment they had monitoring her. She looked up to see him, her pretty eyes bloodshot and tired. The minute she saw him, tears welled up. He was by her side instantly, gathering her up in his arms and holding her against his chest as if he would never let her go.

"I love you too," she rasped out, her voice thick and so weary that it broke his heart to hear it. "Thank you. Thank you so much for stopping me."

"You stopped yourself, although I wasn't going to let you do anything you'd regret. You know I don't work that way. And I do love you. It's the damndest thing, something so alien to me in so many ways, and yet it came so naturally with you. Only with you." He pressed gentle kisses to her upturned face, then kissed her lips so gently that her numbed body could barely feel it. "You almost killed yourself, you know. I don't think I need to tell you to never do that again. I don't care how much you think you're helping. The price you pay is not worth it. You got me?"

"Okay," she sighed softly, burrowing her cheek into his chest. "Believe me, it's the last thing I ever want to do again."

"Can you give us the room?" he asked the technicians standing over her head. They seemed to hesitate. "I promise if she so much as blinks the wrong way, I'll call you back in."

"Just watch her speech. If she slurs, there's trouble."

The medics exited the room.

"Okay, we're alone now," he told her softly. "Which is good because I'm about to do the one thing I swore to myself I would never, ever do again in the whole of my life. I want you to know that, so you know just how important this is, okay? And I think I'm asking because you're a little out of it and I'm not above using dirty tricks."

"What is it?" she asked with a giggle.

"Will you join with me? Become my wife? I promise not to change a damn thing about myself and be exactly the same person you see sitting here today."

She laughed at him. "Good. Because I wouldn't want you any other way. Even if things change and we end up on separate missions all the time. I won't care as long as we come home to each other and my family."

"Our family is going to be huge," he promised her. "I have a lot of uncles and cousins. You have a boatload of Chosen Ones. Holidays are going to be enormous."

"I would really, really like that. But aren't you afraid of what the top brass will say about it?"

Bronse kissed her softly, then gave her a sheepish grin. "We weren't as clandestine as we thought we were. Greays knows. And he's fine with it as long as it doesn't interfere with our work."

"I think it will just make it better." She hugged him as tightly as she could. "I'm so glad I waited for you. Every moment of pain was well worth it. This was so worth it."

He smiled into her hair, but then he sighed. "Your brother hates me."

"My brother isn't the one you have to worry about. You just worry about making me happy. I'll take care of Kith."

"How can I make you happy?" he asked, his smile almost wolfish as he kissed her cheek, her jaw, and then the side of her neck.

"You really want to know?"

"Always."

"Get the medic. I have a bitch of headache."

"Damn. Not even joined yet and you're already using the headache excuse." He chuckled.

She slowly wrapped one hand around his neck and then laid the other over his heart.

"You better do it or I'm going to tell you your fortune and it won't be good."

"None of that," he said, grasping her hands and pulling them down to a safe place against his chest. "I don't need my fortune told. I already know exactly how lucky I am and how happy I'm going to be."

Read on for an excerpt from
SEDUCE ME IN FLAMES
by Jacquelyn Frank

Published by Ballantine Books

Her heart beat rapidly, her breath rasping in the back of her throat. What could it mean? What could he want? The same questions swirled around her head again and again as she strode through the palace hallways with an air of confidence she did not feel. There had never been a sense of confidence, a sense of security in her life. Even when her father had supposedly loved her, she had never felt that sense of cocooning comfort that a child was supposed to feel when in the presence of her protector.

She supposed his treatment of her these last years had proven her very intuitive, even at toddling age.

He had once professed a great love for her mother. There were those in her household who swore, to this day, that her mother had been the great love of his life. But then his eminence the emperor had tired of his favorite concubine. Some said it was because a newer, younger woman had caught his fancy. Others said her mother had overstepped herself with him one too many times, that she'd grown proud and arrogant, making the mistake of thinking that being the mother of his heir apparent made her as good as being empress.

Whatever the reason, Emperor Benit Tsu Allay had put down his common-law wife like a dog. Unafraid of the possible repercussions he might face at the hands of the Interplanetary Militia, he'd had her tried for treason, proclaiming her an enemy to his crown and a conspirator in a plot to have him killed. Her mother's trial had been a whirlwind of, some said, preponderously damning evidence, spurious accusations, and one of the cruelest and most horrific executions in the history of their realm. Then, before she could understand that her mother would never touch her again, hold her or hug her, she'd been declared fruit of a poisonous tree and packed off into the back of nowhere where she had been languishing ever since.

More or less.

She'd been called into his presence twice since her exile at the age of four. Once when she was twelve and once when she was fifteen. Both times he had hurled accusations of treason at her, accused her of knowingly plotting with his enemies to overthrow him and take his throne. However, lack of evidence, or, perhaps more likely, his unwillingness to slaughter a child, had spared her life . . . but not before she had spent over a year each time in his prisons.

Then there had been silence. After some time, news had filtered down to her through her more trusted attendants that the emperor had sired a male heir. Her brother. And her only living sibling. This decided lack of proliferation the emperor had blamed on his weak-blooded concubines, however with medical technology at such an advanced state that in vitro could have been performed at any time with any viable uterus, it was widely believed that Emperor Benit was the one with the problem. But Benit wasn't about to prove anyone right by having himself tested.

All of this swam through her mind in a ceaseless stream as she was led by a cadre of guards through the grand halls of Blossom Palace, the emperor's most favored of his seven residences. The astounding opulence of just the corridors would take one's breath away. She could still remember playing in these halls, running the maze-like lengths day after day . . . her rich little gowns inlaid with Delran platinum, her bed so big and soft she had needed help getting in and out of it and she could lay all six of her attendants on either side of herself comfortably.

Now, her bed was narrow and serviceable, the sheets a bit worn in places. She had only two personal attendants (one of which was, she believed, her father's spy) and a household totaling four, when the maid and cook were taken into account. Her gown was threadbare at the seams, her father having neglected her household stipend, and when he did remember to pay her servants, there was nothing left over for new clothes. She balanced the books herself since, years earlier, she had been forced to let her secretary go. As it stood, her servants stayed on because of their love of her, because they certainly did not stay for the value of the living she could provide.

Still, it was a damn sight better than the cold, bleak dampness of the emperor's prisons.

The fact of the matter was, she was the emperor's daughter whether he wanted to acknowledge that or not. The blood in her veins meant his enemies could use her to stage a coup. So, he had to control her and keep her close enough to keep an eye on her. At least, she believed, until he could contrive of a way to be rid of her like he had done with her mother.

Now she was twenty-five cycles old and more than adult enough to be a threat to her decade younger brother and heir apparent. She was also old enough now to be executed without making her father look too much like the monster he was. Truthfully, she had been living in anticipation of this day ever since her last incarceration. The day when she would be called into his presence for the last time.

* * *

They reached the presence chamber and the guards before her threw open the doors. She had expected to see him at the end of the bamboo runner that led through a sea of courtiers and ended at the foot of the throne where he was usually sitting in much state and pompousness. But the throne lay empty and there was an eerie quietude among the courtiers. Her chin rose proudly as she realized all eyes were upon her. She might be terrified of what the emperor had in store for her, but she would be damned if she would let anyone else see that. No matter what he decreed, as far as she was concerned she was the heir to his throne. She had lawfully been his firstborn child. The law of their land demanded she be his heiress. She did not recognize the laws he had hastily passed in order to put her aside.

But neither would she raise a hand against her innocent half-blood sibling. She knew there were factions willing and able to overthrow the young prince if she so much as nodded in their direction, but she would not exile another to the fate she had been exiled to.

Out of the corner of her eye she saw Prelate Kitsos step to the edge of the runner as she was being hurried past the roomful of prelates and paxsors. He tried to catch her eye, his look full of some kind of meaning and intent. She remained staring full ahead, not wanting in any way to be associated with the man's plots and plans. He was too obvious in his avarice. He would be the death of them both if he were not more careful.

Now her heart was lodged firmly in her throat, although it seemed to beat twice as fast. She was led past her father's throne and into his private visitation chamber. The difference in the brightness from one room to the next was shocking, and she was nearly blind in the sudden darkness. She clutched the prayer book she held between her hands, hoping the Great

Being was watching over her. As her eyes adjusted to the darkness she was grabbed roughly around each of her arms and shoved hastily forward. She tripped over the skirt of her gown, making her fall to her knees in an obesience she did not truly feel, may the universe forgive her for her angry heart.

She was now kneeling at the feet of the man who had tormented her throughout her life in one way or another. She would have bowed to him on her own power, but she would never have groveled before him. She clenched her teeth in anger, forcing her countenance to remain cool and serene. She could not afford to be prideful. She could not risk any show of backbone in front of an emperor who had no compunctions about killing off anyone who ticked him off.

Silence ticked by, the only sound in her ears was the rasp of her own breathing. She kept her eyes trained on the bamboo runner that ran through this room as well. The woven, decorative mats were used to protect flooring and, in this instance, hand-malleayed carpeting. Artisans created malleay rugs on great looms, working teams of people in some sort of concert of creativity. She had not seen one of the rich creations in completion since childhood, and even now the mat thwarted her. True, the bamboo was cleverly wrought, colorful threads and Delran platinum decorating the plain tan fibers and creating something quite spectacular, but she would much rather see the rug.

Far more than she wished to see her father just then. Even now all she could see of him was his slippered feet.

"Sister."

The pubescent voice startled her, as did the address, and she forgot herself and looked up. Instead of her father, she found herself at the feet of a brother she only knew from images in VidMags and other media. He was tall and gangly, all sharp joints and a physical awkwardness that rolled off him even though all he was doing was standing still. But he also had that imperious air and confidence of a prince born and raised. The luxurious cloth-of-platinum robes he wore were robes of state and, though they seemed to weigh heavily on his narrow frame, he wore them perfectly straight and with the exactness of someone used to such finery.

"My good brother," she said, inclining her head again. "I am honored to meet you at last."

"Are you?" he questioned her. "Or are you as much a traitoress as your mother was? Now that our father is dead, will you drive a knife in my back at the first opportunity?"

"Our father is dead?"

"He will be long remembered," everyone in the room said solemnly, the ritual confirming the fact.

The shock was so tremendous, so unexpected, that she forgot she was not allowed to acknowledge the emperor as her father. There was also such a shocking release within her psyche, the relief of almost a decade's worth of stress and tension, that she immediately felt lightheaded. Blackness rode over her, forcing her to drop her prayer book and brace her hands out on the floor. She fought off the faint that was tugging at her and used her seemingly obeisant position to touch her forehead to her brother's slipper.

"My great lord and emperor," she said, "I am so utterly sorry for your loss."

"So, you acknowledge me to be our father's heir?" He was clearly fishing and she had learned to tread carefully around such dangling worms.

"I have always done so, Your Eminence. Is it not so decreed? I am the fruit of a treacherous woman who conspired to murder our lord and master, the late emperor. Her shame is my shame. I do not deserve to be heir or empress."

"Then you will not mind signing this document to that effect."

Her brother's hand swept out to the left and she raised her eyes to see a secretary reach down with a carefully drawn up document, its gilt edges brightly obscene as she quickly read the contents.

I, Ambrea Vas Allay, do swear from this day forward, that I renounce my blood and any connection to the Allay throne. Thus, I will now be known only as Ambrea Vas, a commoner and subject of this realm. I sign this of my own free will with both signature and retinal scan to prove beyond a shadow of a doubt that these are my wishes and desires. Any attempts on my part to take the Allay throne, from this day forward, will be considered an act of high treason and will result in the immediate forfeiture of my life.

Ambrea Vas.

Ambrea, it meant . . . "daughter." Ambrea Vas Allay meant "daughter of this realm." In all these years, her father, though he had alienated her and stripped her of her rightful place in the succession, had never taken this step, stripping her of her name. She had always wondered why. Perhaps there had been some part of the former emperor that had been, after all, loath to deprive himself of his spare heir while his only living son was still young and susceptible to the many illnesses and dangers of youth. Perhaps he had not, in the end, wanted to leave her without any claim to anyone. But clearly her brother had no such reservations.

To sign such a document would mean she could never, even in the event of her brother's death, lay claim to the throne. She would be cut loose. Set free. She could then do anything. Go anywhere. Her brother would be renouncing all ability to hold power over what she did or where she went, except that of a sovereign over his subject. He would no longer be responsible for her upkeep. She would, in essence, be her own woman.

The rush of the idea was a heady one. The thought of it, of being able to walk away, perhaps leave the planet altogether, where she could explore any part of the three worlds, it was remarkable. She could hear her blood rushing against her eardrums. She was a signature and a scan away from turning her back on this stifling existence forever.

Except . . .

"I beg you to forgive my hesitation, Your Eminence," she said quickly, not wishing to anger him, knowing nothing of his temperament that she didn't see in the media. But all hints thus far had pointed to a spoiled, rich, and powerful youth who was used to getting his way, just like his father had been. "I am merely in shock at the news of the emperor's death."

"He will be long remembered," her brother's attendants chorused respectfully. But there was a decided lack of enthusiasm in their voices. The fact was, Emperor Benit had been a tyrant, and these attendants that were now flocked at her brother's back had been the previous emperor's attendants and advisors. When Emperor Benit had raged, which he had often done, these were the people that had borne the brunt of it. Now they were eagerly supporting a child they probably felt would be far more malleable than his father had been. There was power to be found by being the advisor to the boy sovereign. These vultures would be clawing at one another for the best position.

"He had been ill for some time," her brother faltered.

There was emotion there. Genuine emotion. Despite how he was portrayed in the media, young Emperor Qua Tsu Allay had feelings. And now his insecurities were also showing. Suddenly those robes of state looked far too big for the boy.

If you love Jacquelyn Frank's sensual
fantasies, look for the latest installment of her
beloved *Nightwalkers* series,

Supernatural,

available from Zebra Books this September.

Kane burned. His mind, his every sense, but most of all his body burned with need and lust unlike anything he had ever felt before. The Samhain moon was growing heavy and full, it would be at its apex in a matter of days, but it may as well have been scorching its full influence into him in that very instant, that was how ravaged by it he was feeling.

Or maybe it was just because of her.

He'd followed her for three days now, stalking her every step since the moment he'd first laid eyes on her, either in person or with the power of his mind. He was Demon, a creature born perfectly into the night, born with powers beyond human understanding. Every Demon favored a specific element: Air, Fire, Water, Earth, Body, or, as in his case, Mind. He was powerful, capable of great feats . . . and yet always weaker than other Demons around him. They called him fledgling. A child. A nearly hundred-year-old child. He was a mere two years from earning a little more respect. Then he would be adult. Not quite the heavily respected Elder that his brother was, nowhere near the astounding Ancient that Gideon was, but it would be better than that accursed title of fledgling.

But however much or little his contemporary

Demons thought of him, this young female, this human, had lived for barely a quarter of his lifetime. She was ignorant of so much, ignorant of his kind and the other Nightwalkers that lived on the borders of her world. Maybe that was why she was so incessantly carefree in the way she lived her life. Granted, she was marred with emotional scars that others had so thoughtlessly burdened her with, but in spite of that she still managed to be vivacious and earthy, as vibrant as her brilliant red hair and sparkling green eyes. As clean and clear as her pristine pale skin.

Someone else had taken notice of her brilliance. He was unworthy. Even she thought so. The inept creature had bored her almost from the outset, and yet she carried on their date trying to find comfort in his plainness and his constancy. Kane had been tracking this absurdity from a distance, pacing furiously as the ridiculousness of it all burned at his patience. But there was little he could do about it. She was human and to him she was forbidden. By all rights he should have turned his back on her days ago. He should have written her off completely. Keeping track of her, whether from near or from far, would only lead to trouble.

That trouble had come. It had come in the guise of this overwhelming burn, this savage sense of lust and ownership that could not be denied. He couldn't bear her being on that useless creature's arm another second. Now he was flying to her side in a series of raging, uncontrolled bursts of teleportation, each jump taking him closer to her and each jump leaving behind an ever more violent burst of smoke and sulfur in his wake. His emotions were out of his control and therefore his powers were also out of his control. But none of that mattered. He was close. Closer. Soon he would put this fiasco to an end and he would rip her from the side of this clown she was trying to make worthy of her.

He materialized on the seedy New York street in a violent flash, only his power to influence the minds of others camouflaging the frightening display from those nearby. His beauteous redhead and her so-called date walked on completely oblivious to his presence.

He stalked after them quickly, his eyes tracking all the shadowy corners and alleys of their location. His distaste for her escort trebled. What male worth anything would bring a woman to a place such as this? Didn't the fool realize the dangers all around them? Did that weak excuse for a human male honestly think himself capable of protecting her should danger present itself?

In truth, the thought wasn't even in his mind, Kane realized as he gave them both a backhanded scan. The shocking fact was, he was barely even focused on the treasure walking by his side! All of this fool's thoughts were eagerly pointed toward the film they were going to see. Apparently its special effects and coveted director warranted more attention that the one of a kind sultry creature on his arm.

Disgusted, Kane seized control of both of their minds at once. They stopped still for a moment and then Kane shaded out any awareness and recollection of her from the human male's mind and sent him on his way to the moving picture that seemed to mean so much to him.

And now he was alone with her. Mere steps away. It was child's play for him to beckon her to him, to bring her to him as a willing, compliant thing. Oh, but that was not what he wanted. He wouldn't take her as a mind-numbed slave. It was the totality of what she was that so enthralled him.

He would only alter her perceptions a little bit, just so she would forget what she had been doing, thus opening an opportunity for him to introduce his presence into her life. But first . . . first he needed to touch her. Just one blessed moment of contact. Something to soothe this burn within him. Something to calm it a little so he could think straight and function properly.

Kane reached for her, his hand trembling as he did so, the vibration indicative of the power of his feelings, of his weakening restraint. His palm burned just with the anticipation of her, prickles dancing the length of his long fingers so that they twitched. Her unknowing smile was soft and serene. It could be anything he wanted it to be. It could be even more beatific, it could be wildly ecstatic. For now it remained that lovely neutral as he touched the tips of his fingers to the curve of her high cheekbone.

Oh, Sweet Destiny. It practically hurt, that overwhelming sensation of rightness and relief that rushed through him. He cradled that gorgeous face against his palm and fought off an emotional wash of tears that pricked behind his lids. His. She was *his*. At last he had her in his grasp, he had crossed the line and, contrary to all the warnings pounded into him for all of his life, lightning had not come to strike him down. What was so bloody wrong about this, he wanted to know. Yes, she was human and he was Demon, but weren't they more alike than unalike? Were they not both made of flesh? Did they not both crave the touch and presence of that special someone . . . that caress of forever knowing each other, that passion that blinded the soul? The world was not coming to and end! It was just beginning!

And then lightning struck.

Like the snap of a magician's cape being pulled away to reveal a tiger in a cage, Jacob the Enforcer appeared before him. Dread and horror rushed into Kane from all vectors, the shock of suddenly standing toe-to-toe with his Elder brother slamming into him like a sucker punch. This was Jacob at his most frightening. His most terrible. Yes, it was still the same brother who had raised him and loved him all of his life, but it was the side of Jacob no Demon saw until they had crossed Demon law. It was the Enforcer. And he had come to punish Kane.

Kane's throat went suddenly and brutally dry, his heart seizing in what he had to confess was fear. The punishment for what he had just done was the most severe a Demon could face, next to being put to death. His hand jerked away from the redhead's cheek as if she'd burned him and his concentration broke from her. She blinked, suddenly becoming aware that she was sandwiched between two strange men and had no idea how she had gotten there.

"Take hold of her mind, Kane. Do not make this worse by frightening her."

Kane obeyed instantaneously and his precious fixation relaxed. The resulting peaceful beauty that washed over her was enough to distract him even from the knell of Jacob's presence. He marveled at how soft and sweet she looked. He knew her mind and nature were matched to her looks. It was only the cold warning look from his sibling that kept him from touching her again.

"Jacob, what brings you out on a night like this?" he blurted out, unable to think of anything else to say. After all, they were blood brothers. If Jacob was going to give anyone a pass, wouldn't it be him?

"You know why I am here," the Enforcer said, nipping that thought right in the bud with a chill disciplined tone that warned Kane not to test his mettle.

"So maybe I do," Kane relented. And still, it didn't seem to be getting through to the rest of him. It was taking everything in his power to keep from reaching for her again. Even though it made him look ever guiltier than he really was, he lowered his gaze to the spotted, dirty sidewalk and shoved his hands deep into his pockets. He gripped hold of the fabric on the inside of those pockets and forced himself to hold on. "I wasn't going to do anything. I was just . . . restless."

"I see. So you thought to seduce this woman to appease your restlessness?" Jacob asked bluntly as he folded his arms across his chest. His entire manner radiated the image of a parent scolding a wayward child. It could be an amusing thought, considering Kane was just about to enter his second century of life, but the matter was too serious by far.

"I wasn't going to hurt her," Kane protested. He could never hurt her. She was precious. She was everything. He would love her as deeply and as thoroughly as he could.

"No?" Jacob asked, his sarcasm very obvious. "Just what were you going to do? Ask politely if you could visit the savageness of your present nature on her? How does one word that exactly?"

Kane fell stubbornly silent. He knew that the Enforcer had read his intentions from the moment he'd decided to stalk his prey. Arguments and denials would just worsen the situation. Besides, the incriminating evidence of his transgression was standing between them.

For a brief, passionate moment, Kane's thoughts filled with vivid mental imaginings of what could have been more incriminating. He suppressed a shudder of sinful response, his eyes falling covetously on the woman standing so beautifully serene before him. Had Jacob been even slightly off his irritatingly perfect game and come into the picture a half hour later . . .

"Kane, this is a difficult time for our people. You are as susceptible to these base cravings as any other Demon," the Enforcer said with implacable resolve. It was as though Jacob were the one who could read Kane's mind, rather than the other way around. "Still, you are a mere two years from becoming adult. I cannot believe you have me chasing you down like a green fledgling." There it was. That word again. That . . . *term*. "Think of what I could be accomplishing if I were not standing here saving you from yourself."

The remark was like a kick in the pants, and it smarted both shamefully and painfully. Sweet Destiny, it was true! Near Samhain his brother Jacob was weighted down by his responsibilities even more than usual. The last thing he had needed was to be chasing after his own baby brother. Jacob had never asked for his mantle of responsibility. He had inherited it suddenly and unexpectedly when their eldest brother Adam had suddenly gone missing, presumed dead at the hands of some necromancer and his nefarious summoning spell many centuries ago. Jacob had lost a beloved brother and inherited a ponderous duty in one fell swoop. Now he was the pariah of his people. A necessary evil, as it were. Sort of like the internal affairs division was with the human police. They were necessary, they were members of the same brotherhood, but oh, how they were held in such contempt.

"I'm sorry, Jacob, I really am," he said at last. Kane felt utter shame washing over him as he appreciated the position he had put his beloved sibling in. It actually surprised him that he hadn't thought of the consequences of his actions and how they would affect Jacob sooner than this. He shot an acidic glare up at the Samhain moon and knew that was where the blame belonged. Kane's throat closed with the sharp sense of remorse that knifed through him.

It was as overpowering as the dread that was welling up within him. He'd betrayed the sanctity of their laws, and there was punishment for that. A punishment that made an entire species catch their breath and back away whenever the Enforcer entered the vicinity. Kane could suddenly feel the weight of Jacob's position, and it sharpened his regret to a point of pain in his chest.

"You will send this woman home safely by reuniting her with her escort and making sure she remembers nothing of your misbehavior," Jacob instructed softly. "Then you will go home. Your punishment will come later."

"But I didn't do anything," Kane protested, a swift rise of inescapable fear fueling the objection.

"You would have, Kane. Do not make this worse by lying to yourself about that. You will only convince yourself that I am the villain others like to make me out to be. That will only cause us both pain."

Kane realized that truth with another upsurge of guilt. Sighing resolutely, he closed his eyes and concentrated for all of a second. Moments later, the redhead's escort loped back across the street with a smile and a call to her.

"Hey! Where'd ya go? I turned the corner and suddenly you weren't there!"

"I'm sorry. I was distracted by something and didn't realize you'd gone, Charlie."

Charlie linked his arm with his date's and, completely oblivious of the two Demons barely a breath away, drew her off, chattering incessantly about that ridiculous movie he was so damn excited about. It grated up Kane's spine to hear it, it set off a screaming sensation in his blood to allow her to walk away from him. But what else could he do? They were forbidden and Jacob would fight him if he tried to do otherwise. Sweet Destiny, fight with the Enforcer? Even Gideon the Ancient had not been able to come out a winner against Kane's powerful brother.

"Good," Jacob commended Kane, unaware of how the fledgling had to struggle to stay where he was, to let her go into a dangerous night and a ridiculous date where she wouldn't be even slightly appreciated for the wonder that she was.

Kane sighed. Nothing about this felt good. Not the position he was currently in, and certainly not turning her back over to that inept buffoon who knew nothing of how precious she was . . . of how exquisitely, painfully she was capable of making a male feel just by her very presence in the room.

"She's so beautiful. Did you see that smile? All I could think about was how much I wanted her to smile when . . ." Kane flushed as he looked at the Enforcer. He had not intended to speak aloud. He had not wanted to confess so much to his brother. Nothing would change the inevitability of the consequences to come, but there was a sanctity to what he felt for his redheaded human torturer. It was private. Nothing to be shared with others. "I never thought this would happen to me, Jacob. You have to believe that."

When it came down to it, Kane didn't want Jacob to think he had purposely brought them to this pass. He loved his brother.

"I do." Jacob hesitated for a moment, for the first time making it obvious to Kane that this had been a terrible struggle for him, no matter how well he projected otherwise. "Do not worry, Kane. I know who you really are. I know that this curse is hard for us to fight. Now," he said, his tone back to business, "please return home. You will find Abram there awaiting you."

This time, Kane brushed away the welling trepidation within himself. He did this for Jacob's sake, knowing how deeply this cut the Elder Demon, even though the Enforcer's thoughts were too carefully guarded for Kane to read. "You do your duty as you would with anyone. I understand that, Jacob."

Kane then gave the Enforcer a short nod of kinship. After glancing around to make sure they were unobserved, he exploded into a burst of sulfur and smoke as he teleported away.

It took everything . . . every fiber of control he could muster, not to stray from the course Jacob had demanded of him.